THE REINCARNATION OF ISAAC BROCK

A.B. Robinson

To Irene Linden
with Thanks

Authors
On Line

Visit us online at www.authorsonline.co.uk

ISBN 0 7552 0238 4

Authors On Line Ltd
19 The Cinques
Gamlingay, Sandy
Bedfordshire
SG19 3NU
England

This book is also available in e-book format, details of which are available at
www.authorsonline.co.uk

DEDICATION

To my children and grandchildren, so they will know how they got here; with thanks to my ancestors for living such interesting lives.

ACKNOWLEDGEMENTS

The Royal Canadian War Museum for the front cover portrait of Sir Isaac Brock.

Thanks to my wife, who allowed herself to be dragged through dozens of national historic sites and museums during the course of my research, and who waited patiently day after day while I wrote the novel.

CONTENTS

INTRODUCTION

British North America, already a jurisdiction of grand proportions, became even grander with the conquest of New France in 1759. Just a few years later, it was rent asunder by the American Revolution. The rump, what was left after the Americans departed, eventually became the Dominion of Canada.

But the Americans were not satisfied with gaining their independence. They believed it was their manifest destiny to rule all of the North American continent. In 1812, driven by that belief and with a plausible excuse for war, they invaded Canada, expecting to annex it easily. Standing in their way was Major General Sir Isaac Brock, who gave his life to stop them.

Brock, a giant of a man blessed with courage, dash and flare, had everything to live for. When the war was over, he planned to marry the woman he loved. Already showered with honours by an adoring British nation, he might have become Field Marshal of all her armies. Equally revered in Canada, he might have elected to stay in this country, here to father a line of military leaders and politicians who would have served us well. Yet he exposed himself recklessly, needlessly, to deadly enemy fire.

Did Brock deliberately sacrifice himself for glory, for the magnificent monument to his honour that stands on Queenston Heights, the site of the battle where he was killed? Or did he believe his life was charmed, that he was somehow immortal, and would never fall in combat? Whatever the answer, there is an aura of mystery about Queenston Heights in the autumn, the season when he met his death. On quiet evenings, the distant thunder of Niagara Falls can be heard there, and mists from the cascading water rise up to embrace the red-leaved maple trees. Perhaps the great soldier's ghost is pacing about, lamenting his untimely demise. Or perhaps his remains, which lie at the base of his monument, are crying out for reincarnation.

PREFACE

British North America, including the part which became Canada, has a rich history, but history to many is a dull subject. In an attempt to make it interesting, I have resorted to fiction, and tell it through the eyes of four distant, modern-day relatives, who come together to write a book about their ancestors. Two of the relatives are Canadian, the woman of French ancestry; one is an Englishman; the other is an American. Naturally, there is a love story, in this case involving the two Canadians, who overcome the gulf between their two cultures, and create the reincarnation of Isaac Brock.

While the modern characters are fictional, some of the historical ones are not. Besides the well-known soldiers and politicians who were involved, members of the Bonney family were real people. Thomas Bonney, for example, did emigrate from England to the Plymouth colony in 1634, and he did father eight children after he was fifty.

As with the fictional authors, you will find the story much easier to follow if you have a large-scale map of North America at hand, or a good atlas.

I ask the forgiveness in advance of those experts, military and otherwise, who will find fault with my version of history. But this is a novel, after all, not an attempt to supplant serious accounts of what took place.

ABR
Kamloops, British Columbia, Canada

Isaac Brock's Memorial, Queenston Heights, Canada.

Chapter 1.

Sandwich

Late winter blizzard blowing down the Ottawa River. Drifts piling up on the deserted street outside. Attic shutter rattling in the cold, gusty wind. A night designed for suicide.

I closed the blinds, poured myself a fourth nightcap, and tried to face the bitter truth. Tomorrow, Monday the 15th of March, 1993, I would not go to my office at the Department of Transport. After 30 years of loyal service, I was a discard at age 55, a sacrifice on the altar of balancing Canada's budget. Oh, they sent me off with a generous severance allowance and a full pension, so that I was financially secure, but that didn't keep me from feeling as if I'd suddenly lost my identity. "What in hell are you going to do with yourself, Fred Bonney? Drink yourself to death, or go crazy? You've already started talking to yourself." I took a swallow of rye, and went through it all again.

Retirement. I stopped looking forward to it when Beth died in 1990. Since then, I had become a workaholic, had not kept up with our friends, had lost all interests outside the job. If only Beth was still alive! Prim, proper, Beth, a saint in her church, but not an enthusiast in bed. Once, she told me, when I suggested we try something different, "God sees us, Fred." But she would have had the answers. We would have travelled. She would have made me do chores. "Get married again," she commanded me on her deathbed. "You need someone to look after you." But would any other woman put up with my attacks of abdominal gas?

Still, there was one woman - I laughed at myself. "No fool like an old fool, Fred." Josée, Josée, French-Canadian Josée, one of the secretaries at the Department, so different from Beth, all curves, paint on her face, brunette one week and blonde the next, the life of the office parties she organized. The word was she was divorced and didn't mind a roll in the hay, but she was much younger than I was, and could never be interested in a social misfit like me. Besides, I rationalized, I would hate to pay for her clothes. She never seemed to wear the same outfit twice.

"Rattle, rattle, damn shutter. Alright, Beth, I'll try to fix it. Now, concentrate." Gather tools, stumble, grumble up the stairs, open the door, turn on the light, pause to survey the cobwebs and the clutter, plot a course to the windows.

Squarely in the way was an old storage trunk with the name 'Lorenzo Dow' painted on the outside of it in faded, white letters. "Uncle Bill's trunk, right where I put it after he died. Should have opened it long ago, I guess, but with Beth sick. Ah, maybe tomorrow."

It might have been the drinks, but I swear the rattling of the shutter fell silent just then, even though the wind continued to howl and moan around the eaves.

The hair on the back of my neck tingled. "Uncle Bill, was that your ghost making that noise? You want me to open your trunk now, is that it?"

The hinges squealed in protest when I lifted the lid, as if something sinister might be inside, but all I could find were old Bill's notes on the Bonney family, along with letters, pictures, portraits and birth certificates, all neatly arranged like the man himself. 'The family name was first spelt Boney, then Bonny', he'd written in his summary. 'They came originally from France, probably at the time of the Norman Conquest, and settled in the English town of Sandwich. Many of their descendants became Puritans, and in 1634, some of them emigrated to the Plymouth Colony in what is now Massachusetts . . . '

I looked at the pictures, one by one. They all looked vaguely familiar, like uncles and aunts. At last, I came to a silver locket, and the woman pictured in it looked decidedly unlike an aunt; in fact, she looked so much like Josée that I cried out, "I wonder who she was?" Hoping to find a clue, I leafed through the summary, but on the last page, in a quavering hand, Uncle Bill had written only this: 'the woman in the locket: ancestor Lorenzo Dow, the Massachusetts militia, the expulsion of the Acadians, 1755, Grand Pré, Nova Scotia.'

"So why did you leave me this stuff, old Bill, instead of money, like you left your other nieces and nephews?" The answer dawned on me slowly. "You wanted me to write a book about the family, the book you never started after all this research, because you died suddenly. Alright. That will give me something to do with myself." I looked at the locket again, and an unfamiliar, wild kind of excitement gripped me. "And I'm going to have that French-Canadian secretary too!"

Before going to bed that night, I took a good look at myself in Beth's full-length mirror. "Overweight, flabby, but nearly six feet tall, and still with a full head of gray hair. Well, almost a full head. Blue eyes that light up when I laugh. Don't laugh much any more. Features kind of craggy-looking, but not unpleasant, even the high bridged Bonney nose - big nose denotes character, they say. So what do I have to do to attract Josée? Lose 20 pounds, firm up my slack muscles, become a social lion? Alright. I'll give the first two a try."

It was hard at first, working out on the exercise machines that had been gathering dust in the basement, skating on Ottawa's unique outdoor rink, the Rideau Canal, and then jogging when the ice went out. I nearly gave up a few times, and then I would think of Josée, and I would keep on going, through good weather and bad, jog, jog under the stately elms in the city's parks, jog alongside the canal and the rivers, the Ottawa and the Rideau, Josée, Josée, jog, jog, and I often wondered, when the time came, if I actually would have the courage to try for her. I knew she played golf, so when the weather began to warm up, I bought a new set of clubs and took some lessons. Then I forced myself to visit public courses in the area, and waited patiently until I could get a game. Soon, I had my handicap down to 20, where it was when I stopped playing - that was when Beth died.

To keep myself from drinking too much in the evenings, I learned to surf the net on my new laptop, a retirement present from my daughters, and in the process, found a lot of background information for the book. At the same time, I became interested in geography and began to appreciate what a marvellous country I lived in, the second largest in all the world. From the Maritime Provinces on the Atlantic Ocean to British Columbia on the Pacific; from the international border to the Arctic Islands: this was an immense and wealthy land to be held by less than 30 million people.

I also bought a history of Canada, the first self-governing Dominion of the British Commonwealth of Nations, the template for one of the most extraordinary political inventions of all time. But how fragile our nationhood was, with the French in Quebec threatening to separate! And then there were the Americans, some of whom still believed it was their manifest destiny to rule all of the continent - they even tried to take Canada by force of arms twice. Outnumbered ten to one in terms of population, how did we manage to hold them off? I became convinced that one British officer, Major General Sir Isaac Brock, had more to do with it than anyone else, and I became engrossed with his character. He lost his life during the battle of Queenston Heights, fought in 1812, just downstream from Niagara Falls, but his example of courage and daring inspired others to hold the Americans at bay. One night I even had a dream about him. Standing in the wind and rain of a dark morning, with his right hand drenched in blood, over the wound in his chest that killed him, he was looking about restlessly. And just as the dream ended, he shouted in a loud voice, "By the Lord Harry, I shall have no peace until I find him!"

At last, on Wednesday, May 12th, the 20 pounds were gone, and I stripped and looked at myself in the mirror again. "Well, Fred, not much to work with, but you've done the best you could. Now for that secretary!"

My heart skipped a beat. Now, I had to confront Josée. All the rest of that day and all the next, I wrestled with myself, unable to take the final step, the one that might save my life, or one that would see me, if she ridiculed me, a broken man, doomed to die at best from cirrhosis of the liver. At last, in a thick mental fog, I found myself at the Department's reception desk on Friday morning, and I asked for her.

Josée was plainly startled when saw me. "Mr. Bonney! You look wonderful! Retirement must agree with you."

After we exchanged pleasantries, I blurted out, "How about dinner some night?"

"Dinner?"

"Maybe some dancing too. I have a proposition I want to make to you."

"A what?"

"Maybe a change of job."

"Alright. I'm free tonight."

I could hardly believe she would be free on a Friday evening, especially this evening; in fact, I was so sure she would turn me down altogether that her sudden acceptance put me off balance. Recovering, I managed, "Uh, I looked up your address in the phone book. Pick you up at seven?"

It was supposed to be fun and uncomplicated, and it started out well enough. I was a terrible dancer, but she was so easy to lead that we whirled around the floor, just as if I wasn't uncoordinated old Fred Bonney. At the same time, she seemed depressed, and kept her head turned to one side as if she were trying to hide something from me. The drinks I bought her before, during, and after dinner should have cheered her up, you would think, but if anything, they seemed to make her even more depressed.

Dessert was long over before I finally found the nerve to tell her about the book, and that I was looking for a travelling companion. I couldn't make myself say 'bed mate'. I was a career public servant, after all, long-schooled in the art of not spelling things out. But she knew what I meant, and she broke into tears. "What's the matter?" I asked, mystified.

She replied, in accented English, "I always admired you because you were so faithful to your wife. I caught you looking at me many times at the office, but you never made a pass at me, and now I find out you're just like all the rest - all you want is sex. And this was my last day at work. I've been downsized, laid off, fired, what-do-you-call-it? I need another drink."

"One more of those and you'll be under the table."

"Nobody thinks I have feelings. Nobody cares how hurt I was when my scum of a husband went out and cheated on me. Nobody thinks that maybe I really wanted to be a faithful wife to a decent man, to have children, instead of just being good old available Josée, the one who organizes the office parties, and who might sleep with you if you give her enough booze. Now I'm almost into menopause, and I'm just a cranky old bitch who's lost her job."

"Almost into menopause! I didn't think you were a day over 29!"

"I want to go home before I get sick."

I took her to her apartment, helped her while she vomited into the toilet, and put her to bed. "You're just an old lecher, like she says. You'd like to pile in there and take advantage of her, wouldn't you? But she's got the rags on - you know, I've hardly even thought that expression before - I'm degenerating. We'll just have to give this one more try tomorrow."

On my way out, I became aware of a pleasant smell in the air, one that defied definition at the time; a mixture of smells, really, including one so delicate that I wasn't sure it was there at all. And I noticed a kind of tray on legs in a corner of the living room, perhaps two feet wide by six feet long, and in it were a dozen or more clay pots, all filled with what looked to be the same kind of flowering plant.

Josée apologized for her behaviour when I phoned her the next morning. "That's alright," I told her. "The offer still stands. I can't pay you what you've been making at the Department, but we'll work out an agreement on finances."

"What happens afterwards, when the book is finished?"

"I hadn't really thought about that. It will probably take a year or more to write. Maybe we'll like the arrangement and just stay together."

"I still don't feel very well. Let me sleep on it, and I'll let you know tomorrow."

"How about lunch tomorrow, then?"

"Alright. Just don't buy me any drinks."

She still seemed depressed the next day, but she did say, "Thanks for not assaulting me the other night. As for your proposition, it's the best one I've had since I got laid off, so I'll take it. It really does sound like fun, and I promise I'll cheer up. When do we start?"

I took her hands, and a kind of electricity shot through my body. "I really appreciate your saying yes. First stop will be England and the town of Sandwich, where the Bonneys came from. Meanwhile, I've rented the house because I couldn't get a decent price for it, and everything should be in storage by the day after tomorrow. I was counting on moving in with you after that."

"O.K. I should be over my problems by then."

She was understanding when I couldn't perform that first night in her apartment. I was devastated. She suggested, "Maybe something a little bit kinky would get you going."

"Oh, God, no! Remember I'm 55 years old, and only ever knew one woman in my whole life. We hardly got beyond the missionary position. Anything fancier might make me blow an artery." She started to laugh and couldn't stop, and I joined in, in spite of my embarrassment.

We shared a nightcap and went to bed. At four in the morning, I woke her, and everything worked - thank God it worked - and it was wonderful, especially since it had been so long, with my partner eager and responsive, unlike anything I ever experienced with Beth!

Josée woke me at eight, and we made love, and made love again, and then she flopped back on her pillow with a smile on her face, apparently satisfied. If she hadn't been, there was nothing more I could have done for her - at least, that's what I thought until we showered together. Afterwards, she confided, "Now I can tell you that I used to wonder what it would be like, with you." She kissed me. "I am not disappointed." Then she exclaimed, "Mon Dieu! I'm hungry! I hope you like to cook, because I'm not very good at it."

Weekend breakfasts were my specialty in the days of my marriage, so I was able to whip her up a Spanish omelette complete with green onions and peppers. "Mmmm! Was that ever good!" she raved, as she scraped the last morsel off her plate.

"Thanks. Let's have another cup of coffee, and you can tell me all about yourself."

"Well, as you know, I am French-Canadian, born near Quebec City in 1953. After graduating from high school, I got a job in a bookstore near Montreal, and that's where I seriously started to learn English. That's also where I met and married that scum, Paul Tremblay. After ten years together, I found out he was

5

cheating on me, and when I confronted him about it, he said he loved me, but he was the kind of man who needed other women too, and not to worry about it. Mon Dieu! I packed up and left the same day, took a secretarial course, and got on with Transport. Now, they kick me out at the unemployable age of 39, without enough severance pay to keep me in groceries for six months."

"Just a minute." I took the locket out of my briefcase and showed it to her.

"Why, it's almost as if I were looking into a mirror! Where did you get this?"

"Out of a trunk in the attic. Do you know any of your family's history?"

"Not really, except I was told that one of my ancestors was a 'Fille du Roi', one of the women the French king sent over to be wives of the settlers, way back in the early days of Quebec. My brother, though, is quite a student of Quebec history."

"I really never thought about a French connection when I decided to write the book. One of my ancestors, Joel Bonney, took part in the conquest of Quebec, and it would be interesting to know if any of your family was on the other side. I'd like to have a talk with your brother sometime."

Josée looked surprised, then smiled wryly. "I don't know if that would be a good idea. Pierre is a rabid separatist, dislikes all Anglais, won't even speak English even though he can, what-do-you-call-it, fluently. He will be most upset when he finds out I am shacked up with an Anglais. And he is so big."

"But surely he should be happy if you're happy!"

We dropped the subject. I wondered how big her brother was, and if he would hit me when we met. I looked at the woman across the table, and decided it would be worth it if he did. She was tall, at least five eight I guessed, and all curves, yes, but athletic looking at the same time, from her sturdy neck to the well-turned calves of her legs. Her skin, still smooth at her age, had an attractive olive cast to it. Her face, featuring a straight, narrow nose, sensuous lips, and a small dimple in her chin, was framed by black, shoulder-length hair. And when I looked into her dark, brown eyes, they looked back at me knowingly, invitingly.

I forced myself to concentrate on some necessary business. "If we're going into a long-term relationship, we need some kind of agreement; otherwise, you will be able to claim half my estate when we split, and that should really go to my kids. To start with, do you own your apartment?"

"No. The rent is $700 a month."

"O.K. On the one most important condition that you stay faithful to me, I will pay the rent on your apartment, feed and clothe you, and give you an allowance of, say, $200 a month, to cover things like cosmetics and getting your hair done. How does that sound?"

"Fine, as far as it goes, but shouldn't the agreement state that you must remain faithful to me also? And I will be giving you the best of the years I have left. Maybe you should give me a severance package, like the government, after it's over."

"It never entered my head that I might stray, but okay on the faithful part. What did you have in mind for a severance package?"

"How about $10,000 a year, to a maximum of $30,000? I could exist for a year on $30,000 in case I had trouble finding a job."

I did a quick mental calculation. It could come out of the house when I sold it without cutting too much into my estate. Besides, both my daughters had married well, and were much better off than I was. "O.K. I'll put that in, and we'll get some lawyers to draw it up. Just one more thing. It's a little late to be thinking of it after all that unprotected sex, but what about AIDS and all that?"

"I had a test recently. Everything was okay, so far as the doctor could tell."

"But you're still young enough to get pregnant. What about precautions?"

"I am, what-do-you-call-it, impregnable? There is no need for precautions."

I chuckled. "Barren would be a better way to put it, but it conveys the message. And how beautifully convenient."

"Oh, when are we going to England?"

"Next Tuesday, the 25th."

"I must arrange for someone to look after my Impatiens while we are away." She made a phone call, then filled a small watering can, and went over to her tray of flowerpots. "Voulez vous un peu d'eau ce matin, mes jolies?" she crooned, and gave each plant a drink.

The intriguing smell in the apartment suddenly grew stronger. Potting soil! That was definitely one of the ingredients, made more noticeable by the watering.

"Josée, there's a faint, sweet scent in the air. Does it come from those flowers in the tray? What kind did you say they were?"

"They are Impatiens of various kinds, and they really don't have much of a fragrance."

I went over to the tray to sniff the flowers. Yes! There was that delicate scent! But there were more ingredients that I couldn't yet identify. Whatever they were, the sum total would remind me of Josée for the rest of my life.

By rights, I should have been exhausted, my back close to spasms, but instead, I was full of energy. It was a beautiful day outside, I finally noticed, and I said, "Hey, why don't we play a game of golf today?"

"Oh. Really, I haven't played much lately. My clubs are worn out, and so are all my golf clothes. I wouldn't be caught dead in them."

I forgot my concern about finances. I was just a giddy old man with a beautiful new toy. "Hell, we'll just buy you a new set of clubs and a new outfit at the first pro shop we come to. Let's go!"

"Oh, you have made me very excited! But I must clean up this breakfast mess first. I can't stand coming home to dirty dishes."

It turned out that Josée was a member of a private course across the river in Hull, and she got us a tee time there. At the pro shop, we bought her the set of clubs she'd long had her eye on, and outfitted her with designer golf clothes, from the shoes up, and I felt murderously jealous when the pro leered at her. She insisted on warming up on the practice tee, something I never did, and I was impressed by her concentration on form and rhythm, rather than on distance.

More than that, I was entranced by the way her breasts responded when she waggled. On the course, she beat me by 15 strokes, but I didn't care. I couldn't get the silly smile off my face each time I watched her swing - so in balance, such solid contact with the ball, the high, graceful finish. I was falling hopelessly in love.

Over lunch in the clubhouse, I asked her where she'd learned to play such a good game. "My father is the pro at a course on the south shore, just across the St. Lawrence River from Quebec City, and he started me playing when I was four. Even though I won all kinds of tournaments as a junior, and played in the interprovincial matches for Quebec, it was always a disappointment to him that I was never good enough to turn professional. Still, he pays my dues at this club, otherwise I could not afford to play."

"You are a five handicap and he's disappointed? How much better would you have to be to turn pro?"

"I would have to improve to a plus handicap, that is, at least six strokes, to have any chance on the tour."

On the way home, Josée tuned the radio to a French station and began to hum along with the music, and when they played a set of traditional folk songs, she began to mimic almost flawlessly the phrasing of the recording artist. I hadn't sung for years, but found myself joining in whenever I remembered the words. Josée raised an eyebrow. "Such a nice baritone! Your French is not bad, either. Have you taken lessons?"

"Such a gorgeous contralto! And thanks for the compliments. Yes, I was high enough up in the public service to qualify for the French language program."

They played 'Vive La Canadienne'. which I knew by heart, and Josée sang a descant, and we made marvellous harmony together. I had never believed anyone could be as happy as I was at that moment.

Before we left for London, I learned more about Josée. She was a poor cook, but, besides being fastidious about her own person, she loved to clean house. Dressed in jeans, blouse and with a bandana around her hair, she vacuumed, dusted and waxed her apartment until it shone, and that's when I became aware of the other ingredients in the intriguing smell: soap and furniture polish. On our first Sunday morning together, she disappeared for two hours without first eating breakfast, explaining when she came back that she'd been to church. And I thought she was an unrepentant sinner. Then she complained that she had nothing to wear, even though her closet was jammed full of clothes, so we went out and bought her three new outfits at one of Ottawa's better stores. After admiring her in each of them, I hardly noticed how much they cost when I signed the credit card slip.

The night flight to London on the 747 was uneventful. Josée ate munchies while we watched the movie, and she offered me some. I declined. "Full of cholesterol and calories," I said. "You'll get fat."

"But I do this all the time when I'm watching TV. I never put on weight."

When the movie was over, she snuggled up to me, and went to sleep with her head on my shoulder, and I was overcome with a feeling of possessiveness.

We landed at Heathrow before noon, took a taxi to the railway station, and boarded a train bound for Sandwich. From our compartment, we looked out on the London suburbs and then the pleasant English countryside, all divided into fields by hedgerows, a landscape long tamed, so unlike our native Canada. To pass the time, I read out to Josée what I'd learned from my research about our destination. "Sandwich lies 12 miles east of Canterbury and two miles from the sea on the River Stour - has been a town since before 1226, when the record of mayors began - population from the latest census about 4,500. It was one of the Cinque Ports during the middle ages, whatever a Cinque Port was, a naval headquarters, a centre of the wool trade, and the chief port of embarkation for the continent, that is, until the harbour silted in and became useless.

"The streets are lined with timber-framed houses and others built by refugee Flemings, religious refugees, I guess, who were allowed to settle there during the reign of Elizabeth the First. The Fisher gate, built in 1384 and restored in 1954, is the only one of four still standing. The Barbican, now converted to an inn, and that's where we'll be staying, dates from 1539, and was one of a chain of blockhouses built along the coast about that time. Nearby Richborough castle, built on the site of a Roman settlement, dates from 43 AD. In the town proper, many medieval buildings are still in use, including the Guildhall, three hospitals, and three churches, one of them St. Peters, where the Bonneys worshipped. As for present day Sandwich, it is an important agricultural and manufacturing centre, and also a holiday town with a fine golf links, Royal St. Georges, one of the courses on the British Open rotation, or, as they call it over here, the Open Championship.

"Too bad we don't have clubs or golf clothes with us, although I doubt we'd be able to get on that course anyway. What we can do is poke around the graveyards and see if we can find any Bonney headstones, then tour the town. I want to get the flavour of the place, try to imagine what it was like in the early 17th century."

"When I was young," Josée said, "my father took us to the graveyards around Quebec City and Montreal, and we found several family headstones. Maybe that's where my brother got his interest in history."

We were bonding now. For the rest of the train journey, we joked about the experiences we'd shared in our short time together, like my latest gas attack. "At first, I thought you'd gone in your pants," she giggled. Watching her expressive mouth and those knowing eyes, listening to her musical laughter, I knew that I was in love with her. What I really wanted to do was get off the train and into our room, so I could tell her in the proper setting.

Our mouths were locked together until we found it impossible to undress each other that way, then locked together again as I pulled her down on top of me. I had to tell her before we started. I managed to stop the kissing and said it.

"Josée, Jos, I love you."

9

She stiffened in my arms and propped herself up on her hands. "Don't ever say that to me. You have my body, but you cannot have my heart. I will not have it broken again."

"But Josée, I mean it. I ... "

"Shut up, Fred! Shut up! I'm going to punish you for saying you love me, so you will not say it again." And she straddled me, and began slowly to wriggle herself across my belly and chest toward my face.

"What do you want me to do now?" I knew, I guess, but I'd never done it before.

"Mon Dieu! It is like going to bed with a virgin boy!"

Josée was not an early riser by nature, and while I waited for her to get up the next morning, I looked through the phone book to see if there were any listings under the name Bonney. "Hah! Bonney, Colonel Sir Richard!" I tried the number, but there was no answer. "Come on, Jos. It looks like rain. We need to get a move on if we want to stay dry."

In the graveyard at St. Peter's church, in the midst of medieval monuments, we discovered a stone marked Elizabeth Rachel Boney, b. Jan 8, 1601, d. Mar 7, 1629. Poor Elizabeth! Such a short life, but not, perhaps, by the standards of the day. While we continued our search, a tall, spare man with close-cropped, iron-gray hair and handlebar moustache appeared. With his hands clasped behind him, he stood looking for the longest time at one headstone, then began to walk about slowly, apparently lost in thought. It was Josée who noticed. "Fred, that man keeps looking at us, but when I look at him, he turns away."

Because I knew loneliness, I sensed that the stranger was terribly lonely, and either so shy or so reserved, by class or upbringing, that he could not initiate contact with us. We approached him, and I put out my hand to him. "My name is Fred Bonney, and this is Josée Tremblay - my secretary. We are from Canada, and we are looking for graves of my ancestors."

Shy, reserved or not, the man's face registered amazement. "How extraordinary! My name is also Bonney - Richard Bonney. Ah! I see you also have the Bonney nose."

We shook hands. "Colonel Sir Richard Bonney, as in the phone book?"

"Yes, I am now retired, but I still masquerade under my old rank." He looked embarrassed for a moment, as if he had said too much, then rushed on in choppy sentences. "I come here every day. You see my wife is buried here. Almost a year ago now, my daughter Sarah was killed in an automobile accident, and my wife, Mildred, was severely injured. She finally passed away three months ago. It seems so much longer than that, somehow. Oh, but Bonney, yes, you must have found Rachel's marker. I know it says Elizabeth first, but it was customary for the female members of the family to go by their second names at that time. Oh, by the way, the name was probably spelt 'Bony' at the time the original family came from France to England. Canada, you say? Then you must be descended from the Puritan faction who went to Massachusetts? Oh, I should explain myself. I do know something about the family. I am a bit of a history buff – actually. I was going to write a book about the Bonneys, but just haven't had the ambition to start since the accident. I've had three books published, you see, all military histories." He looked embarrassed again. "Oh, forgive me for going on so." He looked longingly at Josée, and I then understood what had attracted him to us.

"Yes, Sir Richard, I am descended from the Massachusetts Bonneys, and funnily enough, I also know something about the family. As a matter of fact, I'm writing a book about the North American branch, and it's interesting that the female members over here went by their middle names. In North America, there is a similar tradition."

"Interesting indeed. Oh, may I call you Fred? And Josée?" We nodded. "Do call me Dickie. All my friends do. But Fred, since I have abandoned the idea of writing my book, perhaps I can help you with yours. In the matter of a publisher, I can put you in touch with the firm that did my histories - good people, extremely helpful, well connected in the trade. Have you a sample of your writing to show them?"

"Yes, I have an outline, and I've roughed out the first chapter. Really, thanks so much for offering to help. I didn't expect to make a commercial venture of the book; rather, I was going to have just a few copies printed for my children and some close relatives."

"Oh, forgive me for becoming possessive of you, but would you be my guests for dinner at the golf club this evening? I'll pick you up at seven, if you'll tell me where you're staying. And Fred, do bring along what you've written. I'm anxious to have a look at it."

We accepted his invitation, told him we were staying at the Barbican, and left him there. On the way back to the inn, Josée observed, "What a coincidence! What do you make of him?"

"I know I'm not allowed to say it, but I can tell he's already in love with you."

She looked pleased. "Don't be silly, or I'll do something a little bit kinky to you again."

"No, thanks. You nearly drowned me last night. That's for when I've really been bad."

"Oh, but I have nothing to wear for tonight! On the way to the church, I noticed a lovely little shop with such nice things in it. Could we stop there?"

We stopped, of course, and bought her a pale pink silk dress featuring a plunging neckline designed to make a man's eyes fall out of his head.

The clubhouse at the golf course reeked of tradition and fine English cooking. Dickie, a gracious host who obviously appreciated a drink as much as we did, soon shed his reserve, and entertained us with stories of the Open Championships played at Royal St. Georges. Josée was nothing short of stunning in her new outfit, and when Dickie complimented her about it, she wiggled and smiled prettily. I knew he was dying to learn what kind of a relationship we had with each other, and over liqueurs, I made a pre-emptive strike. "Josée and I are more than platonic."

She blushed down to her cleavage and looked daggers at me, while Dickie smiled and raised his glass. "Congratulations! You are a fortunate man."

Changing the subject, I asked, "Dickie, can you tell us about the Cinque Ports?"

"They were a confederation of English Channel ports formed in medieval times to furnish ships for the King's navy. Cinque, of course, means five in French, and Sandwich was one of the original five. In return for providing a navy, these ports were granted certain privileges."

"What were those privileges?"

"Let me see if I can remember them all: tax and tallage, sol and sac, tol and team, blodwit and fledwit, pillory and tumbrel, infangentheoi and outfangentheof, mundbryce, waives and strays, flotsam, jetsam and ligan, guild and portmote."

I looked blank, and he laughed. "Essentially, Fred, those Old English privileges amounted to relief from taxation, rights to salvage, and a good deal of self government."

Again, I changed the subject. "I really should know, but I'm not much on religion. Who were the Puritans, and why did they leave England?"

"The Puritans were a faction within the Church of England who wanted to distance themselves more from the Church of Rome."

Josée interrupted, "You bloody Anglais, setting up your own church, and persecuting Catholics!"

"Of course, you are Catholic, Josée, as are most French-Canadians," Dickie responded. "Well, yes, we did set up our own Church, because the Church of Rome was guilty of the most outrageous practices, such as selling indulgences. But we were talking about the Puritans. They came in many forms, but in general, they wanted less ritual in the church, less in the way of hierarchy - certainly no bishops - and more attention given to the scriptures. They themselves were persecuted at various times by Catholics, Josée, and in hopes of gaining more religious freedom they supported the rebel Oliver Cromwell against King Charles the First in the 1640's. Poor Charles, of course, was eventually beheaded. After the restoration of the monarchy in 1660, there was a period known as the Great Persecution, when many Puritans were killed or driven into exile. When did your ancestors leave, Fred?"

"In 1634, so they must have missed the worst of it. Would you like to look at my material now?"

"By all means." Dickie read quickly and began to smile. "Yes, yes. Thomas Boney, as it was then spelt, a cordwainer - what a delightfully archaic word for shoemaker! Born in Sandwich 1604, emigrated to New England in 1634 on the vessel Hercules, 200 tons, John Weatherley master. Settled in the town of Duxborough, now Duxbury, Plymouth County, Massachusetts. Married first to Mary Terry, who died childless, then to Mary Hunt when he was 50, who bore him eight children."

Josée made a strange little noise. "Had eight children after he was 50? Mon Dieu!"

Dickie chuckled "Josée, I think that truth, as always, is more fascinating than fiction. Fred, I think, with a little work, you could produce something saleable out of your material. How much time have you left in England?"

"We're booked out on Air Canada on June 3rd, a week today. I thought, as long as we're over here, we might take a tour or two. I was going to make some arrangements in the morning."

Dickie looked guilty. "I took the liberty of phoning my publishers this afternoon on the hunch that you might have something good. Will you come with me tomorrow to see them?"

Foolish pride clouded my brain. "Why, thanks. Of course."

"And do you play golf, by any chance?"

"Josée does. I thrash."

"Delightful. How about a game day after tomorrow then, here at St. Georges?"

Before I could answer, Josée accepted for both of us. "Oh, I never thought I would ever get to play on a British Open course! But we have no clubs, nor suitable clothes," she added.

"Oh, heavens, don't worry about that. I will line both up for you."

We were hardly out of Dickie's car before Josée was on my case. "You didn't have to tell him we were sleeping together. You embarrassed me terribly."

"If the shoe fits, you'll have to wear it."

"I'll get even with you, just wait."

We met Dickie at the train station that Friday morning, travelled with him to London, and took a taxi to his publisher's offices in the high fashion district. He introduced me to Basil Hall, the man he dealt with, then asked, "Do you need me? If not, I thought I'd take Josée for a walk."

I could feel my jealousy level rising, but I really didn't need him. "Go ahead. Just remember to bring her back." He laughed, and said of course he would.

Basil ushered me into his office strewn with manuscripts, I gave him my material, and he scanned it quickly. "Interesting," he opined. "Let me digest this for a few moments." He leaned back in his chair with his hands behind his head, and looked at the ceiling. At length, he said, "I see that you are well organized, with lists of letters, pictures and so on. Did you do the research yourself?"

"No, actually, an uncle did it. I inherited his work when he died."

"How long and detailed are some of those letters?"

"A couple of pages, at the longest."

"Pity. What I have in mind is to reincarnate these ancestors of yours in flesh and blood, and more detail would have been helpful. To put it another way, your ancestors should be real, not inanimate objects created on a computer. For example, 'Thomas Bonney sailed from Dover to Duxbury, Mass., where he settled and had eight children by his second wife' will not sell. 'In 1634, Thomas Bonney embarked on the tiny sailing vessel Hercules with his frail wife, Mary, in high hopes for a better life in New England, and the chance to freely practise his religious beliefs. He had no idea of the ordeal that faced him, the twelve week passage to Massachusetts Bay on the stormy North Atlantic, or the great loss he would soon suffer.' That might sell."

"You're asking me to write fiction."

"Not entirely. You have these ancestors who did these things. It is a matter of imputing motives, expectations, emotions. You are a Bonney. Imagine yourself leaving Dover on that leaky, wooden tub, with your wife, who will die, and who therefore may have been frail."

"I see. Well, I'll give it a try. When I get something ready, I'll send it along."

"Good. I'll look forward to it. By the way, a woman has more insight when it comes to emotions than a man. Josée, if I may say so, should be a great help to you."

Not you, too! Jesus! Every man in England is falling for her!

Basil continued, "I'll give you a file number. Put it on the envelope and on each page of your material when you send it in, and it will be sent straight to me. Otherwise, it will get lost in the mountain of trash that you see lying around in here."

We talked for another half hour about deadlines, the timing of publication, and assorted other details, and said goodbye. Basil then showed me out to the reception area, and there was Josée, Josée in a brand new and obviously expensive outfit, and on the floor beside her were two boxes obviously full of clothes as well, with Dickie grinning at her. I managed to control myself and ignored her. "Dickie, you promised us lunch. We'll take you up on that."

Back in our room in Sandwich, I yelled at her. "Jesus Christ, Josée, how did you con him into buying those clothes?"

"Mr. Bonney, such profane language."

"Don't call me Mr. Bonney! How?"

"I didn't con him into anything. We went for a walk, we passed this shop full of pretty things, he said was there anything there that I wanted, that he would buy it for me if there was. And there was."

"Fuck! There, you've made me say it. For the first time in my life, I've said fuck in front of a woman. Don't you know you can't go around letting strange men buy you things? Don't you know that he will expect something in return? Do we have an agreement or don't we?"

"I told you I would get even with you. Now it is your turn to be angry. Dickie said not to worry about the cost, and if it gives him pleasure to buy me nice things, why not?"

"Thank God we're going home in a few days, and will probably never see him again. But what's in the other two boxes?"

"Oh, my old clothes in one, and golf clothes for tomorrow in the other. And we are to be at the pro shop tomorrow morning at eight o'clock to be fitted with clubs. Dickie said he would find some old clothes for you, since you are about the same size."

"Dickie's going to buy us new clubs for one game of golf?"

"Probably two or three games. Ah, mon cher Fred," she said sarcastically, "I won't torture you any longer. He told me I remind him of his dead daughter, that is all."

I looked at her for an excruciating moment, then she came to me, and I crushed her in my arms. "Josée, Jos, being with you is like blasting off in a NASA shuttle. What happened to my quiet, sheltered life?"

She pushed herself away and looked at me with those knowing brown eyes. "Do you want to go back to that life?"

"Not on your life do I want to go back! Come here and let me appreciate you."

I appreciated her at some length, and after we were finished, I lay back and thought about Dickie. Whatever his opinion of Josée, I perceived my distant relative as a rival, one I certainly couldn't compete with financially, and if she started to work on him, I had a hunch his daughter image of her might vanish in a hurry. And after all, wasn't she, innocently or otherwise, already working on him - the pretty smiles, the musical laughter, the appreciative touch on his arm, those damn wiggles?

Josée interrupted my thoughts. "Dickie wants to talk to you some more about your book. You've got him interested in writing again."

"What, are you his messenger now?"

"Just talk to him. He has some ideas."

I was still disgruntled the next morning when Dickie picked us up. The only good thing was that Josée got up without any urging, because when it came to golf, she was deadly serious. We made small talk on the way to the club – wasn't the weather wonderful, and so on - with no mention of the book. When we got there, Dickie introduced us to the pro, and told us to pick whatever clubs suited us without looking at the price. We both found sets identical to the ones we owned, and after the pro checked to make sure they were of the proper shaft length and lie, we were treated to new shoes as well. Dickie's old clothes fitted me well enough, while Jose's new outfit, although in compliance with the dress code, showed off her figure dangerously.

We started off by hitting some practise balls, and I noticed that Dickie looked to be a fair golfer. All of a sudden, I was seized with mischief. "Handicap, Dickie?"

"Seven."

"Josee? Five, isn't it?"

"You know that."

Dickie was impressed. "Five!"

I said, "Alright, I'm out of your league at 20, but Dickie, I'll bet you that Josee beats you by those two strokes, and two more besides."

"Fred!" Josee waggled, and her breasts did tantalizing things.

"Alright," Dickie said. "I play from the members' tees and Josee from the women's. What for a wager?"

"The price of Josée's clubs."

"Oh, Fred!" Another delicious waggle.

"A sporting man, I see. Agreed, then."

Three caddies appeared and made off to the first tee with our clubs, we following, I wondering how many strokes the stiff breeze blowing off the English Channel was going to add to my score. Dickie and I hit first, his ball barely finding the left side of the fairway, mine slicing weakly into the right rough, and we then listened to Josée while she talked to her caddy. I'd never had one before, but she obviously knew what she wanted from hers.

"Now pay attention. We have a serious match on, I don't know the course, and I'm depending on you to give me distance to the yard, advice on where to place the ball, and line on the greens. To start with, how should I play my first shot?"

The caddy smirked and eyed her up brazenly. "Oh, don't worry about it, miss. It is almost impossible to hit this first fairway. Just aim for the middle and hope."

Josée looked at him blandly. "But it is possible to hit it?"

"Well, you have to aim right and hit it at least 240 yards with a slight draw, but... - "

"Just keep your eye on the ball, *cretin*, not on me. Give me the driver." She teed up her ball and approached it from behind and to the right. One look toward her target, one glorious waggle, one perfect swing, and the ball sailed high into the sky, curving slightly to the left, and came to rest on the fairway, 250 yards away. The caddy opened his mouth as if to say something, then closed it. Finally, he managed, "Shot."

While I hacked myself out of knee high rough and head high sand traps, cursing the architect, if there ever was one, who designed this fiendish layout, Josée proceeded to win my bet for me. She was one up after the first hole, two up at the turn, back to one up when Dickie birdied the tenth, then four up when she birdied the eleventh to his double bogey. There were the two strokes plus two, and she added two more before the finish. All the while, her caddy became more and more solicitous, and at the end, shook her hand warmly. "A pleasure to carry your clubs, miss." He hesitated. "Ah, what does *cretin* mean?"

"Loosely translated, that's French for asshole."

Over a late lunch, Dickie brought up the subject of the book again, looking at me in an ingratiating, almost pleading manner before he began. "Fred, I don't want to usurp your turf, but your notes on the family have started my creative juices flowing. I have decided to write another military history, this one about British North America, but several have already been published on the subject. What I have in mind is to do something more than the purely military aspects, that is, about the diplomatic manoeuvring, the personalities, as well as the wars and the battles leading up to the creation of Canada."

Like so many Brits, he pronounced the name of my country 'Canader.'

"There is more to it than that, Dickie. Beyond the creation was the preservation of it."

16

"Yes indeed. I thought we could end after the settlement of the boundary with Alaska, the last real crisis in determining the size and shape of your country. In any case, it seems to me that what you propose to do might well complement my history, lend a human dimension to events that might otherwise seem dispassionate. Alright so far?"

My guard was up, but I said, "Go ahead."

"So it seems to me we could go at it independently, or work together as co-authors. In the latter case, you would not have to worry about a publisher, because Basil is enthusiastic about the idea. No doubt you won't want to make a snap decision one way or another, but will you think about it?"

I was about to make a snap decision against co-authorship when Josée broke in. "And I will act as secretary for you both, and not only that, I will translate the book into French so that it can be published in both languages. You Anglais are too quick to forget that one quarter of the people of Canada speak French, and I can give you their view of things through my brother's eyes. Perhaps we should write my ancestors into the book, too. That would give both sides of the wars between the French and English."

"A capital idea, Josée." Dickie looked from one to the other of us with what seemed to be equal fondness. "You two look as if you are going to have such fun. I hope you will allow a lonely old man into your plans."

"Dickie, I don't know how you see this happening, but I imagine it will be necessary to visit New England, travel across Canada from coast to coast, visit several archives, museums, and National Historic Sites, to assemble all the necessary material."

"Agreed. I can certainly help with the expenses - in fact, I'll pay them all."

I was trapped. I couldn't help liking him, and Josée had practically invited him along. Besides, my severance allowance was already half gone. "I will think about the co-authorship part, but in the meantime, you might as well come over and join us when we go to Boston."

Dickie looked ecstatic. "Thank you so much." He shook my hand, and was about to shake Josée's when she reeled him in, kissed him, and gave him an enthusiastic hug.

During our remaining four days in England, we played two more games of golf with Dickie at St. Georges, and we all laughed when we learned that the nickname 'Cretin' had stuck to Josée's caddy. On the Sunday, after Josée first went to church, Dickie took us on a walking tour of Sandwich in a drizzle, pointing out likely spots where Thomas Bonney may have had his shoe shop. And on our last day, we toured the museum in the old windmill, a thatched roofed Kentish Oast house where they used to dry hops, and Richborough castle.

Leaving Dickie to start his research in England, with the arrangement that he would join us in Boston in two weeks, we caught our flight for home on schedule, I looking forward to another blissful interlude alone with Josée. It started out that way. We were hardly in the door of her apartment before she was cleaning again, and then she washed and ironed a mountain of clothes, and when

17

she had finished that, she stood in the middle of the front room, aglow with perspiration and with a satisfied look on her face, and she said, "Fred, it's time for a shower."

We had less than a blissful week, as it turned out, because her period came, an event that completely changed her. On the second day, I caught her crying, and I took her in my arms. While she sobbed against my shoulder, I said, "Josée, Jos, I don't care what you do to me, I love you. Tell me what's wrong."

"Fred, shut up Fred." She wiped her eyes and tried to smile. "Every time I have a period, it makes me feel so guilty. From when I was a little girl, I was told by the Church that it was wrong to use contraceptives, but I did when I was first married. Then, when I stopped using them, I couldn't conceive, and I wonder if that wasn't God's punishment for disobeying the Church. And I feel guilty because I must have been a bad wife, because Paul needed other women. Maybe it was because I'm such a poor cook. And I feel guilty because of all the times I've committed adultery."

"Josée, Jos, you are the most beautiful woman in the world. I'm so jealous when other men like Dickie and Basil fall in love with you. Please marry me."

"Shut up Fred, shut up! I am not divorced. It is against the Church."

I held her close while she cried herself out, and then in a muffled voice she asked, "Now that you know all about me, would you really marry me?"

"I would."

"How many children did Thomas Bonney have after he was 50?"

"Eight."

"Mon Dieu!"

Chapter 2.

New England, New France

The way to my heart was not through my stomach, or my affair with Josée would soon have been over. I cooked breakfast every day and lunch too, unless we were out somewhere, or playing golf. After she cooked supper a couple of times, I did a stirfry in self-defence; after that, we decided to eat out in the evenings. Three days before we were to leave for Boston, we tried the neighbourhood pub, and that turned out to be a painful mistake.

Josée by this time was over her period and in a more cheerful state of mind. We had a couple of beers with the special, and since we had nothing else planned, we then moved up to the stools at the bar for a couple of long, tall ones. As the evening wore one, the crowd became less working class and more pleasure bent, more her age than mine, and it became evident that she knew many of the late-comers, some of the men on an intimate basis. One of them, a big stud with a ring in his ear, pinched her bottom and said, "Hey, Jos, your plants still OK? I watered them like you said, twice a week. What're you doing tonight?"

"Thanks again for looking after the plants, Gino, but I got a steady date now."

Gino looked at me, then back to her. "Not this old fart? You gotta be kidding! Hey, old fart, how you get a piece like Jos?"

I was not a violent man. The last fight I had was in primary school. I had no training in boxing or wrestling, but reason deserted me the moment this big slab of meat pinched Josée. I stood up and said, "Because, Gino, knucklehead, I got more brains than you."

He looked surprised, then mad. "Oh, ho ho! More guts than brains, old fart!" He pushed me in the chest once, twice, three times, and then I swung a left at his head. Had to be an advantage, being left-handed, I heard somewhere. It was like hitting a concrete abutment. The room exploded around me, and the next thing I knew for sure I was in a hospital.

Josée was by the side of the bed, looking anxious. "How's your head? The doctor said you have a mild concussion."

"I agree with the doctor. Got a headache, and my hand feels like it's broken. Josée, did you go with that Gino?"

She looked upset. "How could you think that? We have an agreement, n'est ce pas? After he hit you, I hit him over the head with a bottle."

"Jos, my head hurts when I laugh. Don't make me laugh."

"There was a riot, and the bill for damages could be a few thousand. We have to appear in court tomorrow."

I couldn't help laughing, even if it did hurt. Josée joined in, and after awhile, a nurse came along to find out what all the noise was about.

In court, the six of us who were ordered to appear gave our testimony, and the judge determined that Gino was the chief culprit. Gino, sporting a black eye and a bandage where the bottle cut him, was ordered to pay $1,000, and to keep the peace for six months, while the rest of us were charged $500 each, enough altogether to cover the damage bill. I paid our share before we left, and we were confronted outside by Gino.

"You old - you old man, look what you did to me." He pointed to his black eye.

"I did that?" I was immensely pleased with myself.

"And you, Jos. You gave me ten stitches in the head." He looked down and shuffled his feet. "Jos, you care for this old man?'

"He asked me to marry him, Gino."

"Oh." He grimaced, and I knew he was in love with her too. "Yeah," he said, nodding his head and looking into the distance. "I would have married you too, except I never got around to asking." He turned and started to walk away, then stopped and turned back. "You take care of her, old man, O.K. You ever need any help with anything, Jos, like looking after your plants, just call me."

We walked to the car, silent at first, Josée, I'm sure, feeling a little sorry for Gino the way I was. Then I said, "I didn't know I could do a black eye." She laughed, and we started to talk in a mixture of French and English, something that was becoming our natural way of communicating. Neither of us was fully versed in the idiom of the other's language, with the result that we mispronounced some words, or put the accent on the wrong syllables, and added to some errors in sentence construction, it all suddenly seemed hilariously funny. By the time we got to the apartment, we were laughing so hard we must have looked like a couple of happy idiots. Maybe that is what saved me from being hit again.

If Gino was big, the man standing at the door of the apartment building was bigger. "Pierre!" Josée gasped. And in French, "Why didn't you tell me you were coming?"

"I tried to phone you last night. No answer. I had to come to Ottawa on business, and I thought we could have lunch together. You with this old man? Is he Anglais?"

Josée's brother was darker of complexion than she, but there was a strong family resemblance, except that his nose must have been broken more than once, by the look of it. That gave him the dangerous air of a prizefighter. He seemed familiar, somehow, but I couldn't believe I had ever seen him before. The two of them began to talk in an animated fashion, both using their arms and hands as the French do, and I knew Pierre didn't realize that I understood every uncomplimentary word he said about me. Suddenly, I lost all concern about his size and interrupted, in French, "Oh, come on in, little brother. I want to talk to you about Quebec."

Recovering from his surprise, he said, "So, you speak French. Eh, bien. I will not apologize for what I have said."

"No need. I'm getting used to being abused."

Josée warmed up the coffee (she did that well), and we drank it in the living room. "So, what is it you want to know about Quebec?" Pierre asked, with a faint, contemptuous smile. That smile - now I remembered! Pierre Bonin, the hockey legend, the Canadiens' enforcer for years, and that was the look he had on his face just before he started beating the hell out of one of the other team's players!

"Pierre Bonin, I just realized who you are. Maybe I'm lucky to be alive."

He grinned, then laughed. "Josée never told you about me?"

"Only that you were big and didn't like us Anglais. Josée, why didn't you tell me?"

"I thought it might frighten you away."

Pierre chuckled. "You needn't have worried. I don't go around beating people up since I quit playing hockey. But Quebec?"

"I'm writing a book about my family. Since I first had the idea, Josée and I have got together, and another relative, from England, suggested we broaden the scope of the book into a military history of British North America, using my notes on the family to make it more authentic. Josée reminded us that Canada is one quarter French, and she offered to give us the French view of things through you. She's also going to translate the book into French, and both versions will be published at the same time."

Pierre's face darkened. "Quebec will not be part of Canada much longer."

A month ago, I might have tried to placate him like a good public servant. I was changing. "That will not alter the fact that Quebec was part of Canada during most of the period the book covers."

"Alright, then. I will tell you about Quebec, about New France, of what might have been." He paused and seemed to compose himself. "It is as simple as this. There came to be many more Anglais than French over here; yet, if France had supported us the way the English supported their colonists, if we had been blessed with good administrators when it counted most, then all of North America might now be French. It was not for lack of courage that we lost, for we fought - oh, God how we fought - to retain what was rightfully ours. We were the first to explore this land, to map it, to extract wealth from it, to make treaties with many of the Indian nations. French blood is spattered all over the continent, from the Maritime Provinces in the east to British Columbia in the west, from the Arctic Ocean to the mouth of the Mississippi River. Yet what are we reduced to? A mere province in Canada, said to have no more power and influence that any other, the same in Confederation as that tiny pipsqueak of a place, Prince Edward Island." He laughed derisively. "You Anglais insult us. We will be our own nation."

I wasn't much of an expert on federal provincial relations, but I thought he had a point. "Alright. I am interested in two battles, the one when Louisbourg was captured the second time, and the one on the Plains of Abraham when Quebec was conquered. An ancestor of mine, Joel Bonney, fought for the British in both. Were there Bonins on the other side?"

"Yes, there were. At Louisbourg, my ancestor," he looked at Josée, "our ancestor, was shipped to France when the British captured the fort, and had to make his way back to Quebec on a merchant ship. The Plains of Abraham? There, we were betrayed by a greedy, womanizing administrator, that pig Bigot, who put into his own pocket what should have gone to the military." He smiled sardonically. "But credit where it is due. You had a better general, and some luck. When the British troops opened fire on the Plains of Abraham that September morning in 1759, it was the most devastating volley ever let loose in history. It was as if every man picked a different target, and his aim was deadly. With that one volley, New France died, and along with it, our ancestor Marcel."

We listened to him talk about New France and Quebec for the rest of the morning, and after a break for soup and sandwiches, long into the afternoon. When he was at last done, I asked him about his hockey career, and why he retired early.

"The Canadiens wanted to trade me, but I didn't want to leave Quebec, so I quit. I could maybe have played for another few years, but I wanted to get on with my history studies. This spring, I graduated from Laval University, and now I'm working on an MBA."

I asked, "What have you in the way of family history?"

"A few letters, a journal."

"Just a minute." I retrieved the locket and showed it to him. He was intrigued. "So like Josée! Where did it come from?"

"Out of a trunk in my attic. The trunk belonged to a Lorenzo Dow, and all I know about him is that he was an ancestor."

When Josée excused herself to go to the bathroom, Pierre said quickly, "I worry about my sister. She is pretty mixed up sometimes, takes religion too seriously, feels that it was her fault that her marriage failed, feels that she failed our father by not being good enough at golf, and not giving him grandchildren. Maybe she is attracted to you because you look a little like our father - oh, I don't mean to suggest anything like an Oedipus complex, nothing like that. I have never seen her happier than she was when the two of you came home this morning. I hope you care for her."

"I love her, Pierre. I will look after her as long as she will let me."

When Josée came back, Pierre observed, "Bonney, Bonin. Very close, the two names."

"Maybe closer than we know. My ancestors came from France, and we were told in England that the name was originally spelt B-o-n-y."

"Josée, maybe you should hang on to this Anglais. He is at least part French, and he makes good sandwiches. And I will be more than pleased to tell you whatever you need to know about Quebec, and the French presence in North America. As a matter of fact, I just happen to have with me a copy of my graduating thesis for Josée - and for you, Fred, here is a copy in English, to be published at McGill University later this year. Perhaps that will be sufficient. And you must come to my wedding in July. Geneviève and I both believe that to save French language and culture in North America, we Quebeckers must return to the ways of our ancestors, and have many children."

"How many do you plan to have?" I asked.

"At least ten. But now I must go."

We spent the evening reading Pierre's thesis, entitled 'The French in North America', which ran to 300 pages. At the end of it, he had written on her copy in a strong hand, "To my big sister Josée, with love. I should tell you there is some mystery surrounding the wife of one of our ancestors. Louis Bonin found her somewhere around Schenectady, New York, while on a military raid in 1696, and as far as I have been able to find out, she was of mixed Anglais-Iroquois blood."

"What did Pierre's nose look like before it got broken?" I asked, idly.

"Like yours."

Josée went out on her own the next morning, saying she had to get her hair done and run some errands. She came back a blonde. "How do you like it?" she asked, posing for me.

"I like you in any shade you come in."

She frowned. "The only blonde clothes I have are so worn. I was looking in that nice store you took me to before we went to England, and they have a sale on. Would you take me there again? And then, I have to buy some more cosmetics, and my allowance is all gone. Could I have an advance on next month's?"

I hadn't yet, might never learn to say no to her. At the 'nice store', we bought her three new outfits, and this time, I noticed the amount of the bill - nearly $1,000. After another $200 for cosmetics, she was ready for our trip to New England.

On Thursday, June 17th, we loaded up my old Chev, headed south to avoid the congestion on the Trans-Canada highway, and crossed the St. Lawrence River into the United States at Cornwall. After passing the immigration inspection, we continued south and east through New York State, across two arms of Lake Champlain into Vermont, and south again on U.S. Route 89. It was a stinking hot, muggy day to start with, the kind when every Canadian who could afford it headed north to his cottage on a cool lake. With no air conditioning, we made the best of it by rolling down the windows, tuning in to a French station, and singing along with the music. Again, I experienced sublime happiness harmonizing with Josée, watching her beside me, so erect, so alert, so beautiful, an unbelievable prize for an old man.

It started to cool off as the radio began to fade, and by the time we climbed up the wooded Winooski River valley to Montpelier, the modest state capital of Vermont, the air temperature was almost pleasant. We settled into a motel for the night, and as I was beginning to learn, unfamiliar surroundings acted on Josée like an aphrodisiac. We were going through the preliminaries when she whispered in my ear, "Maybe something different this time, something a little bit kinky. What did you do for yourself when you had no woman to look after you?"

"Well, you must have heard." I didn't want to admit to masturbation at my age - the old public servant coming out in me again.

"Something like this?"

"Well, yes, but Jos, I don't need you to do that."

"Something better, then. Like this?"

"Oh Jos, you don't need to do that - unless you want to. Oh Jos, that's nice."

"Now you can do the same for me, if we turn like this."

"Promise you won't drown me again?"

"Promises, promises."

After we finished, and were nestled together under the covers, I reflected on the joy this woman had brought to me. I just hoped she wouldn't leave me when my money ran out. "It is like Pierre said," she murmured drowsily. "Lake Champlain, named after the founder of Quebec City, once part of New France, now mostly American. And Montpelier? Named after Montpellier, a town in France. The Americans cannot spell it properly, let alone pronounce it. We should make love the old fashioned way in this place as a kind of protest."

"Alright, this is for New France, and Old France too."

We continued down Route 89 the next day through the mixed forests and granite mountains of Vermont, until we were greeted with signs bearing the words 'Bienvenue à New Hampshire'. Josée cheered. "It is like Pierre said. Thousands of Quebeckers have emigrated to New England over the years, and their descendants number in the millions. The French will yet win!"

South of Concorde, New Hampshire, we branched onto Route 93, and followed it all the way to Cambridge, Massachusetts, just short of the city of Boston. As arranged with Dickie, we were to book into a hotel near Harvard University, but it wasn't all that easy to find, especially since Josée proved to be something less than a competent navigator. We spent most of an hour cruising up and down narrow, one-way streets dodging jay walking pedestrians before we stumbled onto it, a lumpy, nine story structure made of the same brick as the university buildings. The doorman looked horrified when he let us out of my old Chev, and the valet who came to take it away to the parking garage turned up his nose, confirming my impression that it was an expensive place. I was thankful Dickie was paying for it.

A bellhop gathered up our luggage and ushered us in, and when Josée saw the lobby, she exclaimed, "Oh, I never thought I would ever get to stay in a place like this! Look at all the quilts hanging by the staircase! Oh, I was born to be rich!"

There were more antique New England quilts in the hall on our floor, and our room was, according to the literature inside, decorated in contemporary country style, with custom designed adaptations of early American Shaker furniture. While I tipped the bellhop, Josée rushed about exclaiming over the amenities, which included two phones, TV, dataport, radio, air conditioning and a mini bar. She pirouetted into the bathroom and cried, "There's even a phone and a TV in here! And listen to what it says in this brochure! There's a glass-enclosed pool, an exercise room and a beauty parlour - oh, I'll just have to get my hair done before we leave! And there are two restaurants, and you can eat in the bar, too, and listen to live jazz!"

The message lamp started to flash: Dickie was waiting for us in the bar. I should have known better, but while Josée put her face on, I browsed through the Boston phone book looking for Bonneys, and one listing in bold print caught my eye: 'Bonney, Joel Robert'. I dialled the number and got an answering service: 'Please leave your name and number after the beep'. I explained who I was, said I was interested in meeting the owner of the name if he were a descendent of Thomas Bonney, and advised that we would be in the bar at the Charles Hotel.

When we arrived at Dickie's table, I controlled myself while he hugged and kissed Josée, forgave him when he shook my hand warmly. "How delightful!" he enthused. "Together again, even if it is in America, where the insufferable 'Lords of the Earth' live. Josée, I hardly recognized you as a blonde, but it suits you. Now, to business. I've booked us in here for four nights to start with."

Josée's eyes were as big as saucers. "Four nights? But it must be so expensive!"

Dickie laughed. "Oh, not really. I'm sure we'll stay in more expensive places before we're finished. What's on the agenda for tomorrow?"

"Harvard University," I said. "I contacted the Widener Library there on the internet. They told me they have a collection of Bonney papers in their archives section, which they will let us go through to see if there's anything Uncle Bill didn't have. That should take care of the first day. Then we'll go down the coast, visit Duxbury, Plymouth and Sandwich, maybe Cape Cod too, if we have time."

"A Sandwich over here?" Josée asked. "And don't forget, day after tomorrow is Sunday, and I have to go to church."

"Can you do it early?" I asked, not wanting to waste half a day waiting for her.

"Yes, I'm sure there will be a service at eight."

"In answer to your question," said Dickie, "Puritans who emigrated from Sandwich in England founded the Sandwich over here. But I have much to tell you. First, I did a rush research job on the military history of British North America, and prepared an outline to show the publishers. Basil was again enthusiastic - oh, before I forget, he sends his love to Josée and his regards to Fred. Together, we marked the places where you, Fred, might fit in your material about the family - but I should have asked you again before I started in. Will you join me as co-author?"

I'd thought about the idea a great deal, and come to the conclusion that I would need money if I wanted to keep Josée. With Dickie as co-author, publication and royalties were assured. "Yes, Dickie. I surrender."

"Good, good." He shook my hand again. "On that, let's have a drink."

Before we could order, the desk paged me, announcing that another Mr. Bonney would be joining us. In a moment, a big, shambling man walked in, instantly impressive because of his large head, bull neck, great mane of yellow hair, and big Bonney nose. He was further distinctive because of his clothes, casual but with that expensive tailored look, and his reading glasses, which were hung around his neck by a black cord. I beckoned to him, and he introduced himself as "Joe-Bob Bonney, born and raised in Georgia, but now a resident of Boston." I was struck by how deep his voice was, and guessed that he'd already had a few by the way he walked. On closer inspection, he was perhaps in his mid-forties, had a ruddy complexion, and was a little overweight. An errant thought struck me. Pierre had the Bonney nose too, if you reconstructed it. No, no. An impossible connection.

We shook hands all around, and Dickie ordered the drinks. Joe-Bob took a generous swallow of his and told us without humour, "I'm a typical American male. I've had three wives and two kids with each of them, and now none of them will talk to me. I was good enough to play in the National Football League till I tore up my knee in my first professional practice - spent two years in 'Nam before that, came out of it a Major with nightmares - graduated in engineering before that, but never engineered anything - went to work selling cars for my daddy instead, after I wrecked my knee. Three months ago, when my third wife left with the kids, I all of a sudden felt as if the air had gone out of my tires - lost all my ambition and aggressiveness - so I sold most of my businesses, including the biggest used car dealership in the south east. Since then, I've been wandering around the country trying to find a reason to keep on living. Now that I've talked to you all, you've got me interested in finding out more about these Puritan ancestors of ours. I already know something about them from my granddaddy. He told me before he died that I was descended from Thomas Bonney, who came over on the Mayflower."

"Oh, no," corrected Dickie. "He most certainly came over on the Hercules in 1634, not the Mayflower in 1620."

"Well, I'm damned."

"Which of his sons are you descended from?" I asked with interest.

"Ephraim. He was the third out of nine children."

"But there is no Ephraim on my list. There were only eight."

"Well, that's what my granddaddy told me. Ephraim, he said, was the black sheep of the family, got expelled from Plymouth Colony for lechery, both adultery and fornication, and pardon the language, Josée, if it offends. I guess the reason he's not on your list is that the family disowned him. Then he went to live among the Indians, got into the fur trade at Fort Albany until he was chased out by the French. Then he went to Massachusetts, and finally to New Hampshire."

"Mon Dieu! Not eight, but nine children after he was 50!"

Joe-Bob looked at Josée with interest. "How do you fit into this crowd?"

"Fred and Dickie are writing a book about the Bonney family in North America. I'm secretary to them both."

" Now I'd call that some good luck for them."

Josée wiggled and smiled sweetly. "Thank you for the compliment."

Why, for God's sake, did she have to wiggle like that? It was like a come-on. I didn't want to have to fight off this unwelcome relative as well as Dickie. Good old Dickie. He wasn't so bad. He said it for me, causing Josée, of course, to blush.

"Joe-Bob, you should know that Fred and Josée have something going."

"Well, damn, Dickie, I am disappointed to hear that. But Josée, you sound French."

"Not French French, I am from Quebec."

"Well hell! One of my ancestors fought the French there, according to my granddaddy."

I took over the conversation. "To change the subject, Joe-Bob, do you realize that you are the namesake of my most famous ancestor, Joel Bonney?"

"No, I sure didn't. What was he famous for?"

"He also fought for the British against the French, and later, he became a United Empire Loyalist."

"What the hell is a United Empire Loyalist?"

"United Empire Loyalists remained loyal to Britain at the time of the American Revolution."

"You telling me he was a traitor?"

"No. You were the rebels. He remained loyal to Britain."

"Why would anyone do that? Must have been some confused about the future. Say, isn't it about time you folks up there in Canada ran the British out, the Queen and all?"

I couldn't believe my ears, even though I'd heard that most Americans didn't know a thing about my country. "Joe-Bob, we've been independent of Great Britain since 1867. Our government is based on the British parliamentary model, except that we are a federation of ten provinces, each with its own legislative assembly, besides the national Parliament based in Ottawa, and we also have two territories which have limited legislative powers. While we have a Governor General, the real power rests with the Prime Minister of the country and the Premiers of the provinces. Our population is nearly 30 million, about one tenth that of the United States, but our country is larger in total area. And we are officially bilingual, that is, both English and French are official languages in the federal parliament."

"Well, I didn't know all that. All I know about Canada is that you sheltered a bunch of draft dodgers from the Viet Nam War, and I sure don't think you should have done that. It is the duty of every able bodied American to serve his country without question in time of war. But say, my stomach is starting to rumble. I'll get the desk to make dinner reservations, and you all are my guests. We've got time for another drink first - waiter, bring another round, and put it on my tab." He dropped two, 20-dollar bills on the table. "And ask the desk to book me into a room here tonight, and make reservations for four at Rowes - just tell them it's for Joe-Bob."

The taxi driver snaked his way through the early evening traffic, crossed the Charles River from Cambridge to Boston on the Longfellow Bridge, and delivered us to a hotel on the waterfront. "I have a suite of rooms here," Joe-Bob told us, "and that does for home while I'm in Boston." The view out the big windows of the restaurant inside was breathtaking, with little ferries scurrying back and forth across the harbour in the fading light, and I was thankful I didn't have to pay for that, or for the upcoming dinner. We all had steak and lobster tail on Joe-Bob's recommendation, and the bill, I was sure, represented a healthy slice out of my monthly pension cheque.

Back at our hotel, we headed to the bar for nightcaps, and listened to the jazz music. One drink led to another, and while Josée and I had our share, the Colonel and the Major, as they started to call each other, seemed to be having a contest to see who could drink the most 'Rusty Nails'. And sometime during the evening, I became 'Canada' and Josée, 'Quebec'. When Dickie turned to Josée and said, "Sarah, you are such a willful girl. Perhaps we spoiled you too much when you were a child. You really should get married again. You know your mother and I would love to have grandchildren," we knew he was on his way out. In Joe-Bob's case, he started in on the man who wrecked his knee and cost him a career in the National Football League. "Blind-sided me, the son of a bitch, when I had my foot caught in a pileup. That's why I ended up as a lousy used car salesman." Then he shuddered and started to sweat, and he was back in Viet Nam. "They pinned us down and lobbed mortar shells at us for three hours before the choppers could get to us. One after another, my men got hit, torn to pieces, screaming, until there were only a dozen of us left." Suddenly, he turned maudlin and, looking pleadingly at Josée, he talked to his three wives: "Cathy, Marcie, Barby, I can't help being what I am. Why'd you have to turn the kids against me?"

Josée and I put them to bed, and as she tucked them in, I noticed some unconscious groping going on. Whether that excited her or the opulent surroundings of the hotel, I wasn't sure, but when we got to our own room, there was no hope of turning in for a good night's sleep.

It was another of those east coast days, the temperature around 80 Fahrenheit, the relative humidity 95 per cent, when we walked the short distance from the hotel to the Widener Library. There, we were given passes, and we spent four hours in the archives looking through the Bonney collection. We divided the material into four parts to save time, and I gave the others a copy of Uncle Bill's summary, with instructions to tag anything he hadn't mentioned. There was little he'd missed, if I could trust my fellow workers. They seemed keen enough.

The archives' staff copied the material for us that we had tagged, and we left in search of a late lunch. Joe-Bob bought us passes at the transit station, and shortly, we were standing at the end of a line-up waiting to get into a restaurant at Durgin Park, famous for its baked beans. "Expect the waitresses to be sassy," Joe-Bob grinned, as we were seated at a long table with strangers. "That's why so many people come here."

Ours, when she finally showed up, was downright rude, and she exchanged verbal insults with Joe-Bob. "Be polite to these nice folks from out of town, can't you?" He implored, with his tongue in his cheek.

"Damn town's too damn crowded as it is without damn tourists."

The dark brown Boston bread and the beans were delicious, and forgetting what they did to me, I pigged out along with the rest. Dickie and Joe-Bob then argued over the bill, after I discreetly dropped out of the bidding, and the conversation went something like this: "Dickie, I might be able to buy and sell you a few times, in spite of all the alimony and child support I'm liable for. Since I sold most of my businesses, I got maybe $100 million lying around in banks or in low risk securities earning nickels and dimes for interest, and the businesses I still have would be worth about the same. I know you're paying for our lovebirds' room, so let me look after everything else. By the way, how did you make your money?"

"I didn't make it, apart from a few thousand pounds a year in royalties and the pittance from my army pension. I inherited it, the only civilized way to come by money. And Joe-Bob, you may be surprised to learn that with $200 million, you could buy and sell me only once. I will agree that you should look after the meals on this trip. I will look after everything else."

"Say, now Dickie, that's hardly a fair division. Somebody's bound to need some clothes along the way - Josée, for instance. How about we split the expenses down the middle?"

Josée wiggled. "You know, I had no idea it would be so hot when I packed for this trip. I really could use something summery to wear."

"Consider it done, little lady," beamed Joe-Bob. "On the way back, we'll take a cab and just go by the best little old dress shop in Boston. Can't have you uncomfortable while we're travelling."

I scowled. It sounded as if he intended to come along with us. This was supposed to be my party. "Do I understand that you are going to come with us when we leave here, Joe-Bob?"

Joe-Bob looked like Dickie did when he asked if he could join us. "Well, cousin Fred, you all look like you're going to have a lot of fun, something I've been some short on the last while. And I can help with the expenses, maybe meals and clothes like Dickie and I were discussing. Besides, I sure would like to see this Canada of yours." And so it was arranged, without my blessing, that Joe-Bob would join the 'team' as he called it.

At an exclusive boutique in downtown Boston, Joe-Bob bought Josée a sleeveless yellow beaded dress made of silk, and a matching, floppy, wide-brimmed hat. Not to be outdone, Dickie bought her an equally expensive purple sundress, while I tried to control my jealousy, and the sinking feeling in my stomach. The outfits I bought her cost in the hundreds of dollars; the ones they bought were in the thousands. I had to give Joe-Bob some credit, however. When we got back to the hotel, he ordered a book on the history of the United States, saying, "I'll read up on it so's I can tell you all what the American view of things was."

About the time we retired to our rooms to get ready for dinner, the beans and the tensions of the day started working on my digestive system, and I suffered a first-class attack of abdominal gas. "God, Fred, you should go to the bathroom!" Josée exclaimed. "Thank heavens there are proper windows in this room!" She threw open the sash and the stink dissipated. "You can't do that at dinner!" She smiled, then laughed. "Maybe you should let one or two go while we're eating. That would be one way of getting even with those two. Do you forgive me for conning them into buying those clothes?"

"Now you admit to a con job. Yes, I forgive you, but Joe-Bob makes me nervous. Don't encourage him any more than you can help, eh?"

"No, mon cher Fred, I will not. We have an agreement, after all."

"You know I would like it to be more than an agreement."

"Shut up, Fred, Shut up. We have what we have as long as it suits us both. What about the gas?"

"I took some pills. They should start working anytime now."

For dinner that night, Joe-Bob took us to a seafood restaurant where we had shark fin soup and fin'n haddie, and for dessert, 'fallen' chocolate cake, delicious but full of calories. Then it was the bar at our hotel until we had to put the military to bed again, followed by something close to a sex orgy in our room.

Josée was back from church by nine that Sunday morning, but it was ten before she finished breakfast. When she was finally ready to go, the valet brought my old Chev to a screeching halt in front of the entrance to the hotel, and insolently tossed me the keys. "Jesus, God, Fred, are we going to have to travel in this?" asked Joe-Bob, his face registering something between a laugh and a sneer.

"Runs good. That's all that matters." It was already muggy hot, and I added, "No air conditioning. You'll have to roll down your window."

With Joe-Bob's help, I found my way through the streets and tunnels of Boston to Highway 3, which would take us first to Duxbury, some 30 miles away, then Plymouth and Sandwich. Josée sang for us on the way, and Joe-Bob complained that he couldn't understand the words. To his further aggravation, it seemed, she said to me in French, "I feel uncomfortable in this land of Puritan heretics. The Protestant churches outnumber the Catholic ten to one."

Duxbury, once a seaport and centre of shipbuilding, then a rural and summer community with an economic base of fishing and agriculture, had become an expensive, upscale residential suburb of Boston by the time of our visit, with a population of about 14,000. There were still many historic and beautiful houses from Pilgrim days in the town, some with views of the sea, but many almost hidden by the trees that had grown up around them. We got out of the car for a short walk-about, Joe-Bob in designer jeans complaining about the heat and mopping his forehead, Dickie in khaki shorts marching ahead, enthusiastic as usual, with camera, binoculars and sketching pad, Josée a fashion plate in her flimsy frock and floppy hat. As for me, I was struck by the number of houses that were either flying American flags, or had them draped over the railings of their balconies.

We found the pioneers' graveyard, but could not find any headstones marking the remains of Bonney ancestors there. Some Pilgrim families were well represented, such as those of Miles Standish and the Partridges, and I wondered if the Bonneys simply didn't care for the grave sites the way some others did. As we returned to the car, one of the locals, an elderly man out mowing his lawn, eyed us suspiciously. Josée gave him a wiggle and blew him a kiss, and we left him there with his mouth hanging open.

Plymouth, in contrast to Duxbury, was highly commercialized, with a trolley running down the main street offering a narrated tour, and a full scale replica of the Mayflower at dock. "The 'Hercules' was much the same size," Dickie advised, as he made a creditable sketch of the ship on his pad with a few deft strokes. "It's a marvel that over 100 people could have crossed the Atlantic in such a tiny vessel." We visited Plymouth Rock, the museum, and several old houses open to visitors, where guides explained the significance of the contents. Again, I was struck by the number of flags in the town, and especially by a man who drove along the street flying one from each side of his car. Otherwise, there seemed to be a lot of fat people waddling from place to place, some of them downright obese, not looking in the least like Dickie's 'Lords of the Earth'.

We continued on to Sandwich, a community much like Duxbury, and finding nothing there of interest, we held a conference to decide if we should drive on to Provincetown at the tip of the Cape Cod Peninsula. "We'll never get back to the hotel tonight if we try that," objected Joe-Bob. "The traffic is bumper to bumper in tourist season and especially on Sunday, take my word for it. I've never been to Hyannis myself. Settle for that instead of Provincetown, and you'll get the flavour of the peninsula."

And so it was that we set off on a nightmare journey of wrong turns and short tempers. I stayed to the right instead of turning left to begin with, and we ended up in Wood's Hole, where thousands of people were besieging the privacy of the oceanographic institute there. Josée got thoroughly confused with her map and by Joe-Bob's advice from the back seat, so I began to ignore them both, and soon had us inching along toward Hyannis on a narrow, two lane road jammed with traffic. It didn't help, either, that it was hot, humid, and long past lunchtime. At least I didn't have to worry about getting a speeding ticket from the police car that was behind us.

"Turn left here," Josée instructed, sounding as if she had finally got her bearings. "That will take us back to the highway, and we can find our way to Hyannis from there." I ignored her, and carried on inching toward Hyannis.

"Why didn't you turn?" she demanded, waving her map at me.

"Because you're usually wrong," I growled.

"Mon Dieu, mon Dieu, mon bloody Dieu!" she screeched. "Find your own bloody way out of here!" And she threw the map out her open window. Instantly, a siren sounded. Joe-Bob started to laugh, and then Dickie, while my face began to burn. There was no need to pull over. I just stopped creeping ahead until the officer behind got out of his car, and approached us with his citation book in his hand.

"Minimum fine for littering in this state is $500," he recited, and began filling out a form.

Joe-Bob, with a grin on his face, took over. "But officer, the lady was just using the map for a fan, and it slipped out of her hand. We'll have the map back, thanks, and be on our way."

The officer looked dubious.

"Besides, officer, these folks are tourists, and we want to treat them right, don't we? You know how much of the state's revenue comes from tourism."

That seemed to convince the law. "Well, alright, but lady, keep a grip on that map, now."

Eventually, we got to the village centre in Hyannis, found a kind of a market where they served light lunches, and gobbled down shrimp sandwiches along with a delicious clam chowder served in plastic buckets. "Within a few miles of here," Joe-Bob told us, "there are some of the wealthiest people in America. Billionaires by the dozens. Someday, I'm going to be one of them."

That ended our visit to the Cape Cod Peninsula, and because Josée refused to help us plot a route back to the highway from Hyannis, Joe-Bob became navigator. Once on the highway and safely on the way back to our hotel in Cambridge, he began to criticize my car. "Fred, you should get rid of this junker. It's not safe to ride in. I can sure get you a good deal on a trade-in."

"Still runs good, like I said. Maybe no air conditioning in the summer, but the heater works like a damn in the winter."

"Say, to change the subject, I thought Canadians ended up every sentence with 'Eh'. I haven't heard you or Josée do that yet."

"The French taught us Anglais that, eh, Josée?"

"Oui, c'est vrai."

"Josée, Jesus, God, I wish you'd stop using that French. I don't know what you're saying. You might be calling me a son of a bitch, and I wouldn't know it."

"If I call you a son of a bitch, I'll give you a translation, eh?"

Joe-Bob laughed. "I see I'll have to find my old sense of humour to keep up with this bunch - eh?"

Over liqueurs that evening, the subject of Joel Bonney came up. I told the others what I had learned from Uncle Bill's notes, concluding with, "Joel was buried in Portland, Maine, in the Pioneers and Heroes section of the Eastern cemetery."

Joe-Bob looked puzzled. "I thought Joel was loyal to the British and went to Canada. How did he get back into the States?"

"Joe-Bob," I said, "the Bonneys in Canada are like the tip of an iceberg. Joel had ten children, nine of them born in Canada, and yet only one of his sons, my great great great grandfather, elected to stay north of the border. Joel returned to the States when he was in his late seventies with no apparent difficulty, and was looked after by members of his family until he died in 1824. I can only guess that the animosities of the wars between us by that time had died down."

"You mean there was another war between us besides the War of Independence?"

"Yes, Joe-Bob, the War of 1812."

"Oh, sure, the War of 1812. I remember now. My granddaddy told me one of my ancestors shot a British general in that war."

Joe-Bob was beginning to remind me of the song, 'I've been everywhere, man'. Perhaps, like his ancestors who came over on the Mayflower, there was some fiction in these stories.

Dickie looked sceptical. "Shot a British General? Not Major General Sir Isaac Brock, by any chance?"

"Brock. That was it. General Brock."

"How extraordinary! During that same war, the British invaded Washington and burned down the White House. Did your granddaddy tell you that?"

"Did they really?"

"They really did."

Dickie's mood changed abruptly. "We seem to have been on a holiday. We must soon get down to some constructive writing, or Basil will be hounding us. Before we leave Boston, we must have the book to the beginning of the War of the League of Ausburg, or King William's War, as it was known on this continent."

"Shouldn't we visit the site of the Boston Massacre and Bunker Hill and all that while we're here?" objected Joe-Bob. "I've been reading about the American Revolution in my book. I do that in the morning, before I read the paper. Can't sleep past five."

Any doubt about who was in charge of our 'team' was dispelled when Dickie replied firmly, "No, no. That comes later. We'll return to Boston when that time comes. When we get to King William's War, our first stop will be Albany, I'm quite sure that is the proper order of things. But I must admit I am at a bit of a loss as to how to proceed with the actual writing of the book, with the four of us now involved."

"Why, it is so simple," Josée cut in. "We will sit down every day, decide what comes next, and I will record it on Fred's laptop."

Dickie looked doubtful. "Oh, you couldn't possibly listen and type at the same time at anything like conversation speed, could you?"

"You haven't tried me."

Mischief again. "You want to bet, Dickie?"

"No, no, Fred. The last time you bet on Josée, you won. I should know better than to doubt her ability, but how about a demonstration?"

"Of course. Let's go upstairs, and I'll show you what I can do."

In our room, Dickie read from notes, slowly at first, while Josée transcribed his words onto the computer. Seeing that she was keeping up easily, he increased the tempo to near conversation speed: "The settling of North America by Europeans may well have been the most significant event in human history . . ." After a couple of minutes, he called a halt, and Josée printed out what she had done. He read a few lines, then exclaimed, "Astounding, utterly astounding. Nothing missing, just a few spelling mistakes, which I'm sure we can attribute to your French background. Josée, you are a marvel!" He gave her a hug, and on that note, we called it a night, and headed to the bar for nightcaps.

Before he started in on the man who had cost him his football career, Joe-Bob told us a little more about himself. "There was one thing my wives wouldn't stand for: other women. Why, women are so pretty I just can't leave them alone, or couldn't. I'm so down on life even they don't excite me any more, well, except, and Fred, I don't want you to take exception to this, but Josée, you sure are a charmer."

Josée, of course, wiggled and smiled prettily. "Merci."

"There you go with that French again. But now, what was this bet that you won off Dickie, Fred?"

"I bet him that Josée would beat him at golf, and she did."

"You folks play golf? Say, that's nice. I have to play with a knee brace now, handicap's gone up from scratch to six."

"Josée's a five, Joe Bob."

"Well, damn! So pretty and charming, and a five? How about you, Fred?"

"I'm improving. I was 19 at last check."

"Oh, well." He sounded patronizing, and I vowed to get better. "How about Dickie?"

Dickie was mumbling to his daughter while gazing at Josée, so I answered for him. "Seven."

"That good! I can get us a tee time tomorrow and fix you all up with clubs. We can play and still get some work done on the book, can't we?"

"Sure, why not. Dickie will have to learn to be patient. Josée and I have our golf gear with us."

"I guess we'll play some more along the way, so Dickie might as well buy clubs and clothes too. I can get him a good deal on both." Joe-Bob drained his glass in two swallows, and 30 seconds later, drifted back to that first professional practise and his knee injury.

That night, I had a vivid, technicolour dream. I was standing in the pioneers' cemetery in Duxbury when an old man in a white robe, an apparition, appeared out of nowhere, and began to read in a loud voice from a long scroll: "And these are the ancestors of Fred Bonney, beginning in the new world: Thomas Bonney, in his 50th year, having lost Mary Terry, his first wife, married again to Mary Hunt, and begat Thomas the second, Mary, Ephraim, Sarah, Hannah, John, William, Joseph and James. And of these, John was the ancestor of Fred.

"And John married Elizabeth Bishop, and begat John, Mary, Elizabeth, Joseph, Ichabod, Ruth, Deborah, Anna, and Perez, all these born to their mother after she was 27. And of these, the ancestor of Fred was Perez.

34

"And Perez married Ruth Snow, and begat Joel, Perez, Titus, Celia, Jarvis, Asa, and James. And of these, the ancestor of Fred was Joel.

"And Joel married Lydia Kenney, and begat Lydia, but her mother died in childbirth, and Joel married again to Elizabeth Sprague, and begat Joel, Perez, Elizabeth, Hannah, Moses, Asa, Ruth, William, Anna and Abiel. And of these, the ancestor of Fred was Abiel.

"And Abiel married Sarah Jefferson, and begat George, Jacob, William, Moses, Robert, Thomas, John, David, Betsy, Peres, and Mary. And of these, the ancestor of Fred was Thomas.

"And Thomas married Cynthia Dow, and begat Thomas, Neil, Judson, Maude, Sarah, and Charlotte. And of these, the ancestor of Fred was Neil.

"And Neil married Marjorie Brittain, and begat Horace, Ethel, Mary, Maude, John, Mabel, William, and Bess. And of these, the ancestor of Fred was John.

"And John married Rachel Heatherstone, and begat Elizabeth, Mary, John, and Fred."

The apparition ceased talking, and rolled up its scroll. "Who are you?" I asked.

"I am Thomas Bonney, of course, wakened from the dead when you trampled on my grave this afternoon."

"I am sorry, but we were trying to find your headstone."

"Oh, that. Someone stole it for a souvenir 100 years ago. Descendant Fred, make sure you beget yourself a son to carry on the Bonney name. Now leave me in peace, so that I may return to my eternal slumbers."

"But forgive me, ancestor Thomas, for I will have no son. My wife passed away two years ago, and I am in love with an impregnable woman."

"But, then, what is this I see in the future? Look!" And there appeared before us a sturdy boy of perhaps six years, with blue eyes and a head of reddish-blond curls. "Never fear, Dad," the boy said in a clear, confident voice. "I will save Canada from the Americans."

I woke with a start. Josée lay beside me, sleeping soundly. She stirred, and I moved carefully to the other side of the bed so as not to disturb her.

I looked at myself in the mirror the next morning, and was surprised to see that I hadn't gained any weight. If anything, I'd lost some, in spite of the lack of exercise, and eating all that rich food. And there were dark circles under my eyes. I concluded that I was slowly being killed by sex, but it wasn't affecting Josée. She was positively blooming. Joe-Bob insisted on taking her for a partner in our four-ball golf match, and as far as I was concerned, the two of them were much too friendly with each other while they beat Dickie and me by five points. Maybe it would have been easier to take if Joe-Bob hadn't rubbed it in unmercifully while smoking a victory cigar.

That afternoon, we finally got down to serious business on the book. Dickie began by reviewing the explorations that preceded colonization; Spanish Conquest and settlement as far north as Mexico and Florida; the search for the 'Northwest Passage' by England, France, and the Netherlands; the incidental discoveries of Newfoundland, the rich cod fishery around it, and the east coast of North America; first contacts with the Indians; the birth of the fur trade. He then set the scene in England on the eve of the Bonneys' departure, and I must admit he was impressive. From a great stack of notes, he summarized the conditions in an animated fashion while Josée clacked it all down on my laptop.

"Yesterday, I said that the settlement of North America by Europeans may well have been the most significant event in human history. Let us now examine why that settlement took place. We must first try to understand the religious fervour that gripped England in 1634, when Thomas Bonney left for Plymouth colony. Roman Catholics, disenfranchised and barred from holding public office, were plotting against the realm. Parliament had been taken over by an array of Protestant sects including Puritans, who were demanding reform of the established Church of England."

"Maybe if we're supposed to understand this religious fervour, we should know more about it," suggested Joe-Bob.

"I will try to acquaint you with it. Picture, if you will, three men of the time, and I stress men, for women then were considered little more that chattels. The first, an Anglican, takes comfort in the ritual of his service, the set form of prayers. He believes that God has left much to the discretion of men, to be exercised by those in authority, whether it be Bishops or Prime Ministers, all acting with the sanction of the King. Membership in his church is for everyman, the lord and the pauper alike.

"The second man is a Puritan, otherwise known as a 'Non-Separating Congregationalist'. While a professed Anglican, he rails against ritual and the rule of Bishops - too much like the hated Roman Catholic Church for him. More, he insists that the Church be judged not by men, but by its adherence to the scriptures, the word of God. Membership in his church is not for everyman, for he believes that the 'unregenerate, natural man', no matter how good, or kind, or public spirited, is nothing but a savage. Rather, membership is only for those like himself who have become 'regenerate' through a traumatic experience of the wrath and redemptive love of God. During this experience, our man is transformed into one of the 'visible saints', he is seized by God to do God's will on earth; he ceases to determine his own future. He believes that saints like himself should band together in covenants to establish self-governing, Congregational Churches, which will maintain only a loose association with one another.

"As for our third man, he is a 'Separating Congregationalist', and in the extreme case, he believes that each individual should determine for himself what his beliefs should be, and that churches are not needed at all.

"That is a pretty sketchy treatment of the subject. The point I want to make is that many Puritans had a monumental faith in their own righteousness, which they perhaps needed to venture across the seas in those tiny sailing vessels, to carve farms for themselves out of pervasive forests full of unfamiliar biting insects, bears, and savage aborigines, to sustain themselves when all around them, others were dying from starvation, pestilence, and Indian arrows. Does that help?"

"I'm sorry I asked," Joe-Bob grinned.

"Returning then to where we left off, the King refused to agree to any reforms, ruled without Parliament, and gave Archbishop William Laud free rein to persecute the Puritans. If they expressed their radical views in public, or dared to wear distinctive dress, such as their narrow crowned, stiff brimmed hats, they were subject to imprisonment, even death. Many of them, therefore, began to meet in secret services, and it was there that the idea of emigration became popular.

"At the same time, England was burdened with a surplus, unemployed population, many freemen having lost their lands as a result of the enclosure laws. Poorhouses and prisons were overflowing, crime was on the rise, and important writers began to promote emigration as a way to rid the country of these problems. There was also a surplus of younger sons of the gentry and nobility, disinherited by primogeniture."

"Primogeniture?" Josée queried.

"The custom prevalent in England of leaving one's estate to the eldest son, rather than splitting it amongst all one's heirs. The younger sons, with the advantages of a good upbringing and an education, were eagerly seeking opportunities to make their marks in life, and were easily persuaded to try their luck overseas.

"As to the method of settlement, proprietors, either individuals or groups, many of them religiously motivated, obtained charters from the Crown to vast and ill-defined lands in North America. In the early stages, the Crown required nothing of these proprietors in return, a point for future reference.

"The immigrants themselves were basically of two types. 'Indentured servants' assigned their labour for a number of years to whoever paid the price of their passage, and were rewarded with land of their own once they fulfilled the terms of their indenture. 'Planters' or 'adventurers' paid their own passage, and purchased or were given lands when they arrived. I think it is important to point out that few of these immigrants seriously expected to return permanently to England.

"Now, Fred, into this scene, you must fit Thomas Bonney as he contemplates emigrating to the Plymouth Colony."

I was speechless for a few seconds, as if I had writer's block. Then, with a great sense of relief, I found words. "Well, I thought we might find Thomas in his shop, driving the last nail in the last pair of boots he will ever make in England. He closes and locks the door and retires to his quarters in the rear, checks his strong box to make sure it still contains the money for the passage to America, and finds his wife, Mary, looking tired and frail."

The keys of the laptop clacked rapidly. Surprised, I turned to Josée. "What did you type?"

"The beginning of the story. I just changed a few words."

"Yes, but -. Oh, well, you can crank out a draft later and we'll all go over it. Where was I?"

Dickie suggested, "You were about to say that Thomas and Mary would give thanks to God for their simple supper, and then prepare to host a secret Puritan meeting. A minister from London arrives with grim news: Archbishop Laud has instructed Justices of the Peace to arrest anyone taking part in Puritan conventicles."

"Jesus, God, Dickie. What the hell is a conventicle?"

"A clandestine meeting."

"Why didn't you say so?"

"Conventicle is the right word. But the minister is also able to tell them that their ship, the Hercules, is in port in Dover, and that they should be there at dawn the day after tomorrow to board her."

"What? Oh, alright. That sounds alright. Type that. Then . . . "

We took a break at three o'clock for coffee, with Thomas and Mary safely across the Atlantic after a harrowing, 12 week voyage. As they step ashore near Plymouth, a few curious Indians watch from the edge of the forest, then go away muttering, while earlier immigrants greet them, and take them in until they can get themselves established. Within days, they have purchased a parcel of land near Duxbury and some cattle, and Thomas is busy trapping beaver, felling trees, and building a new home. And in his spare time, he makes new boots for everyone in his host family.

Josée looked wistful. "So surely, all this time they must have been praying for children. How sad for her to be barren!"

"Besides," Joe-Bob added, "children were needed as workers to help the family survive. In those days, every man was a farmer, or a fisherman, except maybe for the few fur trappers."

Dickie was pleased, but not yet satisfied. "Now, we must set the scene in the colonies - the pattern of settlement - the political and religious climate, the beginnings of trouble with the French, up to the beginning of King William's War - but we must focus primarily on the New England Colonies, particularly Massachusetts, or we will become hopelessly bogged down."

Joe-Bob looked disappointed. "Don't you want to talk about the settlement of all the colonies? I've been reading it up in my book, and I bought this big map of North America so we can see where everything is. Virginia was the first one, started in 1606 . . ."

"Yes, we need to mention Virginia, and you've just done that, because it was involved in the first armed conflict with the French in the New World. To speed things up, we can omit any further discussion of the Plymouth Colony because it was culturally dominated by Massachusetts, and in fact was taken over by the bigger colony when the constitution was amended in 1691."

Joe-Bob shrugged. "What about New York? New York gets involved in King William's War."

"Oh, go ahead, but be brief."

"It started out Dutch in 1614, surrendered to the English in 1664. That brief enough?"

"Just right."

"But I should have mentioned New Sweden. There was a New Sweden."

"Yes, yes, there was a new Sweden. It was taken over by the Dutch. Do get on with it."

"Alright. Now, this won't sound like me, because I'm quoting some from my book."

"That's fine for now. Later, we will have to do some rephrasing to avoid the charge of plagiarism."

"Whatever you say, Dickie. A couple of generalities to start with. As each colony, or province, was established, the people who came to it brought with them the seeds of English freedom, and the heritage of self-government. In all cases, legislative assemblies in one form or another were soon established, and they shared authority, particularly in matters of finance, with the proprietary governor and his appointed council. In addition, the colonies were eventually divided into counties in the English fashion, and as towns developed, meetings were held by the citizens to decide important issues. The people also brought with them the tradition of citizen soldiers, the militia."

"Ah, yes, the militia," Dickie interrupted. "Stemmed from the 'Muster Act', passed by Parliament at the time of the Spanish Armada."

"Yes, yes, Dickie. Let's get on with it. And all these colonies were inhabited by Indians. In most cases, they were treated without respect and their rights were ignored, and when they realized their lands were being taken from them, they rose up to murder, pillage and burn. The most famous of these uprisings became known as 'King Philip's War,' which took place in New England in 1675-76, and as in all the other cases, the whites reacted swiftly and without mercy. After King Philip's War, Indians in general were looked on as enemies, and attempts to convert them to Christianity virtually ended. It was these hostile natives, just beyond the borders of settlement, who slowed exploration of the country inland.

"Massachusetts started up when the first Governor brought the charter with him from England in 1630. That's where most of the immigrants started going, nearly all of them Puritans, and they began to make covenants, and establish churches all over the colony. They also, according to the charter, elected a legislative assembly which was known as the 'General Court'."

We ordered in supper, and carried on into the evening. Someone would start out with an idea, the rest would offer suggestions, and Josée would clack on the computer intermittently, never looking at the keys, but rather, at each of us in turn. At one point, I mentioned that Thomas Bonney, according to Uncle Bill's notes, was also known as 'Goodman Bonney', and was constable in Duxbury in the years 1643-44, 'an office of high trust and responsibility, and none were elected to it but men of good standing'. And in 1652, he was surveyor of highways.

"But we must try to give Thomas a personality, "Josée suggested. "Pious, yes; hard working, yes; faithful to his wife and kind to her, we must assume that, because he was looked up to in the community. A strong, stocky man dressed in what kind of clothing?"

"Homespun," offered Dickie.

"Yes, homespun. Was he good looking or plain?"

"He would likely have had the Bonney nose. Probably a homely man."

Josée glanced at me, then quickly away. "Not homely. Rather, a man with a strong face, one that would make others trust him."

We paused when we came to the year 1677; Thomas had lost his first Mary, married the second, and fathered Thomas Junior, Mary, Ephraim (the banished and disowned lecher), Sarah, Hannah, John (my ancestor), William, Joseph and James.

Dickie observed, with a smile on his face, "A fine piece of work, a fine piece of work. Josée, tomorrow you can tell us about New France, and we can go over a draft of what we did today."

"I have already done New France, up to the time when my ancestor arrived in 1663. It comes straight from Pierre's essay. Let me go over the highlights with you."

We men groaned collectively. The thought of a drink at this hour was much more enticing than the history of New France. This woman had more staying power than any of us.

Josée read our mood. "It will not take long. Dickie, you have already told us about searching for the Northwest Passage. Jacques Cartier thought he found it when he sailed up the St. Lawrence River in 1535, until he was stopped by the rapids at Lachine, near Montreal. Let me take it from there." She paused for a moment, and there was a far away look in her eye when she began again, using Pierre's English translation for background.

"La France Nouveau - plus de quelque arpents de neige. New France - more than just a few acres of snow, as its detractors claimed. A rugged land, yes, with the granite of the Canadian Shield pressed close to the St. Lawrence north shore."

"The Canadian Shield?" Joe-Bob queried.

"Ah, the Canadian Shield," responded Dickie. "A great mass of primordial granite rock, full of minerals, ground down during the ice ages to generally less than 2,000 feet in height, that covers almost half of Canada, and dips down into the United States to form the Adirondack Mountains, etcetera." I could have told them that.

"A harsh climate too," Josée resumed, "but a land of wild beauty, and endless promise.

"There were many differences between the settlement of New France and the English Colonies. To begin with, French Protestants, the Huguenots, were not allowed to emigrate to any French colony, and as they became increasingly persecuted, they fled to the American Colonies instead. Neither was there any

40

great surplus population to export from France, or any pool of disinherited younger sons, for there was no such thing as - what-do-you-call-it - primogeniture. In contrast to English custom, the French legal code required that estates be shared equally among heirs. As you will see when we travel along the big rivers in Quebec, some fields were divided and divided again into narrower and narrower strips as settlers sought to comply with the law.

"The King of France also granted rights to individuals and groups, but not to land, to the fur trade. It became profitable after 1600 when the beaver hat became vogue in Europe. In connection with the trade, the first European settlement in North America was established in 1604 at Port Royal in Acadia."

"Hold it," objected Joe-Bob. "I don't remember seeing any place called Acadia on my map."

"Acadia was never really defined on a map, but it did include Nova Scotia, and that is where Port Royal was built. It was attacked in 1614 by your horrible Virginians, Joe-Bob, who claimed the country belonged to England.

"In contrast to the English experience again, colonization was actually discouraged at first, because the proprietors of the fur trade needed only a handful of 'engages', or indentured servants, to help bring in the pelts from the Indians. With few settlers, farming was not very extensive, so the Indians did not perceive, as they did in the English Colonies, that the French were threatening to take their lands. Even more, the French lived with the Indians, sought to convert them, intermarried with them, and treated them with respect, with one important exception. When Samuel de Champlain established Quebec City in 1608, he chose as allies the Indians who lived nearby - Algonquins, Montangais, and Hurons - and joined them in their battles against the Iroquois Confederacy, an association at first of five, then later six tribes."

"Ah, yes," Dickie interjected. "North America's most famous natives. And the original five tribes were the Seneca, Cayuga, Oneida, Onondaga, and Mohawk."

"And of these, the Mohawk were the most terrifying to the French. Collectively, the Confederacy numbered only about 30,000 people and could field less than 3,000 warriors, but it exerted an influence far greater than those numbers would suggest. The Iroquois never forgave the French for siding with their enemies, and that had grave consequences, as I will tell you later. I should mention here that the Iroquois and the Huron, unlike hunter-gatherer tribes such as the Montagnais and the Algonquin, practised slash and burn agriculture, and grew corn, which they used as a trade item. And rather than tents, they lived in longhouses built of saplings covered with cedar bark.

"A short vignette of Champlain now, the father of New France. He was of common birth, but a skilled artist, cartographer and explorer. He must also have been a persuasive orator, for he talked the King into supporting his explorations and plans for colonization. After founding Quebec City, he extended the knowledge of the country as far west as Lake Superior and as far south as the Hudson River, all that before he died in 1635. It is so sad! In 1610, he married a girl in France just 12 years old, with the understanding that the union would not be consummated until she was 14. They had no children - she only lived in Quebec from 1620 to 1624 - and then she returned to France to become a nun.

"In 1627, the King granted a monopoly over the fur trade to a private company. At the same time, to encourage more settlers, the colony was divided into Seigneuries, each with a Seigneur in charge, usually a member of the minor nobility, a military officer, or a member of some religious order. He would build a grist mill for grinding grain and a church, and organize a militia from the men on his seigneury, so you see, the English had no monopoly on citizen soldiers. It was to the Seigneur that the tenant farmers, the 'Habitants', owed rents, and they were also required to support the church, paying a tithe in kind rather than in money. The land, however, still belonged to the King in the feudal fashion, as opposed to the title English settlers obtained from the proprietors of their colonies, and there was no elected legislature.

"Meanwhile, after the founding of Quebec City and Montreal, the fur trade was developing in this fashion." And Josée painted us a picture in words, of intrepid Frenchmen venturing far into the interior of the continent in their canoes, aided by rivers and lakes strung together as if the creator had intended them for that purpose; the tribes of Indians they encountered, and the attempts to convert them to Christianity; the romantic outlaws, the 'Couriers de Bois', who lived with the Indians and poached furs; the position of the Huron Nation as middlemen, buying furs from the remote hunter-gatherer tribes with corn, and selling them to the French for European trade goods.

The Iroquois dominated her narrative, as they materialized out of the primeval forests to visit horrors on French settlers during treacherous raids. In the mid 1600's, they massacred the Huron in a vain attempt to become the middlemen in the fur trade, and to divert the flow of furs to Albany. In 1660, they were prevented from destroying Montreal and Quebec City by Adam Dollard Des Ormeaux, who, along with a mixed band of Indians and trappers, gave his life to stop them. In 1667, decimated by war and disease, they were forced into a 20-year peace by the first regular soldiers sent to New France, the Régiment Carignan-Salières.

"Damn long French names," grumbled Joe-Bob.

I joined in. "And Des Ormeaux and his men had just stolen a shipment of Iroquois furs bound for Albany. They were common thieves, made into heroes because the Iroquois killed them all."

Josée tossed her head. "But they killed many Iroquois, and the furs reached Montreal, and New France was saved. Let me continue without any more interruptions."

"The private company's attempts to colonize were largely a failure. In 1663, the population of New France was still only 3,000, compared to 100,000 English and 10,000 Dutch to the south, and no matter that the birth rate in New France was unbelievably high, the massive immigration into the English colonies doomed the French to be outnumbered many times over."

"How high was that birth rate?" asked Joe-Bob.

"In Canada now, the rate is 13 or 14 per 1,000 population, and I am ashamed to say that of all the provinces, it is the lowest in predominately Roman Catholic Quebec. In the early days of New France, it reached as high as 56."

"Say! That's a lot of kids to help with the family farm!"

"By 1663, the private company had been bankrupted by the wars with the Iroquois, so the King took over the colony, administering it through the Ministry of Marine. In Quebec City, the capital of New France, a Governor and an Intendant shared power in this new regime, an untidy arrangement as compared to the individual authority of the governors in the English colonies.

"The advent of Royal rule turned New France into a military society. Soldiers sent out to fight the Iroquois were encouraged to take their discharges over here, and to become tenant farmers under their officers. A mini court developed at Quebec City complete with power intrigues and mistresses, and it was fashionable for the ambitious to live 'le vivre noblement', the noble life, to be in debt, to settle arguments by the sword. Young men vied for commissions in the military in the hopes of being placed in charge of a trading post, where they might become wealthy by taking a cut of fur revenues. Few were so fortunate; many spent their lives away from home on military raids. Finally, officials sent out from France dreamed of making a fortune through their postings, then returning home to live in luxury.

"Now, into this milieu I have introduced my ancestor, Jacques Bonin, who came to New France as a sergeant in the 'Troupes de la Marine' in 1663."

"No reflection on your ancestor, I am sure, but the 'Troupes' were a kind of second class army recruited from dockyard slums in France to protect the colonies. Not to be confused with 'Troupes de la Terre', the regular French army," Dickie clarified.

"As you say. In 1670, Jacques married one of 'Les Filles du Roi', who were mostly orphan girls sent out to the colony by the King. Although he was still subject to military duty, Jacques then settled on a farm in the Seigneury of Longueille across the river from Montreal, and raised 15 children. Mon Dieu! Fifteen children, and I cannot manage even one!"

The next morning, we went over drafts of what we had done the day before, spending most of our time revising Josée's English, a criticism she accepted with good grace. But we were careful not to tamper too much with the poignant story of Jacques Bonin, then 35 years old, as he waited anxiously on the Quebec City docks for the next ship carrying 'Les Filles' to arrive. The girls, all from the poorer districts of Paris and dressed in charity clothing, come ashore unsteadily, still suffering the effects of the rough ocean crossing. Jacques spots a pretty one; perhaps she looked a little like Josée. His heart nearly bursting, he struggles through the crowd to the church where the girls will be staying, and asks what he must do to claim her for his bride.

We then roughed out a chapter advancing the Bonneys and the Bonins through the years remaining before King William's War. My ancestor, John, the sixth child of Thomas, married Elizabeth Bishop in 1684, a woman seven years older than himself. Josée appeared to be intrigued. "Why? Was there a shortage of girls? What was she like? Saintly? Thin? Fat? Short? Tall? What was it that attracted John to her?"

"A marriage of convenience?" I suggested. "Her father was Deputy Governor of Connecticut, probably a wealthy man with a lot of influence."

"Ah! And John's younger brother James married Elizabeth's sister, Abigail, but not for convenience, for love. Abigail was pretty, with a figure that made men stare, flirtatious, funny, an exasperation to her parents."

"How do you know that?"

"Could it not have been so?"

As for the Bonins, Jacques eldest son, Louis, grew to be a huge, powerful man, according to Josée, and I knew she was using her brother as a model. When he was hardly 16, he paddled off into the wilderness to seek his fortune in the fur trade, and returned a year later a relatively rich man. While Josée was talking about him, I drifted off into a daydream, imagining myself a Courier de Bois with broken teeth and long, dirty hair, careering down the rapids of a mighty river with shouts of joy, paddling in quiet waters to a village on the shore of a lake, being greeted by a beautiful young Indian woman, who led me to her longhouse, and made love to me.

"Fred, wake up!" Dickie broke the spell.

Again, we had room service for supper, and while we were eating, Dickie posed a question. "As I said, there are now four of us involved. A book with four authors is awkward. Hardly room on the cover to put all the names."

Josée objected. "There are really five, because we are using Pierre's essay for background. I won't mind being left out if we include his name."

For once, I had what I believed was a brilliant thought. "Why don't we invent a pen name for the author? Bonney for sure. How about Bonin Bonney?"

"Sounds odd," Dickie complained. "I think Bonney Bonin would sound better. What do you think, Joe-Bob?"

"Well, I don't really care if I'm included as author either, but I'm coming up with an idea. How about the rest of you give me the North American publishing rights to the book, including movie and TV rights?"

"Oh," Dickie said, "I'm sure our publisher already has those. I'd have to check with Basil."

"Tell you what. When you're finished talking to him next time, let me have him."

"Getting back to a pen name for the author," I persisted, "how about combining our names? If Josée and Joe-Bob don't mind being left off, we could have 'Pierre, Frederick, Richard, Bonin-Bonney.'"

"Too long," the others all agreed.

"Alright, then, let's just use the initials - P.F.R. Bonin-Bonney."

They looked at each other. "Still too cumbersome," Dickie decided.

"Wait a minute, wait a minute. Who's really writing this book? It's Josée, isn't it? All we're doing is correcting her English. She's the one who's turning it into a romantic generational novel. Are we all satisfied with that?"

"Satisfied," Dickie and Joe-Bob said at once.

"Alright, the author is Josée Bonin-Bonney."

"Agreed," the two men said, and Josée looked pleased. In my mind, I would be happy to combine our names if she would marry me.

"We don't even have a title yet," I reminded them. "What are we going to call this book?"

"Why, 'British North America', of course," said Dickie, with an air of finality.

We worked on into the night until all but Josée were out of inspiration, and then it was down to the bar - thank God for the bar - and our usual nightcaps. When we were somewhat revived, the subject turned to religion. "I can't believe that our ancestors were so all-consuming pious," marvelled Joe-Bob. "And moral. In my book, I read about a ship's Captain who'd been away from home for three years, and got put in the stocks for kissing his wife in public!"

Dickie agreed. "As we have discussed, the process of being reborn, of becoming regenerate, was necessary for membership in the church, but the process itself became controversial. Who was to judge whether or not a man had gone through it? And no such strict code of conduct could last. By the time the second generation grew up, few were becoming 'visible saints', and so it was necessary to devise a compromise. The 'Halfway Covenant' allowed limited membership in the Church to non-regenerate but baptized children of the saints."

"Maybe that's why there was a mass baptism of Bonney family members on April the 12th, 1713, so that they could become members of the Church," I offered.

The subject, at length, turned to the Iroquois. Joe-Bob observed, "They must have been something different, those Indians."

Josée shook her head. "I sometimes wonder, when I have violent feelings toward that scum of a husband of mine, if it isn't the Iroquois coming out in me." "What, you part Iroquois?"

"According to my brother."

"According to my granddaddy, old Ephraim shacked up with an Iroquois woman while he was up there around Albany. Said he had a family by her before the French chased him out."

My ears pricked up. "Do you know when that was, Joe-Bob?"

"Well, let's see. Ephraim was the third child, born about 1658, got expelled out of Duxbury in his early twenties, I'd guess. Let's say about 1680. "So, let's say that 's when he got to Albany. Spent some time in Schenectady, too."

I looked at Josée. "When and where did your ancestor find the part Iroquois woman?"

"It was Louis who found her somewhere south of Lake Ontario during a military raid in 1696, when the French were destroying Iroquois villages and burning their crops. The girl had been abandoned by her father and her mother had been killed in the fighting, according to my brother. Louis brought her back with him, and, I suppose, fell in love with her, and married her."

"Hey, somewhere south of Lake Ontario - Lake Oneida - Oswego River - my granddaddy said Ephraim spent some time up there after the French burned out Schenectady."

How much of what Joe-Bob told us could we believe? If what he said was true, a little arithmetic suggested that Josée might be a descendent of Ephraim Bonney!

Dickie raised his glass. "Well, then, it is time to go to upper New York State, where an important part of King William's War took place."

Chapter 3.

Les Petites Guerres

After a morning of editing, we set off for Albany, New York, on Highway 2 otherwise know as the 'Mohawk Trail'. "Say, this will take us past Deerfield, where my ancestor Ephraim settled after his time with the Iroquois," noted Joe-Bob. For some reason, he seemed more aggressive than usual this particular morning, and his steady litany of complaints about my car began to irritate me.

"I bet this tin can won't go 80," he challenged.

"I bet it will!" I retorted, slamming the accelerator to the floor. The needle just passed 80 when a patrol car with its lights flashing appeared out of nowhere, and pulled in behind us. Joe-Bob laughed uproariously.

Dickie, bless him, paid my fine. He was in a much more relaxed mood now that we'd actually made some serious progress on the book, and readily agreed to a game of golf along the way.

"So, how do we decide who gets to play with Josée next?" Joe-Bob asked.

"Oh," I said, "we'll take her in turns." I was totally unprepared for the roars of laughter that followed, and it really stung when Josée laughed just as hard as the others. I blushed and tried to limit the damage. "I meant, we'll share her," and the laughter doubled. "For Christ sake, forget that. We'll throw up our balls each time we play." The laughter doubled again. "Our golf balls, and the two balls closest to each other get to play together."

The Mohawk Trail goes through some really pretty country, and as elsewhere in Massachusetts, it seemed we were driving through unexploited forests rather than a populous American state. The closer we got to the New York border, however, the rougher the country and the worse the road became, with sharp curves, steep grades, and few chances to overtake slower vehicles.

We stopped for the night at Greenfield, where Joe-Bob booked us into the best hotel in the place, and announced that he was looking after the bills. Dickie argued briefly, but gave in when the two of them agreed to alternate as hosts.

In the bar, Joe-Bob led the kidding about sharing Josée. By the time we got to our room, I was feeling really peevish, and I turned my back on her when we got into bed. "Mon cher Fred, what is the matter?" she asked sarcastically, but she did rub my shoulders.

"You know what the matter is."

"Oh, yes, I know, but you did make a 'faux pas'. Turn over and let me make you feel better."

"Josée, I don't think I can tonight."

"Let me see. Ah! You are wrong! You are simply angry with me, and you want to punish me."

"Stop that, will you? Oh, hell, alright."

Joe-Bob got us a morning tee time at a local course, and I began to wonder if he had friends in every town who could do that for him. He had to play with me the way the balls fell, and by the time we finished our game, he was fuming. "Josée," he demanded, "where did you find this loser, this Fred? With a big handicap like his, we should have waxed you two. Instead, even though I shot 76, we have to buy lunch because he shot 105. Fred, I should make you pay."

"I thought Greenfield was on you."

"What the hell did you do for a living while you were working?"

"Airports. I looked after airports till the government decided to privatize them."

"I'm sure glad I didn't fly out of a Canadian airport while you were doing that."

From the golf club, we drove to the small community of Deerfield, just to the south of Greenfield on the Connecticut River. The times dictated that Ephraim Bonney probably lived on the riverbank, so we walked along it where we could, and we did find some depressions in the ground that might have marked the site of his cabin. Joe-Bob looked disappointed, and I began to believe he was really becoming interested in what we were doing.

We piled into my old Chev again and wound our way up into the ruggedness of the Appalachian Mountains, the road becoming narrower and the alignment poorer the farther we went, with only the occasional 'climbing lane' to allow passing. For a break along the way, we stopped at a tourist trap that advertised Mohawk souvenirs, and we were all impressed by the owner, a tall, powerfully built man with high cheekbones and skin the colour of copper. "Mon Dieu!" observed Josée. "No wonder the French were terrified of the Mohawks! Imagine being chased by one of those with a tomahawk in his hand!"

Joe-Bob, meanwhile, bought a small fortune in trinkets, which he said he was going to send to his children. "Makes me feel good to do this," he said sadly, "but the kids will probably never get to see these things. Their mothers will most likely throw them out with the trash."

Past the Appalachian crest, a violent thunderstorm pelted us with rain and hail, forcing us to close the car windows, and we had to suffer not only the heat and humidity, but also the gas attack I was having. "Jesus, God! Who let that go?" demanded Joe-Bob, as lightning lit up the sky, and the rain came down in sheets.

"Fred, you will have to take some pills." Josée let the cat out of the bag.

"But I can't take them without water," I protested. "I'll try to hold it till we get past this damn storm." It was a long wait, because the rain didn't stop until we'd driven through the squalid streets of Troy, New York, and crossed the Hudson River to Albany. With all the windows finally open again, I let go the accumulation with a sigh of relief.

In our four star hotel near the State Capitol in Albany, we began another chapter that evening in Dickie's room, the story of King William's War, and the part the Bonneys and the Bonins played in it. Dickie set the stage. "From the beginning, it was inevitable that the two empires would clash in North America. Consider the differences. First, England and France were traditional enemies, vying at the time for control of ocean-borne commerce, and for colonial dominance. Second, and obviously, was the difference in language. Third and perhaps most important was the difference in religion, for in England, and even more so in the New England colonies, there was an all consuming fear and hatred of 'Popery', or Roman Catholicism. Josée, I'm sure you will be able to confirm a corresponding hatred of Protestants on the French side."

"Oui, yes, it was so."

"Until King William's War, the struggles between France and England, with Spain often a participant on France's side, resulted in little more than skirmishes in North America; yet, during a major European war that started in 1627, England captured Quebec City and Acadia. Both were returned to France at the peace in 1632."

"Yes," added Josée, "and after the capture of Quebec, Champlain and his men were imprisoned in England for three years."

"Josée, my notes suggest he was allowed to go to France during the English occupation, just an example of how the historical record is inconsistent. Whatever. I must point out here that the nations of Europe were exhausted by the wars of religion that followed the Protestant Reformation, and by tacit agreement, had begun to fight for limited objectives, and only under favourable weather conditions. Armies, for example, retired to winter quarters, and waited until spring to launch new campaigns. Coincidentally, it became common practice to exchange prisoners during hostilities, and to trade conquered territory back and forth when peace came. A final observation - armies that traditionally had to forage for food were, by the mid-seventeenth century, being fed by special units or by private caterers.

"The next major war started in 1689 - we have finally come to King William's War, as they called it over here, but more properly, the War of the League of Ausburg. You see - oh dear, how difficult it is to decide how much history to include! Just for the record, then, James the First, the first Stuart King of England and a great persecutor of Puritans, was succeeded by Charles the First, who was forced to recall Parliament for money to fight Scottish rebels, and then Charles the First was beheaded in 1649 by Oliver Cromwell, who led a Puritan republic in England until 1658. The Monarchy was restored in 1660 when Charles the Second, a secret Catholic, came to the throne, to be succeeded in 1685 by his brother James the Second, who was openly Catholic, and who was driven into exile in France in 1688 by his Protestant sister, Mary the Second, and her husband, King William the Third of the Netherlands, who was also known as William of Orange."

"Just for the record," the rest of us choroused.

"Yes, but to complete the record, King William's War started because France wanted James the Second back on the English throne. Now Josée, in order to understand the war as it was fought in America, I think we need to fill in what was happening in New France."

"Oui. By the advent of royal rule, that is in 1663, Jesuit priests and fur traders had already explored far into the continent, as I have already indicated, founding posts and missions wherever they went. Royal rule brought more legitimate exploration sponsored by merchants and another of New France's heroes, Governor Louis de Buade, le Comte de Frontenac. In 1682, Rene Robert Cavalier, Sieur de la Salle, followed the Mississippi to its mouth, and claimed all the country draining into it for France, that is, nearly all of what is now the United States that lies west of the Appalachian Mountains and east of the Rockies."

"Jesus, God, Josée," Joe-Bob complained. "Why do you French have to have such long names?"

"Frontenac may have been a hero to New France," I said, " but he sponsored exploration for his own benefit, and skimmed a fortune from the fur trade."

"But it was accepted that people in positions of influence would take advantage of their opportunities," countered Josée.

"And France's claim to the interior helped convince the English Colonies that they must dispose of the French if they wanted to expand westward."

"You greedy Anglais."

"Fred," Dickie admonished, "don't be too hard on the French until you hear about all the profiteering that went on in the English Colonies. Carry on, Josée."

"By 1689, the Iroquois were raiding again, and 1,500 of them attacked the Seigneury of Lachine near Montreal, only to be held at bay by a mere woman, Marie-Madeleine Jarret de Verchères. Years later, her daughter followed her example. In the early 1690's, the Iroquois forced the French to abandon their remote trading posts when the arrogant but capable Governor Frontenac was replaced by lesser men. Meanwhile, the Governor of New York, heavily invested in the fur trade, encouraged the Iroquois to keep up their attacks on the French for his own profit.

When it became obvious that the Governors sent out to replace Frontenac were incompetents, he was re-appointed to deal with the situation, and that brings us again to the beginning of King William's war."

I added a postscript. "Just one more note. There was hardly a peace between wars. In 1670, the Hudson's Bay Company received a charter covering all lands draining into Hudson Bay, which cut off some of the best furs from the French. In 1686, at a time when England and France were not at war, a force from Montreal seized the Company's posts on James Bay."

"And in that force was Pierre Le Moyne, Sieur d'Iberville, who went on to conquer all of Newfoundland, and become Governor of Louisiana."

"Yes, Josée, yes," said Dickie, looking exasperated. "Returning to where we were, the French concluded that they would have to eliminate New York in order to stop the Iroquois attacks. Late in 1689, Frontenac sailed from France with enough ships and men to conquer the English Colony, but he was delayed by unfavourable winds, and forced to abandon his plans. Landing at Quebec City instead, he launched raids by militia and Indians against the English Colonies, operations which became known as 'Les Petites Guerres', or 'Little Wars', and they were very effective. During the winter of 1689-90, Schenectady, on the Mohawk River in upper New York, was destroyed, and communities in the New England colonies were attacked. Also during this period, Portland, Maine, which was known as 'Fort Loyal' at the time, was captured by the French and their Indian allies, the Abenakis. The garrison surrendered on the promise that it would be spared, but about 100 were massacred by the Abenakis before the French could intervene. The French then tried to justify the killings by claiming the dead were rebels against James the Second! Oh, you do remember who James the Second was, don't you?

"These savage raids un-nerved the English Colonies, but not enough to make them bury their petty rivalries and take concerted action. Instead, Massachusetts was left to go it alone. William Phips and other wealthy Bostonians assembled a fleet, captured some settlements in Acadia, and launched an unsuccessful attack on Quebec City in 1690."

"Ah, New France's finest hour!" exulted Josée.

"Yes, one must admire the style of Frontenac," Dickie admitted.

"When asked to surrender the city, he replied to Phip's emissary, in words like this, 'Tell your general he will receive my reply from the mouths of my cannon'."

"But it wasn't Frontenac's cannon that stopped Phips. It was smallpox, and the threat of the on-coming Canadian winter."

"Stop right there, and backtrack a bit," Joe-Bob interrupted. "It's time to write old Ephraim into the story again. There he is in Schenectady when the French attack, living with this Iroquois woman. By then, I guess, they have some kids, and Ephraim manages to get them away to some village where she has relatives."

"Did he love her, then?" asked Josée.

"Oh, I suppose he loved her, the way I love women, anyway. But maybe she was all that was available."

"And you suggest that he was heroic?"

"I do believe he might have been, being as he was an ancestor of mine. I got a drawer-full of medals from 'Nam. That should prove something."

"Yet, if we believe in coincidences, it was his daughter that Louis Bonin found abandoned a few years later."

"Well, maybe Ephraim was off fighting, maybe got wounded or something."

Dickie looked at his watch. "Let's call it a night. As for tomorrow, perhaps we should see what Schenectady and the Mohawk River look like before we write any more."

"I tell you, that village Ephraim took his family to was up around Lake Oneida," Joe-Bob remembered. "We should go up that way too so we can write about the country properly." We all agreed and it was added to the agenda, and then we went through our usual ritual in the bar before going to bed.

Suddenly, it was June the 25th; Josée and I had been together for over a month; Dickie and Joe-Bob had already been with us for a week. The summer was flying by. On the morning of that day, we headed west on U.S. Route 90 with Josée, having by this time forgiven me for the map episode at Hyannis, again acting as navigator. Actually, she seemed to be getting the hang of it, but right or wrong, I followed her directions without argument. By three in the afternoon, we'd driven all around Lake Oneida, and Joe-Bob decided that the tiny community of Brewerton would make a likely site for the village Ephraim took refuge in.

On the way back, the Friday afternoon traffic became heavy and slow, and it was close to five o'clock before we turned off the highway to Schenectady. The street we found ourselves on led us through a depressed looking neighbourhood thronged with black people, who seemed to be jay-walking aimlessly back and forth across the road. Joe-Bob grumbled from the back seat, "You can see that these people have ruined this town. Same thing happens when the damned Spanish move in."

"Why so many blacks?" I asked.

"Probably descended from the ones who worked on the Erie Canal. And hey, Fred, it's dangerous to drive through places like this with your windows down."

I thought he was being overcautious.

The Mohawk River, that important historical transportation corridor, and long since part of the Erie Canal system, turned out to be a shallow, muddy stream perhaps 150 yards wide. Joe-Bob looked fascinated. "Right here is where old Ephraim may have brought his family, and then escaped the French by paddling upstream in his canoe!"

Not wanting to get lost in this depressing place, we drove back to the highway the way we had come, arriving back in Albany just in time to admire the State Capitol before it got dark. But on the way to our hotel, we took a wrong turn, and found ourselves lost in streets lined with ugly brick buildings. Josée tried to reorient herself with the map when I had to stop for a red light, but she apparently failed, for she gave me no directions.

A black family was still in the middle of the intersection when the light turned green. I waited for them to cross, but one of them, a girl perhaps ten years old, stopped in her tracks and glared at us defiantly. "Fred, punch it!" yelled Joe-Bob. I hesitated. "Go now! Run her down if you have to!"

I hit the gas pedal, narrowly missing the girl. Out of the rear view mirror, I saw two black shapes hurtle across the road. "What the hell was that?"

"Two thugs who would have killed us if you hadn't got out of there. Jesus, God, that does it, that does it!"

In the bar that evening, I listened contritely to Joe-Bob as he lectured me about crime in the United States. After he calmed down, he suggested a golf game for the next day, and insisted on playing with Dickie, because, he joked, nobody could be as bad as me. He made a couple of phone calls after that, then started drinking double Rusty Nails until he got that glassy look in his eye, but this time, he added something to his routine that really made me nervous. "You know, with all my money, you'd think I'd be entitled to the comfort of a woman. I don't think I'm into marrying again, and I sure don't want any more kids - my heart just broke when their mothers took those little rascals away from me. But a woman to look after me, like you have, Fred. I sure wouldn't mind having that." He downed the last of his drink. "Yeah, I sure wouldn't mind having Josée. You know, I was good enough to play football in the NFL until . . . "

When we got to our room, instead of giving me the warm, passionate embrace my fragile self-confidence badly needed, Josée grabbed me by the shoulders and shook me till my teeth rattled. "We play together tomorrow, and we are not going to lose. You sway when you swing back, Fred, so you can't shift your weight properly, and then you hit weak shots all over the golf course. Tomorrow, you are not going to sway, because I hate to lose. If we lose, I will punish you. Now let me show you how to swing back without swaying."

One thing about travelling with millionaires who didn't mind spending their money, we were seeing the country first class. Well, except for my car, and although he wouldn't admit it, I'm sure Joe-Bob fixed that because he was concerned for our safety. We were about to go out for our game the next morning when the desk clerk smiled at me and said, "Sir, you will find your belongings in that mini-van that just pulled up to the door."

"What do you mean? Where's my old Chev?"

"I don't know, sir. It disappeared from the parking garage last night. Oh, yes, and there's something here for you."

The thief must have been honest. Inside the fat envelope the clerk handed me were 50, 100-dollar bills, far more than the car was worth.

The Chrysler van was brand new, on its first trip off the rental company lot, it had the long wheelbase, and the third seat had been removed, giving us plenty of room for our luggage and clubs. Besides that, it had all the bells and whistles including electric windows, air conditioning and automatic transmission, and in comparison to my old Chev, it was a pleasure to drive. As for the golf match, Josée and I won, not much thanks to me I have to admit, although I did make better shots by concentrating on my balance. She shot 74, and Dickie and Joe-Bob could only smile and shake their heads as they watched her. And to save further controversy, we threw up the balls at the end of the match to decide who would play together next time.

Over lunch, Joe-Bob said with enthusiasm, "Say, Saratoga is just north of here. That's where old Gates beat the hell out of Johnny Burgoyne during the American Revolution. And north of that is Ticonderoga, not a hundred miles from here, where Ethan Allen surprised the British in the middle of the night and stole their cannon. We should visit those two places while they're handy."

"Oh, heavens, that's the American Revolution. We mustn't get ahead of ourselves." Once again, Dickie prevailed.

We spent the rest of the day and the evening advancing the book to 1696, when the French and their Indian allies attacked the Iroquois in their heartland south of Lake Ontario, burning villages and crops. Ephraim Bonney and members of his wife's family stage a diversion, trying to draw the French away from their village, but Ephraim is severely wounded, and without his leadership the rest of his party is beaten off. Their village then suffers the same fate as the others. Huge Louis Bonin, a captain in the French militia, finds Ephraim's 14-year-old daughter in the ruins of her longhouse, her face black with smoke and her clothes still smouldering, and she is cradling her dead brother in her arms. Louis is overcome with pity and tries to lead her away, but she is defiant, even in the midst of the tragedy, and she spits at him before surrendering herself to her fate. Meanwhile, Ephraim crawls back to the Mohawk River, finds a canoe, and in the dead of night, slips past the French sentries.

That night I drank too much, I mean, really too much, so that I couldn't remember what happened. I guess it was Joe-Bob's depressing philosophy about the human race that got me started. After we'd had a couple, he stated emphatically, "The United States is being ruined by blacks and Spanish immigrants."

Dickie looked mildly shocked. "You don't mean to say that you are racially prejudiced?"

"You won't believe this, but I'm not. I fought in 'Nam and played football with lots of blacks, and I call some of them friends." He chuckled. "According to my granddaddy, some of them might even be my cousins. But what I'm saying is that a certain percentage of humanity is going to sink into the gutter, and there's a higher percentage of blacks down there than whites. I have trouble with blacks who can't make their own way in white America, who resort to drugs and crime, who end up on the streets and turn our cities into slums, and who don't even know who the President of the country is."

"But I've heard," Dickie argued, "that many whites don't know who the president is either."

"And I have trouble with them, too. As for the Spanish, it's more than just drugs and crime and street people. Some of them are demanding language rights, and if we give in to them, it will be the end of the country."

"But Canada is a bilingual country," I protested, and then my slow moving brain realized that the separatists were adding credence to Joe-Bob's argument. "Never mind," I conceded. "I understand what you're saying."

"The United States started off with the premises that there be one language, one flag, and one God, the Christian God. That is what made us great, everybody going in the same direction. Now, I think we're losing our way, allowing anybody into the country no matter what baggage they bring with them in the way of funny religions and ethnic hatred. We're becoming weak and vulnerable, and wherever there's weakness, there's going to be someone to exploit it. Think about history, weak countries being over-run by strong ones, think about the protection rackets in our cities, think about pimps and prostitutes, think about drug dealers and addicts, and you'll have to agree with me. Now, talking about drugs, some people want to legalize them, but as far as I'm concerned, we have to get tougher with the dealers and suppliers. The death penalty is too good for them. Say, while I think of it, I'm sure glad none of you people smoke. Alright, I have the odd cigar, but only while I'm playing golf, or after I've closed a big deal."

"But what about alcohol?" I asked. "We tried prohibition, and that didn't work."

"Fred, alcohol is our inheritance, something handed down to us from our ancestors, something we've learned to live with over the course of time, except for the few who can't leave it alone. And don't think I drink like this all the time. It just happens when one of my wives leaves me and takes the kids, or when it's time for a party. I'll straighten out when I get my ambition back."

"What would you do with the problem blacks and the Spanish?" I asked, and I think that was my last coherent question.

"Back in colonial days, the Indians were a problem to the settlers, so they killed them off or drove them out."

"I believe you are what they call a red-neck in this country," Dickie observed. "Surely, such drastic action isn't possible any more."

"Believe me, there's lots that agree with me. You have to realize there are far too many people in this country, let alone the rest of the world. We need to be getting rid of some of them."

"Do you know that there are millions of people in the United States, mostly in New England, who are of French-Canadian origin?' Josée asked. "How do you feel about them?"

"Why, Josée, I didn't know that, but maybe that's part of my answer. I guess they've never been a problem, so I have no problem with them."

And that is the last thing I remember hearing that night. I don't know how I got to bed, and I certainly don't think I was in any state to help the relatives to their rooms. I woke up in the middle of the night, half sober again, to find that Josée wasn't there. "Josée, Jos, oh for God's sake, you haven't left me!"

She came quickly out of the bathroom. "Fred, what is the matter? I am right here."

"Thank God, thank God." And I went to sleep again.

It was Sunday again, and after Josée came back from church, and after we had brunch, we drove back to Cambridge on Highway 90, the Massachusetts Turnpike. Periodically, we had to stop and pay a toll for the privilege, but it was worth it, since my head wasn't up to handling the curves and hills of the Mohawk Trail. Anyway, I wasn't footing the bill. I was ready for bed by the time we got back to our hotel, where free spending Dickie had retained our rooms while we were away, but he insisted on a meeting to finish up King William's War. Before he had a chance to say anything, however, Joe-Bob suggested, "Say, now, that trip to Albany was worthwhile, except for the time I was partnered with Fred. Maybe we should start visiting more places."

"Joel Bonney was buried in Portland," I said. "Maybe we should go there and see if we can find his grave."

"But Fred, that would be out of sequence. Joel wasn't even born at the time," Dickie pointed out.

"Well, Deerfield was out of order, wasn't it? Ephraim hadn't got there yet. And are we going to go back and forth to places time after time just to keep the sequence right?" I was tired and belligerent.

"Actually, that is the right way to do it, and certainly, we will go to Portland on our way to Canada. That will be after the start of the French and Indian War."

"But you are being inconsistent." I was like a dog with a bone. "Following your logic, we should have gone to Port Royal first, the first European settlement in North America."

"And shouldn't we have gone to Lachine to see where Marie Verchères held off the Mohawks?" Josée joined in.

"But we are writing a book about the Bonneys - and the Bonins - and as far as we know, no member of either family was in either place."

"Well, yes that's true," I admitted. "But surely, we want to see all of Canada before we're finished, whether Bonneys and Bonins were involved or not."

"Yes, yes, but not until we have all the wars looked after. To continue, then, King William's War ended in 1697 with the Peace of Ryswick, and to underline its futility, all captured territory was returned."

"Alas, and within a year of the peace, the great man, Louis de Baude, Le Compte de Frontenac, was dead," Josée interjected.

"And by then," Dickie went on purposefully, "the Iroquois had grown tired of fighting battles for the English, and made a separate peace with the French in 1701. Now, we must tackle Queen Anne's War, or the War of the Spanish Succession, which began in 1702 after less than five years of peace. In many ways, it was a carbon copy of King William's War, with raids by French and Indians into New England."

"Say, one of those raids was on Deerfield, in 1704. The French and Indians killed over 60 people, including old Ephraim's second wife, I guess you would call her, and her children by her first husband. Ephraim was off with the militia at the time with a fellow by the name of Ben Church. With nothing left at Deerfield to go back to, Ephraim moved to New Hampshire when the war was over, and started a lumber business."

"There were counter raids by New Englanders on Acadia, during which the village of Grand Pré was burned by Ben Church, so Ephraim was probably involved in that. They captured Port Royal in 1710, and an attempt was made on Quebec City by a British fleet in 1711, that ending in disaster when some of the ships were wrecked on Egg Island in the Saint Lawrence River. Now, how alert are you?"

Josée answered immediately, "You said a British fleet, not an English fleet."

"Congratulations, Josée! By the Act of Union in 1707, England, Scotland and Ireland were united into one country. Henceforth, it would be the Union Jack flying over Great Britain's possessions around the world."

"What is this, a bloody history class?" I was still out of sorts.

Dickie looked at me with a hurt expression on his face. "But there was one major difference between the two wars. Governor Philippe de Rigaud de

Vaudreuil of New France made a truce with New York which allowed him to ship furs through Albany, and thence past the British blockade to Europe."

"Dickie," Joe-Bob objected, "I can understand Josée reciting the alphabet when she gives us a French name, but do you have to do the same? Couldn't you just say, 'Governor Voudrou', or whatever his name was?"

"I try to be correct. Just to conclude, by the treaty of Utrecht at the end of the war in 1713, France lost the fortress of Plaisance on Newfoundland, all its rights to Newfoundland, really, and that part of Acadia that is now Nova Scotia, save for Cape Breton Island, which the French called Ile Royale. Almost immediately, they built the fortress of Louisbourg on that Island to offset the loss of Port Royal. And after the war, there were three decades of peace during which both New France and the American Colonies flourished. Now, what kind of a story can we build around these events?"

"Well, Louis Bonin was probably involved in those raids on New England. Maybe he was at Deerfield," Josée offered.

"Alright, then, he was one of the butchers of Deerfield," Joe-Bob accused, "killing innocent women and children."

"I don't like the idea of him being a butcher. I think it is more likely that he could not control the Indians."

"Alright, let's say he was in charge of the raid, and whatever happened, it was on his head."

By this time, I was long past ready for a drink, but the others still had life, and they sketched out most of a chapter while Josée clacked it down on the laptop. During the period covered, my ancestor, Perez Bonney, left Massachusetts and settled in Goshen, Connecticut, and we guessed that he had a falling out with the church. As for Louis Bonin, we first had to invent a name for the half Iroquois woman he married, the daughter of Ephraim Bonney. "Oh, her surname would have been Bonney," presumed Joe-Bob.

"Not so," disagreed Josée. "The Iroquois were a what-do-you-call-it, a matriarchal people. She would have taken her mother's name."

"Jesus, God, what would that have been?"

"We have to invent it. What would sound Iroquois? Something from nature. Something pleasant to the ear, like 'Running Waters'."

"Good enough. Now, for a first name, Ruth has always been popular in our family."

"Alright. Ruth Running Waters. After Louis married her, he took her to Detroit where there would be less prejudice against her. Still, they had a what-do-you-call-it?"

"Tempestuous union?" suggested Dickie.

"Yes, a tempestuous union. She was conscious that she was neither white nor Iroquois, and she needed constant reassurance. Worse, she hated the French for what they had done to her family, and she took it out on Louis. They had ten children in spite of these difficulties, but she died having the last one."

"Do you know all that, or is it fiction?" I asked.

"It could well have been that way. And after she died, Louis, by now a tall, gaunt man in his 60's, brought his family back to Longueuil."

Finally, they were out of inspiration, and we retired to the bar. Joe-Bob phoned somebody and got us a tee time for the next day, and Dickie said to me, "Right. Tomorrow it's our turn, Fred."

I grimaced, knowing what my fate would be if we were to beat Josée and Joe-Bob, but the more I thought about it, the angrier I became, and I made up my mind to give it my best shot, no matter what the consequences. I looked at the drink in my hand, and determined it would be the only one I had that night, so that I wouldn't get stressed out during the game.

Joe-Bob laughed. "You two haven't got a chance. By the way, I'm going to get you all a membership in the USGA, so you can use their computer to keep your handicaps up to date. Say, Fred, after that last game, you might be down to an 18."

"I've kept all our scores since Josée and I got together. Can we plug those in?"

"You bet, so long as you got the course ratings and slopes."

And so I nursed my drink until the others had their fill, and then Josée and I put the other two to bed, with the usual unconscious groping. At least, I thought it was unconscious. And I began to wonder about these relatives, and how they could go on day after day with no sex, because I was sure that, being Bonneys, they would be far from impotent. And that night I had another dream, after Josée let me get to sleep, and in it, I found myself in the pro shop of some golf course, and the pro was telling me to get to the tee because my group was waiting for me, but my clubs were still in the storage room, and the rotten kid who was supposed to be bringing them out had disappeared for a smoke. Josée, Dickie, and Joe-Bob teed off without me, and when I finally got my clubs, I tried to catch up to them, but there were too many players in the way, and they wouldn't let me through because I was a single. And when I finally finished my game, I found my three partners in the clubhouse, and someone was playing the organ, and there was a man with a big smile on his face and his collar turned backward at one end of the room, and Dickie was giving Josée away to Joe-Bob. I shouted, "No! No! I know just cause and impediment why these two should not be joined together in Holy Matrimony!" And the shouting woke me up, and Josée put her arms around me, and I went to sleep again without dreaming any more.

It rained heavily overnight, and the course played long as a result, something I didn't need, but I concentrated as hard as I could on what Josée told me about swaying, and I played what for me was a good game. We were even at the turn; on the back nine, both Dickie and I sank a couple of putts, and we were two up with two to go. Josée became sullen and stopped talking altogether, while Joe-Bob tried to rattle me by reminding me I wasn't that good. We lost the 17th hole but hung on to halve the 18th, and Dickie shook my hand vigorously. "By Jove, we did it Fred, we beat the champions!" And Josée never said another word to me all day.

The golf game and lunch over, we assembled in Dickie's room to carry on with the book. "Now," he began, "we must turn to the last of the 'Petites Guerres'. Believe it or not, this conflict began in 1739 after Spanish Inquisitors cut off an English pirate's ear. From the 'War of Jenkins' Ear' between Spain and Great Britain, it developed into the War of the Austrian Succession, or King George's War, as it was known in America. In King George's War, prompted by mutual self-interest, the colonies took concerted action on their own without the sanction of the British government, in these circumstances.

"After Britain acquired Nova Scotia in 1713 under the terms of the Treaty of Utrecht, New Englanders took over the old French fishing outpost at Canso, near the strait of the same name, the one that separates Cape Breton Island, or as the French called it, Ile Royale, from the mainland of Nova Scotia. To protect the town, the British installed a governor and a small garrison, but it was perilously close to Louisbourg, and thus highly vulnerable.

"When France entered the war against Britain in 1744, the temptation was obviously too great, and forces from Louisbourg attacked Canso, and destroyed it. In so doing, they took a number of prisoners, including the captain of a merchant ship and a Lieutenant Bradstreet of the Canso garrison, who were imprisoned at Louisbourg. The captain and Bradstreet escaped at the end of the year, and brought details of Louisbourg's defences back to Massachusetts, where they convinced Governor William Shirley that the fortress could be taken. He requested and was given permission by the Massachusetts General Court to raise an army of 3,000 volunteers, and an armed colonial fleet for the attack. In an unprecedented example of colonial co-operation, Connecticut and New Hampshire also offered men, New York promised cannon, while New Jersey and Pennsylvania, both pacifist Quaker colonies, would provide only supplies.

"The promised cannon would not be heavy enough to mount a proper siege, so Shirley had balls cast in the calibre of the French guns at Louisbourg, believing, on the basis of the information the ex-prisoners had given him, that some of those guns might be captured. But he needed bigger warships for his expedition than were available in the colonies, and that is where Commodore Peter Warren of the Royal Navy came in. On his own initiative, he agreed to blockade Louisbourg with his squadron." Dickie paused. "Now, Josée, with some misgivings, I must confess that there is the stuff of novels here. Englishman Peter Warren, you see, was in the process of making a fortune from his investments in the colonies, and had married Susannah DeLancey, a daughter of the rich and powerful Huguenot family of New York."

Josée brightened. "Oui! We can make something of this! Being of French origin, though a misguided protestant, she would have been beautiful."

"But," I interrupted, "where are the Bonneys in this?"

Josée looked away from me, as if she was talking to the others. "If there wasn't a Bonney, why can't we invent one?"

"No, No!" I protested vehemently. "Ever since Basil told me to give my ancestors flesh and blood, I've been afraid of this. Outright fiction!"

"Alright," Dickie said in a voice designed to calm. "Peter Warren and Susannah DeLancey are not fiction. What is wrong with giving Josée a little licence to build a short part of the story around them?"

"Say, it's alright, Fred. There was a Bonney involved. Ephraim married a white woman when he moved to New Hampshire, had a family with her. His second son, my ancestor, name of Ichabod, was with the expedition to Louisbourg. He was a captain in the militia, and he got to meet Warren."

"Something to work with." Josée pursed her lips, and looked intent.

"Alright," Dickie continued. "Shirley appointed William Pepperell, merchant, ship owner and militia officer, as commander of the expedition to Louisbourg. On April 4th, 1745, he left Boston with nearly 3,000 men, and sailed to Canso to join the New Hampshire and Connecticut volunteers, already there. Warren arrived May 4th with four ships of the line, then sailed north to blockade Louisbourg.

"We have the background. Imagine how it was as the expedition took shape," Dickie exhorted us. "Fred, why don't you start?"

"Alright. How about this? I'm a volunteer, caught up in the excitement of the times. We came straggling out of the forests and the outlying districts, all of us raw-boned, husky lads, brothers together, friends laughing at the prospect of a diversion from the humdrum. And when we arrived in Boston, we gawked at its marvels: 15,000 people crowded together into one great town, the imposing houses of the rich, the shops, the businesses, the tall ships in the harbour. All these we passed on our way to the bustling waterfront, where we filed onto the transports and began exchanging stories and germs with our fellows. Someone broke open the liquor stores, and bottles were passed around."

Josée began to type furiously. "The ships made a brave sight as they set sail, the escorts firing farewell salutes, girls on shore waving and crying; but once out of the harbour, the party atmosphere vanished. The early April swells of the Atlantic began to toss the transports about like corks, and some of us became so seasick we would as soon have jumped overboard as stay afloat.

"On and on we sailed to the north and east, to the wretched remains of the Canso settlement, so recently burned to the ground by the villainous French. Waiting for us there were the militiamen from New Hampshire, a different lot, frontier-raised, taciturn, self-confident. One of their officers, Captain Ichabod Bonney, stood half a head taller than the rest, a man who commanded respect without asking for it.

"Ah! But to be on the ground again! We were so thankful to be off those wretched transports that none of us grumbled when we were set to work building a blockhouse, as much to keep us occupied as for the need of it. And each day, when chores were done, the liquor flowed, and many of my mates were set on a drunken course for the rest of their lives.

"By the end of April, boredom was setting in and we became restless, cursing the bad weather and wondering what the delay was. At last, in early May, we were heartened by the arrival of Commodore Peter Warren with four ships of the line, led by the 60 gun 'Superbe'. What a magnificent sight she made as she announced her arrival with a salvo from her port side! We set up a great cheer. Now, there would be action!"

"So," Josée paused. "How did Ichabod, Bonney and Peter Warren meet?"

"Like this, according to my granddaddy," Joe-Bob said. "The following evening, Warren invited the senior officers of the expeditionary force aboard for dinner: General Pepperell and his supporting cast of brigadiers; Lieutenant Colonel John Bradstreet, who survived imprisonment in Louisbourg; and because his commanding officer was indisposed, Captain Bonney of New Hampshire. Warren was quite taken with the tall captain, and spent much of the evening conversing with him about the resources of his colony, and how they might be profitably developed. At the end of the evening the two drank a toast, vowing to keep in touch with each other. *Commodore, do come and visit us in New Hampshire, and bring your wife with you. I understand she is the most charming woman in the colonies.*"

"*News of Suzannah's beauty has reached the wilds of New Hampshire, has it?" Warren smiled." Indeed, we shall come, and see first-hand your lumbering business*"

"Excellent," said Dickie approvingly. "May I carry on? Morning dawned cool and clear, and Warren's small fleet was already gone, slipped out on the early tide to blockade Louisbourg, the mighty French fortress only a few leagues away. He sent back word later in the day that the harbour was ice-free, the word Pepperell had been waiting for. Back onto the transports we crowded, some of us spoiling for a fight, others I think trying to throttle their fear, all thankful we had only a short distance to go.

"On May 11th, the ships' crews rowed us ashore at remote Gabarus Bay, and we then struggled on foot the several miles to Simon Point, brushing aside a small party of French soldiers on the way. From there, we could see our objective across a broad area of swampland: Louisbourg, gray-walled and formidable, aware of us, cannon spitting fire at us from inside, and from the Island Battery in the harbour. "Pepperell decided first to loot and burn the warehouses outside the fortress walls. John Bradstreet was assigned the task, and advanced with a company of us across the swamp to his objective, meeting little resistance on the way. We soon gutted the buildings and set them ablaze, but more importantly, as Bradstreet had hoped, we found that the Royal Battery across the bay from the fortress had been abandoned. The guns, having been spiked hastily, we soon made ready for action again, and in a matter of hours, they were lobbing Governor Shirley's cannon balls into the enemy stronghold.

"Louisbourg, however, was not to be taken so easily, and Pepperell knew his own small guns were ineffective at their present range. They had to be moved closer to the target. Beset by clouds of biting insects, battling fever, and working like navvies, we pushed and pulled the guns across the swamp, to the astonishment of the French defenders, and were soon mounting a devastating fire over the fortress walls. Pepperell also needed to silence the Island Battery, which

61

was preventing Commodore Warren from joining the bombardment, and this we were able to do on June 21st. Meanwhile, at intervals, units of us, often with a healthy inhalation of Dutch courage, would storm the fort to no avail, and retire with casualties. Captain Bonney was often in the vanguard of these assaults, and for such a big man, it was remarkable that French musket balls never touched him.

"On June 28th, denied reinforcements and gunpowder by the blockade, Governor Duchambon surrendered to marines from Warren's ships. And can we end," Dickie suggested, "by saying that Peter Warren was promoted to the rank of Rear Admiral, and named the new Governor of Louisbourg."

"Say, that's not the end. He was less than a hero to the New England volunteers, because he wouldn't let them loot the fortress."

"Just to complete the record," added Josée, "a relief expedition of Troupes de la Marine from Quebec City failed to reach Louisbourg in time to help, so it attacked Grand Pré instead, and then withdrew. My ancestor Jacques Bonin, eldest son of Louis, was with that expedition. As for Louisbourg itself, everyone there was deported to France after the surrender."

"Say, now, that was a smart thing to do."

"And a year later, a French fleet sent to retake the fortress never arrived because of contrary winds and illness. Meanwhile, French militia and Indians were ravaging through New England and upper New York, destroying settlements, including Saratoga, and bringing back prisoners."

"Worst of all," Joe Bob finished, "the British gave Louisbourg back to the French when the Treaty of Aix-la-Chapelle was signed, and that really upset the colonies, especially the people of Boston. France was in the driver's seat because she had whipped Britain pretty soundly in Europe. But say, what's at Louisbourg now, Dickie?"

"It has been completely reconstructed by the Canadian government."

"We should go and have a look at it."

"But in going there, we would drive past all kinds of places that I want to save for the proper occasion. We should go to Louisbourg in connection with its second taking in 1758. Here, let me make a sketch of the place for you. Perhaps that will do for the present." And in a matter of minutes, Dickie produced a remarkable drawing. "Bastions here, here and here, powder magazine here, Governor's residence here."

"Say, Dickie, that's nice, but I'd still like to see it. Why don't we fly there so we don't have to go past all those places you're saving?"

I knew what I was talking about, now. "To get to Louisbourg from here, we would have to change planes three times, and we'd end up in something you wouldn't want to fly in."

Joe-Bob shook his head. "Hell, no. I'm talking about flying there in my executive jet. Where's the nearest airport where an executive jet can land?"

"Well, Sydney, on Cape Breton Island, but we would have to land at Halifax first to clear customs."

Dickie capitulated. "An executive jet! Why yes, if we fly it will be alright. But as long as we are going to Louisbourg, I would like to see Canso too. Can we do that, Fred?"

"There's an airport at Port Hastings. That would be closest." I looked at the map. "It's about a hundred kilometres from Canso."

"A hundred what?"

"Kilometres. We went metric in Canada, Joe-Bob, because we thought you were going that way too. But you didn't, and now we're stuck with it."

"Say, how far is that in miles? And do they have any golf courses up that way?"

"A hundred kilometres is roughly 63 miles. And there are some good courses near Sydney, but you won't find any caddies there. It will be golf cars pretty well all the way in Canada."

"Why, then, let's throw our clubs and golf clothes in the plane too."

The rest of the afternoon and evening passed in writing about the period from the end of Queen Anne's War to the end of King George's War. Joel Bonney was finally born, in 1740, the eldest of Perez' seven children, and I wondered if he had blue eyes and reddish-blond curls like the boy in my dream.

Later, in the bar, Josée continued to ignore me, and by the time we got Dickie and Joe-Bob to bed, I knew I was in for it. In our room, still without a word, she undressed us both, pushed me down on the bed and straddled me. The punishment lasted longer than usual, and by the time it was finished, I was gasping for air. "I forgive you for beating me at golf, now," she said. "And for every punishment, there is a reward."

I had flown in small jets before, the government kind, stark and utilitarian craft in keeping with the low status of public servants. Joe-Bob's, in contrast, was entirely luxurious, with room for a dozen passengers, seats upholstered with leather, a galley, and a well-stocked bar. The crew consisted of the pilot, a muscular co-pilot who doubled as security officer, and a cute attendant named Jacqui, who looked as if she might provide any other services necessary. She fixed us an eye-opener and breakfast, while I briefed the others on present day Nova Scotia from my automobile club tour book. "To sum up," I finished, "the population is something less than a million, the area is over 21,000 square miles, the highest mountain is less than 2,000 feet, the chief industries are fishing, forestry and subsidized coal mining, only eight per cent of the land is suitable for agriculture, and they grow good apples in the Annapolis Valley. And it would have been the 14th colony to rebel at the time of the American Revolution if the British Navy hadn't been stationed in Halifax."

"Say, just so I can appreciate what you're talking about, how does the size and population relate to Texas?"

I threw up my hands. "How should I know?"

Dickie, the fount of all knowledge, leapt into the breech. "Texas has about 17 million people, and an area of some 267,000 square miles."

Joe-Bob looked smug. "Therefore, it has 17 times the population and 13 times the area of Nova Scotia."

By that time, we had crossed the Canadian border, and were flying across the Bay of Fundy, the wide inlet that almost completely separates Nova Scotia from New Brunswick. From our vantage point, we could see the two provinces at the same time, both bathed in the summer sunshine, and Joe-Bob looked puzzled. "Say, where's all the snow? I thought Canada had winter twelve months of the year, and that you folks got around by dog team."

"Think about it," I said to him. "Why would there be winter here, just north of the border, when it's summer just to the south? If you want ice and snow and dog teams, you won't find any at this time of the year this side of the Arctic Islands."

On the ground in Halifax, Joe-Bob stopped and stared at the big Canadian flag flying over the entrance to the airport building, and I can only describe the look on his face as a mixture of suspicion and envy. Inside, I smoothed our way past a customs officer who looked as if he might cause us trouble, and we were cleared to go the short distance to Port Hastings. From there, in a rented van, we crossed over the causeway connecting Cape Breton Island and the rest of Nova Scotia, turned onto secondary Highway 344, and drove south along the Strait of Canso. On the other side of the strait rose the smoke stacks of Port Hawkesbury's industrial area, and visible in the distance were the small islands of the archipelago known as Isle Madame, where Acadians had settled centuries before. Joe-Bob was impressed with the causeway, but not our roads. The farther down the Strait we went the worse they became, until grass and weeds were sprouting out of cracks in the pavement. "You Canadians need some American advice on how to build roads."

I told him, "Maybe you're right, but we have universal health care. Trouble is, it's hard to get into a hospital if you need one. Anyway, wait till you see the 401 in Ontario."

"And why are all the highway signs in French as well as English? I thought all the French were in Quebec."

"Have you forgotten the Acadians?" asked Josée. "They make up a large part of the population of both Nova Scotia and New Brunswick, and there are pockets of them on Prince Edward Island and even Newfoundland."

At the bottom of Chedabucto Bay, we branched onto Highway 16, a decided improvement over Route 344, and followed it to the village of Canso, and the National Historic Site there. The girls inside the reception centre showed us around the displays, and we watched a video about the history of the old settlement, located not where the present town is, but on Grassy Island, a low-lying patch of ground at the mouth of the harbour. For a small fee, we took a converted fishing boat out to the once bustling village for a self-guided tour of the ruins. Not much was left intact after the French bombarded, looted and burned the place in 1744.

Back in town, we stopped for a snack at a run-down café memorable only for the music that was playing in the background. Josée began to hum along with one of the catchy songs, I unconsciously joined in, Dickie added a tenor descant, and Joe-Bob began to imitate a tuba with a 'boom, boom, boom' in perfect harmony. When the song was done, we looked at each other and laughed. "Say, that was good. I used to belong to the glee club in college. Where did you folks learn to sing like that?"

The answer was the same for all of us: church choirs.

"What was that song?" I asked the waitress.

"That was 'Barrett's Privateers', written by Stan Rogers. He wasn't born here, but we kind of adopted him, have a festival every year in his memory. Poor Stan! He was only 33 when he was killed in a plane fire in 1983. Would you like to buy the tape? I've got one if you do."

Joe-Bob threw four American 20s on the table. "That enough for the snack and the music?"

We played the Stan Rogers' tape twice on our way back to Port Hastings, and began to learn the unusual words of his ballad, the story of a sailor who lost both his legs in an engagement with an American ship during the revolutionary war: 'The year was 1778 (How I wish I was in Sherbrooke now), When a letter of Marque came from the King, To the scummiest vessel I'd ever seen.' And the chorus went: 'God damn them all, I was told we'd sail the seas for American gold, We'd fire no guns, shed no tears, I'm a broken man on a Halifax Pier, The last of Barrett's privateers.'

So engrossed did we become with the tape that I made a couple of wrong turns, and at dinnertime, when we should have been back at Port Hastings, we found ourselves in the village of Havre Boucher on St. George's Bay. Josée spotted a restaurant advertising authentic Acadian food, and on the waitress's recommendation, we had pea soup served with big slices of warm, brown bread, and a kind of bouillabaisse made with cod, crab, lobster and scallops. I just hoped I could get away with the pea soup. It affected me like beans.

From Port Hastings, the jet hardly stopped going up before it started going down again to land at Sydney, where we booked into the best hotel in the place, courtesy of the reservations made by Jacqui. And in the long summer evening, released by our leader from further toil that day, we drove the Cabot Trail that circles Cape Breton's northern peninsula, a spectacular route along the Gulf of St. Lawrence, with rugged highlands and scrubby forests inland.

Later, over drinks in the bar, I asked Joe-Bob, "What do you do with the jet and the crew when you aren't using them?"

"I make money by chartering them out. You'd be surprised how many people want to ride in those things, maybe a once in a lifetime experience like going on a cruise, or to Hawaii. Hell of a deal, too, for a tax write-off."

Dressed in our golf clothes the next morning, we drove to Louisbourg, a short hour away over roads not much better than the ones we'd taken to Canso. At the National Historic Site, we spent some time in the reception centre looking at murals and displays, which told the story of Louisbourg from the time it was built until its ultimate demise. A bus then took us to the reconstructed fortress itself, where we were first interrogated by the guard at the gate to make sure we were not 'Anglais'. Once past that mock hurdle, we joined a tour along a route replete with costumed animators, college kids playing the part of townsfolk or soldiers, all earning a few dollars to help them through the next school year. Our guide was a plump, jolly Acadian girl who told us, among other things, that there were no prostitutes or brothels in old Louisbourg, but it wasn't hard to find enthusiastic amateurs.

To me, the fortress looked formidable with its bastions and cannon, its dark stone buildings and walls, but Dickie pointed out weaknesses. "Louisbourg could only be defended if French ships controlled the harbour, and if French ships could bring in fresh supplies and ammunition. In 1744, Warren controlled the harbour, and intercepted the supply ships."

We had a Louisbourg lunch after the tour in one of the three restaurants on site, and I chose a kind of fish chowder instead of the pea soup, it having caused me grief the day before. Finally, we took in a cannon firing preceded by a roll of drums and a musket demonstration, during which several of the ancient weapons failed to fire.

To conclude our brief visit to Nova Scotia, we played two matches that afternoon at a course near the airport in the cool, damp breeze coming off the Atlantic Ocean, Josée against Joe-Bob, me against Dickie. She won and I played well but lost by a stroke, but that meant a tie and no punishment!

The return flight to Boston that evening was without incident, and this time, Joe-Bob smoothed us through customs. Back in our 'own' rented van, we made it from Logan airport to the hotel in time for a planning session over nightcaps. "Where to next, Dickie?" Joe-Bob asked.

"To Pittsburgh, or Fort Duquesne as it was known to the French, where George Washington started the French and Indian War."

Chapter 4.

The French and Indian War

On the morning of July 1st, 'Canada Day' at home, Joe-Bob plotted a route to Pittsburgh for us on my automobile club map. It was far from a straight line: U.S. 90 to Sturbridge, Massachusetts; U.S. 84 to Scranton, Pennsylvania; U.S. 81 to Harrisburg; U.S. 76 to Pittsburgh. According to the driving distance inset, it was 633 miles, and it would take about 12 hours to get there, not counting stops for gas and so on. "Say, let's make it a comfortable trip, stay over one night, catch a game of golf tomorrow morning. I know some folks up around Wilkes-Barre, Pee-aye - that's about half way. I'll give them a call, get them to make us a tee time. And Fred, you play with me this time. You play like you did the other day, now, and we'll smoke them."

Dickie wasn't entirely happy about the idea of a relaxed trip. "I must phone Basil this morning and report our progress. We've been doing well, I believe, but Joe-Bob, I wonder if we shouldn't fly to Pittsburgh to save a day?"

"Dickie, it's all part of getting to know the country, isn't it? You can't see it the same way from a 'plane window as you can on the ground. And let me talk to Basil when you're finished."

Dickie picked up the phone at our table, dialled London, and talked animatedly with Basil for a few minutes. Then, with a worried expression on his face, he held his hand over the mouthpiece. "He wants us to send over what we've done so he can get started on the editing. He's revised the publication list, moved us up, so the book will hit the market this fall. Lord! We are really under the gun. Here, Joe-Bob. He's waiting for you. Oh, by the way. He sends his regards to Fred, and his love to Josée."

"Say, Basil - yes, it's Joe-Bob Bonney. Let's get right to it. How are you going to market the book on this side of the water . . .? Haven't decided yet? How about giving me the North American rights . . .? Not a problem. I got a few million in the bank looking for a good investment. How's your company off for operating funds? . . . I can understand your hesitating - you don't know me from Adam's off ox, but over here, we don't mess around with formalities. Think it over, and I'll talk to you again from Pittsburgh day after tomorrow. About the same time? O.K. 'Bye."

Out on the turnpikes and freeways, it wasn't as easy as it looked on the driving distance inset, which didn't allow for construction delays, or heavy traffic around the major cities. A slow waitress in the café we chose for lunch didn't help either, so Joe-Bob's decision to make a two-day trip out of it looked better and better as the afternoon wore on. Dickie continued to fret, however, and kept mumbling about wasting time when our deadline was so short.

At Wilkes-Barre, Joe-Bob found us a comfortable place to stay, and to pacify Dickie, we had supper brought to his room, and there we worked long into the night, setting the stage for the French and Indian War. Dickie, as usual, provided the background. "The French and Indian War started in America, not Europe. Let me explain why.

"While the English in the American Colonies pushed slowly inland from the Atlantic coast, generally having trouble with the Indian tribes in their way, the French, as Josée has indicated, using the Indians as allies, were leap-frogging ahead of them, cutting them off from the country beyond the Appalachian Mountains. The Peace of Aix-La-Chapelle in 1749 solved nothing. A north-south boundary following the Appalachian crest was agreed to, but neither side was satisfied with it, and it was almost impossible to define on the ground. Josée?"

"Let me tell you about the French claim to the country beyond the Mountains. First of all, La Salle - you remember that René-Robert Cavalier de La Salle, Sieur de Lachine - claimed all the Mississippi drainage for France, after he followed that river to its mouth in 1682. In the 1730s and 40s, Pierre Gaultiers de Varennes, Sieur de la Verendrye, reached the Black Hills of South Dakota. In 1739, Pierre and Paul Mallet saw the Colorado Rockies. Where were you Anglais all this time? Sitting in your armchairs or killing Indians? Whatever our claim, we were determined to control North America beyond the English Colonies, starting with the Great Lakes and the Mississippi valley. We therefore built a string of forts on the Lakes, down the Ohio River, and down the Mississippi, thus establishing a link with the new Louisiana colony, and wherever we found any Anglais, we chased them back over the mountains."

"Meanwhile," Dickie resumed, "the main area of conflict became the 'Ohio Country', which lay south of the Great Lakes and west of the Appalachian Mountain chain. As Josée explained, it was claimed by the French on the basis of La Salle's explorations. It was also claimed by the Iroquois by right of conquest, by Britain through a treaty with the Iroquois in 1744, and by another treaty signed with the Shawnee, Wyandot and Delaware Indians in 1748. Indians still dominated the area until 1750, because neither France nor Britain had much in the way of military presence there. The difference was that the French actively courted the tribes present, assuring them that they were only interested in trading, and warning that the British would come not to trade, but to settle. They were so successful in their efforts that even the Iroquois were wavering, and they might have switched sides except for the efforts of a man called William Johnson. He was the nephew of Peter Warren - you all remember who he was, don't you - the Commander of the British fleet at Louisbourg? Johnson had an estate on the Mohawk River and always dealt fairly with his neighbours, and when his first wife died, he married a Mohawk woman, and was made a member of the tribe. The Penns of Pennsylvania also were a positive influence, because they bought land from the Six Nations of the Iroquois Confederacy instead of stealing it.

"Still, there were serious concerns about the Iroquois' leanings, so the British called a meeting in 1754 to settle grievances. In that year, representatives from New York, Pennsylvania, Maryland, and the New England Colonies met with 150 representatives of the Iroquois tribes at the Albany Congress."

"We don't have to go back to Albany, do we?" I protested.

"No, not now. At any rate, the Iroquois were sent away with wagon loads of presents, Johnson was named Indian Superintendent, and he, for the rest of his life, kept troubles with these important tribes under control.

"At the risk of getting ahead of ourselves, I will mention that Colonial Union was discussed at this Albany Congress, as suggested by that extraordinary American-to-be, Ben Franklin. The idea was rejected.

"We now have to backtrack a bit. In 1749, Virginians chartered a company with the objectives of trading in the Ohio Country, and promoting settlement. Governor Robert Dinwiddie was heavily involved in the scheme, and expected to make a fortune speculating in land. That same year, the French sent an expedition into the area with instructions to build forts, and to bury lead plates along the border proclaiming French sovereignty. Agents of the Ohio Company followed behind and dug up the plates."

"When you say 'fort', Dickie," Joe-Bob interrupted, "what kind of structure are you talking about?"

"The word sounds like something pretty formidable, but few in the wilderness were. There certainly were no Louisbourgs." Dickie reached for his pencil and sketchpad. "A typical one might consist of a sapling stockade with catwalks inside, bastions on the corners, and earth ramparts outside, like this. The enclosures were only large enough to include the few buildings necessary for the situation - barracks here, blacksmith shop there, a trading store near the gate, as I've shown. But back to Governor Dinwiddie. He protested to Great Britain about the French occupation of the Ohio Country, and was ignored. He then decided to take matters into his own hands, and we'll stop there for the night."

When we finally got to the bar, I became aware of a change in Joe-Bob, as if he had found that reason to live he'd been looking for. He only had a couple of drinks, and that seemed to rub off on Dickie, too. "The party's over," Joe-Bob grinned. "I don't care what Basil says, I'm not going to take no for an answer. I'm buying myself a piece of this action, and I'm going to know what I'm getting into, too, so I can drive a hard bargain. The hotel got me a book on the publishing business - that's tomorrow morning's prescribed reading."

"You are right about the party, Joe-Bob," Dickie sighed. "Time to sober it up. Can't afford another fuzzy moment because of the Rusty Nails. Besides, I'm embarrassed that we've imposed on Josée and Fred so long."

"You mean about them putting us to bed? Joe-Bob's grin widened. "Say, that's something I sure will miss." Josée blushed, and I knew then that his groping was not entirely unconscious.

We all played well the next day on the lush, rolling fairways of the private club near Wilkes-Barre. I couldn't begin to match the skill of the others, but I held up my end of the partnership with Joe-Bob, and shot to my 18 handicap. The result was another tie, and I breathed a sigh of relief. Escaped punishment one more time!

Back on the road again, the traffic was light, and the van climbed swiftly over the Allegheny Mountains. To pass the time, we sang 'Barrett's Privateers' and other Stan Rogers' songs, and tried to imagine what it was like crossing these rugged hills in colonial days, when there were no roads. The only way through the thick forests then was by way of trails made by game animals, or by Indians as unpredictable as the weather. It would have been necessary, too, to cross dozens of raging torrents that might sweep you away in one careless moment.

When we reached Pittsburgh, in spite of the rush hour traffic, Josée navigated us to our hotel on Fifth Avenue without a hitch, and we were afforded the VIP service we were becoming accustomed to - doorman, valet parking, and courteous bellhops with their hands discreetly extended for tips. From the windows of our room, we could see where the Allegheny and Monongahela Rivers met to form the mighty Ohio, one of the principal tributaries of the Mississippi, while beyond were the rolling plateaux, narrow valleys and precipitous bluffs of the upper Ohio Country, the bone of contention that sparked the French and Indian War. We didn't have much time to enjoy the view, however. Dickie was waiting impatiently for us, and room service was on the way up to his suite.

When we had eaten and were settled in our chairs, Josée at a table with the laptop, Joe-Bob's map fastened to the wall with masking tape, Dickie began. "The French have a penchant for fighting above their weight "

"What do you mean by that?" Josée looked suspicious.

"That is," continued Dickie, "in this context, warring with a stronger opponent. One must none the less admire their temerity. There were just 80,000 of them in North America, and they were trying to hold back over a million English speaking colonists. But we were at the point where Governor Dinwiddie was trying to enlist the aid of Great Britain in his difficulties. Now, here enters on the scene one of the most interesting characters in history - George Washington."

"The father of our country," breathed Joe-Bob, and he placed his right hand over his heart. I almost expected him to crack out an American flag.

"He entered the world in Virginia in 1732, the first son born to his father's second wife. When his father died in 1743, George went to live with his half-brother, Lawrence, for whom he had a great affection. Lawrence had served in the Caribbean in 1739, and in honour of the British admiral in charge of that expedition, he named his estate on the Potomac River 'Mount Vernon'.

"George became a surveyor in 1748 when he was only 16 years old, and was engaged by Lawrence's father in law, the wealthy Lord Fairfax, to map his holdings in the Shenandoaugh Valley. In 1751, Lawrence became ill with TB, and George accompanied him to Barbados, where the climate was thought to promote recovery from that disease. Sadly, however, Lawrence died in 1752 after they returned home, and George was left with a face disfigured with the smallpox he contracted on the Island. A few years later, he bought Mount Vernon from Lawrence's widow.

"George's real ambition was to become a senior officer in the army, and to further that end, he joined the militia in 1752, and became an aide to Governor

Dinwiddie. A 'braw laddie' he was, according to Dinwiddie, sturdy, intelligent, and obliging, but his superior officers had a different opinion of him: a brash, vain, opinionated young pup, who wrote critical letters to them.

"Having received no offers of help from Great Britain, the governor dispatched George Washington to tell the French to quit the Ohio Country, if you can imagine it! Accordingly, George left Williamsburg, then the capital of Virginia, in the late summer of 1753, and trekked almost all the way to Lake Ontario, a distance of 360 miles as the crow flies. There, he found Fort le Boeuf near the present town of Waterford, Pennsylvania, right there on the map, where he was received graciously by the French, who told him they would not quit the area, but promised to deliver his message to Quebec City. Washington, much impressed with the demeanour of the French officers, marched back to Williamsburg, arriving there late in the fall, three and a half months after he left."

"That means he averaged about seven miles a day through the wilderness, the kind of country we were looking at today, coming over the Alleghenies - and when we drove to Albany on the Mohawk Trail," Joe-Bob calculated. An engineer would figure that out.

"As you say. Dinwiddie next tried to get the other colonies to co-operate in an attack on the French, but even though they shared his concern, they refused to help. He tried Great Britain again, and was instructed to confront the French, and stop them from building forts in the Ohio Country. The question was, how could that best be done by a colony with limited resources and an inexperienced militia?

"In early 1754, Washington proposed a fort where Pittsburgh now stands, here at the forks of the Ohio River. Settlers from Virginia were already present, and the fort would serve not only to protect them, but show the French that Virginia meant business. The governor agreed, so Washington set off with 160 militiamen to do the deed, only to find when he arrived here that the French had expelled the settlers and built their own fort, which they named after the then Governor of New France, the Marquis Duquesne. The French turned Washington around and quickly marched him back over the border, the border as they had defined it.

"When poor George arrived again in Williamsburg, Dinwiddie ordered him to return and avenge his humiliation by driving the French out of their fort. Gathering some 400 green militiamen about him, he again set out for the Ohio Country, stopping to construct the makeshift 'Fort Necessity' at Great Meadows on his way. He then pressed forward, hoping to even scores with the arrogant French in a surprise attack.

"Alas, fate was not on George's side. Friendly Indians - the Shawnees and the Delawares - informed the French that he was coming, and the commandant at Fort Duquesne, Captain Contrecouer, sent a party of 30 to parlay with him. Then, the worst of disasters befell poor George. His men stumbled on the French party. The green militiamen panicked and began to shoot. When the smoke cleared, ten Frenchmen were dead, including their leader, Sieur de Jumonville. Worse, one of

George's Indians had scalped him. There was nothing to do but take the other Frenchmen prisoner, and carry on.

"But again, friendly Indians informed the French of what had transpired. Led by Captain Contrecouer, they came storming out of Fort Duquesne, 500 of them with 400 of their Indian allies, all thirsting for revenge. When the two forces met, Washington and his men were soon routed and fled back to Fort Necessity. The French laid siege. The militiamen got into the liquor supplies. George surrendered on July 3rd 1754, nine hours after the attack on his fort began. The French forced him to sign a confession of murder; later, he claimed he didn't realize what it was he was signing. They then let him go, and he retired in disorder leaving behind supplies, equipment, and evidence of Governor Dinwiddie's plans to colonize. That evidence cemented the French-Indian alliance.

"Oh, I'm sure I could have loved the gallant Captain Contrecouer!" Josée exclaimed. I was glad he wasn't around any more.

"Say, Dickie, I don't take kindly to the way you're belittling George Washington," complained Joe-Bob. "In my book, he comes across as a hero in that engagement with the French."

"I am merely embellishing the historical record according to my research, but only slightly, and that record will show, by the time we finish with the American Revolutionary war, that Washington was as hopelessly incompetent a general as ever commanded an army."

"If you were a younger man, I'd thrash you for suggesting that!" Joe-Bob's face was flushed with red.

"That would not change the facts. But don't let my age stop you." One of the handlebars of Dickie's moustache twitched.

"Shut up, *vous cretins*, shut up!" Josée shouted, and the two of them looked at her with their mouths open. "We have a book to write. It is going to make me rich. I hate being poor, don't you understand? I'm not going to let you two screw this up!"

Ever the conciliator, I tried to get us back on track. "So, Washington went back to Williamsburg, and?"

"Well, yes, sorry, Josée," Dickie apologized. "Quite juvenile of me, really. Yes, Washington went back to Williamsburg, after having started the French and Indian War."

"War would have started anyway," Joe-Bob snapped. "But say, Josée, what does that *cretin* mean?"

"Loosely translated, that's French for asshole," I said.

Joe-Bob looked stunned for a moment. "Well, now, I wouldn't take that from anyone else," he said, and he began to laugh. We all joined him, and the tension was broken.

"Where were we?" Dickie scratched his head. "Oh, yes. Back in Williamsburg, Dinwiddie, beside himself at the prospect of not making bags of money from his speculations, again appealed to Great Britain for help. This time, he was heard; and here, we have an important change in Imperial foreign policy. In October 1754, Britain sent Major General Edward Braddock to the colonies with instruction to eradicate French power in North America, even though no state of war existed between the two countries.

"A word about Braddock - an officer in the Coldstream Guards, he was already 60, a blunt man, quick to take offence and to hold a grudge, given to duelling to settle arguments, inflexible in military tactics. He shortly formed a dim view of colonials, who tried to profit from his expedition; in fact, Ben Franklin, he swore, was the only honest man in all of America, for he was the only one who delivered supplies as ordered, on time, and for the price quoted. Curiously, considering his prejudices, he took a liking to Washington, and made him his aide de camp with the rank of colonel. That was doubly curious, for it was policy that colonial officers, no matter what rank, had to serve under British officers, no matter how low the rank. In fact, because of that policy, Washington had resigned from the militia after the fiasco at Fort Necessity.

"Braddock made his plans in consultation with the Governors of Virginia, Pennsylvania, Massachusetts and Maryland. They called for a three-pronged assault: take Fort Beausejour, in Acadia; take Montreal in what we can call Canada, and Fort Niagara at the head of Lake Ontario; take Fort Duquesne in the Ohio Country. Leaving aside the first two prongs for the moment, we will concentrate on Fort Duquesne, with Braddock himself leading the attack. He had two regiments of regular soldiers, the 44th and 48th Foot, only battalions, really, altogether about 1,500 men, or rather, hastily trained, overgrown boys. In addition, he had 700 Virginia militiamen, and George Washington."

"The 44th and 48th regiments of foot? Do we need all that detail?" asked Josée.

"It is partly a military history, is it not? Naming the units lends credibility to the story."

"But it is now much more than a military history," I said.

"Can we leave that aside for the moment, and get on with Braddock's campaign? Thank you. Braddock set out on June 21st, 1755, for Fort Cumberland, 100 miles away, in the north western corner of Maryland, arriving there 19 days later, after hacking a path through the forests for his guns and wagons. Then his progress slowed to two miles a day as he fought his way through, as he recorded in his diary, 'an uninhabited wilderness of steep rocky mountains and almost impassable morasses'. He had already made two mistakes. He would not use Indian scouts, and he stubbornly chose the more difficult of two routes to his objective. It was at this point that he made his third mistake, and Joe-Bob, please do not threaten me with violence. It is historical fact. He listened to the advice of George Washington, and split his force in two so the forward column could move faster."

Joe-Bob grimaced. "My granddaddy told me that my ancestor, Josiah, son of Ichabod, grandson of Ephraim, was on this campaign, and he said Washington was a hero."

"The French, of course, through their Indian allies the Shawnees and Delawares, knew Braddock was coming, and Captain Contrecouer prepared to abandon Fort Duquesne."

I said, "Why not just Indians, instead of Shawnees and Delawares? Same argument as for naming the military units."

Dickie summoned up his hurt look. "Why not be accurate? We know who the tribes were. Again, let's leave that. Captain Contrecouer was going to evacuate, but at the last moment, decided to let one of his officers, Captain de Beaujeu, make a stand. De Beaujeu, with a force of 108 colonial regulars, that is Troupes de la Marine, 148 militia, and 637 Indians, ambushed Braddock's advance column of 1,200 on July 9th, 1755, near the Borough of Braddock, just eight or nine miles south of here, as the British were struggling across the Monongahela River and up a steep trail."

"Mon Dieux! Now 108 Troupes, 148 militia, 637 Shawnees and Delawares! Dickie! We drown in detail!"

"Oh, do let me finish! The French, spread out behind tree cover, began by firing a volley at the head of the British column, then concentrated on picking off the officers and drummers. The poor British lads in the van fell back on the middle. In the confusion, Braddock yelled and thrashed about at his men, while Washington on his horse tried to rally them. During the battle, de Beaujeu and 23 of his men died, Braddock was mortally wounded, 877 or 977 of his men were killed, depending on which account you read, Washington escaped unscathed, and only one cannon shot was fired. Fortunately, the Virginia militiamen took to the trees, and their fire allowed retreat. Over Washington's protests, the army, now under Brigadier Dunbar, withdrew to Fort Cumberland and then to Philadelphia, destroying its equipment before leaving, but Braddock's plans for the three-pronged assault fell into French hands. That, then, was the battle that became known as 'Braddock's Defeat', and it opened the frontier to French and Indian attacks.

"And yes, Joe-Bob, Washington was the hero of the occasion, at least in the colonies. He was made commander of all Virginia forces, but the British army would not accept his authority, thus denying him the respect he felt he deserved. He took part in one more campaign, which we will talk about later, and then, when he could not get a royal commission, he resigned a second time from the militia, this time with the rank of brigadier. In 1758, he was elected to the Virginia legislature, the House of Burgesses, and played no further part in the wars, and he was left with a grudge against the British. Now, how are we going to turn all this into our story?"

Josée had that faraway look in her eye, and the trace of a smile on her face. "We have Joshua Bonney on the one side, and Marcel Bonin, the grandson of Louis, on the other. Tall, lean Joshua will experience the humiliation at Fort Necessity, the disaster of Braddock's Defeat. Stocky, strong Marcel will be a key player in these French victories. Let me fill in the details."

"Joel Bonney was born in Goshen, Connecticut, in 1740," I volunteered. "As a boy of 15, he was probably following news of Braddock's campaign. Can you work him into the story now?"

"Your most famous ancestor, soon himself to be involved in the wars with the French? Let me see. Perhaps I can tell part of the story through his eyes. Yes, yes. And Braddock's Defeat will convince him to volunteer for military duty. Now, what would he look like?"

Without hesitation I replied, "He would have been a sturdy lad with blue eyes and reddish-blond, curly hair."

"How do you know that?"

"I just know."

We had our nightcaps in the bar, two each, and said goodnight, and after Josée reminded me that we were partners in the next golf game, and lectured me on the consequences of losing, and after she finished using me as a sex object, I fell into a troubled sleep, and had another crazy dream. In this one, I was a private British soldier with a huge pack on my back, struggling through a canyon on the Monongahela River, and I could not keep up with the others, and an officer, who looked remarkably like Dickie, kept wacking me across the buttocks with the flat of his sword, saying, "Come on, Bonney, you must catch up." The rest of the army disappeared ahead of me; and suddenly, the sound of small arms fire filled the air, and the screams of wounded and dying men, and I finally made my way around a bend in the river, and there, in front of me, was the carnage of Braddock's Defeat. Nearby was a cannon with no crew to fire it. I didn't know anything about cannon, but I swung the barrel around, aimed it at the trees beyond the battle scene, and fired, and the sound of the shot, at least, that is what I imagined, woke me up.

Joe-Bob talked at length with Basil on the telephone the next morning, and I listened to one side of the conversation with interest. So, that was how a big wheel made a deal - brusque, to the point, always probing for vulnerability. When he hung up, Joe-Bob had a grin on his face. "Got him!" he exulted. "I knew when he moved our publication date up that his company was in trouble. A couple of books they hoped would be big sellers have bombed. I'm going to advance them a couple of million so they can get square with their suppliers, and in return, I become one of the preferred shareholders in the Golden Lion Publishing Company. Got to make another call to get some money moving."

That business out of the way, we visited the blockhouse, the last vestiges of the colonial forts built near the forks of the Ohio River, and drove to the Borough of Braddock where the ignominious defeat took place. On the way back to the hotel, Dickie and Joe-Bob found an exclusive ladies wear shop and bought Josée a couple of new outfits - a peace offering for their bad behaviour the day before. That just about shot the morning.

The afternoon found us on one of Pittsburgh's better golf courses, as arranged by Joe-Bob, and we played a scramble, which I hate, because it's an alternate shot format in which my partner, in this case Josée, had to depend on me more than usual. I hit a lot of bad shots, and she had to play the next from wherever I put the ball - in the rough, in the bunkers, on downhill slopes close to the water hazards. But she kept scraping the ball out of the trouble I put her in and getting it on the greens, and I was able to sink a lot of putts, and between us, we got around in 78 strokes. That was good enough for a one-up victory.

Dickie, the slave driver, had us back in his room for supper, and we edited Josée's text from the night before. She had done a masterful job, I thought, of introducing Joel Bonney into the story, and she also sifted out what was unnecessary in the saga of Braddock's Defeat. Dickie, of course, complained that she had omitted important facts, so Joe-Bob and I told him, in unison, "Dickie, there isn't room for all that."

Over drinks afterward, Joe-Bob asked, "What's next, Dickie?"

"We are going to do some serious travelling. Tomorrow, we go back to Boston and then to Portland, Maine, where we will find Joel Bonney's grave, and visit Longfellow House, the shrine to that wretch who wrote the poem, 'Evangeline'."

Joe-Bob looked belligerent. "Dickie, now, why are you calling one of our most famous poets a wretch?"

"That will become clear by the time we finish this trip. From Portland, we will take a ferry to Yarmouth, Nova Scotia, Canada, then visit Port Royal and Grand Pré, where Evangeline was supposed to have lived, both those places on our way to Beausejour, the second prong of poor, dead Braddock's plan. By the way, Governor William Shirley of Massachusetts was appointed to take his place, but as we shall see, he didn't last long."

"Say, how do you like my vest?" Joe Bob asked us the next morning. It was all covered with stars and stripes in honour of the fourth of July.

Personally, I thought it was hideous, but I wasn't about to say that. Dickie had more gumption. "If you are looking for a compliment, I suggest you ask a fellow American."

It was a long drive back to Boston, with no overnight stop, and we didn't get away until after ten because Josée had to go to communion first. It rained hard most of the way, and I had to concentrate more than usual in the heavy traffic, especially when there were transport trucks around. They were the worst - aggressive drivers, cutting in so close they almost forced me off the road - and then, for thanks, they would spray, or better, deluge the van with water. The resulting stress may be why the drinks at the familiar bar in our familiar hotel in Cambridge hit me so hard, and for the second time in a week, I really didn't remember how I got to bed. Joe-Bob wasn't around to help. He begged off with the excuse that he had some business to attend to, and I wondered if it was with Jacqui, the cute attendant on his plane. The last thing I remember was the crafty look on Dickie's face when he ordered me another drink.

The only good news was that I didn't have much of a hangover in the morning. Josée was still asleep when I woke up. I leaned over to smell the sweetness of her breath, and that made me remember the haunting smell in her apartment: the mixture of potting soil, soap, and furniture polish, with the delicate, almost non-existent fragrance of Impatiens. She stretched, yawned and opened her eyes. "Did we do anything nice last night?" I asked her.

"You don't remember? Why, I might as well have went with Dickie."

"Gone with Dickie. You wouldn't!"

"Don't ever take me for granted. I hope you will never be so drunk again that you cannot remember making love to me."

By the time we hit the road that morning, the rain had stopped, and traffic was moving smoothly. It thinned gradually as we headed north into New Hampshire, where U.S. Route 95 became a turnpike, and we made good progress until we crossed the border into Maine. There, we began to run into construction delays - more lanes, more concrete overpasses - and I was suddenly struck with a gloomy thought. The Americans, and to a lesser extent, ourselves in Canada, had become slaves to the automobile and the truck. How many billions of dollars went into building, improving and maintaining roads each year, and at what cost to the environment, in terms of lost habitat and pollution?

We were in the minor seaport of Portland for lunch, bought from a take-out place on the docks along Commercial Street. Dickie asked me, between bites of his lobster roll, "Where, again, was Joel Bonney buried?"

"In the Pioneers and Heroes section of the Eastern cemetery," I replied.

"There's an information place across the street," Joe-Bob pointed. "They should be able to tell us where that is."

Information places, sometimes called visitor centres or interpretive centres, are a boon to travellers, at least in my experience. Most are staffed with pleasant, knowledgeable people who are more than glad to give you not only advice, but free maps and brochures advertising the attractions of their area as well. In this case, an old gentleman volunteer knew where the cemetery was, and marked the best route to it on a map for us. Following his directions, we found it easily enough, but it was surrounded by an iron fence and the gate was locked. There was a number posted to call if you wanted a key, so Joe-Bob tried it on his cell phone, but all he got was a recorded message telling him to call back before noon the next day.

We walked along the street and followed the fence around a corner, looking for another way in, and there we met a middle-aged woman, who turned out to be the self-appointed caretaker of the cemetery. "I just crawl in here, under the fence," she told us, "but if you go across to that building over there, you can get in through those arches." She promptly slithered under the fence, followed by her dog, and began to pick up the litter that had blown inside since her last visit.

It was plain that Josée would ruin her clothes if she tried the slithering routine, so we opted for the arches across the way. Still, I had to help her up onto a low wall, and she had to jump into Joe-Bob's arms on the other side in order to get in. I thought he held on to her a lot longer than he needed to.

We then began the search for Joel Bonney's grave, not an easy task, because many of the headstones were illegible. Fortunately, others must have been made of a harder material, and by looking at the dates on these, we narrowed down the search until we found what we were looking for. 'Joel Bonney', his marker read. 'Died 1824, Aged 83 years.' And that was all. No mention of his service in the Connecticut militia or with Wolfe at Louisbourg and Quebec. I looked around with sadness. The Stars and Stripes fluttered over many of the grave sites, and on the headstones, records of service against the British in the War of Independence or the War of 1812 were inscribed, and I suddenly realized that for Americans, the world started with the Revolution. Even before that, they created their own names for the colonial wars - King William's, Queen Anne's, King George's, the French and Indian War. They were England's wars and Britain's wars, not their wars.

Josée made the sign of the cross. "We must get some flowers. Perhaps none have been placed here for a hundred years."

We inquired in a bookstore across the street where the nearest flower shop was, and the proprietor gave us directions, and told us he had a key to the cemetery, which he would let us have when we came back. Josée chose the flowers, an arrangement of yellow gladioli and red carnations, with a spray of some kind of evergreen shrub, and I wrote on a card, 'From a grateful descendant'. Entering the cemetery by the gate this time, we skewered the card with the stem of the shrub, poked a hole in the ground next to the headstone, and pushed the flowers into it.

There was more to do in Portland and not a lot of afternoon left to do it in. Using the map and the directions given to us at the information office, we found our way to Wadsworth-Longfellow House, a handsome, three story Georgian structure. In the reception office, we arranged for a tour, which was conducted by a thin, middle-aged woman with a terrible cold. She didn't seem upset by the wrangling between Dickie and Joe-Bob that went on as we followed her around. Perhaps she was on tranquillizing medication.

"Say, Dickie, why again did you call Longfellow a wretch for writing 'Evangeline'?"

"Do you know the poem?"

"Just bought a copy."

"He was a wretch because, 90 years after the fact, he wrote the poem, and in it he was unjustly critical of the British for deporting the Acadians."

Our guide blew her nose forlornly. "Notice the fireplaces in all the rooms."

I knew Joe-Bob had his tongue in his cheek when he said, "Well, that was a pretty drastic thing to do, wasn't it?" If he'd been in charge, he might have drowned the Acadians instead of deporting them.

"But we did it to protect the English Colonies from the French. Longfellow was an ingrate, like most Americans."

"Whoa, now, those are pretty strong words."

"More than that. We deported most of the Acadians to the English Colonies where they were treated like dirt. They could get no work, they had to beg to survive, and as many as were able slipped back into Acadia or into the swamps of Louisiana, or to France, or to French possessions in the Caribbean."

"And this was Henry's office," sniffled our guide.

Next door to Wadsworth-Longfellow House was a library of a sort, or an archive, really, where the history of Maine was kept in many volumes. We went there after our tour and browsed around for a few minutes, until I spotted the name, 'Dow', in one of the card files. The girl at the desk brought me what it referred to, a thick volume entitled, 'The Book of Dow', and in it was the history of all the branches of the family in the new world. Josée was hissing at me to hurry up, so I leafed through the pages quickly, hoping to stumble on some information about my ancestor Lorenzo, the one-time owner of Uncle Bill's trunk. And I found it. One family moved to Nova Scotia after the French and Indian War, and took up lands confiscated from the Acadians near Grand Pré. I quickly made some notes on a scrap of paper, hoping I would be able to decipher my left-handed scrawl later.

Outside, Josée tugged at my sleeve. "We must find a grocery store."

"Why?"

"Because we will all catch that woman's cold unless we take some garlic and drink some orange juice."

"You really think that will help?"

"An old family recipe."

She led the three of us, protesting, along the street until we found a green grocer, nor was she satisfied until we had all swallowed a clove of garlic, and washed it down with a small bottle of orange juice. I hoped it would prevent the cold. I hoped it wouldn't start a gas attack.

We used the rest of the afternoon to tour downtown Portland, described by Longfellow as 'The beautiful town that is seated by the sea'. These were my impressions: hilly streets; policemen on horseback; dirty, old, red brick buildings; a lot of fat people, some of them outright obese, just like in Plymouth; a lot more looking as if the rest of America had left them behind, and not at all like 'Lords of the Earth'.

I wasn't the only one to notice these people. Joe-Bob grumbled, "No use to the country at all. Might as well be dead, instead of living and reproducing like flies."

Dickie noticed too. "But surely, rather than destroy them, Joe-Bob, you should re-invent the indentured servant. If someone falls through the cracks of society, why should they not be able to bond themselves to someone who would feed them, clothe them, and otherwise look after them, in return for domestic service for example? The bond or indenture would be for a finite number of years, as in the old days, and when the term was served, the individual concerned would be entitled to some kind of a payout. They would then be free to leave, or to enter into another indenture."

"Alright, Dickie, but what kind of servants would they make? Would masters be able to beat them to make them do their work? I don't think so, with all the bleeding hearts in this country."

We turned in the van at the rental agency and boarded the ferry bound for Yarmouth, a gleaming white, pocket-sized version of the love boat. That evening, we tried the onboard casino, and Joe-Bob, who didn't need the money, was the only one of us who won, but I was the one who bankrolled Josée, and it was almost as if I had reclaimed her from the clutches of my, or our, rich relatives. Later, we all danced with her, even Joe-Bob with his gimpy knee, and I again experienced that wonderful feeling of floating around the floor with her in my arms, as if I were Fred Astaire. And again, the unfamiliar surroundings excited her, and she attacked me hungrily when we got to our cabin.

The ferry docked at Yarmouth at eight in the morning, and we stowed our belongings in another rented van. Joe-Bob was itching for a game of golf, it seemed, and he said, "Must be a course around here we can get on."

"As one of the shareholders in Golden Lion Publishing, you should be anxious to get on with the book, not fritter away our time," Dickie chided.

"Dickie, there isn't a problem. We could feed Josée a few lines now and then, and she'd have it finished in a week."

Highway 101 in Nova Scotia was basically a two lane affair, with the odd stretch of four lanes, and the surface, I was happy to see, was free of cracks, grass and weeds. We drove along for a few miles until Joe-Bob noticed a golf sign. "Turn off here, Fred," he ordered. There were more signs, and we soon found the course, half of it on one side of a rural road and half on the other. In the pro shop, we were greeted first in French, then in English, and were told we could get on the tee in about half an hour.

"We are in Acadian country!" Josée enthused. "See? The golf club is flying the Acadian flag."

"Now, how can your government allow these people to fly their own flag like that?" Joe-Bob asked. "Someone did that in the States, they'd soon have to take it down."

"That is one of the differences between Canada and the United States," I suggested. "It's a matter of maintaining cultural identity, rather than pouring everybody into a melting pot."

The course was pretty rough compared to the ones we were used to playing, designed by an amateur, by the look of it, and the fairways were brown because they depended on Mother Nature for water. But golf is golf, whether on a silk purse or a sow's ear, and the match was intense. Joe-Bob and Josée both hated to lose. Dickie and I were much less aggressive, but the other two brought out the competitive juices in us, and the lead changed hands every few holes.

On the 13th tee, we caught up to the group ahead of us, three flat bellied, laconic young Acadian boys, perhaps 16 years old. When the traffic ahead of them cleared, they hit in turn, each smashing his ball 250 yards down the middle of the fairway. "Bien coupés!" Josée congratulated them, as they shouldered their bags. They turned, swept their caps off their heads, bowed to her in appreciation, and walked briskly on.

We tied the match on the 17th for the fifth time, and backed into a draw on the last hole when Joe-Bob missed his birdie putt. "Worst greens I ever played on," he complained. "Dutch treat for lunch, though, because nobody won."

While we were eating our sandwiches in the clubhouse, Joe-Bob looked about with a scowl on his face. Everybody was speaking French. "Say, you Canadians have got yourselves a big problem. How can you be a country when you let these people speak French?"

"I am one of these people," bristled Josée.

"But you speak English, too."

"Voila!" She turned to the table beside her, and spoke to the three Acadian boys sitting there. "Bon jour. Comment ca va aujourd'hui?"

"Tres bien, merci," answered the tallest.

"How did you play today?"

"Awful! The only thing I could do was drive the ball - couldn't hit my irons, couldn't putt. How about yourself?"

"Trés mal aussi." And Josée glared at Joe-Bob. She <u>was</u> out of sorts.

"You mean to say that all you French can speak English too?"

"No, I do not mean to say that, but most Acadians can."

There were many more tricolour Acadian flags flying along Highway 101: blue at the staff, with a star in the upper left corner; white in the centre; red in the fly. We were passing through the heartland of Acadian settlement, and in recognition, the highway between Yarmouth and Grand Pré was designated the 'Evangeline Trail'. As we drove along with St. Mary's Bay on our left, we could see Digby Neck in the distance, the low lying finger of land half covered with the remains of once commercial forests, that juts out into the Bay of Fundy. And when we caught a snack and bathroom break at the Tim Horton's doughnut shop in Digby, I began to feel at home again.

Annapolis Royal, the British capital of Nova Scotia before it was moved to Halifax, was our destination for the night. Our hotel was the most modest we had stayed in yet, with no doorman and an old man for a bellhop, who looked as if he would expire if he had to carry one more bag up the stairs. But it had a dining room and a bar, the main ingredients. That evening, we gathered in Dickie's room for our nightly writing session, and he began, "There was a rapid build-up of French forces in North America after King George's War, and as part of that buildup, Fort Beausejour was built in 1751 to protect French interests in what was left of Acadia. You will remember that in 1713, by the Treaty of Utrecht, which ended Queen Anne's War, or the War of the Spanish Succession, the Nova Scotia part of Acadia, except for Cape Breton Island, was ceded to Great Britain."

The rest of us groaned. Now, maybe we would remember.

"That left Britain with the colony of Nova Scotia, or a province, as it was also called, peopled by 10,000 French-speaking Acadians, who were concentrated around the Bay of Fundy, which we saw on our way here today. To help counter that fact, and to end criticism by New Englanders over the return of Louisbourg to France by the Peace of Aix-La-Chapelle in 1749, the British founded Halifax in that same year, and sent out 1,400 debtors under Governor Edward Cornwallis to settle the town. New Englanders also came, and soon, the population of Halifax rose to 5,000. In 1753, still with the objective of reducing the percentage of French, the British invited German and Swiss Protestants to settle in the colony."

Josée interrupted, "Details, details, Dickie, but you omit one important one. The 10,000 Acadians were descended from only 500 immigrants, and it became necessary for the church to waive the rules of consanguinity."

"Consanguinity, the rules governing marriage, as, thou shalt not marry thy mother or thy father or thy brother or thy sister, etcetera, but thou mayest marry thy first cousin, if it is not possible to find a more distant mate. Where were we? Ah, yes. As you can see from the map, Fort Beausejour lay just across the Missaguash River from Nova Scotia, and it was a thorn in the British side. While they, the British, were demanding the Acadians take an oath of allegiance, the French at Fort Beausejour were pressing them to remain loyal to France. Unable to deal with these conflicting forces, many Acadians left their homes in the early 1750s, and resettled in French-held territories elsewhere, while those who remained tried to maintain a neutral position. I should say also that Fort Beausejour harbored Abbé Le Lutre, a soldier-priest of the Spiritan Order, who encouraged his Micmac Indian converts to terrorize the British.

"Just two miles from Fort Beausejour, on the other side of the Missaguash River, lay the British Fort Lawrence. There were polite exchanges between the two outposts until the British, in 1755, determined to carry out the second prong of Braddock's plan.

"The commander at Fort Lawrence at the time was Lieutenant Colonel Robert Monckton of the 47th Regiment of Foot. On June 1st of 1755 he was reinforced by two battalions of provincials, that is, colonials, 2,000 men altogether, under Lieutenant Colonels John Winslow and George Scott, and by a contingent of regular army artillery from Halifax.

"On the other side of the Missaguash, the commander at Fort Beausejour was Louis Du Pont Duchambon de Vergor, a sleazy character, by all accounts, and a friend of the infamous Intendant of New France, François Bigot. De Vergor's forces consisted of 175 Troupes de la Marine, Le Loutre and his Micmacs, and 300 Acadian militiamen. We will hear more of both Monckton and de Vergor, but for the moment, Fort Beasejour is our topic.

"De Vergor was well aware of the impending attack, and tried to slow Monckton by destroying a bridge across the Missaguash, and by breaking dykes to flood his path. After some days spent overcoming these obstacles, the British began a bombardment, which made Beausejour untenable. De Vergor was forced to seek terms, part of which allowed him to withdraw to Louisbourg with his Troupes. Abbe Le Lutre and the Micmacs disappeared into the forests, while Monckton pardoned the militiamen, pending a ruling from Governor Lawrence in Halifax. Oh, just an aside. The French had built another fort, Fort Gaspereau, on the shores of Baie Verte just to the north of Beausejour. It surrendered to Winslow without a fight on June 18th."

"Yes, Dickie."

"Yes. Now, the decision of the 300 Acadians to fight for the French had dire consequences. That, coupled with the refusal of most of their colleagues to take an unconditional oath of allegiance to the British Crown, prompted Governor Lawrence to expel them. He hired a fleet of ships and ordered Winslow to round up the Acadians at Grand Pré for deportation to the English Colonies. And while the people were boarding the ships, taking only those possessions that they could carry, Winslow burned their village to the ground."

Josée looked as if she were close to tears. "It was called 'Le Grand Derangement'. Oh, the cruelty of it! Women separated from their children, husbands from their wives, all sent into an alien, uncaring sea of English."

"But Josée, don't you see, the British had no choice. There could be no security for Nova Scotia or the New England colonies while the Acadians threatened to support the French."

Joe-Bob appeared to stifle a grin. "Say, I read that poem, 'Evangeline', this morning. Josée's right. You awful Brits lured those Acadian men into the church, then locked the doors, leaving their poor women and children outside wondering what was happening."

"As I said before, it was a difficult but necessary decision. Grand Pré, of course, was only the beginning. Until peace came in 1763, some 7,000 Acadians were rounded up and deported. Others hid in the woods and conducted sporadic raids on the British, while still others fled to Canada, that is, what is now called the Province of Quebec. And further, the American colonists celebrated the deportation, and as I have already intimated, treated the Acadians worse than animals. Because of that, many Acadians returned to Nova Scotia, took the oath of allegiance, and were allowed to re-settle. After the war, when they were no longer required to take the oath, many more came back."

"But Dickie, their lands had been what-do-you-call-it, confiscated, and taken up by New Englanders, and so the centre of Acadia shifted to New Brunswick," Josée pointed out.

"Yes, Josée. Shall we stop there for the night? I have suddenly developed an acute thirst."

We began the next day by visiting the historic gardens in Annapolis Royal, where most of the flowers were past their peak. Enough remained, however, to captivate Josée, and she cooed and sang to them until some of the other visitors stopped to look at her with curiosity, or to smile. In walking around the gardens, we were able to look over a marsh, which the Acadians, by dyking and with the help of an ingenious type of valve, had reclaimed from the salt waters of the Bay of Fundy.

We next visited nearby Port Royal, now a National Historic Site, the earliest European settlement in North America, if you discount the Viking outpost on Newfoundland's northern peninsula. The original 'Habitation', destroyed by

Virginians in 1613, had been completely reconstructed by the Canadian Government according to the original plans, unearthed in France centuries later. We were greeted by an Acadian fellow dressed in the costume of the time, complete with wooden shoes or 'Sabots', a most engaging character who hugged and kissed Josée when she spoke to him in French.

The steep roofed, two storey buildings of the Habitation completely surrounded a small, central courtyard with a well near the centre. Armed with the usual brochure, we entered through one of the buildings, and walked up and down dowelled stairs, through dormitories, forge, chapel, kitchen, bakery, storerooms, guardroom, and finally, cannon platforms. One of the Parks' people told us that the reconstruction of the Habitation was spurred by an American woman who used to spend her summers nearby. She decided that, since Americans had destroyed the place, they should rebuild it, and she raised a considerable amount of money for the project herself, donating it to the Canadian Government once they agreed to go ahead. Joe-Bob was of two minds about that. "Well, I can see her point of view in one way, but then, why resurrect a monument to the damn French, who terrorized us all through those 'Petty Gurrs', or whatever Dickie called them."

From Port Royal, it was a short two hours to Grand Pré, a pleasant drive through the orchards and small, neat towns of the Annapolis Valley, where some of my ancestors had settled. At Grand Pré, another Parks Canada historic location, we visited the unconsecrated church built on the site of the one that Winslow burned to the ground in 1755. Inside were paintings and exhibits illustrating Acadian life and the expulsion, and Parks' staff to answer questions, while outside were extensive gardens, monuments, and two statues, one of Longfellow, the other of Evangeline. Hers was mounted on a stone pedestal and her head was turned to the right, as if to look back over her shoulder at the ruins of Grand Pré, and the comfortable pastoral life she was forced to leave. There was something about her, something so appealing, so familiar, that I stood before her, transfixed. What was it? The head turned, like Josée on our first date? The face? The form? The others approached, Joe-Bob and Dickie arguing, Josée scolding them, and the spell was broken.

Halifax was to be our home for the night, and we would look the town over the next morning. Then, Joe-Bob had some business to attend to, he said, that required him to fly back to Boston. "Say, Dickie, why don't you come along? We'll leave the lovebirds to themselves for a few hours."

"Thank you, I believe I will, Joe-Bob."

Jacqui booked a hotel for us on Barrington Street in the downtown core, but Halifax wasn't the easiest place to find your way around in, and there were some heated exchanges between Josée and me before we reached our objective. We convinced Dickie that we were really doing quite well with the book, and to let us eat in the dining room instead of choking down room service while we tried to write. But after dinner, he had us back at it, and this is how the story continued: Marcel Bonin, an officer in the Troupes de la Marine, falls in love with

Evangeline, an Acadian girl, while stationed at Fort Beausejour. He fights valiantly but in vain when the British attack, and following the surrender, he and the rest of his detachment are exiled to Louisbourg. He begs leave from his commanding officer and strikes overland to find his beloved, only to learn that the people of her village have been deported. But some, he learns, are hiding in the woods, and at last, he finds a band of starving Acadians living in make shift huts, and Evangeline is one of them. Vowing vengeance, he leads the ragged band back to Louisbourg, where, for the moment, they find security, and the marriage of Marcel and Evangeline livens the gathering gloom over the fortress, if only for a moment.

"And Evangeline was her real name, Josée?" I asked.

"Yes," she answered. "My second name is Evangeline. I am named after her."

"The girl in the locket?" The statue! That was it! Evangeline, the statue, was Evangeline, the girl in the locket!

"Oh yes, the girl in the locket. Why not? Now, again, how did it end up in your trunk in the attic?"

"What the devil are you two talking about?" asked Dickie.

"Maybe Dow, Lorenzo Dow, my ancestor, was one of Winslow's men. Maybe he was a soft hearted wimp, like me, took pity on this beautiful girl, and allowed her to escape in return for the locket."

"Say, it sure would be nice if you'd let us in on this," Joe-Bob grumbled.

"Alright," I explained. "My great great grandfather, David Bonney, married Cynthia Dow. I inherited this trunk with the name 'Lorenzo Dow' painted on it, and Lorenzo, I believe, was Cynthia's grandfather. Anyway, in the trunk was a locket. Here, see for yourself." I fished the locket out of my briefcase and showed it to them.

"Well, I'm damned!" our co-authors exclaimed in unison. "It's Josée!"

"Then, when we were in Portland, I read that one family of Dows emigrated from Massachusetts to Nova Scotia after the expulsion, and were given lands that formerly belonged to the Acadians here at Grand Prè. Maybe Lorenzo came back, hoping to find the girl again."

"Alright. Let's develop this, then," commanded Dickie.

"But there is more," Josée said. "John Bradstreet, who was captured by the French at Canso and later fought them at Louisbourg, had an Acadian mother and a British officer for a father. It would be interesting to know what her feelings were when the other Acadians were deported. We should do something with that as well."

We did the walking tour of downtown Halifax the next morning, then took a guided tour through the Citadel, another Parks Canada Heritage Site. While we were there, the student soldiers were going through their paces, and Dickie was quick to point out that they were impersonating the 78th Highlanders Regiment of Foot and the Royal Artillery, both from the 1869 era. Also on Citadel Hill was the four-faced town clock, a landmark of the city of Halifax, erected by one time Governor Prince Edward of Kent.

Lunch was a hurried affair, as Joe-Bob seemed anxious to be off, and Dickie seemed agitated too. At the airport, we waved goodbye to them as they walked out to the jet, where Jacqui waited, smiling, in the hatchway. I should have been glad to be rid of them, but somehow, they had grown to be a kind of family, more than just the distant relatives that they were.

Josée and I spent the rest of the day taking a tour of the harbour, and crossing over to the naval base at Dartmouth on the ferry. We had supper in a nightclub close by, and danced a little afterward, but the musicians, who were jerking around the stage as if they had mad cow disease, were not playing our kind of music, so we left. On the way back to the hotel, we heard the familiar strains of 'Barrett's Privateers' wafting out of a pub, and we found the last two seats in the place. The band was playing a medley of Stan Rogers' songs, including 'North by North West', and 'Johnny Green', and we stayed until the last standing ovation faded into the rafters.

Back in our room, we watched a little television before going to bed, and I found out why Jos was out of sorts. Her period had started, and with it came the feelings of guilt, and the melancholy, and the tears.

The two of us watched Joe-Bob's jet coming in late the next afternoon, from the time it was a tiny speck in the sky until its engines whined to a stop on the tarmac. Our co-authors stepped out smiling, waving, and looking refreshed, and we greeted them with hugs and handshakes, as if they had been away for a month. On our way to Amherst, Nova Scotia, Joe-Bob didn't talk much about his business trip, saying only that he had closed a deal he'd been looking at before his third wife left him. I did notice, when I glanced in the rear-view mirror, that both he and Dickie looked at Josée as if they had missed something.

The best we could find for accommodation in Amherst was a second-rate motel with sprung beds. It was already nine o'clock by the time we checked in, and we sat around in Dickie's room for an hour drinking nightcaps out of a bottle of vodka, which we mixed with orange juice and tonic water from the pop machine outside his door. Perhaps it was the orange juice that prompted Josée to ask, "Maintenant, now, did anyone catch a cold from that woman at Longfellow House, or did they not? You have my family's remedy to thank for your good health."

Dickie insisted on discussing the last prong of Braddock's 1755 plan, which was to take Fort Niagara on the Niagara River, and Crown Point on Lake Champlain. With Joe-Bob's map taped on the wall as usual, he began: "You will recall that Governor Shirley of Massachusetts, who had proved himself an able commander in organizing the conquests of Louisbourg and Fort Beausejour, was appointed to take Braddock's place, but he faced problems that he was unable to overcome. Powerful factions in New York led by Governor James de Lancey and his family - you remember that Suzannah de Lancey was married to Rear Admiral Peter Warren - did not want their favourable trade connections with the French to be disrupted, and were otherwise hostile to New England. Shirley also had difficulty getting support, supplies and men from other governors, who did not feel threatened by the French. He therefore did not assault Fort Niagara, contenting himself with strengthening and garrisoning the fort at Oswego on Lake Ontario.

"Meanwhile, William Johnson, the Indian Superintendent, was appointed a general in charge of the attack on Crown Point, or, as the French called it, Fort St. Frédéric. He, too, was faced with problems: he had to compete with Shirley for resources, and the New York and Massachusetts militias seemed rather more inclined to fight each other than the French. Still, he managed to assemble an army of over 9,000 men, 6,000 of them from New England, the rest from New York and the Iroquois Confederacy.

"But the French were ready. Under General the Baron Jean Armand Dieskau, they staged a pre-emptive strike against Johnson, and mauled his advance force of 1,000 men. There followed the Battle of Lake George, an inconclusive engagement in which both Johnson and Dieskau were wounded, and Dieskau captured. Johnson then built Fort William Henry at the site of the battle, and resigned his commission."

"Say, an ancestor of mine was with Johnson at Fort William Henry, according to my granddaddy."

"How convenient. We can work him into the story, then. Any Bonins?"

"Yes," answered Josée." Two younger brothers of Marcel, Philippe and Claude, survived these battles."

"Alright, then. Thus ended the unofficial war of 1755, in which the only British success was Beausejour. Tomorrow, we will visit the Fort, as partially reconstructed by Parks Canada."

At Fort Beausejour, we first looked at the art work in the museum adjacent to the reception area, big paintings by Lewis Parker illustrating life at the fort after it was taken by the British, smaller portraits of officers who had been stationed there, and others of civilians who promoted the restoration. The fort itself was a small, stone walled affair which would have been lost in a corner of Louisbourg, and far from completely rebuilt, but it was possible to see that it had been shaped like a five pointed star, allowing fire to sweep all the outside walls. "Like Louisbourg, a difficult place to defend," remarked Dickie. "At the same elevation as the surrounding ground, which meant it was easy to lob shells and mortar bombs into it.

"Let's now go on to Moncton for the night, good old Monckton without the 'k,' because some clerk misspelled it 200 years ago. We can finish writing and editing William Johnson's campaign while we are there, and then we should visit Lake George, and Ticonderoga, or Fort Carillon, where the greatest French victory of the French and Indian War took place."

Chapter 5.

The Seven Years' War

Moncton, New Brunswick, with a population of 60,000, still had a strong French flavour, having begun as an Acadian settlement under the protection of Fort Beausejour. We booked into a hotel there in the early afternoon of July 9th, and shortly after were at work in Dickie's room, tidying up our story of the Acadian expulsion. Dickie then introduced the Seven Years' War, the European conflict starting in 1756 in which Austria, France, Russia, Sweden, and some German states were opposed to Prussia and Great Britain.

"In 1756, in spite of the opposition of King George the second, William Pitt became the Prime Minister of Great Britain. Unlike the King, who wanted to protect his German possessions, Pitt was determined to concentrate on the war in America, and leave the fighting in Europe to Prussia.

"After his failure to mount a campaign against Fort Niagara in 1755, Governor Shirley of Massachusetts was sacked as Commander in Chief in America, and replaced by John Campbell, the fourth Earl of Loudon, also spelt Loudoun. He arrived in New York City in the summer of 1756, and very soon proved that he could not get along with colonials. Josée?"

"At that time, New France's native son, Pierre de Rigaud, the Marquis de Vaudreuil, was Governor and Commander in Chief in Quebec, a cold, humourless man who was committed to La Petite Guerre to protect his far-flung holdings. But in 1756, France sent out a professional soldier, the Marquis de Montcalm, to take over command of the regular army, that is, the Troupes de la Terre. All other military units remained under the control of the Governor. There was also the Intendant, François Bigot, who was supposed to procure supplies for the colony, but while he was doing that, he pillaged the Royal Treasury, and used the money to buy himself mistresses.

"Like Vaudreuil, Montcalm came from the old aristocracy of southern France, and had first served his King in the War of the Spanish Succession when he was just 15 years old. In contrast to Vaudreuil, he was a lively, witty man who inspired loyalty and courage in his men. Now 47, he was a traditionalist, I guess a little like Braddock, and he abhorred the treachery and savagery of La Petite Guerre; neither was he committed to saving all of New France - in fact, he wondered openly if the colony should not be used as a pawn when peace came. From the beginning, he and Vaudreuil never got along, and some accounts suggest they even detested each other.

"But Montcalm was a good soldier, at least, until the battle for Quebec City. He took over the attack on Fort Oswego when he arrived, and captured it, thus extinguishing the only British presence on the Great Lakes. Then, in August of 1757, he captured Fort William Henry, so recently built by Sir William Johnson, and along with it a large supply of military equipment. The garrison surrendered on Montcalm's promise that it would be spared, but his Indian allies had other ideas. Before Montcalm or his men could stop them, they killed and scalped several of the prisoners. Dickie?"

"While Montcalm was achieving these successes, Loudon was suffering failure. In the summer of 1757, he arrived in Halifax with 6,000 regulars and 6,000 militia, intending to attack Louisbourg, but the attack never took place. Citing rumours of massive French reinforcements, bad weather, and colonial legislatures unwilling to support his efforts, he returned to New York City with his tail between his legs. On the positive side, he was responsible for establishing the Royal American Regiment of four battalions, all its men recruited from the colonies.

"William Pitt was not amused. He recalled Loudon in December of 1757 and replaced him with his second in command, Major General James Abercrombie. Accounts suggest that Abercrombie, who was overweight and suffered from dyspepsia, was too slow-witted for a command in the field, but at least he would fight, was the opinion given to Pitt by senior military staff in London. Pitt gave him the resources needed for victory - men, resources and money - and instructed him to treat colonials as equals, and to recognize the rank of militia officers.

"Again, the British developed a plan for a three-pronged assault: against Louisbourg; against Fort Duquesne; and against Fort Carillon on Lake Champlain, or as we will call it, to save confusion, the English name for it, Fort Ticonderoga. Abercrombie himself would lead the attack on Ticonderoga assisted by his second in command, Brigadier General Augustine Viscount Howe, and his Quartermaster, Colonel John Bradstreet of Louisbourg fame.

"In the early summer of 1758, Abercrombie assembled his forces at Albany, eight battalions altogether, only battalions, really, even though some of them were called regiments - the Royal Scots, the Inniskillings, the Black Watch, the 34th, 44th, and 46th Regiments of Foot, and the 1st and 4th battalions of the 60th, or Royal American Regiment. There were also 8,000 provincial militia, including companies of Rogers Rangers."

"Say, Joshua, my ancestor, was with Rogers Rangers, now that's a fact."

This was the first time Joe-Bob had said anything about fact concerning his ancestors. But I wondered about Dickie's exhaustive listing of military units. "Oh, Dickie, how many men altogether?" I asked.

"Well, 15,000, but you aren't going to discard the detail again, are you? Josée? Montcalm had?"

"Just for the record, his second in command was Brigadier General the Chevalier de Levis, and he had 3,600 Troupes de la Terre, eight battalions altogether, from the regiments La Sarre, Langdoc, Bearn, Guyenne, Royal Rousillon, La Reine, 1st Berry, and 2nd Berry. And Marcel's brothers, Philippe and Claude, acted as scouts for this French army."

"Badly outnumbered, then, but in a strong position at Ticonderoga, as we shall see, the Fort having been built in 1755 on a promontory overlooking Lake Champlain. Montcalm further reinforced it with log and earth walls and abatis, that is, felled trees and large branches placed so as to impede attackers."

"I always wanted to know what abatis were," I quipped. I was ignored.

"Abercrombie's army paddled upstream to Fort Edward at the great bend of the Hudson River, right there on the map, in bateaux, that is, large, open, wooden boats. They then marched overland some 10 miles to Lake George, arriving at the ruins of Fort William Henry on July fourth, it having been destroyed by Montcalm the previous year. At the head of the lake, they embarked on more bateaux, and paddled north, towing rafts laden with horses, wagons and cannon. There were some 900 boats on the lake, and one can imagine some of them flying regimental flags, with bands playing, the regulars in coats of red, the Rangers in green, many of them soon to face enemy fire for the first time.

"On July 6th, the army disembarked at the foot of the lake, and an advance guard under Howe set off to scout the territory along the Riviere des Chutes, the stream that drains Lake George into Lake Champlain. Shortly, the guard surprised a detachment of French soldiers who had become lost trying to find their way to Ticonderoga. In the ensuing skirmish, Howe was killed, a pity really, because he was an able soldier who knew how to work with colonials.

"The next day, William Johnson, the Indian Superintendent, arrived with 100 or so Iroquois, all he could raise in the face of their treaty of neutrality with the French, but they were not to be a factor in the coming battle.

"On July 8th, Abercrombie attacked Fort Ticonderoga without first bombarding it with his cannon. Some historians claim that he had word of French reinforcements, and he therefore decided to proceed without waiting for the guns to come up. Time after time, he ordered frontal assaults by his regulars, and time after time, they were thrown back from the abatis, until 1,600 of them were killed or wounded, including most of the 42nd Highland, or Black Watch Regiment. On the other side, the French suffered only 400 casualties, dead and wounded. The Iroquois, meanwhile, had been sniping at the French without effect from a neighbouring hill."

"A glorious victory for New France!" Josée cheered. "And the Fleur de Lys flag that was flown on that day became the flag of Quebec."

"Yes, Josée. But even while Montcalm and his men were celebrating, the noose was closing on New France. Louisbourg was already under siege. Brigadier John Forbes with George Washington was advancing on Fort Duquesne. Incidentally, Washington, in this, his last action for the British, remained true to form. He tried to convince Forbes to change his route, but was rebuffed."

Joe-Bob reacted immediately. "There you go, slamming Washington again. What about those fools that were running the British army? Braddock? Loudon? Abercrombie?"

"Point taken. Abercrombie did one intelligent thing, however. He sent John Bradstreet to take Fort Frontenac, near the present site of Kingston, Ontario, and he captured it on August 27th. Not only that, but he smashed the boats there that constituted the French navy on Lake Ontario, and marched away with tons of spoils, thus impairing the ability of the French to supply their chain of forts in the Ohio Country, and down the Mississippi.

"I can say at this point that we are out of British fools, for the command of British armed forces fell to two capable generals, Jeffrey Amherst and James Wolfe, the latter to become the victor at the pivotal battle for Quebec City. But before we move on to the conquest of New France, we should visit Ticonderoga. I want to go there by the most direct route so that we don't go past Saratoga, or up the Richelieu-Lake-Champlain corridor from Montreal, because that should wait until the American Revolution. Joe-Bob, is it possible to fly to Glens Falls, for example, so that we can bypass these places?"

"Never flew there myself, but I'll get the crew on it." Within minutes, the word came back: yes, it was possible to land at Glens Falls, and the jet would pick us up at nine in the morning.

"What comes after that?" Josée asked. "You are all invited to Pierre's wedding next Wednesday, and I want to be in Quebec City at least one day before that."

"And that is exactly where we need to be after we see Ticonderoga," Dickie affirmed.

"Are we going to sit around Quebec City for five days waiting for the wedding?" Joe-Bob wanted to know. "If that's the case, I'll arrange a business trip."

"We have much to do at Quebec, but it won't take five days. Let me see. Perhaps we should use the time to see some of Canada. We could drive from Moncton to Quebec City, for example, have a look at the lower St. Lawrence River."

"We are going to fly back here from Ticonderoga?" I was incredulous.

"Why not, Fred?"

Josée warmed to the driving idea. "We could follow the New Brunswick coast up to Caraquet, where there is an authentic Acadian village, then around the Gaspé and up the St. Lawrence."

And so it was decided.

Our flight from Moncton to Glens Falls included a circle over Albany, Lake George, and Ticonderoga, so that we could appreciate the logistics of the battle that was fought there in 1758. "One of the most interesting pieces of geography in the world," Dickie observed, exuding enthusiasm. "Two great river systems just 10 miles apart, the Hudson and the Richelieu, forming a corridor vital for travel and war for the aboriginal peoples, and also for the white man during the colonial wars and the American Revolution."

Within an hour of landing at Glens Falls, we were in a rented car driving slowly down the long, tree shaded driveway to Fort Ticonderoga. Here and there were plaques honouring individuals and military units important in the history of the place, and indications of Montcalm's outer defences. And this was an historic site with a difference. The Fort was abandoned in the mid 19th century, and gradually fell into ruins. Early in the 20th century, Stephen Pell, a wealthy

American, purchased the property, restored the Fort, and for years after ran it as a private tourist attraction. Members of his family carried on, until they eventually turned the site over the State of New York.

The Fort itself was built of stone, somewhat larger and more elaborate than Beausejour, but of basically the same five star design. Dickie rushed about exclaiming over the demi-lunes, glacis walls, and other details of construction, while the rest of us walked the battlements and talked to a half naked Iroquois, who acted his part as a warrior with conviction. Inside the buildings was a museum of sorts with period artifacts, including engraved powder horns, muskets, and military uniforms.

It was another hot, humid day with thunderclouds gathering and rain already falling, but on the way out, Dickie insisted that we stop at the scene of the 1758 battle. "You see," he said, when we got there, "here were the abatis where the Black Watch was so badly mauled. And there." He was cut off by a flash of lightning and a loud thunderclap, and in an instant, we were soaked to the skin by a torrential, wind-driven downpour. On our way to the gates, our car was pelted by falling branches as well as rain, the wind causing it to lurch from side to side like a drunken sailor, while near Glens Falls, it looked as if a tornado had cut a swath across the country. Crews were out clearing the roads of fallen trees, and we passed a house trailer that had been overturned, leaving its foundations exposed to the sky.

By the time we got to the airport, the rain had slackened off to showers, and the wind was reduced to occasional gusts, but the jet was nowhere in sight. "Probably took off when he got word of the storm, and went somewhere safe," Joe-Bob guessed. He limped into the terminal to contact the pilot on the radio, and found that he was on the ground in Springfield, Massachusetts, waiting for clearance to take off.

We sat around in the airport snack bar drinking coffee while we waited for the jet to show up. After the second cup, Josée stood up abruptly and began to pace up and down "Are we to be prisoners here and miss the wedding?" she fretted, and without waiting for an answer, took her anxieties outside. While she was gone, Joe-Bob questioned me about her brother.

"Pierre? He'd be the all-Canadian boy if he weren't a rabid separatist. He's even bigger than you, Joe-Bob, and he was the enforcer for the Montreal Canadiens for years."

"Separatist?"

"Something like 40 per cent of the people of Quebec want to leave the Canadian Confederation and become a separate country."

"Enforcer? And what kind of game do the Canadiens play?"

"Hockey. It's a rough game played on skates with lots of body checking, six men aside, in an arena with the ice surface surrounded by boards. The object is to put a hard rubber disk called a puck into the other team's net by shooting it with a curved stick, and the enforcer is the guy who beats up guys on the other team who take liberties with his team's stars."

"Say, I tried to watch a game on TV once, but couldn't follow that puck. But this Pierre. He's a goon, then?"

"Far from it. Has a degree in history from Laval University, and by now, should have his MBA. I have to tell you that I really like him, even if he is a separatist."

Josée burst through the doors, singing, "The jet's here, the jet's here!"

We didn't get away from our hotel in Moncton until late the following morning because it was Sunday, and Josée did her disappearing act. With her looking her serene, after church self, we followed Highway 11 north from Shediac through gently rolling country, a mix of pastoral and forested landscapes with occasional glimpses of the sea, and past places with names like Richibucto and Kouchibouguac, echoes of the aboriginal past.

At the town of Chatham, with its huge pulp mill, we crossed the broad Miramichi River and continued north along the low-lying, sandy coast. There were many Acadian flags flying along the way, which caused Joe-Bob to grumble, that is, when we weren't singing choruses of 'Barrett's Privateers', or some other Stan Rogers' composition. "But the music is all wrong for this part of the country," objected Josée, her morning serenity starting to disappear. "This is the heart of Acadia, and we should be singing French songs. In Caraquet, we must buy a tape."

Joe-Bob wanted to know what kept this part of the world going. "I saw that big mill back there in Chatham, or Miramatchee."

"That's Miramishee!" corrected Josée, "with the accent on the last what-do-you-call-it, visible."

"Ha, ha! Alright. Accent on the last visible."

"Jos, that's syllable," I said gently. "Joe-Bob, just for reference, New Brunswick is one of the smaller provinces, about one tenth the size of Texas, with a population of about three quarters of a million people. Forestry is one of the main industries, with fisheries also important, especially the lobster. This stretch of coast is attractive to tourists, because the water is supposed to be the warmest north of Virginia."

"But there are no big towns, hardly anything more than villages. No heavy industry or high tech that would support more people. That right?"

"That's about it. Most people make their living off the land or the sea. Oh, while we're talking about it, I should mention that the Cunard steamship line got its start in Chatham."

"You mean a Canadian started that?"

"That's right, Samuel Cunard, back in the 1820s."

A few miles beyond Caraquet, we came to the Acadian village, another historic site maintained by the Federal Parks Department. We watched a slide presentation inside the visitor centre, then walked the long main road past dozens of old buildings, including several farmhouses, tavern, blacksmith shop and print shop. Costumed animators were cutting hay with scythes, dyeing bolts of cloth, cutting shakes with froes from blocks of spruce, making horseshoes in the smithy, printing handbills in French at the print shop, and serving Acadian food in the tavern. Near the far end of the road was a water-powered gristmill, and we joined the crowd as the animators there opened the valves, and ground up a small amount of wheat. The village church was last in line, and Josée made us wait while she knelt to pray, emerging with that serene look on her face. But then she made us drive back to Caraquet to find a tape of Acadian folk music. While we were there, she tried on an authentic Acadian costume consisting of black slippers, dark blue petticoat, dark red skirt, black vest laced from her waist to her breast, long sleeved white blouse, and white lace cap. She looked good in whatever she wore, but I had to admit there was something special about that outfit, so I paid for it. It reminded me of the statue of Evangeline.

While we hummed along with the music on the Acadian tape, the vocal numbers alternating with dazzling instrumental work on fiddle, accordion, piano, and mouth organ, we continued on Highway 11 to Bathurst, another small pulp mill town. Beyond, we took secondary Highway 134 along Chaleur Bay, which separates New Brunswick from Quebec's Gaspé Peninsula, and we passed through pretty little villages with names like Nigadoo and Petit-Rocher, Pointe-Verte and Jaquet River. And there was a subtle change in the countryside, from flat or gently rolling to hilly, as the long bulk of the Gaspé rose out of the sea on our right. "Say," Joe-Bob said, "we haven't had a game of golf for days. They got any courses up this way?"

"I don't know this part of the country very well," I told him, "but there must be some."

"Hey! There's a golf sign there. We're going in the right direction."

The course was near Dalhousie, another pulp mill town and deepsea port on Chaleur Bay. We made a tee time for the next morning, and went on to Campbellton for the night, not a pulp mill town, but a transportation and outdoor recreation centre with a population of 8,000. Here, we seemed to be pinned between highlands characterized by the domed top of 1,000 foot Sugarloaf Mountain, and the head of Chaleur Bay, where the Restigouche River finds the sea.

There wasn't much left of the evening, so we abandoned the idea of work, and went to bed after our nightcaps. In our room, Josée seemed restless and disinterested in sex, and I asked her what was the matter. "Here we are, only in Campbellton, Pierre is to be married in three days, I need a whole day before that to get ready for the wedding, and we have a golf game tomorrow. Do we really have time to go all around the Gaspé?"

"It would be a shame not to, now that we are so close. Let's see." I got out my map and added up the distance. "It's about 1,000 kilometres to Quebec City via Gaspé. I see there's a shortcut we can take, and a ferry from Dalhousie to Miguasha that will save us coming back to Campbellton to get around the end of Chaleur bay. Settle for half a day, and we'll have you in Quebec City Tuesday afternoon."

"Alright, but I hope we don't have any car trouble."

Josée's concerns carried over into her golf game the next morning on the hilly Dalhousie course, and she shot 85, but her partner for the day, Dickie, seemed inspired, either by the surroundings or by having her to play with, and more than made up the difference. So I escaped punishment again, but had to put up with Joe-Bob's ill humour at losing. With take-out sandwiches in hand, we just caught the next ferry to Miguasha on the Gaspé peninsula, and headed east on Highway 132, which skirts the rocky north shoreline of Chaleur Bay. "Now that we are in Quebec, we must call it Baie des Chaleurs," Josée insisted.

The names of the villages we passed through were in many cases of English origin, but the region had long since been taken over by French speaking Acadians. Every village had its own Roman Catholic Church, always the largest and most imposing structure in the place, and I wondered how the few parishioners could have paid for such monuments to their faith. Certainly, there was little evidence otherwise of wealth in these communities. As we drove along, we passed dozens of roadside stands, where people were selling model sailing ships made of wood and other folk art. At length, Josée made me stop so she could buy something, saying, "Maybe I can find a different kind of wedding present for Pierre."

Two youths were minding the stand we chose, and it soon became clear that they were mentally retarded. Josée dealt with them sympathetically, and paid them more than they asked for one of their model ships. Back in the car, Joe-Bob, with a look of revulsion on his face, said, "That was absolutely scary. Those boys were morons, real morons! How did they get that way?"

"I hate to hear you call them morons," Josée objected, "but it is a sad fact that some in this area are that way. It is the result of too close marriages, the relaxing of the rules of consanguinity."

The experience with the retarded boys cast a pall of gloom over us, which lasted until we came to Percé, the fabled limestone rock just offshore at the eastern end of the peninsula, with a hole in it big enough to sail a ship through. Bathed in the light of the setting sun, it was almost blood red in colour, and Dickie, exclaiming superlatives, shot off half a roll of film at it. That proved to be the highlight of our day because, as the sun faded and disappeared, Josée began to fret again about the wedding, and made it known that she would make our lives miserable if we were late for it. Over dinner in the town of Gaspé, we finally decided to stay there for the night and get an early start in the morning, because Dickie wanted to follow the St. Lawrence River all the way to Quebec in the daylight. That would mean abandoning any idea I had about taking a shortcut.

Josée wasn't sexy again and couldn't sleep, and kept me awake half the night with her tossing and turning. I gave up the struggle at five o'clock and staggered, numb and hollow-eyed, into the bathroom to shave. We were on the road again before seven, and I found it an effort to stay awake, and for the first time since we began travelling together, I asked for relief. Joe-Bob volunteered to take the wheel and that woke me up in a hurry, because he turned the narrow, winding road into a rally course, taking the curves by brinkmanship and with obvious relish. I was glad to get into the driver's seat again.

We stopped for a coffee break at the village of Les Méchins where the St. Lawrence River, now some 30 miles wide, becomes the Gulf of the same name. Later, from a vantage point, Dickie shot off the rest of his roll of film and started another, intoning, as he pressed the shutter release, "North America's river of destiny. Think of Cartier, Champlain, the Kirkes, Phips, Wolfe, and all the others, un-named, who sailed on her waters, and made their own small contributions to history."

Matane, Mont-Jolie, Rimouski, we passed through these, the larger villages among dozens of smaller, all with their great churches, some situated so as to be visible for miles. At Rivière de Loup, we crossed the St. Lawrence, still over ten miles wide at that point, to the north shore on a ferry, and breezed past the spectacular Montmorency Falls into downtown Quebec City at three in the afternoon.

In my mind, Quebec City, where the St. Lawrence narrows to less than a mile in width, with its wealth of history and the fairy-tale castle known as the Chateau Frontenac as its centrepiece, is the most beautiful and interesting city in Canada. In terms of atmosphere and outright elegance, no hotel we had stayed in could match the Frontenac with its massive walls, soaring turrets, and verdigris copper roofs. Inside, good-natured security staff tolerated the crowds of tourists that filled the spacious foyer, knowing that few of them were hotel guests, and bilingual clerks at the reception desk switched easily from French to English.

Josée was awe-struck. "Oh, I never thought I would ever get to stay in the Chateau Frontenac!" Predictably, she had nothing to wear for the wedding, and while the rest of us were registering, she peered into the exclusive shops in a corridor adjacent to the foyer. Predictably, also, Dickie and Joe-Bob indulged her for the privilege of seeing her model several outfits, and they each bought her one: for the wedding, a burgundy coloured sleeveless ankle length boat neck dress of silk with side slits and stitching detail; for the reception, white palazzo pants and tank top of cotton with drawstring waist and side pockets, and a deep-orange, tunic length shirt to be worn over. These shopping sprees always made me nervous, made me think that I was losing Josée, but that night, with all her anxiety gone and the excitement of staying at the Frontenac, she almost convinced me I had nothing to worry about.

In a rented car the next morning, we drove over the Pierre Laporte Bridge to Levis on the south side of the St. Lawrence River, where Josée's family lived. Pierre greeted us at the door, hugged Josée, and welcomed the rest of us warmly. In contrast, their parents were quite reserved, and I guessed it was because neither of them spoke very good English. The father's name was Jean, and as I was led to expect, we looked enough alike to be father and son, or more likely, brothers, considering the few years between us. He appraised me suspiciously, but the mother, Isabelle, melted when I called her 'Mama', and gave me a hug and a kiss.

Dickie trotted out his best Parisian French, leaving Joe-Bob as the only pure Anglophone in the party. He looked rather glum at the prospect of listening to nothing but a foreign language for the next day, until Pierre abandoned his stubborn refusal to speak English, and struck up a conversation with him. They seemed to get along, and soon, Joe-Bob had a working knowledge of Quebec and its resources. I listened in on part of the conversation.

"Say, Pierre, Texas is about 267,000 square miles in size, with a population of about 17 million. How big is Quebec in relation to that?"

"Over twice as big, with less than half the people, but nearly everyone lives close to the St. Lawrence River."

"That big! What's this I hear about you French wanting to separate from Canada?"

"That is true. We are 'un peuple', a people different from the rest of the country."

"But you know, bigger is better. Now, this free trade between us. You would lose that if you went on your own."

"Oh, we would expect to make our own deal with you."

"Son, I'd say that's wishful thinking. Why would we want to be bothered with a small country like Quebec? You better think hard before you jump."

I was afraid Pierre would take offence at these blunt words, but he seemed to realize that Joe-Bob knew what he was talking about. "We do think about that, and just how we would make out without such a trade deal."

"Say, I hear, too, that you used to play this hockey. Don't know much about the game myself, football was my sport in college, good enough to play in the NFL before my knee got wrecked. But I hear your sport is pretty rough and entertaining."

"It is our national game."

"There you go. Your national game. Enough to keep the country together?"

Pierre laughed. "I don't think so. All the countries that play soccer have not joined together."

"Alright. Getting back to this hockey. I hear that you were pretty tough, used to look after the stars on the team. Anybody hit them, you called him out and got him to think the right way."

Pierre laughed again. "Who told you that?"

"Why, Fred. He thinks you're the best thing since sliced bread."

"I am flattered, Fred. Thank you."

"Fred has been telling me a lot of things, like that you probably know more about the history of Quebec than anyone else, and that you just finished your MBA."

"Fred, you must not be so complimentary."

"Say, Pierre, I'm thinking of investing in Canada, but before I do that, I need to know something about your commercial laws. How'd you like to come to work for me? I would expect you, to begin with, to give me a summary of what's involved, especially any restrictions on foreign takeovers. Then, I would want a list of companies that are short of capital but have growth potential, and that could be anywhere in Canada. I'd start you out at a guaranteed 200 grand a year, and any companies I buy an interest in, you would get a percentage of any profits earned over ten per cent. That could amount to more than the guarantee."

Pierre was taken aback. "Again, I am flattered that you would want me, but I already have a good job. I could not leave it without severe inconvenience to my employer."

"Loyalty. I like that. Hardly anyone has it any more. A man who is loyal, yet meaner than a junkyard dog when he has to be, that's the kind of man I need. I think you fit the mould. Say, how big is this business you're working for?"

"I suppose you would call it small, by American standards. We grossed about ten million last year."

"And is it successful?"

"Yes, I believe so. Profit after taxes in the range of 15 per cent. I think, with a little more capital and by developing markets in the United States, we would be even more successful."

"How about I buy the business, and you along with it?"

Now, Pierre seemed upset. "Do you not even care what it is the company does? And I must tell you that I would not be happy to be bought in this way."

"Don't be too hasty. When I buy a business, I have a simple philosophy. Whatever it is the company does, if it's well managed and making profits in excess of ten per cent, I leave things alone. If not, I move in and appoint my own people. And don't think of it as being bought. Just remember what it was like being a professional athlete. You played for the team that offered you the best deal, didn't you?"

"That is where our philosophies differ. I played for the Montreal Canadiens because it was Quebec's team. When they wanted to trade me, I hung up my skates."

"You are a different kind of cat. But promise me you'll think about it. Think about expanding into the States with me supplying your company the capital it needs, and arranging for markets. And say, what are you going to call your hockey team after you separate?"

"I never thought about the team's name. But they have a nickname - Les Habitants. An easy choice. As for your offer, may I talk to my employer about it?"

"Sure, Pierre. Go ahead. Now, how old a man is he?"

"I believe he will be sixty this year."

"How many hats does he wear? I mean is he president, chairman of the board, managing director?"

"Both president and chairman, and he manages the company."

"I'd like to have a talk with both of you when you come back from your honeymoon. How long you going to be gone?"

"I will be back at my desk in two weeks."

"Alright, let's say I'll call you on July 29th at eight in the morning."

"I'll set that up, then. Here is my card. Now, I must be on my way."

This was no ordinary, run of the mill wedding, for Pierre was a famous native son who was marrying into one of the richest families in Quebec. The vows were to be exchanged at Our Lady of Victory Catholic Church, built on the foundations of Champlain's original trading post, and the list of invited guests included the Premier of the province. Significantly, the Lieutenant Governor, the representative of the Queen and the Government of Canada, was not on the list.

On Wednesday, July 14th, at the appointed hour, a limousine paid for by Pierre's employer arrived at the door, and it took us, along with Josée's parents, across the St. Lawrence River by ferry to the old part of Quebec City. I hadn't been inside a church since Beth died, let alone a Roman Catholic one, and I felt extremely nervous, as if my puritan ancestors were frowning down on me. It was the graven images, the paintings, the icons that separated me from this world that was so important to Josée. Using the end of a pew for support, she genuflected gracefully, and we took our seats in the area reserved for family. My eyes were then drawn across the aisle where the Premier was talking to his wife. He had a satisfied look on his face, the same I had seen on television so many times.

The organist played some introductory music, then the wedding march, and as he pulled out all the stops, the sound filled the church, and reverberated off the walls. At the stroke of mid-day, Geneviève Gaspereau, Pierre's fiancée, appeared at the doors on her father's arm, a tall, striking, brown-eyed blonde, and the people assembled gasped and murmured at her beauty, and the undoubted cost of her wedding dress. Slowly, she walked up the aisle, making the most of her moment, while Pierre, with his best man beside him, looked steadfastly ahead until she was beside him. Then he turned to look at the vision of her, the woman who would bear him those ten children, if not more.

The priest took them through the service, and they murmured "Oui," etcetera, at the appropriate moments, until he pronounced them man and wife, in French, of course; and with a rejoicing of organ music, they kissed and walked out into the sunlight, to be showered there with confetti and the good wishes of the guests. Before we had a chance to pay our respects, however, another limousine arrived, and swept them off to a photography session. Josée was furious. "I bet Geneviève did that on purpose."

The reception was to take place in the Chateau Frontenac beginning at five in the afternoon. "What are we going to do with ourselves in the meantime?" Joe-Bob wanted to know.

"What we should do is get out on the St. Lawrence so that we can see what Wolfe saw in 1759, when he sailed up the river to conquer Quebec," Dickie suggested.

"Say, it's only a block or so to the river. Must be some boats for hire down there. Let's go."

We had walked alongside the docks for more like half a mile when we came to a gleaming white power boat at least 40 feet long named the 'Lady Joyce', with an American flag flying on the stern. "Why don't we try this one?"

"But Joe-Bob, it must be a private yacht," I objected.

"Well, let's just see." Joe-Bob climbed aboard, and hailed, "Anybody around?"

A man well past middle age appeared on the flying bridge. "What can I do for you?"

"Say, is this boat for hire? We want to pretend we're General Wolfe, and see what he saw in 1759."

The owner of the yacht grinned then started to laugh. "You must be an American. No Canadian would have the brass to ask that."

"That's right. My name's Joe-Bob Bonney, and I live in Boston right now, but I was raised in Georgia, and that explains my accent. These here are shirt-tail relatives from Canada and England. Alright. I won't offer you any money for taking us on a cruise, but I'll just ask you for the favour, and I promise I'll return it. You ever need to fly anywhere on an executive jet, for example, just let me know."

The man laughed again. "Alright. I'm Roger Patterson, and here comes my wife, Joyce. Come aboard, the rest of you."

The Pattersons showed us around their floating palace complete with four staterooms, galley, saloon, and bridge that shone with steel and brass. The steward hustled about, we soon had drinks in our hands, and good smells started to waft out of the galley.

"Say, Roger, I'll have to get me one of these someday. You have time to enjoy it?"

"Haven't worked a day in five years. Used to own a foundry business in Massachusetts, but when my ticker started acting up, I sold it. You still slaving away?"

"Never did think of it as slaving. Nothing gets me going like closing a deal, buying a business that's on the way up, or even, when I started, selling a used car."

"But you're not working on this trip, are you? What's it all about?"

"The four of us are writing a book about our Bonney ancestors in North America. Well, Josée is actually writing the book. The rest of us just feed her information."

"Are you a Bonney too, Josée? You sound French-Canadian."

"We think I'm related, way back. But the book also features my Bonin ancestors."

"Must be quite a book. What's the title?"

Dickie, used to being our spokesman, seized the stage. "British North America."

Roger's raised his eyebrows in surprise. Then his face darkened. "Dickie, no sense beating around the bush. My ancestors came from Ireland at the time of the potato famine, my great grandfather was killed in Canada during a Fenian raid in 1866, and I just plain don't like anything British. As far as I'm concerned, Canada should be part of the United States."

100

Joyce admonished him. "Oh Roger, get off that hobby horse of yours. And don't be so rude." She was a pretty woman with carefully preserved, strawberry-blonde hair, and a figure that suggested she was much younger than her husband.

Dickie wasn't phased. "Thank you, Joyce, for coming to my defence. For my part, I don't dislike Americans, but I easily could, if only because an ancestor of mine spent six years in an American prison camp during the Revolution, an experience he was lucky to survive. Regardless of our feelings, it is a fact that before the Revolution, Great Britain did rule most of settled North America."

Roger raised his eyebrows again, then started to chuckle. "Alright, let's call a truce, and talk about the book some more. You are an odd group. How did you ever get together?"

We explained ourselves from my initial idea for the book to meeting Joe-Bob in Boston. Dickie told them how he lost his wife and daughter, Joe-Bob talked about his three wives, his children, and his aborted football career, and Josée blushed when it was impossible to hide our relationship. "Quite a story," Joyce smiled. "Almost enough to make a book in itself."

"Which way you want to go first? Upstream or down?" Roger asked.

"Down, by all means," answered Dickie.

Roger, with the twin diesels throbbing quietly, eased the 'Lady Joyce' out into the river, while Josée leaned on the rail of the flying bridge and exclaimed, "I never thought I would ever have a ride on a boat like this!"

Below Cap Diamant, the promontory jutting out from the north shore that is the site of Quebec City, the St Lawrence widens and splits into two channels, one on each site of the Ile d'Orleans. As we neared the Island, Dickie told us, "That's where Wolfe had his headquarters to begin with. Now, across from us is the Beauport Shore, where the first British assaults were so bloodily repulsed."

For the next two hours, we made our way slowly up river, past Levis, "where the British set up batteries," and past the cliffs of Cap Diamant, "imagine how daunting that escarpment was to an invading army. And there is where Wolfe's men landed, at L'Anse du Foulon, prior to climbing the cliffs to the Plains of Abraham." Dickie was grinning from ear to ear. "How exciting to finally see it!"

The Pattersons took us as far as Cap Rouge, about as far up the river as the British carried on operations. When they delivered us back to the docks, we thanked them, and Joyce said to us, "I hope you will keep in touch. We want to be the first to buy the book." We took their phone numbers, one for the boat and the other for their residence on Long Island, New York, and promised to call them.

Back at the hotel, Josée changed into her other new outfit for the reception. "I cannot believe it, my little brother married. They are staying at the hotel tonight. Maybe we could get together with them."

"Your little brother is 35 years old, and this is their wedding night! I'm sure they won't want to get together with anyone."

"But Pierre and I see so little of each other. Surely, an hour or so."

"Josée! Surely not. Did you know Geneviève before?"

"Not well. I think she is a spoiled brat."

"Not good enough for Pierre?"

"No woman is good enough for him."

"Well, she's his wife now, and I'm sure neither of them will want to visit tonight."

The reception in the 'Salle de Bal' of the Frontenac, with its massive chandeliers and draped windows, was lavish and lively. Starched linen cloths, gleaming silver cutlery, and ornate candelabras graced the tables in the half of the room set aside for dinner, while in the other half, a string quartet played Mendelssohn from a stage, and waiters circulated with trays of hors d'oeuvres and champagne for the enjoyment of the 300 guests. And everywhere, the conversation was in French. Josée was occupied with some old friends, Dickie had been commandeered by a formidable dowager who looked as if she would like to eat him for breakfast, and so I found myself talking to Joe-Bob, since there was no one else there for him to talk to. "I never knew," he said, "that you had this kind of a language problem here in Canada. It's just like I said about the Spanish in the States. If we were to give them language rights, the buggers would soon want to carve themselves out a piece of our country."

To my astonishment, the premier appeared at our side and introduced himself. Ignoring me, he said to Joe-Bob, "Pierre tells me you are an American. Welcome to Quebec! We look forward to good relations with you after we separate."

"I can't speak for the Government of the Unites States, Mr. Premier, but as a private citizen and businessman, I can say that I believe you will only hurt your trade with us if you leave Canada."

"We do not share your opinion. Why, in my discussions with your government, I am encouraged that we will quickly have our own free trade agreement with you."

"Mr. Premier, believe what you like. I am thinking about investing in this country, in Quebec, but I may have to rethink that if you continue to threaten separation."

"I hope you will not dismiss the opportunity just because we aspire to nationhood. Meanwhile, enjoy your stay." And with a smile and a nod, the premier took his leave.

The bride and groom appeared at last dressed for travelling, even though they were staying the night in the hotel. Josée, to my embarrassment, immediately commandeered her brother, and dragged him away to a gaggle of his former girlfriends. Geneviève looked abandoned for a few seconds, and I could see the anger rising into her face - not an auspicious beginning for relations between the sisters-in-law. She looked imperiously over the crowd until her eyes lit on me. "Fred, isn't it? You are with Josée? How did the two of you get together?"

I explained as best I could, and she feigned fascination. "A book! Yes, Pierre mentioned something about it. How interesting! And the other two authors are here? I would like to meet them."

I beckoned to Joe-Bob and to Dickie, who left the dowager with obvious relief, and during introductions, they made it obvious that they were enchanted, just the medicine Geneviève seemed to need. "Dickie, your French is too impeccable for Quebec. I will try my English on you, Joe-Bob, but only because you are from America." She managed at least as well as Josée, and she questioned us about the book. "What is your point of view? Do you glorify the conquest? That would not be popular here in Quebec."

Dickie answered, "Not at all, my dear. We are writing about the Bonneys and the Bonins, and how they experienced the history of North America."

"You will publish it also in French?"

"Yes, my dear, although we haven't looked for a publisher yet. We were going to do that while we were here in Quebec City."

"Look no further. My father owns a company that can do that for you. How exciting! Perhaps you are writing a - what-do-you-call-it?"

Joe-Bob usurped Dickie's place. "It will be a best seller, little lady. I've got money in it, and I don't invest in losing propositions."

Pierre appeared, looking a little flustered, dragging an unwilling Josée behind him. "Ah! I see you have met the authors, Jen."

"No thanks to you, my errant husband. And Josée. How do you do?" It was an icy and formal greeting.

"I have a headache. Fred. Excuse us, will you?"

"But Josée! Dinner will be served in a few minutes, and I'm starving."

"Fred, please!"

We went up to our room in silence, where Josée threw herself on the bed with a sour look on her face. I was more than annoyed with her. "How could you be so rude? It's your brother's wedding day!"

"I hate her!"

"How could you possibly hate her? You hardly know her."

"I hate her because she is going to have children, and papa will love her more than me."

"Oh, Jos, it's not her fault. Besides, she hasn't had any children yet."

"Rub my shoulders. I have a kink in them."

"Your shoulders?"

"Begin with them."

That night, I had another strange dream, in which I found myself in a magnificent room with high ceilings and murals on three walls, and at one end was a throne of purple, and on it sat the Premier of Quebec, all swathed in silk and ermine, with an imperious look on his face. On the fourth wall was an electronic scoreboard which was flashing a series of messages over and over again in large, red letters: OUI, 50% ET UN; NON, 50% MOINS D'UN; DEMAIN NOUS SONT SEPARÉ; VIVE LE QUÉBEC LIBRE!

At a blast of trumpets, three young men entered the room dressed as the three musketeers, with golf clubs for swords, and I recognized them as the Acadians who were so gallant with Josée where we played in Nova Scotia. Behind them came two boys, each carrying a carved sailboat, and I recognized them also, the poor creatures we saw on the Gaspé.

The musketeers bowed low, and swept their hats off their heads as they had done for Josée. "M'sieur Le Roi de Québec," the tallest said, "we petition you to remain in Canada, for if you do not, we fear that the resulting backlash in Acadia will rob us of our language, and the genes of the Anglais we need to prevent this from happening." And he stood aside so that the king could see the poor creatures from the Gaspé.

"Silence!" roared the King, looking fierce. "On this, the eve of separation, how dare you suggest that I give up my throne to become a mere provincial premier! As for these," he said, pointing at the mentally retarded boys, "I cannot bear to look at them! The fruits of relaxed consanguinity terrify me! Take them away!" Two guards appeared, roughly seized the poor creatures, and dragged them out of the room, breaking their wooden boats in the process.

"But M'sieur Le Roi de Québec," the tall musketeer began again, "there is an increasing tolerance amongst the Anglais that will continue to grow so long as you remain part of the country. Already, New Brunswick is officially bilingual. In the west, parents by the thousands send their children to French immersion schools, and in Ontario and the Maritimes, there are whole regions where people speak both languages fluently."

"Silence! It is not enough! Look in any phone book in Canada outside Québec and you will find hundreds, even thousands, perhaps hundreds of thousands of French names. What do the owners of those names speak now? English, nearly all of them, English! They are Vendus, sold out to the arrogant Anglais sons of bitches, who will never accept us as equals! I must proceed with separation so that I can save French language and culture in North America! I alone can do this! Now, out of my sight!"

The guards appeared again, but they began to cry for mercy when the musketeers drew their club swords. "M'sieur Le Roi de Québec," the tall one said, "you do not speak for all the French in North America. We Acadians have been persecuted, deported, relocated and reviled, but still we retain our language and culture. Ultimately, we are concerned that without Québec, the rest of the country will be annexed to the United States, where they are determined to speak only English. You can stop this from happening with a vision broader than the independence of Québec."

"What? What are you suggesting?"

"What you propose to do will rob all Québecois of the rest of this magnificent country, from the Atlantic to the Pacific, from the international boundary to the Arctic Islands, the prairies, the Rockies, the Maritimes and Newfoundland. Do not fence yourself into such a minor jurisdiction as Québec."

"You are surely babbling, musketeer. Are you saying that I should take over the other provinces and the territories? How can I do that?"

"By the Francophonation of all of Canada."

"The Francophonation of all of Canada? How absurd! How impossible!" The King rose from his throne and began to pace up and down. After some moments, he shouted, "How noble! What a cause! They only out number us three or four to one. Such good odds for a people who are used to fighting above their weight! I shall embark upon this mission immediately! We will dispatch artists to the rest of Canada, musicians and the like, export our rich culture to the poor Anglais, who have none of their own except for Don Cherry and Hockey Night in Canada. We will appeal to the Vendus to remember their French roots, to form Francophone societies, to teach their children to speak our splendid language. And you will be my lieutenants for the Maritime Provinces."

"Bravo, Le Roi de Quebec!" rejoiced the musketeers.

When I woke up, it was just starting to get light.

The newlyweds slipped out of the hotel early in the morning, bound for the airport and a honeymoon in France, while we authors assembled in Dickie's suite for a continental breakfast and a writing session. "At last, we have come to the conquest of New France. Now is when we should have gone to Louisbourg, the site of the second great British victory, the first, of course, coming at Beausejour, but we really don't need to go there again. You will recall how Pepperell and his men took Louisbourg in 1745. Major General Jeffrey Amherst did it exactly the same way in 1758 by bottling up the harbour, and seizing the Royal Battery. In other words, the French learned nothing between wars about defending their fortress."

"Dickie," Josée objected, "now you are slamming the French the way you slammed Washington."

"Oh, I haven't finished with Washington yet. But, to proceed. Abercrombie, as could be expected, was fired by Prime Minister Pitt on September 18, 1758, after the debacle at Ticonderoga, and replaced by Amherst, a colourless but capable officer. On the other hand, one of his brigadiers, James Wolfe, just 31 years old at the time, was a most complex character. Born into the professional officer class, he had his first taste of battle when he was only 16, and was already a colonel by the time he was 23. A tall, gangling hypochondriac who suffered from kidney stones and rheumatism, and who was obsessed with visions of an early death, he made himself into a caricature by wearing his red hair in a queue, and walking with a cane. It was said of him that he was an infuriating subordinate and a difficult superior, but a soldier he was, a brilliant strategist who could be ruthless if the situation demanded it.

"And now, the second taking of Louisbourg. On June 2nd, 1758, the British Admiral Boscawen sailed into Gabarus Bay with a fleet of 157 vessels, including 20 ships of the line, 18 frigates, and 100 transports carrying 9,000 to 12,000 men, depending on which account you read. On June 8th, just as Pepperell had done before him, Wolfe landed in the Bay unopposed. The siege began on July 19th with British cannon in the same places as in 1745, and they, along with Boscawen's guns, began to reduce Louisbourg to rubble."

Josée looked heroic. "You remember, Marcel and Evangeline were within the walls. A priest in the Fort wrote in his diary on July 20th, 'In the last 36 hours, over 1,000 shells have fallen within the town, yet the Governor's wife, Madame Courserac de Drucourt, mounts the ramparts every day to fire cannon at the British, and Captain Bonin's sweet Evangeline goes with her'."

"Yes, heroism there was, no doubt, but the French position was impossible. By July 25th, all French ships in the area had been destroyed, the town was in ruins, and its guns were out of ammunition. The next day, Governor Drucourt surrendered, but he accomplished one thing - he delayed the British victory long enough to preclude an assault on Quebec in 1758. As a postscript, the French were deported back to France, and the fortress of Louisbourg was razed to the ground. Josée?"

"Marcel and Evangeline were among those deported. They took the next available ship back to Quebec City."

"Yes, Josée. For the rest of the summer and fall, Wolfe was sent off to round up the remaining Acadians, a task which he abhorred, but which he executed with dispatch."

"With the utmost cruelty," Josée said vehemently. "He burned houses and ships, killed off the livestock, and allowed his men to murder, torture, even scalp the poor, innocent people."

At last, one of my ancestors was involved in the North American wars. "There were 500 colonials with Wolfe at Louisbourg, Joel Bonney among them. He was only 18 years old at the time, and an ensign in the Royal American Regiment. According to Uncle Bill's notes, he was strong, handsome, and over six feet in height, which would have made him stand out in a crowd in that day and age. During the battle, he was promoted to lieutenant. Josée?"

"So we have ancestors as officers on both sides of the battle. We know of Marcel and Evangeline's heroism. Joel's promotion should indicate the same quality, but did he take part in the persecution of the Acadians?"

"Unfortunately, probably, yes."

"It will be hard for me to treat him fairly, then."

Dickie resumed, "Wolfe returned to England for the winter to nurse his ill-health, leaving his men to dismantle Louisbourg and suffer out the winter, while Amherst went on to organize another campaign which we will talk about later. Now, shall we turn this bit of history into our novel?"

All day, we proposed, rejected, adopted and modified text until we were satisfied with the way it read, and it was room service for lunch and again for supper, as Dickie whipped us on toward the climactic battle for Quebec City. "We can now finish with 1758," he said. "In spite of the bad advice George Washington gave him, Brigadier John Forbes arrived at Fort Duquesne on November 24th. Yes, Joe-Bob, I can hear you muttering. Along the way, Forbes wooed the Indians away from the French, leaving the latter little choice but to destroy their fort and retreat. Forbes stood at the forks of the Ohio the next day, and began the construction of Fort Pitt, which, of course, as we know, since we have been there, became the city of Pittsburgh."

"Yes, Dickie."

"We now arrive at the crucial year of 1759. Let me set the stage. A new, three-pronged strategy was formulated to which Prime Minister Pitt committed 20,000 to 25,000 British regular troops, depending on which account you read, to be supported by a like number of colonials. The objectives this time were Fort Niagara, Fort Ticonderoga, and Quebec City. Amherst would be responsible for the first two, and would delegate responsibility for Niagara to Brigadier John Prideaux. Poor Prideaux! On July 25th, with 2,000 men, including Sir William Johnson and some 100 Iroquois, he achieved his objective after a 19 day bombardment, but Prideaux himself was killed by fire from his own guns. Amherst, meanwhile, with 11,000 men, occupied both Fort Ticonderoga and Fort St. Frédéric, or Crown Point, by the end of July, the French having abandoned them without a fight to withdraw for the defence of Quebec City.

"The King and the Prime Minister wanted Wolfe to lead the assault on Quebec, in spite of his ill health. When the Duke of Newcastle became aware of their choice, he warned the King, 'But he is quite mad, Sir'. To which the King replied, 'Mad, is he? Then I wish he would bite some of my other generals.' Wolfe acquiesced under the pressure and was promoted to Major General, the same rank as Amherst, and I suspect Amherst's nose must have been somewhat out of joint over the appointment of his former subordinate. At any rate, he halted his advance at Crown Point, not wanting to be caught in the Canadian winter if Wolfe failed.

"So at last, we come to the assault on Quebec City. Wolfe left England on February 17th, 1759, with an invasion fleet under the command of Vice Admiral Sir Charles Saunders. After a delay caused by ice in the harbour, Wolfe picked up his troops at Louisbourg, some 9,000 British regulars, two battalions of colonials, and a company of Rogers Rangers, and loaded them onto transports. The fleet consisting of 49 warships, 500 sailors, and 119 transports, then sailed up the St. Lawrence River to anchor on June 26th near the Ile d'Orleans, which, as we have seen, thanks to the Pattersons, is just four miles below the city of Quebec."

"And old Joshua was with the Rangers," Joe-Bob interjected.

"Yes, and I will have something to say about the Rangers in a moment, but first, a word about Vice Admiral Sir Charles Saunders. Besides the fact that his fleet stood in the way of reinforcements and supplies from France, he was a brilliant naval man who would prove invaluable in the campaign. Now, I hope you were all paying attention yesterday when we cruised the river. There, before you, was the sight, although now considerably modified, that greeted Wolfe and Saunders that June of 1759 - the city on the promontory of Cap Diamant, protected by walls at the time as well as the steep cliffs, the river upstream guarded by formidable batteries of cannon, the easier route of attack downstream heavily fortified and defended.

"Hostilities began on June 27th when Montcalm sent fire ships against the British fleet, but sailors managed to commandeer them and beach them harmlessly. That same day, Wolfe successfully landed troops at Levis, not far from the ferry dock on the south shore, and set up a battery of 32 pound guns and 13 inch mortars. It opened fire on July 12th, and although at extreme range, it slowly battered the city into ruins over the next seven weeks. During that time, the French tried to dislodge the British and their guns from the position several times, but they were unsuccessful. Joe-Bob? You look sceptical."

"You mean to say those old guns could fire shells all the way across the river? How far is that?"

"About one and a half kilometres, or one mile. Josée, I think you should outline the French position at this point."

"Oui. To go back a bit, New France was greatly reinforced as a result of King George's War. Military expenditures increased 12 times between 1743 and 1755, and would increase again another five times by 1759, but it must be remembered that some of this extra money was siphoned off by Intendant Bigot, who was a member of a merchant house that imported goods and supplies from France. He would then buy those goods and supplies for the colony at greatly inflated prices, and put the difference in his pocket. It was these actions of his, as much as any, that sparked a vicious spiral of inflation, making paupers out of not only the colonists, but also military officers from France. To make matters worse, along with the inflation came poor crops, rationing, small pox and malnutrition. Still, we must give the devil his due. Bigot continued to bring in food and supplies, in spite of high insurance rates and the British blockade, while others did not.

"Returning to the military situation, we have already mentioned the enmity between Governor Vaudreuil and General Montcalm which was brought on, in part, by the murky chain of command imposed on them from France. An attempt was made to clarify it at the end of 1757, when Vaudreuil was told to 'defer' to Montcalm in military matters, but Vaudreuil obviously chose to ignore that instruction, as we shall see.

"Montcalm had about 16,000 troops, but many were colonials in the Troupes de la Marine and the militia. In his view, they could not be relied on, and in any case, they were the Governor's to deploy. Because of his attitude, his regulars from France looked down on the locals, who were, in fact, much better at fighting in the wilderness than they. In addition, because of alliances formed by Vaudreuil, Montcalm had several hundred Indians he could call on, but he never trusted them after they broke his word to the garrison at Fort William Henry. Dickie?"

"But we are done with wilderness fighting for the moment, because the climax to the struggle for New France was to be a confrontation between massed armies, albeit small armies, in the European tradition. Yet for months, it appeared as if that confrontation would never take place. Quebec City, in spite of the bombardment from Levis, appeared to be impregnable. On July 31st, Wolfe attempted to penetrate its defences to the east, on the Beauport shore, remember the Beauport shore, only to be thrown back with 400 casualties, while the French lost not a man.

"As the summer wore on, Wolfe probed here and probed there, but with no success. He became irritable, blaming his lack of success on his Brigadiers, Murray, Townshend, and Monckton, the last of Beausejour fame, even on Saunders, who was his greatest supporter. One might say he even became irrational. During the Louisbourg campaign, he condemned 'those hell hounds of Canadiens' for their barbarity. Now, in retaliation for the attempts of Habitants, or tenant farmers, to silence the battery at Levis, he unleashed on them 'the dirtiest, most contemptible cowardly dogs', who were none other than Rogers Rangers. They terrorized a 50 mile stretch of the south shore, burning villages, killing and scalping where they were resisted. Ah, an objection from Joe-Bob."

"Jesus, God, Dickie, but you sure know how to get a man's goat. That's Joshua you're talking about. My granddaddy never mentioned a word about terrorizing those villagers."

"An oversight, perhaps?" Dickie grinned.

"And Fred, what the hell was precious Joel Bonney doing all this time?"

"I haven't the faintest idea. He left no journal, no diary. He was with one of the battalions of the Royal Americans, that's all I know."

"But we must get on," resumed Dickie. "As the summer wore on - did I use that phrase before? Josée, leave that out. Rather, as time passed, the British army was fading away with desertion and disease. Deserters, you see, could easily find shelter and support in the American colonies to the south, an indication, perhaps, that those colonies were already in a rebellious frame of mind. Whatever. Wolfe fell ill with fever, if not frustration and disappointment, and took to his bed, leaving his Brigadiers and Saunders to solve the riddle of Quebec. And it was Saunders who came up with the key. On July 18th, he succeeded in running two of his frigates upstream past Quebec's batteries; by August 9th, ten more had joined them, putting the French defenders in a difficult position. Now, Wolfe might attack from above the town as well as below.

"Montcalm responded to this new threat by sending Louis-Antoine de Bougainville with 3,000 men to watch the British ships upstream, and prevent any landings. There followed a pantomime in which Bougainville marched his men along the top of the cliffs, while the British ships drifted up and down the river on the tide - oh, by the way, did I say that the St. Lawrence River was still tidal at Quebec City? And did I say that Bougainville was already, at 28, a fellow of the Royal Society of London, and that he would undertake extraordinary Pacific voyages, much like Captain James Cook, who commanded one of Saunders' vessels?"

"For God's sake, Dickie!" I complained. "What's that got to do with it?"

"Oh, what indeed, just some flavour. At any rate, Murray, Brigadier Murray, staged hit and run raids along the shore below the cliffs, forcing Bougainville to respond to the point of exhaustion.

"At last, on August 20th, Wolfe rose from his sick bed and consulted with Saunders and his Brigadiers. They convinced him that they must attack from up the river, because the French defences downstream had already been tested, and found to be too strong. Land at Cap Rouge, ten kilometres upstream - remember Cap Rouge? - and march back to the city, they decided, and while the army was being deployed for the attack, keep the French off balance by feints and ruses.

"And so began the game which ultimately warped the judgement of Montcalm. Ships probed here, then there, as if looking for a spot to land troops, and bombarded the shoreline randomly, while transports loaded with red-coated soldiers scuttled about, and staged diversionary raids. Meanwhile, a solitary figure in a rowboat could be seen riding the tides up and down day after day, looking like a common soldier out fishing. It was Wolfe, with a glass, and he scanned and examined the cliffs, looking for a way up from the river that was closer to the city than Cap Rouge. And finally, he spotted it. "On the night of September 12th, while Bougainville marched wearily westward along the top of the cliffs, following the flotilla of British ships riding the incoming tide, Wolfe had his men loaded on the transports. In the early morning darkness of September 13th, they were rowed ashore at L'Anse du Foulon, where the path up the cliffs began. Fate was with them. A fleet of canoes carrying supplies was supposed to arrive that night from Montreal, and sentries were told to let them pass. The supply run was cancelled, but the sentries were not told about it, and so they were not alert.

"Led by Colonel William Howe, the advance guard of Rogers Rangers and regulars crept up the path, 180 vertical feet to the top. Legend has it that a Scottish officer, Simon Frazer, answered sentries' challenges in French, and before they realized what was happening, enough troops had reached the top of the cliffs to overpower their outposts. One of the officers captured at that time was Louis du Chambon de Vergor, who surrendered Beausejour to the British, and survived the court marshal that followed, but he did manage to get away a messenger to warn Montcalm.

"With the path to the top of the cliff secured, the rest of the army clawed its way up in the darkness, and marched the remaining two kilometres to the Plains of Abraham, directly outside the walls of Quebec City. A detachment of Royal Artillery dragged two field guns up with them, a feat that still boggles the mind. When dawn broke, Wolfe's army stood shoulder to shoulder on the Plains waiting for the French reaction, and Josée, what was that?"

"News that the British were on the Plains reached Montcalm at five thirty in the morning. Neither he nor Vaudreuil believed it, because a low rise called the Buttes a Nevue hid the troops from view. Montcalm rode out, saw that what he was told was true, and exclaimed, 'I see them where they have no business to be!' And immediately, he made a decision. Whatever prompted him to make it - the weeks of sleepless nights under the incessant bombardment from Levis - the constant probing of his adversary - the conviction that if he delayed, the Plains before him would soon be filled with cannon that would batter down the walls of the town - the fact that supplies of food were almost exhausted - the burning desire to be done with this game of wits - we will never know - but, over the objections of Vaudreuil, he decided to come out and face his enemy. And here, we have the real tragedy of New France. Vaudreuil, still convinced that Wolfe's real intention was to attack the Beauport shore below the town, refused to allow the Troupes de la Marine and militia there to be brought up to the Plains."

"Thank you, Josée. Let's leave it there. The road known as Cote Gilmour follows the same path that Wolfe's men took up the cliffs. We will drive up it tomorrow to Battlefield Park, or what is left of the Plains of Abraham, and reconstruct the events of September 13th, 1759. Anybody else for a drink, as if I need ask?"

Next morning, we drove west along the north shore of the St. Lawrence on Boulevard Champlain until we came to Cote Gilmour. Dickie insisted on getting out at the bottom and walking through the trees to the top, so that he could experience first hand what it had been like for Wolfe's men. Josée, dressed in blue shorts and white halter-top, decided to join him. "Better time those two, Fred," Joe-Bob warned, with a grin. Josée didn't help my state of anxiety, either, when she wiggled and smiled prettily. I have to tell you that when she wiggled, it was hard to keep your mind on what you were doing. I checked the odometer when we started up the hill, and again at the top. Less than half a kilometre. Joe-Bob must have done the same. "If they don't show up in 15 minutes, Fred, they're up to hanky-panky."

They took 30 minutes, but neither of them looked ruffled, as if they'd had a quick one on the way up, so I relaxed. Dickie looked ecstatic. "I've always wanted to do that, to walk where Wolfe walked, ever since I first read about this campaign when I was a boy. Do you know that he was supposed to have recited 'Grey's Elegy in a Country Churchyard' as he climbed these cliffs? I believe, by then, he was convinced that he was going to die."

Battlefield Park, when we came to it, was a peaceful green space of lawn and trees wedged between the St. Lawrence River on the south and the Grande Allée on the north, one of the main thoroughfares to downtown. Citizens of Quebec City came here to walk, jog, bicycle, roller blade, and picnic, and to enjoy pleasing views of the river and Levis on the other shore. A kilometre or so east of the top of Cote Gilmour, we found a place to leave the car and, dodging skaters and joggers, we started to walk across the park. Close to the Grande Allée, Dickie stopped, seemingly satisfied, and we sat down on the grass to hear how the battle on the Plains of Abraham was fought, that fateful September 13th of 1759. Josée began, "The exact number of troops available to Montcalm is subject to dispute. Earlier, I said that he had 16,000. Some accounts say he had as few as 15,000, even as many as 21,000, but that would have included the Troupes and the militia that Vaudreuil refused him, the 3,000 with Bougainville, and another 3,000 who were the garrisons of the remote forts. He probably had not more that 4,500 on the Plains, and about half of that number were from his five regular regiments, or battalions - La Sarre, Languedoc, Bearn, Guienne and Royal

Rousillon. The rest were Troupes, militia, and some hundreds of Indians. As for cannon, some say that Vaudreuil withheld all of them from him, but he definitely did have three. Dickie?"

"Again, Wolfe's strength has been estimated to be from a maximum of 8,000 down to a minimum of 4,000. On the Plains, he definitely had ten regular regiments, or rather, battalions - the 15th, 28th, 35th, 47th, 48th, and 58th regiments of foot, the 2nd and 3rd battalions of the Royal Americans, the 78th Highlanders, and a company of Rogers Rangers. At full strength, that would have amounted to in excess of 5,000 men, but not more than 6,000. In addition, he had the two light field guns. Oh, yes. Do you know about grenadiers?"

"Soldiers who throw grenades," I guessed.

Dickie roared with laughter. "No, Fred, no. Grenadiers were the tallest men in the army. In each regiment, they were formed into the lead company to impress the enemy, and they usually took the brunt of the casualties. In Wolfe's case, the tallest men were formed into a single battalion called the 'Louisbourg Grenadiers'.

"So, to the battle. Remember that the field at the time was twice as wide as what we see today; in fact, we are sitting precisely in the centre of the action. On the south were the cliffs above the St. Lawrence. To the north was the escarpment above the St. Charles River. In between was a distance of perhaps 1,000 yards. Now, the deployment."

I balked. "You mean, you are going to tell us which regiment was where?"

"Of course, Fred."

"Is that necessary to our novel?"

"Don't you want to know where Joel Bonney was on the battlefield? Joe-Bob? Where the Rangers were, and what they did?"

"The way you tell it, maybe I don't want to know what the Rangers did. According to my granddaddy, they practically won the battle by themselves. But go ahead, as far as I'm concerned."

"I take that as a vote of confidence. From the south then, the British right, above the cliffs on the St. Lawrence side, Wolfe arrayed the 58th, the 78th highlanders, the 47th, 43rd, and 28th, and the Louisbourg Grenadiers. The 15th was in the second line, the Royal Americans protected the left flank, and the 35th protected the right flank. In reserve was the 48th. The men were instructed to line up only two ranks deep instead of the usual three, to load two balls into their muskets instead of one, and not to fire until the enemy should be within 40 yards."

"What about Rogers Rangers?" demanded Joe-Bob.

"They were not deployed, by which I mean that they were not in the line of battle, nor were they counted on as a reserve. Josée?"

"Montcalm's army began streaming out from behind the walls of the city at eight o'clock, and formed into a battle line. He placed his regular regiments in the centre, while Troupes de la Marine guarded the right and left flanks. He kept no units in reserve. In addition, militia and Indians snipers were placed in the thick woods on both flanks."

"Wolfe had no Indians?" asked Joe-Bob.

"No," Dickie answered. "He had Rogers Rangers instead."

"One of these days, you arrogant Brit, we are going to have a reckoning."

"Anytime, you overbearing Yank."

"I am warning the two of you to shut up!"

"Yes, Josée."

"That's better. The snipers began to inflict casualties on the British."

"Wolfe's flanking companies, including the Royal Americans on the left, responded with sorties against the snipers. Joel Bonney would have seen action then."

"The battle proper began with a barrage from Montcalm's three cannon."

"Wolfe ordered his men to lie down, an unheard of tactic, but one which largely negated the cannon fire."

"At precisely ten o'clock, Montcalm began to advance. What a sight it must have been! The regulars magnificent in their red waistcoats and white surcoats, the Troupes in their uniforms of blue!"

"At Wolfe's command, the British army stood, a sudden, solid line of red."

"Montcalm's men began to run forward. The centre surged ahead, while the left lagged behind. Their cohesion was broken. Some of the Troupes began to fire at 130 yards where no musket could be accurate, and to drop to the ground to reload, as if they were in the forest fighting Indians."

"The British began to move forward, every man in step, not one in front of another, a disciplined, formidable advance."

"And then, at 40 yards, came the devastating volley that broke the French line, and killed my ancestor, Marcel. In 15 minutes, it was all over."

"No, Josée. There was no one, single volley. It would have been almost impossible for Wolfe to order such from his position near the St. Lawrence, with clouds of smoke from the guns billowing about. Rather, each unit fired when their commanders felt it was within the 40 yards."

"But it is the legend of the conquest that our men were decimated by that one volley."

"Not so, again. The French casualties, at less than 700, were no more severe than the British. My dear Josée, it was the undisciplined line of advance that cost New France the battle, not a devastating volley."

Josée began to weep silently, her brother's essay in her hand. "But why did Montcalm not wait for Bougainville to come back down the river? They would have had the British trapped between them. And why did Vaudreuil deny him the men and the cannon he needed to assure victory?"

I took her free hand and drew her to her feet, and the four of us walked slowly off the Plains of Abraham.

Back in the car, we drove east along Avenue Ontario until we came to Wolfe's monument, close by the walls of Quebec's citadel. Josée didn't join us when we got out to look at it. "Revisionists at work," Dickie observed. "Twice, this monument has been destroyed by those who want to obliterate the memory of the conquest."

We left the park and turned east onto The Grande Allée, which soon turned into Rue St. Louis, and that took us directly back to the Chateau Frontenac. On foot now, we crossed the broad expanse of Dufferin Terrace, took the funicular tramway down the cliffs to the old part of Quebec, and soon found ourselves on the narrow, 17th century street called Rue Petit Champlain. Josée's eyes were dry by the time we sat down at a street side table outside a restaurant, but she seemed detached, and took no part in the conversation. Dickie finished off New France while we were waiting for lunch: the deaths of both Wolfe and Montcalm from wounds suffered on the battlefield; Vaudreuil's escape with most of the army to Montreal; the surrender of Quebec City on September 17th. "There is more, but it can wait until this evening."

"When do we leave here?" I asked.

"How about a game of golf first?" suggested Joe-Bob. "I sure like to play a game of golf everywhere I go."

Josée broke her silence. "I arranged to play a game with my parents tomorrow. The three of you can go out on your own. The tee times are already made."

Lunch, at length, arrived, steaming hot bowls of minestrone, and croissants filled with an assortment of seafood. We ate without talking much, Josée's gloom hanging over us like the conquest itself, and I wished in vain that the noise and gaiety of the crowds passing by would cheer her up. When we were finished eating, she said, "Fred, walk me down to the ferry dock. I will stay at home tonight. I will meet all of you on the other side at nine in the morning, and take you to the golf course."

A shapely Quebecoise dressed all in black, her hair dark red in the fashion so popular locally, minced by with a come-hither smile. "Say, Dickie, if our chief author is taking off, we can't do any writing, so why don't we poke around this tourist trap? Might find some souvenirs."

"Souvenirs? Oh yes, souvenirs. Splendid idea. See you in the morning, Fred, in the lobby at say, eight?"

I walked Josée to the ferry, just a couple of blocks away, past throngs of tourists who were pouring off buses it seemed at every corner. I bought her ticket, and we stood facing each other like strangers. "If it helps, I love you, Jos," I said.

"Shut up Fred, shut up. Right now, I hate all Anglais." And she turned, without a hug or a kiss, and disappeared into the boarding lounge.

Not having the least idea what to do with myself, I wandered around the old part of town on the cobblestone streets, past quaint little shops selling everything imaginable at inflated prices, not wanting to run into Dickie and Joe-Bob, or to interfere with whatever it was they were up to. For something to do, I bought an ice cream cone and ate it in a little park, where children were playing on old cannon left over from the days of the conquest. Nearby was the church where Pierre and Geneviève were married, and on impulse, I walked to it, and entered. There were many others there, tourists mostly, who were drinking in the artwork and the atmosphere. I sat in a pew and tried to imagine myself a devout Roman Catholic like Josée, but I soon realized that would not be possible, because my ancestors, whether I liked it or not, had bequeathed to me a powerful Puritan ethic. 'Thou shalt not make unto thee any graven image, or any likeness of any thing that is in heaven above or that is in the earth beneath, or that is in the water below the earth: Thou shalt not bow down thyself to them, nor serve them.' So thundered the preacher from the pulpit in my mind.

I left the church and climbed up the street called Cote de la Montagne until I came to the Musée du Fort, an austere stone building just a few yards from the Chateau Frontenac. Inside, for a few dollars, I took in the slide and diorama presentation of all the battles for Quebec City, from the Kirkes in 1629 to Wolfe and beyond. It was most realistic, with tiny ships in the painted river, lights flashing to indicate cannon firing, toy soldiers in the uniforms of the combatants, and an excellent running commentary. When it came to the battle on the Plains of Abraham, the various units of the British army fired in quick succession, and quite suddenly, I became convinced that the legend of the devastating volley could still be true. I resolved to become stubborn about it, that I would not be bullied by Dickie, and that we would tell our story that way.

Out in the sunlight again, with hours still left in the day let alone the evening, I strolled along Dufferin Terrace, looking across the broad expanse of the St. Lawrence to Levis where my love was. How foolish of her to think that I would ever stray! Clumsy old Fred Bonney straying! Who else would want me, anyway? I sat on a bench, feeling sorry for myself, when the same Quebec-style redhead we had seen on Rue Petite Champlain swayed by, the same come-hither smile on her lips. She was young and pretty, and her face was all covered with makeup, and her black dress clung to her in such a revealing fashion that I imagined it might have been sewn onto her. She turned the smile on me as she passed, and to my utter disbelief, I felt myself reacting. To my utter horror, she stopped and said, in French, "Oh, monsieur, do not think me a professional, but one who is attracted to mature, successful men such as yourself. I desire nothing more from you than the pleasure of your company, but if you should be pleased with me, and want to reward me with a meal or some spending money, that is your choice."

"Merci, merci, mais non!" I croaked, and I sprang up from the bench, and fled into the hotel.

Dickie and Joe-Bob looked rested and fit the next morning, and were exchanging good-natured jibes. They were developing a kind of Jekyll and Hyde relationship, buddies one minute, at each other's throats the next. We went down the tram again to the sleek ferry that would take us to Levis, and in a matter of minutes, Josée was greeting us on the other side. She seemed marginally more cheerful than the day before while she drove us to the golf club, but only marginally. She and her parents teed off before us, joined at the last minute by a tall, dark man, just starting to gray at the temples. Where the hell did he fit into the picture? I looked at Dickie and Joe-Bob, and they looked just as envious as I'm sure I did.

We played skins for a dollar each a hole, and I only won four, which meant that I lost ten dollars. Actually, none of us played well because we kept being distracted by the group ahead of us, and when we weren't trying to keep track of them, we argued about the devastating volley, truth or fiction, on the Plains of Abraham. "Dickie," I asked, "where did you get the idea there was no such volley?"

"Fred, I've read a dozen different accounts of the battle, and only one suggests that there was 'one, final volley' that broke the French line. Most authors and eye witnesses say there was 'steady fire' as the two armies approached each other."

"Then Wolfe's order to hold fire until within 40 yards was fiction, or was not followed?"

"One or the other."

"Say, I know a thing or two about muskets," Joe-Bob offered. "Now, let's reconstruct the scene. Dickie, how many Brits were there advancing against the French?"

"Oh, dear. Discounting the battalions on the flanks, in the rear, and in reserve, I'd say about 3,500."

"Then I'd say, if they waited until they were within 40 yards before they fired, they must have been bad shots. Muskets aren't rifles, but they aren't that inaccurate, either. At 40 yards, especially if they were loaded with two balls, they should have blown the French to hell and back. Think of it. We're about 40 yards from that green ahead, just a little pitch shot, a quarter of a wedge. Why, I believe I could hit someone standing that far away with a rock. Any way you look at it, there certainly should have been more than 700 French casualties."

I was determined to win this argument for the sake of my relationship with Josée. "Let's look at it this way," I said. "The Brits are no different than the French. They hold their line, alright, but they are pretty nervous too, so most of them start firing from, say, 80 yards in. But the Grenadiers on the left end of the line, all guts, no brains, hold their fire until they really are within 40 yards. Then, altogether, that one battalion lets fly at the Troupes on the right end of the French line. That line, already broken by the uneven advance, disintegrates, and the rout is on."

Dickie scratched his chin. "Yes, it could have happened that way. Proud, veteran troops like the Grenadiers would hold their fire longer than the others, perhaps. That might have been the 'devastating volley'. Alright, Fred. You win." When we got back to the clubhouse, we found the tall, dark stranger having lunch with Josée and her parents, and she seemed to be enjoying his company far too much. Just about the time I was wondering if she would ever introduce him to us, he got up, kissed her soundly on the mouth, and left. Only then did Josée beckon us to come over. I was furious, but I had to contain myself for the time being. We talked for a few moments with her parents until they also left, and then I hissed, "Dickie and Joe-Bob, get lost for a minute, will you? Josée, who the hell was that fellow you were playing golf with?"

"An old - what-do-you-call-it, flame? He is a partner in a law firm now. He is already married, but he wants me to be his mistress."

"So where does that leave me?"

"Right where you are, standing all angry in front of me."

"Are you coming back with us?"

"Beg me, and I might."

"It may interest you to know that a really good-looking woman tried to pick me up yesterday afternoon. I nearly went with her."

"Was she the one dressed all in black that passed our table when we were having lunch?"

"Why, yes."

"An enthusiastic amateur, I suppose. You should have went with her."

"Gone with her."

"Gone, then. Are you going to beg me to come with you?"

"Yes. I'm begging."

"Not good enough. Give me another reason why I should come."

"There <u>was</u> a devastating volley on the Plains of Abraham, fired by one of the British battalions. I saw the diorama at the Musée du Fort, and the re-creation of the battle gave me that idea. And that's the way it's going to be in the book, I've convinced Dickie of that."

"Mon cher Fred! Then the French did not invent the volley as an excuse!"

"That's right."

"Alright, I will come, and besides, if I don't, the three of you will make a mess of my book."

I can't begin to describe how good it felt to have her at my side again, to put my arm around her, to look into her knowing eyes, to kiss her, but there was little time for romance. Dickie was nervous again about progress on the book and in no mood to allow another night off. As soon as we got back to his room at the hotel, we worked the ancestors into the conquest, Joel Bonney leading his platoon against the snipers on the left, Joshua Bonney and the Rangers chafing for action in the rear, Marcel Bonin dying on the Plains. The saddest part of the story concerned Evangeline, Marcel's Acadian wife. Pregnant, with a three year old tugging at her skirts and a baby suckling at her breast, she flees Quebec with Vaudreuil and his army, and finds her way to Longueuil, the ancestral home of the Bonins. There she is received by the matriarch of the family, Marcel's great-aunt, who welcomes her with open arms.

Over a room service dinner and far into the night, we laboured on to the conclusion of the Seven Years' War: the desperate winters of 1759 and 1760, when the surviving Canadiens nearly starved to death; the Chevalier Levis' heroic attempt to retake Quebec City in the spring of 1760 at the battle of Sillery; Murray's stubborn defence and the siege that followed; the arrival of the British ship, the Lowestoft, that dashed the last remaining French hopes; Levis' retreat to Montreal; the final surrender to Amherst and his three converging armies in September, 1760; Britain's decision not to deport the Canadiens; Amherst's guarantee to them of religious freedom, property rights, and equality in trade.

Joe-Bob had a resolute look on his face when he said, "Now, that last part is where Britain made its big mistake. Should have deported those French right then and there, like they did the Acadians. Look at all the trouble they're causing now."

Josée looked furious. "You would have deported 80,000 people, wouldn't you?"

"I sure would have."

"Oh, let's get along," chided Dickie. "Joel Bonney would have been with Murray, Fred, so he lived through the battle of Sillery and the siege. And he would have gone with him to Montreal. After the surrender, Joe-Bob, Rogers Rangers were sent to take over the remote forts such as Detroit from their French garrisons, but there was no bloodshed involved."

"Arrogant, damn Brits, didn't believe colonials could fight, put the Royal Americans on the flank, wouldn't use a perfectly good outfit like Rogers Rangers for anything but terrorizing defenceless civilians. I can hardly wait for the Revolution."

"You won't have to wait long. That comes next. Incidentally, is your jet available tomorrow?"

"I don't know, on such short notice. The crew has a pretty full schedule. Why?"

"We must fly back to Boston for the start of the revolution, and to Montreal the day after that."

"I'll try and arrange it. Otherwise, we'll have to go commercial." We took a break while Joe-Bob phoned his dispatch centre, and he came back with a frown on his face. "They can fit us in tomorrow afternoon by juggling a couple of flights. I won't ask them to do that again. On time, on budget, always reliable, that's the way I want my customers to think of my businesses. Dickie, how about giving me a little more notice next time? You're running this outfit like a mystery tour."

Dickie grinned. "Makes it fun, doesn't it? But to conclude. Great Britain declared war on Spain on January 2nd, 1762, after Spain decided to join France and her allies in their struggle with Prussia. Spain, long since a spent military force, promptly lost Cuba, some other islands in the West Indies, and the Phillippines to Britain. France, in one last desperate attempt to gain bargaining territory, invaded Newfoundland, only to be chased out by a force under the command of Colonel William Amherst, brother of Jeffrey."

"So when do we go to Newfoundland?" I asked.

"Let that be part of the mystery, if you like. But do let me finish. My throat is getting dry. By the treaty of Paris, which ended the war on February 10th, 1763, the status of Canadiens as British subjects was confirmed. Spain, meanwhile, gave Florida to Britain in return for Cuba and the Phillippines. As for France, she might have retained Canada if she had really wanted it, but she elected instead to keep some islands in the Caribbean. In return, she ceded all her territory north of the Great Lakes and east of the Mississippi River to Britain, save for two small islands off Newfoundland from which she would be able to continue fishing. As for her claims to the country west of the Mississippi, she ceded these to Spain in the secret treaty of Fontainebleau in 1762, hoping that she would be able to regain them at a later date.

"And so, the French menace was removed from the American Colonies, and for a few short years, all of North America east of the Mississippi drainage was British. I can say it no better than Major Rogers of the infamous Rangers. The taking of New France was, according to him, 'A conquest of perhaps the greatest importance that is to be met with in the British Annals'. Ah, how short a time was Britain to enjoy the fruits of victory!"

We thankfully adjourned to the bar after these final words on the Seven Years' War.

Chapter 6.

The American Revolution

I reached over, half asleep, to lift the phone receiver and silence our wake-up call. Another sound jarred me awake: the shower was running. Josée was already up, Josée who usually only got up on time when there was a golf game on. The showering stopped, and she came out of the bathroom wrapped in a towel. Ignoring me, she disappeared into the walk-in closet, then reappeared in a smart looking avocado suit I hadn't seen before. "Where did you get that?"

"Yvan bought it for me. It was delivered to the room."

"Yvan? Your lawyer friend?"

"Oui."

'Why up so early?"

"Since we don't fly until afternoon, Yvan is taking me to breakfast, then to church."

"To church, when he is planning to commit adultery with you?"

"The Catholic religion is very understanding and forgiving."

"How can you do this to me, make love to me like you did last night, then go out for breakfast with a man who wants to take you away from me? I bet I look as green as that suit."

"You do. Maybe it was something you ate."

"Are you going to say goodbye to him?"

"No. I will keep him on the what-do-you-call-it, the string, just in case."

"You are coming with us, then?"

"Yes, you bloody bunch of Bonney Anglais. I have to for the sake of the book."

"Not for my sake?"

"We have an agreement. That is all."

"I love you, Jos."

"Shut up, Fred, shut up." And she left.

I skipped my exercises, using my hurt feelings as an excuse, and when I showed up with a long face in the restaurant, Dickie and Joe-Bob asked in unison, "Where's Josée?" I pointed to a far table where we could see Yvan's animated, passionate face, and the back of Josée's head. At least, she brought him over and introduced him to us on their way out. He was wary and spoke only in French, and I could imagine his anger and confusion. What was his mistress to be doing with the three of us? Joe-Bob said pointedly, "Say, when I want a Quebec lawyer, I'll sure go looking for one who speaks English."

Yvan looked startled. "Look no further. Here is my card. Let me know if I can be of service." He managed a smile, then took Josée by the arm, and led her off to church.

"Where are we going to stay in Boston this time?" I asked Dickie, when we were airborne in Joe-Bob's jet.

"Be precise, Fred. We stayed in Cambridge last time, a suburb of Boston, certainly, although I'm sure the citizens of Cambridge don't think of it that way. This time, we are going to stay downtown."

Josée was having a catnap in one of the back seats while Joe-Bob was in the cockpit, and I took the opportunity to satisfy my curiosity. "Dickie, what's with Joe-Bob and Jacqui?"

"Nothing, old boy, nothing. She's an employee, and he doesn't, as they say, mess with employees. And Fred, you aren't very observant. It is obvious to me that she has something going with the co-pilot."

"What do the two of you do when you go off on these business junkets?"

Dickie looked uncomfortable. "We, of course, or I should say Joe-Bob, does have things to attend to. I must admit he is quite remarkable in the way he is able to juggle all his interests, and keep them going forward." He paused and looked at me almost apologetically. "Fred, you don't know how lucky you are to have Josée." We stayed in the hotel where Joe-Bob took us to dinner the night we first met him, the one with the spectacular view of the harbour. We had only a few moments, however, to enjoy the scenery before Dickie had us tackling the American Revolution in his room. "Curiously," he began, "the conquest of New France became one of the principal causes of the Revolution. Oh, in the beginning, of course, there was the predictable euphoria, the war finally, successfully over. A number of artists eulogized the death of Wolfe on canvas, while the English lit bonfires, and struck a commemorative medal to mark the acquisition of Canada. New Englanders also celebrated, happy to have the French neutralized, not only because of the recurring raids they staged, but also because they were Catholic. The American Colonies, collectively, now looked forward to expanding to the west without interference, except, of course, from the Indians.

"By Royal proclamation in 1763, five new colonies were established: Quebec, Nova Scotia, Newfoundland, and of lesser importance to our subject, East and West Florida. At the same time, it was confirmed that Rupert's Land, or those lands draining into Hudson Bay, was under the sole jurisdiction of the Hudson's Bay Company. "

"Is that worth mentioning?" asked Joe-Bob.

"My dear fellow, do you realize the size of the area we are talking about? Do you know that it was five times the area of France, and included millions of acres in the United States?"

"Well, damn, I didn't know that, but I'll study up on it."

Josée broke in, "I think it is important here to point out that the name Quebec was chosen by the British, not the French, who for generations continued to call themselves Canadiens."

"Yes, Josée. With the French no longer able to help them, the Indians became fearful that settlers from the English Colonies would come pouring over the Appalachian Mountains. Amherst, the military commander in charge of the conquered territories, would give them no assurances to the contrary, and made matters worse when he abandoned decades of custom by refusing to give them gifts. As a result, under a chief called Pontiac, the Indians began to terrorize the frontier in a desperate attempt to retain a homeland. To mollify them, Britain closed the country west of the Appalachians to settlement, and it was marked 'Indian Country' on maps. The closure upset the colonies and their expansion plans until 1768, when, with Pontiac dead and the Indian rebellion crushed, they were allowed into a part of the Ohio Country. Finally, in 1774, the notation 'Indian Country' was removed from maps.

"Now, what really bothered the English colonies was the Quebec Act. It guaranteed the French their own civil code, their language and their religion; thus, it guaranteed the establishment of popery in North America, and that was anathema to New Englanders, in particular. In 1774, the act was amended, and the boundaries of Quebec were expanded to include the area north of the Great Lakes, thereby cutting it off from possible expansion by the older colonies. And so another grievance was added to the growing list being compiled by future Americans. Josée?"

"The architect of the new Quebec Act was the governor, Sir Guy Carleton, who first took up his duties in 1766. He, like many other Britons, was captivated by the people, believing them to be simple and gentle and amenable to a benevolent type of autocracy. Nothing, incidentally, could have been farther from the truth. Over the ensuing years, he completely misconstrued the attitudes and desires of Canadiens, with the result that the new law obliged them to pay the tithe to the church, and left them still bound by the chains of the Seigneurial system. Equally reprehensible was the fact that they had no assembly, and therefore no popular representation in government. Carleton was also mistaken in his belief that thousands of Canadiens would enlist in the militia at the wave of his hand."

"Thank you. Today, Carleton's name is remembered in towns, universities and historic sites, but as we shall see, he proved no more astute in war than in politics. In fact, he was largely responsible for the failure of a critical campaign against the American rebels. Joe-Bob? And do be brief, in your usual style."

"At last, I get my say. Yes, the Quebec Act was a cause of the Revolution, but it was only one of the straws on the camel's back. From the outset, first England, then Great Britain, and let's just say Britain, was completely unconcerned about the political and economic well-being of the colonists in North America. It never provided for their representation in the House of Commons, as, for example, it did for Jamaica. Our only voice in the old country was by way of agents for the several colonies, and by 1771, those agents had to be approved by the governors, not just the elected assemblies. By a series of Navigation Acts and a Customs Service, Britain attempted to control trade both in and out of the colonies to its own benefit, and tried to stifle manufacturing within the colonies as well, so that it could sell its products over here. And finally, it attempted to make the colonies pay for the Seven Years' War, and the military needed to guard the frontier against the Indians."

"My word, that is brief. Would you care to add anything?"

"Yes. On the edge of the frontier, Americans became self-reliant and wary of authority. They began to despise 'Placemen', those appointed rather than elected to political office, and the 'Civil List' of lackeys that came with them, and they feared standing, professional armies as a possible agent of oppression. Because of these attributes and attitudes, Britain's attempts to control trade were largely a failure; rather, they prompted many Americans to turn to smuggling and piracy."

"Could you be specific about the events, albeit within the context of your terse remarks, that finally sparked the Revolution?"

"I would blame first the Trade Acts of 1762 and 1763, which resulted in a stepped up campaign against smuggling and piracy. Second, I would blame the Sugar Act of 1763, designed to force imports of sugar, rum, and molasses from other British Colonies, rather than from the cheapest source. Third on my list would be the Quartering Act of 1765, which required the colonies, at their own expense, to provide barracks and provisions for 10,000 British soldiers. Fourth would be the Townshend Acts of 1767, which introduced, among other things, new duties on tea. Fifth would be the Currency Act of 1764, which strangled colonial commerce by outlawing the issue of paper money. Sixth was the Stamp Act of 1765, which required that stamps be purchased and pasted on all newspapers, legal documents, and commercial papers, the first direct tax ever imposed on the colonies. Seventh was the introduction of Admiralty Courts to try pirates and smugglers. But the list goes on. That enough, you arrogant Brit?"

"Quite, you overbearing Yank. But in Britain's defence, it was deeply in debt after the Seven Years' War, which it felt, quite rightly, was fought to the benefit of the colonies. It therefore felt that the colonies, none of them in serious debt because of the war, should help to pay for it. And everywhere in America, the colonists seemed determined to profit from the presence of the military by charging outrageous prices for goods and supplies. Lastly, Britain did repeal the Stamp Act, and the Townshend Acts, except for the duties."

"Those were the exceptions. Otherwise, the more we tried to assert our case against oppression, the more Britain tightened down the screws."

"A matter of argument. But what was the last straw?"

"It was a long straw, beginning in 1768 with the arrival of British troops and ships in Boston. In 1770, British soldiers killed five men in what became known as the Boston Massacre."

"But a drunken mob provoked them."

"In December of 1773, as a protest against the duties still in effect from the Townshend Acts, Bostonians dumped three ships' worth of tea into the harbour. In retaliation, Britain passed three bills into law which became known as the 'Coercive Acts': the 'Boston Port Bill', which made it illegal for anyone to load or unload ships in Boston harbour; the 'Bill for Better Regulating of the Government of Massachusetts Bay', which annulled the constitution of 1691; and the 'Bill for the Impartial Administration of Justice', which provided that trials of officials charged with capital crimes could be moved to Britain, or other colonies, to assure they got off. As if those acts weren't bad enough, the Brits also amended the Quartering Act, requiring the colonies to provide better billets for the military."

"But the British government did offer to rescind the Regulating Act if Massachusetts would behave."

"Fat chance of that. Citizens had their backs up. They were not going to be pushed around any more by an irrelevant, corrupt government thousands of miles away."

"In April of 1774, the new Governor of Massachusetts, General Gage, sailed into Boston with orders to use force, if necessary, to bring the colony to heel."

"In June, the new Quebec Act was passed, sparking outrage against the British Government for expanding the French Colony's boundaries, and supporting popery in North America. In July, the citizens of Boston held a town meeting, where they initiated a movement to ban the import and consumption of British goods, and to stop exporting to Britain the commodities it needed. They then petitioned the other colonies for support, while the General Court called for a meeting of all colonies to support Boston. A second town meeting approved a declaration to 'Great Britain and all the World' listing grievances against the British Government, and calling for the establishment of a 'Committee of Safety'."

"What was a 'Committee of Safety', Joe-Bob?" I asked.

"A council of war, I guess it was. Dickie?"

"Whatever it was, Governor Gage banned all future town meetings, and refused to call the newly elected General Court."

"Radicals called for county conventions to take the place of town meetings. And Massachusetts wasn't the only colony with grievances. There was unrest everywhere, and that culminated in the election of delegates to a 'Continental Congress', which met for the first time in Philadelphia in September and October of 1774. The delegates from the original 13 colonies were in no mood to give in to the mother country. They decided that no obedience was due the Coercive Acts affecting Boston, and advised the people to elect their military officers, and prepare for war. They compiled a list of rights and grievances, and details of the Acts, which infringed on and violated the rights of colonists. In particular, they asserted that the Crown had no right to maintain soldiers in America without consent, or to appoint members of colonial councils, and they attacked the Quebec Act. In addition, they prepared four addresses: to the people of Great Britain, in the hope of rallying sympathy; to the King, asking for intervention against his corrupt government; to the colonists, justifying the actions of the Congress; to the French in Quebec, pointing out that Britain withheld from them their political and legal rights, and asking them to join with the other colonies. The Congress also voted for an embargo on imports to be effective December 1st 1774, and on exports effective a year later, unless parliament repealed a list of acts. Finally, it created a form of association to be signed by all American Colonists."

"But the Congress did not declare independence at that time. In fact, much of its work was devoted towards reconciliation with Britain."

"That's true, but the seeds of rebellion had been sown."

"But public opinion was sharply divided. It has been said that only one third were for independence - the radical, rowdy third – one third were against it, and one third were neutral."

"The percentage for independence was much higher in New England, especially in Massachusetts. In November of 1774, members of the General Court there met in defiance of the governor, and voted to raise troops and money."

"News of the Continental Congress reached London in mid-December, and plans were made for war. Through the gloomy winter months and on into the spring of 1775, friends of the colonies, like Edmund Burke and former Prime Minister Pitt, now Lord Chatham, tried to promote compromise, but failed. So, too, did Ben Franklin, proposing at one stage that colonial assemblies be recognized as the equivalent of Parliament. He finally gave up in March, and sailed for home."

"Meanwhile, another clandestine - like that word, Dickie? - meeting of the General Court took place in Massachusetts, and it voted to raise taxes, and established a code of conduct for the army. Also, meanwhile, the colonists were clandestinely stockpiling weapons and supplies."

"And a lot of those weapons and supplies were stolen from British magazines. In the late hours of April 18th, 1775, Governor Gage, in the face of all this disobedience, sent 700 troops to Concord to seize a military cache, his intent to cow the colonials with a show of force."

"Paul Revere made his famous ride that night to warn the citizens that the British were coming. On the morning of April 19th, on their way to Concord, the British were confronted by a group of minutemen at Lexington, and killed eight of them."

"Please, what is a what-do-you-call-it, minuteman, Joe-Bob?"

"Josée, that was a selected militiaman who was supposed to be ready for action in one minute, more or less."

"Merci."

"You mean, thank you."

"Oui."

"Stubborn French. Dickie?"

"The British carried on to Concord, but they found nothing, because the citizens had already moved their arms and supplies. The soldiers then turned for home, only to be harassed by the Massachusetts militia all the way from Concord to Boston, a distance of about 20 miles."

"The first shot fired at Concord became known as the 'shot heard round the world'. Within days, 15,000 militiamen had the British in Boston pinned against the sea. And now, I can call us Americans! We had no cannon to begin with, but

Ethan Allen and the Green Mountain Boys, together with Benedict Arnold, captured Fort Ticonderoga, and shipped the cannon to Boston."

"They didn't capture Ticonderoga. They surprised the garrison in the middle of the night and bamboozled them into surrender. Not a shot was fired."

"Isn't that capturing?"

"Just the first in a long line of treacherous acts committed by you Americans."

"May I continue? Thank you. At Bunker Hill near Boston, the Americans threw up earthworks for protection. On June 17th, 1775, the British tried to dislodge them."

"Major General William Howe, the same who was with Wolfe at Quebec, although only a Colonel then, was the British commander. Time and again, he threw his regulars against those earthworks, only to have them repulsed with severe casualties."

"Remember I said I knew something about muskets? The Americans, because they used them almost on a daily basis, really learned how to shoot those old guns. I believe their accuracy was a factor in the battle. Not only that, but according to legend, our boys held their fire until they could see the whites of the Brits' eyes."

"I grudgingly concede your point about accuracy. The British were much better at fighting with bayonets. In any event, the rag-tag bunch of American militia was dubbed the 'Continental Army' by Congress, and George Washington was appointed Commander in Chief. He arrived in June with six companies of riflemen, but he was not able to dislodge the British from Boston."

"But by March, 1776, under constant bombardment by the guns taken from Ticonderoga, the British had enough. They abandoned Boston and sailed to Halifax, taking 1,000 Loyalists with them."

"Who had to leave behind everything they couldn't carry in their arms, just like the poor Acadians," Josée sympathised.

"Yes, Josée. Now, what family members were involved at Bunker Hill?"

"As soon as he heard about the fighting, my ancestor Moses, son of Joshua, came running from New Hampshire to get in on it."

"Alright. Anyone else? Fred?"

"By this time, Joel Bonney was in Maine."

"Yes, but that is another story, is it not? We will be dealing with that in due course. So Josée, what can you do with Moses and the battle of Bunker Hill?"

"He would have been, as Joe-Bob said, self reliant, a good shot. He would have helped make the earthworks, then he would have stood behind them, courageous, defiant, a rallying point for others of lesser courage."

"Don't forget the boom of the cannon, the whizzing of howitzer shells, the smoke, the rattle of musket fire, the British with fixed bayonets, ah, the poor devils, dying on the slopes below the earthworks."

"And don't forget the smell of gunpowder and gangrene, and soldiers crawling through pools of blood and pieces of human flesh. War isn't pretty."

"Alright, then. Joe-Bob, we will need a car and driver after lunch for a tour of revolutionary sites."

Our guide that afternoon, a garrulous little Yankee, took us to Paul Revere's statue, the Old North Church, the Paul Revere House, the site of the Boston Massacre, the Boston Tea Party Ship and Museum, and Faneuil Hall, where Massachusetts radicals met to plot against the British. Our man then took us the few miles to Lexington and to Concord, both with interpretive centres and statues of Minutemen, and finally to Bunker Hill in Charlestown, across the Charles River from Boston. There wasn't a hill there any more, it having been excavated away for fill decades earlier, but the site was marked by an obelisk over 200 feet high, with a spiral staircase inside leading to the top. Dickie, of course, was determined to climb it, so I joined him, leaving Josée and Joe-Bob, with his gimpy knee, to explore the gift shop. I soon found myself several turns of the spiral behind my British relative, who was seven years my senior, and I marvelled at his energy and enthusiasm. I didn't catch him until we reached the top, and I stood there, puffing, while he exclaimed over the view. By the time we got to the bottom again, my leg muscles were complaining, and I resolved to take our exercise sessions more seriously.

"This is really a monument to the incompetence of General Howe."

Our fellow travellers joined us. "You figure it was Howe's fault that the British lost at Bunker Hill?" asked Joe-Bob.

"Precisely. Silly ass underestimated you Americans. Thought he could overcome your earthworks and run you off the hill, just like Abercrombie at Ticonderoga thought he could fight his way through those abatis. Worse, once beaten, Howe was left with the opposite problem - too much respect for you and your earthworks, which led to his woeful performance later."

Our guide delivered us back to the hotel, and over Dickie's objections, we took time off for steak and lobster tail in the dining room. We paid for it later, however, because he kept us at it until the British had left Boston, and Moses Bonney, now a militia captain, was waving them a sarcastic goodbye. Even then, Dickie insisted that Joe-Bob bring us up to date on the politics of the Revolution.

"All the way through 1775, Congress still hoped for reconciliation with England. Shortly after the fighting started, it issued a declaration setting out the necessity for taking up arms, and denying any 'ambitious designs for separating'. It also petitioned the King again, avowing loyalty and devotion to him, and asking for his intervention. Even by the end of the year, most states were still hoping for an end to the conflict, and in the meantime, their delegates to Congress voted for only limited resistance. The New Englanders were the most radical and republican, as I've said, but they were looked on with suspicion by the south.

"But there was to be no reconciliation. At the end of 1775, Parliament in England passed still another act, this one declaring the colonies to be in rebellion, and prohibiting trade. As a consequence of that, Congress threw open American ports to all shipping in March of 1776, and sent Silas Deane to France to seek aid in the form of gunpowder and armament. Both France and later Spain were happy to oblige, in the hope that it would cause Britain trouble."

"Remember, Fred, when I told you not to be too hard on Frontenac? France and Spain gave these items to America as a gift, but Silas Deane sold them to his own country. So much for patriotism."

"American free enterprise, that's all. Meanwhile, the Republican Movement gained force as Americans designed ways to govern themselves without royally appointed overseers. Finally, in April of 1776, North Carolina told its delegates to Congress to seek independence, and others followed suit."

Dickie sighed. "It is really unfortunate that so few in Britain could see how difficult it would be to control the colonies. One who could was Lord Camden, who warned parliament in 1775." (Here, Dickie rose to his feet and assumed a pose, with one hand behind his back as if under a coat-tail), "'To conquer a great continent of 1,800 miles (of seacoast) containing three millions of people, all indissolubly united on the great Whig bottom of liberty and justice, seems an undertaking not to be rashly engaged in . . .'"

"A Whig bottom? A Whig bottom! Qu'est ce que c'est?"

"Josée, let's get rid of bottom first. In this context, it means foundation. And a Whig was one who wanted to limit royal authority and increase the power of parliament, that is, the opposite of a Tory."

"Say, that's not right, in this context. A Whig was a supporter of the independence movement in America."

"Quite right, Joe-Bob. To continue with Lord Camden." Dickie resumed his pose and waved his free hand about theatrically: "'It is obvious, my lords, that you cannot furnish armies, or treasure competent to the mighty purpose of subduing America . . . but whether France or Spain will be tame, inactive spectators of your efforts and distractions is well worth the considerations of your lordships.' Ah! Prophetic, those final words!"

At last, we were permitted to find our way to the bar. "'Plane's all set for nine in the morning," Joe-Bob assured us. "Should be in Montreal before eleven. Where to from there, Dickie?"

"We will book into our hotel, and review the events surrounding the American attempts to capture Quebec in 1775 and 1776, then follow the route of the British army which invaded New York in 1777."

The routine was now familiar. Wake-up call, shave, throw on sweat clothes, shake Josée, who finally gets up, down to the exercise room where Dickie and Joe-Bob are already perspiring, a mile on the treadmill and two miles on the bike to warm up, ten minutes on the weights, six laps in the pool, thirty seconds in the hot tub, shower, back to the room, shower again with Jos, time and inclination permitting, throw on street clothes, down to the restaurant for breakfast. On travel days like today, we would take the limousine or a taxi to the airport, where Jacqui would be waiting for us, smiling, with an eye-opener, and the pilot would then take us up above the bumps, and we would sail smoothly to our destination, in this case, Montreal's Dorval Airport. On the ground, it was the usual delay at customs, and this time, at the car rental kiosk. A quick lunch in the cafeteria and we were on our way to downtown Montreal, Canada's second largest city, but still barely big enough to be major league, a place where French and English co-existed uneasily together.

Josée knew the city well and directed me without any re-runs to our hotel, which featured convex windows that provided a panoramic view of the city, and easy access to upscale shops and the Montreal subway beneath. We were allowed time only to have our bags put in our rooms, and then the captain of the mystery ship put us to work. "We have already mentioned that Benedict Arnold together with Ethan Allen and his gang of thieves took Ticonderoga by treachery in May, 1775. Then they launched the first assault of the Revolution against Quebec."

"The traitor, Benedict Arnold."

"Joe-Bob, let the jury remain out on that charge. Arnold occupied Crown Point, made his way by boat down Lake Champlain and the Richelieu River to St. Jean, which is on the other side of the St. Lawrence from here, and took it after a brief struggle. Allen, with a handful of men, next attempted to take Montreal. He was captured, the clown."

"Dickie, you're slandering the name of one of America's heroes."

"A clown is a clown, no matter where he comes from. You Americans must have your heroes, men, even women, who single-handedly can defeat a whole army. You have made Allen into one of these heroes, but he was nothing more than brash, overconfident, arrogant, self-righteous, and stupid. In fact, this invasion was little more than a stunt. The Americans, short of supplies and wrong in their belief that the Canadiens would support them, withdrew when attacked by a small force of militia. Joe-Bob?"

"It sure beats me how you pass judgement on people, especially Americans. What gives you the right to do that? How the hell did you ever get to be a colonel, anyway? And what about your knighthood, Sir Dickie?"

"Knowledge and the advantage of hindsight allow me to pass judgment. As for my colonelcy, I was a one-pip wonder at Suez in 1956. An Egyptian shot my helmet off, and they gave me another pip. Later that day, my captain was wounded, and they gave me the third pip. After Suez, I served as military attache in a succession of embassies around the world, and I guess those up there were impressed with some of the things I discovered. A little clandestine - right, Joe-Bob? - espionage, shall we say. But you had better carry on with the Revolution."

"Alright, alright. Congress was still determined to take Quebec, because that would prevent the British from invading from there. A much more serious attempt was made later in the year when two armies marched north, one under Richard Montgomery, an ex-British officer, who mobilized his forces at Albany, and invaded Canada via Lake Champlain and the Richelieu."

"Now there's a traitor for you."

"No interruptions, please. Again, Montgomery took Fort St. Jean as well as Fort Chambly."

THE REINCARNATION OF ISAAC BROCK

"Carleton allowed the bulk of his forces to be trapped at St. Jean, while he cowered in Montreal."

"Montgomery then continued down the Richelieu to Sorel, cut communications with Quebec City, and took Montreal."

"Which had been abandoned by Carleton. On November 20th, he escaped by boat and floated past the other American army on his way to Quebec City."

"Wait a minute. I haven't even told you about the other army yet. It was under the command of Benedict Arnold, who took a much more difficult route, up the Kennebec River in Maine and down the Chaudiere to Quebec City. By the time he got there, he had only 600 men left out of his original 1,000, and they were exhausted, and close to starvation. Meanwhile, Montgomery, with 1,400 men, marched down the St. Lawrence, occupying Trois Rivieres on the way, and joined Arnold."

"As for Carleton, he had 1,800 men, including only 90 regulars, and 500 sailors and marines. And here, we encounter a severe problem for the Americans - their terms of enlistment."

"You stick to the British side of things. But yes, enlistment. Most of the men with Montgomery and Arnold had signed up only until the end of the year. Besides that, the Americans had no cannon to breach the walls of the city of Quebec. But they attacked anyway, on December 31st, in the midst of a blinding snowstorm."

"Montgomery came from the west along what is now the Boulevard Champlain, which you will all remember, as we drove along it on the way to Cote Gilmour. British gunners, through the snowflakes, thought they saw figures approaching, and opened fire. A blast of grapeshot killed Montgomery, and his men fled. On the east end, Arnold advanced into the St. Roche District, where the British discovered him lost amongst the warehouses - we were near there when we got on the Patterson's yacht. During the ensuing counter-attack, Arnold was wounded and escaped, leaving one of his officers and 400 men to surrender."

"But the Americans were not done. Congress sent replacement troops and a new commanding officer, General John Thomas, and the siege continued until May 5th, 1776."

"That is when a fleet of British warships arrived with reinforcements, including seven battalions of infantry, four batteries of artillery, and a new second in command for Carleton, Major General John Burgoyne. When the Americans saw the fleet, they melted away into the forests so quickly, legend has it, that General Thomas' uneaten dinner was still warm on its plate when a British patrol discovered it."

"But the Americans were still not finished. They sent General John Sullivan to take Thomas' place."

"Timidly, Carleton started back up the St. Lawrence, re-taking Trois Rivieres and Montreal, but he failed to capture General Sullivan as he should have. Sullivan made a desperate stand, then retired to Albany."

"Let me say a word," Josée broke in. "One of Sullivan's troubles was that the Canadiens were hostile and unco-operative. At best, they would only supply food at outrageous prices."

"Yes, Josée," agreed Dickie. "It seems that the Canadiens decided they were better off with the British than the Americans, who always preached to them about freedom and the evils of popery."

"Now, I disagree with why Sullivan retired. His men were being hit with smallpox."

"And desertion, Joe-Bob. Of course, no American would ever desert, would he?"

"Dickie, you're getting my goat again."

"Baaa! Back to Carleton. He kept advancing against minimal opposition, making it to Crown Point on October 14th before he stopped. He then quartered his men with the Habitants for the winter, to punish them for not enlisting in the militia the way he thought they would. And that ends the campaign for Canada. Were there any family members involved?"

There was silence. "Well, it may interest you to know that an ancestor of mine, Miles Bonney, served as an ensign with Carleton - one of those 90 regulars. Josée, what can you make of that?"

"Was he critical of Carleton?"

"Most decidedly. Left a journal which I have inherited to prove it. And at the risk of putting you off the trail, there was a hint that he became infatuated with a Canadien girl. Of course, nothing could come of it."

"Why not?"

"Junior British officers were discouraged from indulging in such delightful diversions with local girls."

"Let me see. Each day, as he goes about his duties, he sees her - where? No. She is the daughter of a Canadien merchant, and he is billeted in her home. Is that possible?"

"Oh, quite, Josée. Meanwhile, Joe-Bob, there were developments. By the end of 1775, the British had formed a grand design for subduing the colonies. They believed that Loyalist support was in the majority in the middle colonies, that is, New York, New Jersey and Pennsylvania, and also in the south, and weakest in New England and Virginia. They therefore planned to isolate New England by establishing control of the Richelieu-Hudson corridor, and put pressure on Virginia by invading the south."

"Right. In February of 1776, an army under General Sir Henry Clinton invaded the Carolinas, expecting support from the people, but the support didn't materialize, and he was defeated at the battle of Moore's Creek Bridge."

"In March, the British abandoned Boston and sailed to Halifax, as we have already said."

"In April, George Washington, anticipating a move by the British, took the Continental Army to New York City, and began to fortify it against attack."

"George, for once, was right. Admiral Lord Howe arrived off the city in June with an army under the command of his brother William, the loser at Bunker Hill. Rather than attack the city immediately, the British set up headquarters on Staten Island, and waited for General Clinton to return from his abortive attempt on the Carolinas. Upon his arrival, Howe had a total of 25,000 men."

"Washington, meanwhile, had only 19,000 volunteers, most of them one year wonders."

"The Howes had been appointed Peace Commissioners by the King, and were authorized to negotiate an end to the revolution on Britain's terms. By the time they met with a delegation from Congress, however, America had already declared independence - on July 4th, 1776."

"God bless America and the glorious fourth!"

"There followed a charade in which General Howe came within moments of defeating Washington several times, only to withdraw or break off the engagement at the critical moment, and that often when he came on American earthworks. George escaped out of New York by the skin of his teeth, leaving behind nearly 3,000 of his men as prisoners, and retreated into New Jersey. That is his only claim to fame, his ability to escape, to run and fight another day."

"But he scored two great victories which helped to turn the war around. On Christmas day, 1776, with only 6,000 of his men left, he routed two regiments of Hessians at Trenton, New Jersey, and captured tons of supplies."

"Routed be damned! The Hessians were in winter quarters, which would have been sacred ground to a European army. They were full of Christmas dinner and drunk as, I believe you say over here, skunks."

"Hessians?" I queried.

"Fred, Britain's army was still undermanned because of the Seven Years' War, so it recruited mercenaries from several German States, including Hesse, to help out. About 30,000 of them served in America before the end of the revolution."

"I don't care what you say, Dickie, it was a victory. So was the battle at Princeton in January, when Washington, on his white horse, inspired his men when they beat up a British brigade."

"The brigade was in winter quarters as well. Sorry, no victory. Back to Howe. After spending the winter dallying with a mistress in New York City, he sailed to the head of Chesapeake Bay in July of 1777, leaving Clinton behind with a token force, and chased Washington about Pennsylvania for the rest of the year. He defeated him whenever he could catch up with him, but Washington, the will-of-the-wisp, always managed to get away with the bulk of his army.

"And now, sadly, we come to America's only real victory of the war, the defeat of Gentlemanly Johnny Burgoyne at Saratoga."

"You finally admit we beat you somewhere. What about Yorktown?"

"Josée, you will be delighted to know that the French beat the British at Yorktown."

"Bien!"

"The hell they did! Washington beat them!"

"But first, Burgoyne, a fascinating character. He was born in 1722 into an upper middle-class family, and like many others of like origin, he joined the military early by purchasing a commission. In 1743, he ran away with and married the daughter of the Earl of Derby."

"Ooh, I can do something with that!" Josée looked like the Cheshire cat.

"Yes, Josée. He was such a charming fellow that the Earl didn't hold it against him, but he was a wild young man, a compulsive gambler, and in 1743, he had to sell his commission to help pay off his debts. He and his wife then lived abroad for seven years, no doubt with the help of the Earl, but at the outbreak of the Seven Years' War, the Earl managed to get him back into the army, where his natural ability was allowed to shine. By 1758, he was Lieutenant Colonel of the Foot Guards, and then commanded a regiment of light cavalry, his own innovation, in operations against coastal France. In 1762, during the waning years of the war, he served with distinction as a Brigadier in Portugal.

"But he had more than a military string to his bow. He became a Member of Parliament in 1761 and again in 1768, and just before he was shipped to Canada, he wrote a successful play called 'The Maid of the Oaks'. By that time, he was a Major General with the just reputation of a wild gambler. Josée, the best, romantically, is yet to come, but I will save it for later.

"Someone in authority finally recognized the incompetence of Carleton, and he was replaced as military commander in Canada, or more properly Quebec, by Burgoyne. This slight did not sit well with Carleton, and as we shall see, that would ensure the failure of Burgoyne's campaign. As I said earlier, the British strategy was to isolate New England by driving a wedge down the Richelieu-Hudson corridor to New York, but it wasn't until June, 1777, that Burgoyne was able to set out from Montreal, the northern end of the wedge, the delay caused by lack of troops. He had with him 7,000 to 9,000 men, according to which report you read, almost half of them German mercenaries, along with some Iroquois and Canadiens. He also had 138 cannon, a dreadful encumbrance in the rough, forested terrain, and only 30 days' worth of supplies. The success of his campaign depended on two things: first, a diversionary attack by Colonel Barry Legere was supposed to draw some American forces up the Mohawk River; second, Howe was supposed to send General Clinton with an army up the Hudson to meet him. The diversionary attack failed, and Clinton, with the few men Howe had left him, only got as far as West Point, where the Hudson River narrows, right there on the map."

"The Americans were under the command of General Philip Schuyler. They slowed Burgoyne down by destroying bridges and setting up log barricades."

"In spite of these delaying tactics, Burgoyne took Ticonderoga on July 6th after a four day siege, and Fort Edward - you remember Fort Edward - on July 29th."

"The Americans intercepted dispatches from Clinton urging Burgoyne to march straight to West Point, still 80 miles away when Burgoyne reached Saratoga."

"At Saratoga, Burgoyne found himself pinned between the Hudson River and low bluffs that had been heavily fortified by the Americans."

"And by that time, Schuyler had been replaced by General Horatio Gates, who had about 9,000 men, with volunteers flocking to his colours."

"You should have explained why Schuyler, a respected and able general, was replaced by Gates. There was much plotting and backstabbing involved. Gates was born in England in 1727, and served in the British army in the French and Indian war, notably with Braddock at Fort Duquesne. He retired at half pay, a common practice in those days, and emigrated to Virginia in 1772, where he bought a plantation. In 1775, he became the Adjutant General of the Continental Army, and thus another traitor, and was promoted the next year to the rank of Major General, one of only four appointed by Congress at the time. One of the others so appointed was Schuyler.

"In order to gain command of the Northern Army, Gates first claimed precedence over Schuyler, that is, asserted that he was appointed before Schuyler, and when that didn't work, he defamed Schuyler by blaming him for the surrender of Ticonderoga without a proper fight. Schuyler was relieved of his command, demanded a court martial at which he was exonerated, but by then, Gates had stolen his army from him. More of Gates later. You should also have mentioned, Joe-Bob, that the heights at Saratoga were fortified by a Polish engineer, Colonel Thaddeus Kosciuszko."

"Now, I don't need to do any explaining. Carry on."

"By this time, Burgoyne's ranks had been thinned by half through desertions and casualties suffered during a foraging expedition, he was low on food, and his remaining men were facing starvation. The evil, jealous Carleton could have sent him massive reinforcements and supplies, but he did not.

"On September 19th, Burgoyne attacked the American entrenchments at Saratoga, but was thrown back. Over the next three weeks, a number of engagements were fought in which the British suffered 1,000 casualties, twice as many as the Americans, and lost large numbers of the cannon dragged all the way from Canada. The greatest hero for the Americans during this period was Benedict Arnold, who fearlessly led men against the British fortifications and overcame them, even after being relieved of command by Gates. It was during one of these engagements that Arnold sustained the famous wound in the foot. I submit that if it were not for Arnold, Gates would not have defeated the British. Gates was another green-eyed monster, jealous of Arnold's success."

"The hell you say."

"The hell I do. Finally, on October 9th, Burgoyne withdrew north to the Heights of Saratoga, but soon he was surrounded by an American army that was now 20,000 strong, and forced to surrender on October 17th. Gates granted him the honours of war, and agreed to let him and his men return home, but when Congress heard of the deal, they cancelled it, and only Burgoyne himself was allowed to go free. My ancestor, Miles Bonney, spent the next six years as an

American prisoner of war. I like to think he was too stubborn to die, as many of the other men did."

"I know why he lived," Josée said emphatically. "He kept thinking of the Canadien girl he met in Quebec City."

"Why, I suppose that could be true. You will develop that idea?"

"Oui. But you were going to tell us more about Burgoyne."

"Yes. His surrender at Saratoga has been called the turning point of the Revolutionary War, in that it encouraged the French and the Spanish to join the Americans. When he returned to England, he found himself the target of much indignation. He was stripped of his rank and other perks, and refused a hearing to clear him of blame. He remained in the military and political wilderness until 1782 when powerful friends took over the government, arranged a colonelcy for him, appointed him Commander in Chief in Ireland, and made him a member of the privy council. In 1783, when the government fell, he returned to private life to concentrate on his writing, and in 1786, he wrote the comedy, 'The Heiress', a huge and lasting success, which was translated into ten languages. And now Josée, the worst and the best. His wife died in 1776 on the eve of his departure for Canada, and he mourned her for five years. He was then befriended by a beautiful young actress, Susan Caulfield, who bore him several natural children before he died in 1792. One of those children became Field Marshal Sir John Fox Burgoyne, the highest ranking officer in the British army."

"Oh, I cannot bear it, it is such a beautiful story!" Tears appeared in the corners of Josée's eyes, and I handed her a Kleenex. "We must now write and rewrite until we do justice to it."

And so we did, through room service and the evening, until our thirst got the better of us. Over drinks, Dickie told us, "Tomorrow, we cross the St. Lawrence to St. Jean and Chambly, and then go up the Richelieu to Lake Champlain, thence on U.S. 87 and New York Highway 4 to the Saratoga National Historic Park. We will probably have to overnight somewhere, Plattsburgh perhaps, but I hope we get as far as Glens Falls. From there, we should continue on to West Point where Clinton bogged down, and on into New York City."

"New York City! Oh, I never thought I would ever see New York City!" Josée was clearly not drained of emotion yet.

"Yes, New York City, where we should cover some of the ground the two armies marched over, Howe and Washington. Then, Joe-Bob. Today is Monday. About Saturday, we should fly to Savannah, Charleston and Yorktown to wrap up the campaign in the south."

"More notice than usual. Should be possible. I'll get on it first thing in the morning."

"Where will we stay in New York?" Josée asked.

"We have reservations at the Waldorf."

"Is that downtown? Oh, I couldn't find my way around downtown. I can't stand it when Fred shouts at me."

"My dear Josée, I wouldn't put you through that. We can find our way to an airport, drop the car, and take the limousine from there."

"I have a better idea," Joe-Bob suggested. "I have to spend some time on business, so why don't we speed this up by doing Saratoga, then back-track to Glens Falls, and fly to New York from there? We can drive up to West Point from New York." And so it was agreed.

On our way to Fort Chambly the next morning, we crossed the St. Lawrence River via the Lafontaine Tunnel and the St. Leonard Bridge, and took a detour through Longueuil. It was now almost an integral part of Montreal, the skyscrapers on the opposite bank making it hard to imagine what it looked like when Jacques Bonin settled there some 300 years before. But try as she might, in spite of my shouting, Josée could not guide us to Fort Chambly. "It has to be right here, on the banks of the Richelieu," she complained, looking at her map.

We gave up the search and settled for St. Jean, more properly known as St Jean sur Richelieu. We could find little evidence of its military history, other than a boulder on Rue Champlain marking the site of the old fort, but it was otherwise interesting for its canal, built to bypass the rapids on the river. After a stop at Tim Horton's, we continued north on secondary highways, past marinas crowded with the yachts and powerboats of the affluent, until we came to Fort Lennox, another National Historic Site. I was conditioned to stop at anything that smacked of history, but Dickie objected. "This fort wasn't built until 1819, and has nothing to do with the Revolution."

"But we are here. Should we not visit it anyway?" Josée suggested.

"But look at the time!" It was already three in the afternoon.

"Let us at least go into the reception centre."

And so we outvoted Dickie, and after Josée discovered that the fort was on the Isle aux Noix in the middle of the river, she insisted we go over to it on the little ferry that shuttled visitors back and forth. Dickie, with a sigh, apparently resigned himself to Plattsburgh for the night.

As we walked around the fort, Joe-Bob discovered Roger and Joyce Patterson in the crowd. "How did you get here?" he asked.

Roger laughed. "You don't know? Up the Richelieu Canal from the St. Lawrence. We're going home by way of Lake Champlain and the Hudson Canal. What direction you heading in?"

"Why, we're heading for Saratoga."

"Why don't you come with us? We can drop you there."

"What a capital way to see the country, by this most historic waterway!" said Dickie, suddenly all enthusiasm again.

Back at the reception centre, we attended to minor details like ditching the car. Expense not being an object, we phoned the rental company's office in St. Jean, and two employees soon appeared in another car to take it away. Then we boarded the Patterson's palatial powerboat, and headed south.

The light was fading when we left the saloon and climbed up to the flying bridge. We were well into Lake Champlain by then, the islands in Vermont to the east, the ridges of the Adirondack Mountains rising to the west. The setting sun put the high, thin clouds afire, and the fire was reflected by the calm water ahead of us, and danced about in our wake.

It was still twilight when Roger guided us into a berth at Plattsburgh, New York, and announced that, because of his heart condition, he had to retire early. The rest of us talked what was left of the evening away, and it was then that I noticed some kind of chemistry working between Dickie and Joyce. They soon went off by themselves to stroll around the deck, and to lean on the rails in conversation.

These strange surroundings excited Josée more than usual, and it was all I could do to keep up with her when we got to bed. When we were finished, she cuddled close to me and asked, "Will the royalties from the book be enough to buy a boat like this?"

"It would have to sell a lot of copies, or be made into a movie. Would you really want a boat like this?"

"First, I would want a nice house. It would not have to be a new one, just big and nice, with two stories and an attic, and four bedrooms, and a den for an office, and two, maybe three bathrooms, counting the en-suite. A big living room, with a real wood fireplace, a dining room and kitchen with a pantry, and maybe a family room where I could put my Impatiens. And a basement to store things in. And a garage for two cars. And a big back yard with a fountain in it, and room for a vegetable garden."

She had described my old house in Ottawa down to the spare bathroom in the basement. "You would rattle around in a big place like that."

"But I would love to have lots of room. And I would spend one whole day a week cleaning it."

"Who would you share this big house with?"

"We have an agreement. Until that is ended, with you."

"What would you say if I told you I already have a house like that?"

"Do not make fun of me."

"The back yard is big enough that I used to flood a rink in the winter for the kids. But I might have to sell the place to support you in style."

"I would rather have the house than the style. Let's move when this is over. Besides, then we can buy a boat like this with the royalties."

Dickie assembled 'the team' on deck the next morning and commanded us to remember Plattsburg's harbour for future reference. Roger joined us and asked, "Where are you going after Saratoga?" He looked a little flushed, as if from high blood pressure.

"To West Point, then New York City," answered Dickie.

"You know, we can take you all the way to New York. We'd love to have the company."

"That would be awfully kind of you." Dickie looked at Joyce, who looked away with a smile. For some reason, the attraction between these two made me nervous, another legacy from my Puritan ancestors. 'Thou shalt not commit adultery!' I could hear the minister thundering from his pulpit. But wasn't that what I was doing? Josée was still legally married, so it certainly wasn't for me to put obstacles in their way.

"Joe-Bob, can we change plans?" Dickie asked.

"Why not? I'll phone Jacqui, and tell her to meet us with a car instead of the jet."

The Pattersons delivered us to the tiny community of Schuylerville early in the afternoon, where Jacqui was waiting for us in a rented minivan. Roger begged off coming, but Joyce joined us, and we were soon whisked the short distance down Highway 4 to the National Historic Park at Saratoga. We toured the museum and exhibits in the visitor centre to begin with, then drove around the nine mile battlefield circuit, a gently rolling landscape of woods and fields. There were ten formal stops altogether, each with plaques telling of their significance, and some had push button audio as well, with actors' voices re-creating stories of the times. The house at Neilson's Farm, once the barracks of American officers, had been restored, and costumed animators acted the parts of the couple who had once lived there.

Dickie's enthusiasm was heightened by the presence of Joyce, I thought, and he added his own colour to the scene: here, on September 19th, the British nearly carried the day; here, on October 7th, Benedict Arnold, already relieved of command by the spiteful Gates, led the Americans to victory; there, in a fenced enclosure, was Arnold's boot with the bullet hole in it. For my part, I detected a general admiration on the part of Americans for Burgoyne, whose campaign evolved, so like the character of the man, into a desperate gamble to reach West Point. That admiration extended also to his subordinate, Brigadier General Simon Fraser, who was mortally wounded in the fighting. Only the Irish celebrated his death, a plaque proclaiming that he had been shot by one of their own.

The gates closed behind us as we left the Park, and Jacqui returned us to the 'Lady Joyce'. We had drinks, then dinner, then more drinks, except for Roger, who, I was glad to see, settled for orange juice and ginger ale, because he had to do the navigating. Our destination for the night was Albany, and on the way there, Joe-Bob amused our hosts with the story of our near mugging in that city, the humour mostly at my expense.

We were under way the next morning by seven, and I was impressed at our speed. I joined Roger on the flying bridge and he told me, "Cruises at 17 knots. Going down the canal like this, we can sometimes do 20, but we have to slow down to 10 when we're passing small traffic." After a short pause, he said, "I'm living on borrowed time. I've had quintuple bypass surgery, and they replaced a piece of my aorta after an aneurism. It's my small arteries they can't do much with, the little ones by the hundreds that are silted up with plaque."

Why he would volunteer this information to me, a virtual stranger, I didn't know, but he went on, "I'm on blood pressure pills. Takes the starch out of a man, you know what I mean? Can't help Joyce out any more. She's a fine woman and I love her very much, but she's much younger than I am, and should be looking for someone else. Don't think I haven't noticed the way she looks at Dickie, or the way you look at the two of them, like you were some Puritan preacher."

I was as transparent as glass!

"She's loyal, and I know she won't stray till I'm gone, but don't get in their way."

I searched for something to say, something diplomatic like a public servant would come up with. Instead, I laughed. "Roger, you going to let your beautiful, loyal wife take up with an Englishman?"

He looked at me with a surprised look on his face, then laughed. "Not much I'll be able to do about it. And better Dickie than some of the hounds that are breathing heavily around home."

My brain sometimes worked in mysterious ways. One down and one to go, I thought. A beautiful widow-to-be interested in Dickie. How could I get rid of Joe-Bob?

Dickie was all for touring the sprawling military college at West Point when we got there, but Joe-Bob convinced him that he couldn't just march up to the gates and get in. "Leave it until the book is finished, Dickie, and I'll get you an invite." We contented ourselves with looking down on the canal from a vantage point near the college, and Joe-Bob told us, "One of General Clinton's problems was that he couldn't get his boats past here, where the Hudson narrows, because the Americans put a heavy chain across it."

Dickie added, "And this is where Benedict Arnold tried to surrender his garrison in September of 1780. He was found out when dispatches were intercepted, and he escaped to join the British, who had the good sense to give him brigadier's rank."

We continued on down the canal, the density of settlement increasing the farther south we went, until it terminated in the Hudson River, a waterway busy with commercial traffic as well as small craft. Roger dropped us off at one of New York City's prestigious yacht clubs, and we said goodbye. Dickie shook his hand. "I was hoping you would help us when we get to the Fenian raids into Canada. That should be in a week or two, after we are done with the Revolution and the War of 1812."

"I look forward to that. Every fall, I make a kind of pilgrimage to Ridgeway, Ontario, where my grandfather was killed. Maybe we can meet there. And I have some of his papers that might help you."

I expected the lights of the big city of New York, the skyscrapers, the opulence of the hotel to excite Josée, and I was not disappointed. For the second night in a row, I was called on to perform heroically, and it seemed to me that I was consuming myself like a starving man in order to meet her expectations.

We spent the next day in a chauffeured car visiting the places where Howe and Washington skirmished in the summer of 1776. At one point, Dickie pointed out, their armies were marching parallel to each other, with only what is now Central Park between them. He appeared agitated. "Bloody fool, Howe. Had George at his mercy half a dozen times, backed off every time when he ran into earthworks, bloody legacy from Bunker Hill. Could have cut him off and surrounded him at least twice. Worse, while he gallivanted off to waltz around Pennsylvania with George, he left Clinton with too few men to march up the Hudson to meet Burgoyne. Why did we have to come up with such an incompetent ass when we needed somebody like Wolfe?"

"Say, Dickie, you don't think you ever would have put down the rebellion, do you? You could have won dozens of battles, but we still would have been here, telling you we weren't going to put up with your oppressive government."

"I suppose you are right. It was one bunch of Englishmen telling another bunch what they could and could not do, and there is no surer way to start a riot."

That evening, we polished off the campaigns in New York, New Jersey and Pennsylvania, in which Moses Bonney fought with Washington, and Howe, utterly disillusioned, resigned, to be succeeded by Clinton in May of 1778. "Clinton was ordered to evacuate Philadelphia and return to New York," Dickie recited, "but the jackals were already circling. The French and Spanish by this time were in open alliance with the Americans, and a powerful French fleet was on its way across the Atlantic. Clinton's transports were diverted to help deal with this threat, so he had to make his way to New York by land, and that opened him up to harassment by the Continental Army. Not only did he have 8,000 troops with him, he also had 3,000 frightened Loyalists to contend with."

"Including my ancestors, Robert and Abigail Robinson," I was happy to contribute.

"Yes, Fred. Fortunately for Clinton, Washington left it to one of his subordinates to do the harassing, General Charles Lee, a self-aggrandizing twit."

"There you go again. But say, you are almost admitting that Washington could have done a better job."

"Almost. At any rate, Clinton taught Lee a lesson when the two collided, then managed to hitch a ride with Admiral Lord Howe from Sandy Hook to New York City. Washington then moved his army to White Plains, on the outskirts, but did not mount an attack. Meanwhile, just to wrap up what was going on in the north, Sir John Johnson, son of the famous Indian agent, with the help of the Mohawk Chief, Joseph Brant, was staging raids into upper New York State from Canada."

"And committing atrocities, just like back in the - back in the 'Petty Gurrs'."

"Washington was just as brutal. He sent an army under General Sullivan to take Fort Niagara, with instructions to use the same tactics as Johnson and his Mohawks. Sullivan was so successful in destroying crops that his army almost starved to death.

"But now, to the campaign in the south, Georgia and South Carolina that is, the so-called 'soft underbelly' of the Revolution, where there were more Loyalists than rebels. Not only that, but the country was kinder and gentler than the north, so that cavalry could be used to advantage, for there was no rugged mountain terrain to contend with, or wide rivers that were difficult to ford. The strategy was to take two important centres, Charleston and Savannah, which would then serve as rallying points for Loyalists, and as springboards for attacks on North

Carolina and Georgia. Now, in order to attack these two centres, it was necessary to take to the seas, which by the end of 1778 were being patrolled by a French fleet under the command of Admiral le Compte D'estaing.

"Major General Archibald Campbell was selected to lead the British forces in the south, and while the French fleet was occupied elsewhere, he slipped down to Savannah and took it in December of 1778. He was joined there by a force from East Florida under the command of Major General Augustine Prevost, and I would ask you to remember that last name for future reference. A month later, Campbell had moved inland and taken Augusta as well, where he was able to recruit a substantial number of Loyalists, but Prevost was not successful in his attempt to take Charleston. At that point, D'estaing showed up with both his fleet and an army in tow, only to suffer a severe drubbing off the coast at Savannah. He withdrew to Boston, leaving Britain once again in charge of the seas, and that allowed Clinton to consolidate his forces in New York City.

"A word about that other jackal, Spain. She entered the war in 1779, and promptly re-occupied the Florida territories she had ceded to Britain in 1763.

"And so we come to the last successful enterprise of the British in the Revolutionary War. Clinton mustered the bulk of his forces, about 8,500 men, and set out from New York City on February 1st, 1780, to besiege Charleston. Why it took him so long to get to it is a mystery, but in any event, Charleston surrendered, largely undamaged, on May 12th, after its outer defences were breached. Clinton then returned to New York, leaving Major General Lord Charles Cornwallis behind with some 5,000 men to hold the territory, and to start moving north. I should mention also that Cornwallis had with him a very able cavalryman, Colonel Banastre Tarleton."

"Say, now there's a name for you. But Dickie, give me a chance here, and let me eat a little humble pie. You were on about Horatio Gates at Saratoga. Seems you were right. Congress, over the objections of George Washington, appointed Gates as commander in the south. Washington objected because Gates, while president of the Board of War in 1777, had been part of the Conway Cabal, by which he sought to have himself replace Washington as Commander in Chief of the continental army."

"Words, words, you Anglais, words! Cabal?"

"My dear Josée, a cabal is a number of persons secretly united to bring about an overturn in public affairs."

"Thank you Dickie. Joe-Bob, you were eating humble pie."

"Alright. Gates started off the summer of 1780 to attack Camden, one of the inland posts the British had set up. He took a real difficult route through the swamps to get there, tried to surprise the garrison but failed, and got his tail whipped by that Banastre fellow. Then Washington got his way. He talked Congress into appointing Nathaniel Greene to take Gates' place, a soldier in Washington's own image. Cornwallis chased Greene all over the Carolinas, but could never give him more than a glancing blow."

"Now, Joe-Bob, I should have some of that same humble pie. It must be remembered that Washington and Greene were inexperienced commanders, with armies of short enlisted militiamen who were facing professional soldiers. Their genius was in learning how to fight while avoiding the destruction of their armies."

"Yes, Dickie, but more than that, Congress, somehow, seemed to think that all this fighting could be done without money, and I hate to admit that patriotism was not much in evidence when it came to supplying the armies with what they needed at a fair price. But back to Greene. He did learn how to fight, and at Guildford Court House, North Carolina, on March 15, 1781, he nearly whipped Cornwallis."

"A pyrrhic victory for Cornwallis, who lost one quarter of his men, and could not follow when Greene withdrew. He regrouped briefly at Wilmington, North Carolina, where he made the decision to abandon the Carolinas, and march north for Virginia and Chesapeake Bay."

"Greene, meanwhile, overcame all the remote British posts, and their garrisons retreated to Charleston and Savannah, the only places in the south left in British hands by the fall of 1781."

"And now we come to the end. Britain by this time was like a wounded animal at bay, engaged in Africa, India, the West Indies, and in the Mediterranean, where she was under siege at Gibraltar. The French fleet had Clinton trapped in New York City, and a French army under General Rochambeau was quartered in Newport, Rhode Island. Clinton still had 17,000 men with him, but felt himself in greater danger than Cornwallis, because George Washington was camped at White Plains and might attack."

"George, however, had come to the conclusion that the city was too well fortified for a successful assault, and was prepared to wait Clinton out."

"Benedict Arnold was already in Virginia when Cornwallis arrived, sent there by the British in January of 1781 to rally Loyalist support, and disrupt the American war effort. By all reports, he was very successful."

"Washington sent the Frenchman, the Marquis de Lafayette, and others to counter first Arnold, then Cornwallis, but by doing so, he weakened his own position."

"Lafayette was outnumbered 5,000 to 7,000, and had little success at first, allowing Cornwallis to roam around Virginia at will until midsummer. Then Clinton, in New York, issued a series of baffling orders, at first demanding that Cornwallis send him reinforcements, and at last, instructing him to fall back to and fortify Yorktown, on the premise that he could be supported there by the British fleet. But the fleet was in no position to help, and Cornwallis was left in a precarious position."

"On August 14th, 1781, Washington received word that French Admiral de Grasse was sailing not for New York, as expected, but for the Chesapeake, with a fleet of 29 ships and an army of 3,000 men, and that he would remain in the area only until mid October. It was then that Washington made the most fateful decision of the war. He wrote in his diary, 'Matters now having come to a crisis, and a decisive plan to be determined on, I was obliged, for the shortness of Count de Grasse's promised stay on this coast, the apparent disinclination in their Naval Officers to force the harbour of New York and feeble compliance of the States to my requisition for men . . . to give up all idea of attacking New York, and instead to remove the French Troops and a detachment of the American Army . . . to Virginia'.

"Gathering Rochambeau's French from Newport with his own men, Washington started for Yorktown, 450 miles away. He reached the head of Chesapeake Bay on September 6th, and by September 26th, 17,000 men, Americans and their French allies, were deployed on the Yorktown peninsula."

"Inside the hastily erected defences of Yorktown were 7,000 British soldiers, caught like rats in a trap. The navy tried to help them but could not, for it was barred from the Chesapeake by a superior number of French ships."

"The Americans threw up earthworks parallel to the British defences, and on the evening of October 9th, they opened fire with heavy guns and mortars."

"Oh, do call yourselves allies. And those earthworks were designed by French siege engineers. The bombardment was so intense that it crippled Cornwallis' artillery, and except for three redoubts, he was forced to withdraw to his inner defences."

"Redoubt?" queried Josée, looking exasperated.

"A rectangular, isolated out-work, my dear."

"The Americans threw up a second parallel of earthworks, and took the last of the British redoubts on the night of October 14th."

"That second parallel was also designed by French siege engineers, and the allied forces took a severe punishment before the redoubts fell. And in a last, defiant thrust, British soldiers sallied forth on October 16th to spike several of the allies' guns. Cornwallis then tried to retreat to alternative defences across the York River, but was prevented from doing so by bad weather. It was then that he decided to surrender, and on October 17th, the request for a parlay was beaten on drums."

"A blindfolded British officer was taken to the American lines, where terms were discussed and agreed to."

"Cornwallis steadfastly refused to surrender to any American, and so it was the French who accepted his offer. They accorded the British the honours of war, by which they were allowed to march out of Yorktown, lay down their arms, and surrender their colours. This they did on October 18th, and they then were imprisoned for the rest of the war.

"For all intents and purposes, the war was over with Cornwallis' defeat. Clinton showed up five days later, after the French fleet had left, but there was nothing he could do by then. He sailed back to New York, which the British continued to occupy until after the peace was signed in Paris in 1783, and that allowed thousands of Loyalists to escape to Nova Scotia. Incidentally, the last

British commander in the city was our old friend Guy Carleton, soon to be Lord Dorchester.

"Britain, negotiating from a weak position at the peace talks, recognized the independence of the American Colonies, and nearly gave them Canada, too, but the French, the canny French, persuaded her to keep your country, Fred and Josée, expecting that the Americans would not be satisfied with the boundaries that were agreed to. And they were absurd, leaving most of Lake Champlain in American hands, for example. Now, who in the family was involved in these campaigns?"

"Well, according to my granddaddy, Moses Bonney was with Washington to begin with, took a beating at Camden with Gates, was with Greene at Guildford Court House, then with Washington again at Yorktown. By then, he was a colonel."

I thought, again, 'I've been everywhere, man'.

"Josée? What can you make of that?"

"Nothing at this time of night."

"Heavens! It's midnight. Let's call it enough. Now, tomorrow, we are off to Savannah, Charleston, and Yorktown."

"But what about New York City?" Josée asked. "I wanted to shop and get my hair done, maybe go to a play."

"Oh, we are finished here," Dickie said with certainty.

Josée looked crestfallen, and I went to bat for her. "Forget about us. Jos and I are going to do New York City while you're gone. You can brief us when you come back." So Dickie and Joe-Bob went on their own to Savannah, Charleston and Yorktown, where they went over the campaigns there, and to Atlanta, where Joe-Bob was to 'tidy up' some loose ends in his businesses. The first morning they were gone, Josée had her hair done, emerging from the salon a Quebec-style dark red, and she said to me, "Now when you make love to me, you can pretend I am that girl you nearly went with in Quebec."

I was horrified. "I would never do such a thing!"

"Men do things like that, you know. Women too."

"You don't, when I make love to you, do you?"

She looked at me with a Mona Lisa smile. "Mon cher Fred, you are so naive. Now, help me find the nearest Catholic Church so I can go to mass in the morning."

I took her shopping after that, and spent the rest of my severance pay on two outfits for her, and in the evening we went to a play, a raunchy, brassy musical that made her laugh from one end of it to the other. And when we were back in our room again, she rewarded me with more passionate love, and I thanked my ancestors for giving me the prowess to keep performing night after night. And then I wondered what Dickie and Joe-Bob were doing about sex.

When our co-authors returned the next evening, they were still arguing about who forced Cornwallis to surrender, the Americans or the French. "Without the help and expertise of the French, including Bougainville, who must have relished his revenge on the British after marching up and down the St. Lawrence River in 1759 until he was exhausted, the Americans would never have won the war. Josée, I am pleased to see you looking rested - and what a becoming choice for a hair colour. Are you ready to start in again?"

"Merci et oui. But can we not find some love in this last part of the Revolution? Was Moses Bonney made of stone?"

"Say, my granddaddy told me Moses was wounded and taken prisoner at Camden, got patched up by a Loyalist nurse, talked her into changing sides, and got her to turn the other way so he could escape. After the war, he went looking for her, found her, and married her."

"Bien! Do you know her name?"

"Hannah, I think it was. Hannah Jackson."

And so we wrapped up the Revolution in a gossamer thread of romance. Over drinks later, I asked, "Dickie, Isn't it time to talk about Joel Bonney?"

"Yes, it is, Fred. Tomorrow morning we fly to St John, New Brunswick, the self-styled Loyalist capital of Canada."

Chapter 7.

The Rump

Saint John, New Brunswick, with a population of some 70,000 people, reminded me of the somewhat smaller Portland in Maine, with its old brick buildings, hills, and docks. But in Saint John, there were signs everywhere indicating pride in the city's Loyalist heritage, something which brought a frown to Joe-Bob's face.

We booked into a downtown hotel featuring a fitness centre, business services, and easy access to shopping. Then we gathered in Dickie's suite, where we listened to his phone conversation with Basil, who gave his love to Josée and his regards to me. Joe-Bob talked to him briefly after that, asking short, direct questions, until he seemed satisfied that the publishing company was going in the right direction.

Dickie wore his worried look. "I suppose we should get right to work. Basil was on about how the future of the company depends on us."

Joe-Bob ridiculed the idea. "Basil's got all he can handle at the minute. First off, we buy Josée something decent to wear, then we tour this place. I hear they have reversing falls, or something like that, and Jacqui's made us a tee time for this afternoon."

Josée wiggled. "I could use a casual suit for travelling." So we took her to a mall and found what she wanted, a white cotton suit with a blue sleeveless blouse from Dickie, with matching accessories from Joe-Bob, including a string of cultured pearls, and when she finished changing into her new things, we got a brochure from the desk, and followed the directions for a walk through the downtown core. I couldn't help but notice the difference in Joe-Bob since that day we walked in Duxbury. Now lean and fit, he looked properly like one of the 'Lords of the Earth', even though he still limped a little. He didn't complain about that any more, and he seemed genuinely interested, if disapproving, of the strong Loyalist flavour that was everywhere.

With a wrong turn or two, we found our way to the reversing falls on the St. John River that afternoon, where we jostled with bus loads of tourists, come, like us, to see this tide-driven natural phenomenon. As for the golf, it was a lovely day, the course was in fine, late summer condition, and we played skins for a dollar a hole, and it seemed to me at first as if we were all relaxed, like old friends, with lots of banter and teasing. I began to wonder if Dickie and Joe-Bob had fallen out of love with Josée, until I saw the look in their eyes when she waggled over the ball. That look preoccupied my thoughts so that I couldn't concentrate on the game, and I ended up paying them all money.

The fun was over. It was room service and work in the evening, and we started on the story of Joel Bonney and the Loyalists. "Fred, the ball is in your court," announced our leader.

"Alright. After the taking of Quebec and Montreal, Joel remained in the Provincial Regiment until 1760. Then, he went back to Connecticut, where he apprenticed as a millwright until 1762. In that year, he turned up in the Connecticut militia."

"Any interesting detail?"

"Just for your sake, Dickie, I can tell you that he was an Ensign in Captain Samuel Elmore's 9th company of Colonel Whiting's regiment."

"Demoted to Ensign, was he? Not from the soldierly side of the family," Joe-Bob needled.

"I don't know about that. Obviously, it was a short-term enlistment, because he was discharged on December the 4th. In 1763, he married Lydia Kenney of Scarborough, Massachusetts, and moved to northern Maine, where he helped found the town of Machias."

"Say, Fred, that's Matchias, not Makias. I happen to know, because I took my eldest son on a fishing trip there once." Joe-Bob wore a sad smile.

"If you say so. Lydia, unfortunately, died in childbirth, in December of 1764."

"What happened to the child?" Josée asked, showing concern.

"Named Lydia, after her mother, she survived. Within a year, Joel was married again, this time to Elizabeth Sprague, daughter of another Machias pioneer. They eventually had nine children, the youngest, Abiel, being my great great great grandfather."

"That's not a record for kids, so what's so interesting about all this?" Joe-Bob asked.

"I'm coming to the interesting part. Joel helped to build the first sawmill in Machias, and several more after that, but as the Revolution neared, he found himself, along with his second wife's family, part of the minority on the side of Great Britain. In June of 1775, some of the local radicals, anxious to show support for Boston, cut down one of the 'King's Trees', and stood it up like a spar in the town square."

"Let me explain what a 'King's Tree' was," offered Dickie. "All white pines over 23 inches in diameter were reserved to make masts for the navy."

Joe-Bob broke in. "Say, I never mentioned those 'King's Trees' as an American grievance, but they sure were. My family was involved in the lumber business in New Hampshire, now partners with Peter Warren, part of the deal he and Ichabod Bonney cooked up after they were at Louisbourg together. They had to leave those trees standing, the best ones there were, just in case some inspector showed up. Didn't make any sense. Could have logged them and sold them to the navy."

"At an exorbitant price," snorted Dickie. "That's why the British reserved them. Go ahead, Fred."

"A short time later, the British ship Margaretta under Captain Moore arrived in Machias to pick up spars for the navy. He ordered the tree in the square removed, but the townsfolk voted to leave it where it was. Moore, sensing trouble, left the next day, but Captain Jeremiah O'Brien and a crew of radicals went after him on the sloop 'Unity', and captured his ship. Moore was wounded in the fighting, and died in Machias the next day.

"Because of this action, Machias became the northern headquarters for revolutionaries, with supporters flocking there from Nova Scotia and elsewhere. In 1776, an unsuccessful attempt was made from there on Fort Cumberland, the former Fort Beausejour, by Colonel John Allan, the son of a former British soldier, and the revolutionary commander at Machias.

"Joel Bonney was logging on the Magaguadavic River in what is now New Brunswick in 1779. Because the Revolution had cut off trade with Machias, he was no longer able to get supplies from that place, and his family was in danger of starving. He therefore went to Machias, but was received with hostility, so he and his two brothers in law, Abiel and James Sprague, took their families to the Island of Grand Manan, right there off the coast of Maine. The Americans sent Indians to harass them, which led to a famous family story. It seems that the women were making soap when a party of Indians descended on them. You know how they made soap? No? With fat and lye. The women dumped the caustic lye on the Indians, who fled back to their canoes and never came back. The Americans then threatened the settlers on Grand Manan with dire consequences, and I have the letter that was written to them from Machias."

(On Public Service.) Machias, June 4th, 1779

Gentlemen - At a Conference with the Merrisheet, Penobscot, and Passamaquoddy Tribes of Indians, on the 28th May past, complaint was made by said Indians, That a Number of Inhabitants, Subjects of America, had Taken Possession, & where making Improvements on an Island call'd Grand Manan the property of said Indians.

Upon Examination It was found you & Familys had Done This & the most Evil Consiquences might be Expected from such proceedings.

You must know Gentlemen, That this Island has Accation'd much Dispute between the Court of France & the Court of Great Britain, in Former times, and now the Court of Great Britain claims it as theres as they say it Belongs to Accadia or Nova Scotia contrary to their Former claims. However let this be as it will, it was Left for the Benefit of the Indians, who had no Concern in the Dispute and who had the original right, in this Case it was Guaranteed to them by promise in Behalf of the United States, till a further Ditermanation of Congress or any other Sutable authority.

I do therefore Warn you to leave without Delay the said Island, as you will answer the Consiquence at your Peril, for a Breech of Treaty between the United States and said Tribes of Indians, and I have farther to Warn you That the Greatiest Threats is thrown out against you by said Indians, The Execution of which will not be in the power of the Superintendent & Agent to prevent.

Therefore if any difficulty befalls you or your Familys it will be your own faults as you now have Sufficient Notice.

I am, in behalf of the Continantal Agent,

Your verry humble Sarvent,

Lew's Fred'k DeLesdernier
A.D.C. and acting Secretary to the
Commanding officer of this Place,* &c.
To Messrs, Abial and James Spragues and Joel Bonny
now Inhabitants of the Island of Grand Manan
*Colonel John Allan

"As a result of this letter, Joel Bonney and his companions returned to the mainland of New Brunswick in the vicinity of Digdeguash, where they were able to survive the rest of the war, and they continued there after it, with Joel working as a millwright and a logger. He received a grant of land at Digdeguash in 1784, and the family name, though the short form, 'Bonny', is still preserved in a community on the Magaguadavic River. Just as a postscript, Britain used the occupation of Grand Manan by Joel Bonney and the others as part of its claim to the Island, but it wasn't until the treaty of Ashburton in 1842 that it officially became undisputed British territory. So that little Island, only about 53 square miles in extent, was an important part of family history."

Josée stopped typing for a moment, then, with dazzling speed, started in again. I opened my mouth to say something, but she cut me off. "I should have this part all done in an hour."

"But we really should go to Machias and Digdeguash before we finish it, shouldn't we? We might pick up some details."

Her fingers still flew over the keys while she looked at me. "I can add any details later."

Joe-Bob watched her with a look of disbelief. "Say, I never had a secretary who could type like that."

"Tomorrow, we'll visit Machias, etcetera, to pick up those details," Dickie pronounced.

That night, after our usual two drinks in the bar, Josée made love to me almost casually, and went to sleep immediately after, leaving me to wonder how long it would be before she left me for one of the others. It would be Joe-Bob, I guessed, with all his money. Dickie was too much of a gentleman - or was he?

Machias was just over 100 miles away, and we drove there the next morning, crossing the border at Calais, Maine. Josée was indignant when she heard it was pronounced 'Callous' by the Americans. "Vous sauvages!" Machias itself, a town of less than 3,000, was neat and tidy, its tree shaded streets lined with the white two storey, shingle or clapboard houses that dominate settlements on the northeast coast. The main point of interest was historic Job Burnham's Pub, now maintained by the daughters of the American Revolution. Outside it, we found a plaque engraved with the names of the town's founders, Joel Bonney among them, while inside, a dark haired young woman named Nancy took us through the rooms, describing the significance of the artifacts, and recounting the events that took place near Machias during the Revolution. For one thing, she told us that Burnham's Pub was where the radicals met to plot their strategy over tankards of beer. One other thing she told us got Josée's attention. In the days before Ben Franklin invented the stove, cooking was done over open fires or in fireplaces, and the second leading cause of mortality in women, after childbirth, was from burns suffered when their clothing caught fire. For that reason, they would wet their long skirts with water before preparing a meal.

Nancy was a beautiful girl, a fact not lost on Joe-Bob. "Say, little lady," he said to her, "this just a summer job for you?"

"Yes. I'm trying to make enough money to pay my tuition at college this fall."

"Are you going to make it?"

Nancy shook her head. "I don't think so. Then, besides the tuition, it would be nice to have a little money for fun."

"Let me help out. How about I write you a cheque for, say, five thousand?"

Nancy looked startled for a moment, then suspicious. "Oh, no, I couldn't let you do that."

"It's not for free. I want you to take a screen test in return. You interested in acting at all?"

"I haven't been, but for $5,000, I will be!"

Joe-Bob got out his chequebook. "Give me your name, address and phone number, and some of my people will be in touch with you in a few days."

We were back across the border in time for a late supper in St. Stephen, where Joe-Bob told us we had reservations for the night at St. Andrews, near the most famous golf course in New Brunswick. "And Jacqui wangled us a tee time for the morning."

"Oh, we haven't time for that," objected Dickie. "We must get on with the war of 1812."

"But Dickie," I pointed out, "there was a long period between 1783 and 1812. Surely we should bridge that period by describing what was happening in British North America."

"The rump of British North America, you mean. Then we best get started on that this evening."

"Say, Dickie, by the time we get settled in, there won't be any evening left. As one of the principal shareholders in Golden Lion Publishing, I declare a night off."

"Heavens, that's all we need, a shareholder interfering with the writing of the book. Fred, what do we still have to do to wrap up the chapter on Joel Bonney?"

"Find Digdeguash; drive up the Magaguadavic River to the settlement of Bonny River; go to Grand Manan Island."

"How long will all that take?"

"The ferry to Grand Manan takes about an hour and a half each way, so I guess we'd need a day for that, and maybe half a day for the rest, because it's handy to St. Andrews."

"So after our golf game tomorrow, we can do Digdeguash and Bonny River, work in the evening, then do Grand Manan the next day, and work in the evening. I shall have a tantrum if we are not then finished with this chapter."

At a fine inn near St. Andrews with all the luxuries we could ask for, including a spacious bar, we unwound from the day's travels. And that night, after another casual encounter with Josée, I had another of those vivid dreams, and in this one, I found myself in Job Burnham's Pub in Machias. A crowd of radicals was arguing with Joel Bonney and his Sprague brothers in law, while Mrs. Burnham, who was unquestionably Nancy, the girl who showed us around the place, poured pitcher after pitcher of water on her skirts. Captain O'Brien, the leader of the attack on the Margaretta, prodded Joel in the chest with a finger. 'It is time to choose sides. Either you are for us or against us.' And he took a large pull on a huge tankard of beer.

Joel, a tall, powerfully built man, dominated the scene. 'But you are asking me to fight against men I fought with at Louisbourg and Quebec. I cannot do that, old friend.'

'The time for friendship is passed. Go while you can, and do not chance this way again.'

Joel and the Spragues left and trudged off to the waterfront, where they climbed into a small boat already laden to the gunnels with their wives and dozens of children, and they rowed off into the choppy waters of the Atlantic Ocean.

The golf game the next day was magical, played in tattered tongues of mist coming off the Bay of Fundy, and accompanied by the bass notes of distant foghorns. In the four-ball match, I was paired with Josée, and I shot the best game of my life, breaking 80 for the first time. Joe-Bob complained about sandbaggers and porch-climbers, while Dickie insisted that I have a saliva test before they bought my lunch.

By contrast, the afternoon was largely a disappointment. The community of Digdeguash, for example, was now hardly more than a few scattered houses in the forest. Hoping for something more impressive at Bonny River, we drove up the narrow road beside the broad, placid Magaguadavic River, no doubt used by Joel Bonney to drive his logs to the coast, only to find much the same situation. We stopped at a bed and breakfast and asked the proprietors if they knew anything of the history of the place, to which they replied, no, they didn't, but they thought some members of the Bonney family lived at Quispamsis, a few miles north east of St. John. Dickie sighed in apparent frustration, but agreed that we should try to contact these relatives before we left New Brunswick. The slave driver had us in his room for supper, however, and we started to rebuild British North America from the ashes of the American Revolution. "Fred, the ball is still in your court," he pronounced.

"The most significant development for British North America was the arrival of the United Empire Loyalists, maybe as many as 100,000 of them, but more likely, about 70,000. Most of them settled in Nova Scotia, which at the time included New Brunswick and Prince Edward Island, while the rest went to Quebec. Joe-Bob?"

"At most, that's less than three per cent of the population of the American states, and the Loyalists were all people we were glad to be rid of. Tories, we called them, men who fought against us, Anglican clergy, and paid officials of royal governors."

"Yes, and you started confiscating their property as early as 1776."

"But when peace came, the United States agreed to restore property to any Loyalist who didn't actually fight on behalf of Great Britain."

"Did that actually happen?"

"Why, I'm sure it did."

"Whatever, the Loyalists arrived penniless, cold, hungry, and unwelcome. In the case of Nova Scotia, Governor Parr got rid of 10,000 of them by sending them to the valley of the St. John River, after expelling the Acadians who lived there."

"More persecution of the Acadians!" Josée noted grimly. "At least, the Governor of Quebec was more sympathetic. Frederick Haldimand, a Swiss-born Francophone, was appointed governor in 1778 after Carleton went to New York, and he protected the French by shipping the Loyalists out to the wilderness in the west."

"Not wanting to have the Loyalists complaining about popery or the French civil code," I said. "At the same time, he made a lot of enemies, like the New York Loyalist leader, John Butler. Haldimand accused him of committing atrocities during the revolution on his raids into Pennsylvania and New York, and refused to speak to him.

"The Constitutional Act of 1791, as passed in the British Parliament, split Quebec into two provinces, Upper and Lower Canada, thus reinforcing the gulf between French Catholics and English Protestants. At about the same time, New Brunswick was separated from Nova Scotia."

Dickie asked, "Fred, you have said that these Loyalists were unwelcome. Why was that, and what was done for them?"

"I guess they were unpopular because they made much of being loyal to the Crown, when, it was popularly believed, the majority of them just made a bad judgement call about the outcome of the Revolution. And it was necessary to look after them in the early stages. Only the army had the resources to do that. Military surveyors laid out tracts of land for them, and the army supplied them with blankets, tents, enough military rations for three years, implements, weapons, and so on. They were then expected to carve farms out of the wilderness and become self-sufficient."

"How much land did each man get?" asked Dickie.

"Many of the men were veterans, and so most areas were settled by regiments. Colonels and majors like you and Joe-Bob got 1,000 acres, captains got 700, other ranks and civilians 100, later increased to 500. The officers got the first pick of land, and were responsible for handing out supplies and weapons. Then there were the loyal Iroquois, mostly Mohawks, displaced from their ancestral lands by the Revolution. With much bitterness, they accepted resettlement along the Grand River and on the Bay of Quinte in what is now Ontario."

Josée asked, "Where did the Robinsons from Philadelphia end up, Fred?"

"The Robinsons were able to stay in Nova Scotia, settling in the Annapolis Valley, where Robert established one of the early orchards in the area. Not that their lot was an easy one. Like the others, they had to clear land of the native forests, and it took a year just to prepare one acre for cultivation. True, they could market the timber, which gave them some cash flow."

"Alright, then. I am ready to write about the arrival of the Loyalists." And Josée began to work her magic on the laptop.

That night, I was rewarded for my prowess on the golf course with passionate, not casual, love-making, and when we were finished, I made the mistake of telling Josée I loved her, and she told me to shut up, and said she would punish me double for saying it the next time we lost a match.

The morning of July 29th, Joe-Bob was already on the phone when Josée and I arrived at the restaurant. The conversation seemed to be laboured, with much repetition, and at times, Joe-Bob seemed exasperated, if not downright belligerent. At length, he hung up with a shake of his head but a grin on his face. "Josée, your little brother is now the president of Archambeault Plastics. I convinced old Archambeault to give up the position and concentrate on the chairman's job, but that wasn't easy - he doesn't speak a word of English, so Pierre had to act as translator. Got to make another phone call and get some money moving."

The day gave a mixed promise, half clear and half cloud, as we drove to Black's Harbour, just one of the numberless, rocky coves on the coast of New Brunswick, this one the terminus of the ferry to Grand Manan Island. The line-up of cars was long and more were coming, and after talking to some of the natives, we decided to park the van and go over as foot passengers. While we waited, I spent some time looking at maps and calculated that, if my dream were fact, Joel Bonney would have rowed about 30 miles to the Island from Machias. More likely, he crossed farther up the coast, where the distance was only eight miles.

The ferry, called simply the 'Grand Manan', announced its arrival with blasts on its whistle, and shortly afterwards slipped into its berth. We crowded aboard the utilitarian craft, hardly like the luxury vessel we took from Portland to Yarmouth. The seas of the Bay of Fundy were calm for the trip, and we could see the low hills and forests of Maine off to our right, and Campobello Island, where President Franklin D. Roosevelt maintained a summer home for years.

The ferry docked at North Head before noon, and Joe-Bob commandeered a taxi to take us to the town of Grand Harbour, the major settlement on the Island. Our driver turned out to be a Mrs. Brown, a pleasant looking, elderly woman who in earlier years had escorted Uncle Bill around. "Have you eaten? No? Then you will be wanting lunch. I'll take you to the best seafood restaurant in the Maritimes, right here on Grand Manan. You will need to spend some time at the museum after that, and I will take you to Bonney Brook, where Joel and the others lived for a year. Let me see. It's now a quarter of one. You will need to be back at the ferry dock in five hours." She was a delight to listen to with her New England accent, and all the local idiom that went with it.

Our lunch consisted of seafood rolls and the second-best clam chowder we had eaten on the trip, right up there after Hyannis on Cape Cod. The museum was close by, and I was pleased when the curator recognized the Bonney name, and exclaimed that most of what he had in local information came from Uncle Bill. He gave me a copy of the 'Grand Manan Historian', which contained a deposition signed by Joel, and a copy of the threatening letter he received from Machias.

Mrs. Brown reclaimed us at three, and took us to Bonney Brook on the Maine side of the Island, an unimposing trickle of water running through a landscape scalped of trees. Yet it was there that the soap incident occurred, and where the women of the family probably saved the whole clan from being murdered.

We said goodbye to Mrs. Brown at the ferry dock, leaving her, over her protests, a healthy tip for the extra attention she had given us. The light was fading by the time we got to the mainland, and was altogether gone when we arrived back at the hotel, but it was back to Dickie's suite and room service, and we edited far into the night. Then, only one thing remained to be done to complete the saga of Joel Bonney: a search for relatives at Quispamsis, likely to be a wild goose chase, Dickie complained, because there were no Bonneys listed in the phone book for that place.

Rain came the next morning, the down-east kind that can soak you in seconds. As we drove through it with the wipers barely able to cope, I reflected on the heritage the natives had left us in place names like Digdeguash and Magaguadavic, difficult to pronounce but unique, never to be confused with any other. We stopped to pay the toll on the highway bridge over the St. John River, near St. John, the city, not St. John's, the capital of Newfoundland, or St. Jean sur Richelieu. And so my mind rambled until we got to Quispamsis, just off the freeway to Moncton.

I asked the attendant at a gas station if he knew of any Bonneys in the area. He said no, he didn't, because he was new to the area himself, but he thought that Mrs. McConnell down the street might know. So we went to Mrs. McConnell's place and knocked, and eventually a tall, straight backed old woman came to the door, carrying herself with such obvious pride that I was instantly impressed. "What can I do for you?" she asked.

"My name is Fred Bonney, and we are looking for anyone by the name of Bonney in this area. Can you help us?"

She looked surprised, then smiled. "I'm Charlotte McConnell. My maiden name was Bonney. Do come in."

It took us only a minute to establish that we were related: her great grandfather was the brother of my great grandfather, Thomas. "The Bonneys never were the kind to maintain strong family ties," she said. "They were born wanderers, so it was typical, Fred, that your great grandfather found his way to

British Columbia. Our great great grandfather's three brothers moved back to the States, to Arlington, Massachusetts, and they all fought for the north in the civil war."

"Say, that's interesting. My great great grandfather also fought for the north. We're related, too, Charlotte, way back to the original Thomas who came over from Sandwich."

"Really? Oh, I'm so glad you came, all of you. I've found it quite lonely here since my husband died, and the children moved away. Let me get you some lunch."

"Let me help," Josée offered, and I hoped she would not be asked to do more than boil the kettle.

Charlotte looked at her closely. "You're French, aren't you?"

"Yes, from Quebec."

"Then I will have to watch what I say."

Josée looked at her steadily. "Whatever it is you want to say, don't let me stop you."

Charlotte returned her gaze. "Later, my dear, I will, as they say these days, let it all hang out. But boil the kettle for me, will you, while I whip up some sandwiches? And how about a little sherry first to celebrate the occasion?"

One sherry led to two, and Charlotte had a third, as she said, to loosen her tongue. "My husband was the editor of a newspaper in St. John, a successful man you would think, but he drank himself to death. There was nothing I could do to stop him."

It was obvious she blamed herself. I took a chance at being light. "You didn't nag him enough about his habit?"

She laughed. "I tried that, but it didn't do any good. It was a problem throughout his family."

Over lunch, we talked about Joel Bonney and his choice to remain loyal to the Crown. "But he went back to the States to die," I concluded.

"Yes," Charlotte said, "I remember that from what my father told me. He was a double-ender, then."

"What in heaven's name is a double-ender?" Dickie wanted to know.

"Here in the east, the border between Canada and the United States is pretty loose. All kinds of people wander back and forth across it, depending on economics, mostly. They are called double-enders. Who was it that said, 'One day British subjects, the next day citizens of the United States, as it best suits their purpose'?"

Joe-Bob looked appalled. "They don't take their citizenship seriously?"

"Not at all. That goes back to 1812, when New England virtually refused to support what they called 'Jimmy Madison's War'."

"It may go back farther than that," Josée suggested. "In the early days, there was much trade between the Acadians and the New Englanders. The Acadians called them, 'Nos amis, l'ennemi'."

"What a clever phrase!" Charlotte applauded. "But Josée, it is time to speak my mind, now that it is uncluttered by the sherry. You see, both sides of my family were United Empire Loyalists, and I am very proud of that fact. They elected to give up their birthrights, to come here and struggle and fight to remain British, to revere and salute one flag; yet we lost that flag, the old ensign with the Union Jack in the fly, because Quebec did not want to be reminded of the conquest. That was bad enough, but now, all around me, I see the Acadian flag flying instead of the Maple Leaf, I am subjected to the French language on road signs, on cereal boxes, and in the media, and my taxes go to support the bilingualism of this province and this country. It is as if the French won the wars between us, and I long for us to be simply English Canadian, if not British, again. Frankly, it has come to the point where I am seriously considering moving to the United States."

"And we would be proud to have you!" Joe-Bob exclaimed.

"We were here first," Josée said quietly.

Dickie tried to salvage the conversation. "Dear Lady, do not abandon us! The Indians were here before the French, and they are still here, are they not? Because I am British, I would, of course, be delighted if this country were as you would want it. At the same time, I can see that you could create in Canada the most extraordinary bilingual society, with tolerance the key word."

"What you say is true, but it does not satisfy this stiff-necked old woman. Both my daughters married Americans and live in New England, and they have been pestering me to come and stay with them. After this conversation, I am more determined than ever to go."

"Here is my card. Let me know if I can help you with immigration," Joe-Bob offered, and he kissed her on the cheek.

We checked into our familiar hotel in St. John for the night and wrote Charlotte into the story, not as herself, but as the despairing wife of one of the Loyalist settlers. When that was done, we repaired to the bar, and Dickie changed our course. "I think it is time we went to Newfoundland, tidy up that loose end before we go on to the War of 1812. Joe-Bob, I know you don't like surprises, but is your jet available tomorrow?"

"Dickie, it's a good thing you inherited your money, because if you tried to run a business, you'd go broke. Where in Newfoundland do you want to go, and when will we want to come back?"

"We should fly to St. John's, the capital, the scene of several clashes between England and France over the course of the colonial wars between them, and we can drive from there to Placentia, or as the French called it, Plaisance, although I'm sure there never was anything very pleasant about the place, particularly in the wintertime. For that, we will need two days."

"Alright. I'll get hold of Jacqui." Joe-Bob made the call from the bar, and, shaking his head, told us that the jet wasn't available until late afternoon the next day. Then he brightened. "Say, that will give us time for a game of golf."

The next morning, we played our game on the same course where I got skinned so badly before, and history repeated itself.

We were over Port Hawkesbury that afternoon when the starboard engine started to cough, and Josée gripped my arm so tight the blood almost stopped flowing to my hand. In a moment, the co-pilot came out of the cockpit with a reassuring smile on his face. "No need to panic. We'll sit her down at Sydney and find out what the trouble is."

The trouble, as it turned out, required parts to be flown in from Chicago, along with a qualified mechanic, which meant we weren't going to fly anywhere in the jet for a couple of days. "Say, that's not a problem," Joe-Bob shrugged. "We can take a sked flight or charter something, and the jet can pick us up when we're finished over there." He went into the terminal building and returned a few minutes later with a frown on his face. "Nothing available this evening."

"Dear, oh dear," Dickie moaned. "But I suppose we could take a room and get some work done on the War of 1812."

"We could go over the way the people do," I suggested. "By ferry."

"How long does that take?" Joe-Bob wanted to know.

"About eight hours, if I remember right. And I think one leaves just after midnight."

"But doesn't the ferry dock at Channel-Port au Basques, on this side of the Island? We'd be faced with a two-day drive to St. John's!" Dickie, all agitated.

"Well, I guess we could make it in a day if we had to, but we should take our time. There is more to Newfoundland that St. John's."

"Such as?"

"A marvellous golf course at Terra Nova National Park, for example, with good accommodation right there."

Say, let's do that one. Must be staterooms on the ferry? I'll get Jacqui on it."

We arrived at the ferry terminal in North Sydney in the gathering darkness, and were directed into one of the waiting lanes. Joe-Bob looked dubious. "Say, Fred, must be hundreds of cars here already. And look at all the trucks! All these going to get on? Hey! Here comes the ferry now! It's big, alright."

"This one's for trucks, and most of them will get on it, or at least the trailers will, plus they squeeze a few cars on as well between the trucks - that's for people who haven't got reservations."

For the next two hours, we watched the ponderous process of loading trucks onto the ferry, with Joe-Bob becoming more critical as the time wore on. "There has to be a more efficient way of doing this," he maintained. "First of all, those tractors they use for loading are too slow. Second, they have to back the trailers on most of the way. Who runs this operation, anyway?"

"The Federal Government."

"I should have known. No profit incentive. I bet there are a lot of complaints about the service."

"Yes, there are."

"And I can't understand it. They could be making a fortune from stateroom sales if they had more of them. They told Jacqui there was a waiting list of fifty. Anyway, I'll look after that when we get on board."

Someone knocked loudly on the door of the van, an official, I supposed, and I wondered what I had done wrong. I rolled down the window to look into the face of a man who obviously enjoyed his food and beer. "Good evening, folks," he began cheerfully. "Squeezin' Tom Yates here with a deal you can't refuse. Ten dollars apiece, two for fifteen, for the best music tapes to be had on the Atlantic coast. It's me and me darlin', Katie O'Grady, singing the songs of Newfoundland and Nova Scotia."

Joe-Bob reached into his pocket and came out with two twenties. "Say, that enough for two?"

In the garish amber light of the dock lamps, Squeezin' discerned that he had a considerable sum of money in his hands. "American, begod! Bless you, me son, bless you! That's worth six of me priceless tapes, but I've only got two different kinds, so that's what you'll get, along with my undying gratitude!" He handed me the goods, and with a cheery wave, went on to the next car.

"My word," Dickie chuckled. "What an odd character. Why does he call himself 'Squeezin'', Fred?"

"Probably because he plays the squeezebox, the accordion."

"Let's try those tapes out," Joe-Bob suggested, and I plugged one into the player. The music was hardly great, and it had a mournful quality to it that made us laugh, but it was fun to sing along with, and that helped to pass the time.

The truck ferry left at midnight. Half an hour later, our ship appeared ghost-like out of the Gulf of St. Lawrence, sure now to be over an hour behind time departing. When we finally got on board, we joined the crowds that were bedding down wherever they could find a spot - on the seats, on air mattresses on the floor - all, that is, except for the fortunate few who had staterooms. Those on the waiting list stood patiently by, hoping someone would change their minds and give up their reservations for the sake of the stiff charge. Joe-Bob stood with them for a few moments until he determined what the process was, then said in a loud voice, "Say, I need a couple of double berths, and I'll pay 200 American for each of them. Here's the money, right here, and it's yours if you want it."

I was embarrassed, and so too were Dickie and Josée, if I could read their looks. The three of us walked away, found a place to sit, and began reading the brochures on Newfoundland we picked up on the ferry dock. A few minutes later, Joe-Bob came up to us, the flush of success written all over his face. He crowed, "Say, I got us berths! Come on."

We looked at him for a moment, then resumed our reading. "Say, what's the matter with you people? I got us berths, didn't you hear?"

"Have a good night's sleep," I said.

"You telling me I've done something wrong? What? The people who took my money are happy."

"You used your wealth to jump the cue, old boy," said Dickie drily.

Joe-Bob looked at us for a moment, shook his head, and left. Five minutes later, he was back looking puzzled but resolute, with the keys to the two berths dangling from his hand. Next to us were two young families travelling together, the four children all snuffling and coughing from colds, the parents looking weary and careworn. Joe-Bob touched one of the fathers on the shoulder. "Say, you all look as if you could use some berths. I got a couple I just figured out I don't need. Here's the keys, and don't say no, or you'll make me feel bad."

The father looked dazed. "You sure? You're not fooling?"

"Sure as my friends here are trying to teach me some kind of lesson."

"I don't know how to thank you, except - you stopping in Gander anytime?"

"Fred, are we going to stop in Gander?"

"Probably Monday night."

"Then look us up," the father said. "We'll have a soiree for you that night. It's Shawn O'Brien I am, the last O'Brien in the Gander phone book."

The two couples, still looking a little uncertain, gathered their young ones and their belongings together, and as they were about to leave with the keys to their staterooms, O'Brien's wife gave Joe-Bob a hug. "Why," he exclaimed, "I never thought I'd turn into a philanthropist, but it feels good!"

None of us slept much that night, with the ferry rolling and pitching on the open waters of the Gulf. Joe-Bob dug some papers out of his briefcase that Pierre had given him: a summary of Canadian corporate tax laws; the same for the Province of Quebec; a prospectus on a new stock offering that Pierre thought was a sure winner. He read them quickly and efficiently, making notes in the margins as he did so. Occasionally, he would take off his reading glasses and let them drop to his chest, and he would sigh, or smile, or grimace, and I wondered what he was thinking. The grimaces, likely, were reserved for our tax laws. While he was thus occupied, the rest of us alternated between catnapping and reading, until Dickie said to me, "Fred, you said that there was much more to Newfoundland than St. John's. Tell us about it."

"Newfoundland? It's actually Newfoundland and Labrador, Labrador being a chunk of the mainland. The two pieces together are more than half the size of Texas, but have only a tiny population by comparison, half a million at most. The island of Newfoundland itself is a big, low-lying rock in the North Atlantic Ocean with a cool, wet climate, and icebergs drift by for much of the year. It was settled by fishermen from England, Ireland and France in the 18th century, who drove the native Beothuk Indians into the interior where they starved to death, died of disease, or were hunted down like animals. The main industry is fishing, especially for cod, but the stocks are dwindling to the point where the future of the fishery is in doubt, and unemployment is chronically in the 20 or even 30 per cent range. One bright light is the discovery of oil off the east coast of the island, which is currently being developed. There is very little agricultural land, mostly rock and bog with scrubby forests that still manage to support some pulp mills, and there are big populations of moose and caribou.

"Years ago, I brought the family over here for a vacation, and we drove up the Northern Peninsula, stayed in Gros Morne National Park - spectacular granite bluffs there - and visited the site of the Viking settlement at L'Anse aux Meadows. I recommend we at least go as far as Gros Morne. And to get the real flavour of the place, to hear the traditional Newfoundland accent, to understand the dependence of the people on the sea, we should visit at least one of the outports, the small villages that ring the coast. For that, I would suggest Twillingate. Besides that, we should go to Bonavista, where John Cabot landed in 1497."

Dickie looked distraught. "Do you realize that tomorrow, or I should say today, is the 1st of August? Gros Morne, Twillingate, Bona Vista, golf at Terra Nova! When I suggested we come to Newfoundland, I envisioned that we would simply fly to St. John's and drive to Placentia. Now, you propose wasting a whole week!"

"Sounds good to me," Joe-Bob grinned.

Josée waved a brochure. "There is what is known as the French Coast at Port au Choix, a few miles past Gros Morne Park. Have we time to go there?"

Dickie, with an emphatic series of movements, cracked open a map of Newfoundland. "A few miles? Good God, it's at least 100 miles past Rocky Harbour. Surely we aren't going past Rocky Harbour!"

The ferry docked at Channel-Port aux Basques too late for early communion, and that meant we had to lay over until after noon so that Josée could go to church. For the rest of us, there wasn't much to see in the small town, so we spent most of our time in the information centre. Joe-Bob monopolized the pay 'phone there, making calls to Basil, Pierre, and a host of other business associates, and when he was finished, Dickie phoned the Pattersons, our hosts on Lake Champlain. He came away with the news that Roger was on some new medication, which they hoped would help his condition.

With Josée back in tow, we drove to Gros Morne Park through the wilds of Newfoundland, past rocks and bogs and forests, past landscapes on the seacoast where wind-swept trees lay almost horizontal, past neat little villages, each with its own snug harbour with room for dozens of boats, and with houses that all looked as if they had been freshly painted. In the villages lived hardy, honest people with an accent forged of West Country English and the Irish brogue, who grew gardens on the side of the road miles from their homes, and piled up ricks of firewood in the middle of nowhere, both as safe for their owners as if they were guarded by armed soldiers. And we experienced the roller coaster ride up and down the stern, granite bluffs of Gros Morne, and spent the night in Rocky Harbour, where Dickie fretted because we wouldn't work on the book, and where Josée, excited as she nearly always was with new surroundings, made our night interesting.

We made Gander, with a population of 10,000 one of Newfoundland's bigger communities, in time for dinner the next day. I had spent some time at the airport there during my working years, and it was always a place I was thankful to leave in the winter months, because the weather could close in without warning and more than once, I'd been stuck there for days. We booked into the hotel I used to stay at, and I looked forward to a restful evening, but the others were all for visiting the O'Briens.

With Josée changed into her Acadian costume, we found their modest house on a back street. O'Brien himself welcomed us at the door, and introduced us to the dozen or more people inside, including his friends from the ferry, and a group of young men with musical instruments. O'Brien's wife shook our hands, and hugged Joe-Bob again, which he seemed to appreciate, no doubt because she had a buxom figure.

The young men tuned up their instruments - a fiddle, an accordion, a tin whistle, a guitar, and a set of drums - and began to play and sing the Celtic-inspired music of Newfoundland in a thoroughly professional manner. A big jug of rum appeared and was passed around, and not too long after, a second jug took its place, and then a third, and we all became mellow and friendly, and we joined in the singing of such Island favourites as 'I's the By that Builds the Boat', and 'I's the By that Sails Her', and 'We'll Rant and We'll Roar Like True Newfoundlanders'. And as the evening wore on, the music became brighter and faster, and O'Brien played the spoons, and he danced with Josée in the Irish manner, with much tapping of heel and toe, until the house shook, and the cheap chandelier in the living room swayed back and forth until I was sure it would fall.

Along about eleven o'clock, O'Brien's wife produced mountains of food including delicious fish and chips, and then the musicians asked Josée to sing something in French for them, and she did an Acadian folk song, and they quickly picked up the melody, and embroidered on it until it sounded as if they had rehearsed it for weeks.

Long after midnight, the musicians packed up their instruments and left, and we held a post-mortem with O'Brien over the last of the rum. "Say, O'Brien, those boys sure could sing and play. They under contract to anyone?"

"No, but they've cut a tape to try the market."

"You have that tape?"

"I do indeed, and I'll give it to you, and don't make me feel bad by trying to pay me for it."

Joe-Bob threw back his head and roared with laughter. "And that's what it's all about, isn't it?"

"That's right, a favour for a favour, and it's the least I can do to thank you, other than letting me wife hug you again."

"That'll be my pleasure. But how can I get in touch with those boys? Do they have an agent? I have a hunch they would go over really well on the Atlantic coast if not across the country, and I can help them out."

"Well, I've been looking out for them in a kind of way since they're all relatives, but I don't know a thing about the music business."

"Never mind. I'll get some of my people to contact you, and they'll make sure you're given a fair deal. Here's my card, and let me have one of yours."

"I believe you will look after us, but a business card? Why would I need such a thing? If anybody wants to get in touch with me, I'm the last O'Brien in the Gander phone book!"

Joe-Bob howled with laughter. "Tell that to someone in New York City!"

O'Brien didn't seem to get the joke, and asked, "Where are you headed now?"

"We'll drive up to Twillingate tomorrow," I answered, "then go on to Terra Nova Park, Bonaventure, Placentia Bay and St. John's."

"Placentia? Be sure to visit the fort there, what's it called, Castle Hill? Me kid sister is doing a skit there about the French times."

The road from Gander to Twillingate made an erratic beeline to Gander Bay, then wound past a succession of tiny outports with names like 'Clarkes Head' and 'Dormans Cove'. It strayed away from the sea here and there to cross a narrow headland, but always returned to it, the sea that in the beginning dictated the pattern of settlement and the source of livelihood on Newfoundland. Along the way, we stopped at Boyd's Cove to visit the Beothuk Museum, dedicated to the extinct aboriginal inhabitants of the Island. How sad, I thought, that not one of these people survived, not even by way of mixed marriages, a whole gene pool eliminated from the face of the earth. Joe-Bob was of the opposite opinion. "Say, now, that was the way to solve the Indian problem. Chase them away from the coast and the most of their food supply, then give them TB and smallpox."

Beyond Boyd's Cove, we left the mainland of Newfoundland and crossed on causeways to New World Island, the site of the town of Twillingate. With a population of 3,000, it was large for an outport, because it was also the commercial centre for a cluster of smaller communities nearby. We had lunch there, visited the museum, and drove out to the lighthouse at Crow Head, where the north Atlantic surged against the bluffs, and sent huge plumes of spray rocketing into the air. A long way off shore, the last of the summer's icebergs drifted southward, all spires and turrets like a castle, and we had a good look at it through Dickie's binoculars.

Terra Nova National Park was our destination for that evening, and we registered at the luxurious, many-gabled lodge by the golf course. Dickie wanted to do some work on the War of 1812, but we out-voted him because it was almost time for the bar. Not only that, but Josée seemed rather moody and not enthusiastic about the golf game tomorrow, and I realized she must be close to another period.

It rained on our game, but not enough to spoil it, a heavy drizzle at worst that didn't soak through our jackets. As for the results, Joe-Bob rescued Josée from defeat with a fine exhibition of shot-making whenever Dickie and I threatened to tie the match.

Later, we drove through the drizzle and low clouds on narrow, winding roads to Bonavista on the north east coast of the Island, where we toured Ryan's

Premises, the historic fish packing house, visited the statue of John Cabot, the first European to set foot on Newfoundland, and climbed up into the old lighthouse at the Cape. On the bluffs nearby, thousands of Puffins were nesting, quiet, gaudy little birds that didn't look sturdy enough to withstand the wild winds that came in off the North Atlantic. Back in our room at Terra Nova again, I comforted Josée as she suffered through the beginning of another period.

We took our time the next day, straying off the highway here and there to absorb the charm of the sea, the snugness of tidy outports on a 'tickle' or a sound, a cove or a bay, and we played the new tape, and sang along with it: 'Lukey's Boat is Painted Green': 'Billy Peddle': 'Black Velvet Band'. We visited Goobies and Come By Chance, and we narrowly missed a collision with a huge moose on our way to the Castle Hill National Historic Site at Placentia. At two in the afternoon, we caught the day's last performance of the skit O'Brien told us about.

The actors were amateurish on the whole, except for the Acadian boy playing the part of a priest, and Amee O'Brien. He had his lines memorized, and delivered them with fire and passion, while she, playing the part of a merchant's wife, came across like a seasoned actress. She was young and beautiful, and her performance was absolutely charming, whether she was pouting because of her outdated wardrobe or lusting after one of the other characters in the play. After the show was over, we mingled with the actors, and Joe-Bob had a talk with her. "Say, little lady, where did you learn to act like that?"

Amee laughed. "I've always liked to dress up and pretend. Now I'm studying fine arts at the University in St. John's, concentrating on drama."

"Can I help you with that? How much are your fees for the year? Will five thousand U.S. cover them?" And Joe-Bob took his chequebook from his pocket.

"Oh, I couldn't take it, not from a stranger."

"Hey, we really aren't strangers. I know your brother up in Gander real well. We've got a business arrangement going."

"Well, in that case." Amee paused for a moment and assumed a theatrical pose. "I am a poor girl, the kind who become victims of predatory men with money," she sighed. Then, looking at Joe-Bob archly, she murmured, "In return, would you want me to be your mistress?"

"Well, ha ha, say, now, I wouldn't mind that at all, but in return, I'd like you to take a screen test. I'll take your address and phone number, and some of my people will get in touch with you in a few days." He handed the cheque to Amee, and with a primp and a curtsy, she tucked it into her bosom.

"St. John's is one of the only two official cities on the island of Newfoundland, the other being Corner Brook on the opposite coast," I told the others as we neared the capital city. "With that distinction, earned because their populations exceed 25,000, both are policed by the Royal Newfoundland Constabulary, whose origins go back to the beginning of the colony's history. The rest of the Island is looked after by the Royal Canadian Mounted Police."

"Yes, Fred."

By the time we found our hotel in the downtown core it was nearly dark, and again, we staved off Dickie's attempts to work on the War of 1812, because of the lateness of the hour and Josée's lack of enthusiasm.

Our tour the next morning took us to Signal Hill, the historic site high above the narrow, rocky entrance to St. John's Harbour, where many colonial battles were fought, and where Marconi received the first transAtlantic radio signal. We had written already about the last military engagement between the French and the English in North America, which occurred on the spot in 1762, when Lieutenant Colonel William Amherst won the day. A short distance away was Quidi Vidi battery as reconstructed from the same time period, and a few miles beyond that was Torbay, the turbulent inlet where Amherst came ashore. In the afternoon, we went to the bluffs at Cape Spear, the eastern-most point of North America, where the full force of the Atlantic winds had shorn the vegetation away almost down to the bare rock, and where the whales played, and lashed their tails against the sea before sounding. As the light faded, we drove slowly back to our hotel in St. John's, I with some regrets, for there was much we would not see on this trip. Newfoundland is an empire in itself, one worth spending a month on, for around every corner, there is some natural or human wonder that will captivate. I was silently thankful that she had, in 1949, decided to join the Canadian Confederation at last.

The jet was waiting on the tarmac for us the next morning, and we flew to Toronto, where, our leader pronounced, "We will continue with the evolution of British North America after 1783, then travel around Ontario, or Upper Canada as it was, and a corner of Quebec, or Lower Canada as it was, to sites of important battles in the war of 1812."

"So, how big is Ontario?" Joe-Bob wanted to know.

I was prepared for the question this time. "More than one and one half times the size of Texas, but with only 60 per cent of the population, that is, about ten million. Most of the people live in the south-eastern quarter of the province, which is the industrial heartland of Canada now - produces as much wealth as the rest of the country combined."

'Toronto the Good', they used to call it, in the days when Ontario's 'Blue Laws' forbade shopping on Sundays. Now it was the largest city in Canada, a sprawling megalopolis with fiendish freeways, professional sports teams in American leagues, and every nationality on earth, probably, represented within its boundaries. And on Sundays, it was sin and shopping as usual.

Our hotel was close to the CN Tower, the tallest, free standing structure in the world, and from the top of it, we looked out on the flatness of the countryside, and the vivid blue of Lake Ontario. By his reaction, I guessed that Joe-Bob didn't want to believe that Canadians could build something taller than Americans. Back on the ground, we walked the few blocks to Toronto's City Hall, another architectural eye-catcher with its two elliptical outbuildings.

A few blocks in another direction was the Skydome, the only sports stadium in North America with a retractable roof, not to mention the hotel enclosed within it. As we stood outside, Joe-Bob said, "Say, I just have to see the inside of this place, and there's a football game on in there tonight. I've heard of the Canadian League, but not the teams that are playing - Toronto Argonauts and Saskatchewan Roughriders. But football is football. Fred, you suppose we could get tickets?"

"In Toronto, you can always get tickets to a Canadian Football League game. No doubt, you could get thousands if you wanted them."

"Is the football that bad?"

"No, but Toronto thinks they're big league. They want a team in the NFL."

"You all going to come?"

"Only on the condition that we get some work done first," Dickie said firmly.

"Ticket office is just inside. I'll be right back."

Joe-Bob returned in a few minutes with a broad smile. "Got us a box, no trouble, real reasonable. We have our own bar, and we can have dinner brought in."

Back at the hotel, we gathered in Dickie's room and advanced the book to the beginning of the war of 1812. "One thing the American Revolution did was to convince Great Britain that she should never again tax her colonies," Dickie began. "She also became convinced that she could not govern them without representative assemblies, because the Loyalists, used to having a say in their affairs, made that very clear to the governors. So did the many Americans who settled here a few years later when they were offered free land, land that had been bought by the government from the Indians for practically nothing. Colonel John Graves Simcoe, the first Lieutenant Governor of Upper Canada, was the moving force behind this wave of American immigration."

"I just don't understand it," said Joe-Bob, shaking his head. "We just finished gaining independence, and Americans were moving back under the British flag."

"Patriotism is skin deep, as the double-enders in the Maritimes demonstrate," Dickie observed. "One's stomach and the contents of one's purse often dictate one's loyalty. Go ahead, Fred."

"I should tell you that many of those American immigrants were religiously motivated and pacifist, like Quakers and Mennonites, and all Protestants other than Anglican, yet in this setting, Simcoe set out to establish an English-style society in Upper Canada. He had his surveyors lay out townships with two sevenths of the lots, in a random pattern, reserved for the Anglican Church, and he gave large tracts as well to prominent people, a kind of colonial gentry, who in return encouraged immigration and settlement. The land itself, as you saw from the tower, is flat and is of good agricultural capability, but what you can no longer see is that it was then covered with predominately broad-leaved forests.

"Dickie, you said that the British realized they had to allow representative government, but they were still not above making mistakes. They gave significant revenues directly to the governors and their appointed councils, which allowed them to act, to a great extent, without the authority of the legislative assemblies."

"Yes, Fred," added Josée. "This was especially unpopular in Lower Canada, where, in the midst of a French majority, the councillors were all of British origin."

"In spite of these difficulties," I continued, "immigrants came from Europe and the United States and cut down the forests to make farms, while Governors concentrated on building roads, canals, and schools to connect and service the developing areas of settlement. As the 19th century dawned, the British North American Colonies had a combined population approaching half a million, while the United States to the south had over seven million. Dickie?"

"As to the question of defence, Great Britain was entirely responsible for British North America, a not inconsiderable burden considering the geography of it. The most obvious and real threat was from the Americans, who viewed the 1783 Treaty of Paris, as the French had hoped, as nothing more than a truce. What made matters even more difficult for Britain was that in 1793, she became part of a coalition of European powers bent on the destruction of the French Revolution, and the resulting war, which extended into the Napoleonic Wars, did not allow her to station many troops over here, nor to keep up the walls and forts necessary for defence. As for the militia, it was supposed that the Loyalists would form the basis of a near-professional colonial force, but they were having such a desperate time surviving that most of them sold their weapons for supplies and seed. Furthermore, governors in Lower Canada were reluctant to arm the Habitants since their sympathies might be for Napoleon, while in Upper Canada, recent American immigrants began to outnumber the descendants of the Loyalists."

"That's it," Joe-Bob said, looking at his watch. "We need to get to the stadium so we'll be finished dinner before the game starts. Say, I sure am looking forward to this."

We had a couple of drinks before the steaks came, fillets of prime Alberta beef au jus, with baked potatoes from Prince Edward Island and green peas from Quebec. Joe-Bob exclaimed, "Why, I can't ever remember eating a better piece of meat." His was so rare it was in danger of jumping off his plate and escaping. The crowd, such as it was, filed in, and at eight o'clock, they played the National Anthem. Joe-Bob stood with the rest of us, looking awkward, until the last 'We stand on guard for thee' faded into the open sky above us. It was about then that he noticed the size of the field. "Say, Fred, I see two 50 yard lines. That can't be right."

"Yes, it is. The field is 110 yards long. The centre is therefore the 55 yard line, and our field is wider than yours as well."

"You mean you play a different game?"

"Watch and see."

The teams marched out on the field and deployed for the kickoff. "Say, there's too many men on the field - on both sides."

"No, 12 is right."

"Hey, the kick's in the air. Everything looks the same, now - people blocking, getting knocked down. Hey! Good runback!"

The defensive team lined up for the first scrimmage, a yard from the ball. "Hey, why are they so far apart?"

"That's the rules. Defence a yard off the ball."

"Hey, look, there's three backs in motion, and one's charging the line. And they snapped the ball! Penalty!"

"No penalty. Unlimited motion allowed in the backfield."

On that first play, the quarterback handed off to the fullback for five yards. Then he tried a pass, which fell to the ground incomplete, and he trotted off the field. "What the hell? He's only had two downs. Why's he going off?"

"It's a three down game."

The kicker hoisted the ball into the air, the receiver caught it in a crowd, and was immediately slammed to the ground. Flags flew in the air and the play was whistled dead. "Why didn't he call for a fair catch? And what's the penalty?"

"No such thing as a fair catch. Guy has to try to run the kick back, but nobody can come within five yards of him before he catches the ball."

After the next play, Joe-Bob asked, "Say, didn't they announce that Deevon Edwards caught that ball?"

"Wide receiver for Saskatchewan."

"Hey, I watched that cat play in college. Thought he might make the NFL. How many Americans are playing up here?"

"Twelve on each team. We call them 'imports'."

Before half-time came, I had to explain the single point 'rouge' to Joe-Bob, and why the team with the ball was allowed to get off a play at the end of each quarter, even when time was expired.

"Where did this crazy game come from? You sure didn't learn it from us."

"No, you learned your game from us. First one like this was played at McGill University in 1870." I couldn't remember the exact date, so I guessed.

"The hell you say."

"And a Canadian invented basketball, too."

"Come on. Next thing, you'll tell me you invented baseball."

"Nope. Abner Doubleday did that in the good old U.S. of A."

"You mocking me, Fred?"

"No, you're too big. But I fought above my weight once, and gave a big guy like you a black eye. Don't ask what happened to me."

"Actually," Dickie broke in, "this game, although very different, stems from rugby, or rugger, which, of course, originated in England. One of the most popular games worldwide, now. Thank heavens this silly version never caught on. The players look like men off the moon with those helmets and all that padding, and the action stops for minutes at a time."

"You ever play that rugger, Dickie?"

"Rather. When I was younger, it was a way of life. Nothing like a match on a Saturday, and then off to the pub for a few, and some good old rugby songs."

"Rugby songs?" Josée asked. "Sing one for us."

"Oh, Josée, they are for the most part so vulgar I wouldn't dare."

"I am a modern woman. Go ahead."

Dickie thought for a moment, then began to laugh until the tears rolled down his cheeks. "Oh, dear. The most polite one I can remember is frightful, but here goes. 'Rule, Britannia! Marmalade and Jam! Five Chinese crackers up your ass go bang, bang, bang, bang, bang!'" And he laughed again so hard it was infectious, and we all joined in.

The only thing remarkable about the second half of the football game was that it started to rain, and the retractable roof of the stadium closed. Half the crowd had gone home before the end of the third quarter, with the Argonauts on the short end of the score, but we waited until the final tackle was made, then walked back to the hotel through the rain for nightcaps and bed.

Josée was kind to me, and when we were finished, she asked, "Did you imagine I was that girl from Quebec?"

"No! I love you, not her."

"Shut up Fred, shut up."

"Did you imagine I was someone else, like Joe-Bob?"

"I will not say."

Incredibly, it was Sunday again, another week behind us, and Josée did her disappearing act in the morning. While we waited for her, Joe-Bob phoned half the people in North America, it seemed, and Dickie phoned the Pattersons. He hung up with a smile on his face. "Roger and Joyce are looking forward to meeting us at Ridgeway. They are starting up the Erie Canal for Buffalo day after tomorrow."

Josée was back for lunch with her serene look, and we started the afternoon off editing what we had done the day before, the lean years of the late 1780's when the Loyalists struggled to survive. "But it should not be supposed," Josée pointed out when we finished, "that the French, meanwhile, had disappeared. After the conquest, the fur trade was taken over by a number of small partnerships, and they continued to bring in pelts from areas not under the control of the Hudson's Bay Company. My ancestor, René, son of Marcel, was one of those partners."

"Josée, they weren't above a little trespassing, either, and that led to conflict with the older company," I added.

"As the case may be. There was also conflict between the small partnerships, which led to a number of murders."

"And the French were joined by Scots and even Americans, who formed the Northwest Company out of the small partnerships in 1776. Led by Alexander Mackenzie and Peter Pond, they forged a trade route up the St. Lawrence River, through the Great Lakes, and all the way to the Rocky Mountains."

"Each spring, a flotilla of canoes laden with trading supplies would leave Montreal for Grand Portage, at the western end of Lake Superior."

"Meanwhile, the 'Wintering Partners', as they were called, would bring the furs to the same place from the remote trading posts."

"When they met at Grand Portage, there was a party to end all parties, and it lasted for three weeks. The liquor flowed, and the Indian girls were accommodating."

"When the party was over, the Montreal flotilla would take the furs back to market, and the wintering partners returned to their posts with the fresh supplies."

"Aren't we getting ahead of ourselves?" interrupted Dickie. We should be getting on with the War of 1812."

"Dickie," I replied, "This is an important part of the history of British North America, and it happened before 1812. Mackenzie had to be one of the greatest explorers of all time. In 1789, he followed the river that bears his name all the way to the Arctic Ocean. In 1793, he became the first European to cross the North American continent north of Mexico, when he found his way from the Great Plains to the Pacific coast. In that same year, Captain Vancouver of the British navy mapped the coast from Washington State to Alaska. In 1808, Simon Fraser explored the river in British Columbia that is named after him, and in 1811, David Thompson followed the Columbia to its mouth. These explorations helped to secure our claim to these territories."

"Say, Lewis and Clark got to the mouth of the Columbia before that. I think it was in 1805."

"You know where President Jefferson got the idea for the Lewis and Clark expedition? He read Alexander Mackenzie's journals!"

"Oh, very well," Dickie capitulated. "How do you intend to develop this part of the story?"

Josée answered, "This fur trade was not for weaklings. Besides the canoes, supplies packaged into 90 pound bundles had to be portaged around rapids and falls, sometimes for distances of several miles, and the voyageurs would often have contests to see who could carry the most bundles. According to family legends, René was one of the strongest men in the trade, and one time, he carried five of those bundles around a waterfall."

"Say, that's 450 pounds. That's hardly possible, I'd bet."

"And they did bet. René made lots of money that way. By the way, few of the partners, other than René, were French. They were mostly transplanted Scots. It was the French, along with a few Iroquois, who did the work, paddled the canoes, carried them and the freight around the portages, put up and took down the shelters, and prepared the food."

"Did René get involved in those orgies at Grand Cache?" I asked.

"One must presume that he did. Perhaps he left some of himself behind in the way of children. If that is so, we, the family, are not aware of it. He did eventually marry and had six sons and six daughters, and after he left the fur trade, he became the owner of a successful hardware business. Oh, I should say also that he had a real gift for languages, seemed to soak up native dialects like a what-do-you-call-it, blotter, and that is why MacKenzie took him along during his explorations."

"Go ahead, then, Josée, and work the explorations up into the end of this chapter. When you are done, we shall finally, thank God, be able to get on with the war of 1812."

Chapter 8.

The War of 1812

Sunday evening in Dickie's room. My mind wandered for a moment, back to those Sunday evenings in the days of my marriage, when we would sit at the table, the four of us, two little girls and their parents, still dressed in our Sunday best. Beth would say grace, and I would carve the roast, being careful not to make the portions too large, for in those days, the roast had to last until Wednesday. Beth always made it interesting, that roast. On Mondays, it might be hot beef sandwiches; on Tuesdays, it could be beef stew; on Wednesdays, like as not, it was hamburgers made out of the ground-up remains. There never was any sex on Sunday nights, and seldom before the roast was gone, but there was always love and affection, even after Beth got cancer, and there was no sex at all. Was I any better off now than I was then? I looked at my companions, a kind of family in a way, all Bonneys, one way or another, the three men in love with the one woman, if what Joe-Bob experienced could be called love.

"Fred?"

"Yes Dickie. I'm here."

"You looked as if you were miles away. How many times have I said we must get on with the war of 1812? The time has finally come. First, we should examine the causes of the war."

"Say, I can do that for you, Dickie. You arrogant Brits were behaving as if you still ruled us."

"I suppose we were, you overbearing Yank, but we had been in a death struggle with France since 1793, first with the butchers of the French revolution, then with Napoleon Bonaparte."

"That didn't justify your actions toward us. You were stopping, sometimes attacking our ships so you could search for deserters from your navy, you were supplying arms to the Indians and supporting their claim to an independent state west of the Appalachian Mountains, and you were blockading European ports, seizing any of our ships that tried to get through. If those aren't causes for war, what are?"

"But we largely rectified these irritants. Shortly after you declared war on us, we cancelled the orders in council authorizing search and seizure of your ships, for example. Greater damage was done to your interests when you closed your ports to British shipping, for that allowed your smugglers to have a field day, taking goods to free ports in British North America such as Halifax and St. John, where they were loaded onto locally built cargo vessels."

"Dickie," I threw in, "that smuggling gave a boost to the timber and ship-building industries in Nova Scotia and New Brunswick, and they got another boost when Napoleon blockaded ports in the Baltic Sea, thus cutting off Britain's usual sources of timber. Between 1804 and 1809, timber exports increased 1,000 per cent, and the first fortunes outside the fur trade were made in British North America."

"Yes, yes, Fred. As for the Indians, Joe-Bob, we had abandoned our far western posts where we had been giving them comfort and hope for that homeland beyond the mountains. Besides, you had largely cured the problem yourselves by crushing the Indians at the battle of Fallen Timbers in 1794, and crushing them again at Tippecanoe in 1811."

"There was one Indian we didn't get, and that was Tecumseh, and he was trying to unite all the tribes against us."

"That is true, but let us not get ahead of ourselves. You say you felt yourselves aggrieved by our actions, but let us look a little deeper into your motives in declaring war. The doctrine of 'Manifest Destiny' was one of those motives, the belief that Americans would one day possess all of the continent, and included in that motive was the lure of all that good land in the Canadas. As one cynic put it, 'Agrarian cupidity, not maritime rights, directs the war'."

"Dickie, what is what-do-you-call-it, cupidity?"

"Josée, that is avarice, or greed, or an inordinate desire for wealth."

"Greed I can understand. What would have happened to the people in the Canadas who already had some of that land?"

"Why, we would have respected their rights to that land. That's what we told the people."

"I wonder," I disagreed. "Maybe you would have driven them off into the wilderness like the Indians, and then harassed them all the way across the continent until they drowned in the Pacific Ocean."

"Fred, that's not a kind opinion to have of Americans."

"It was you who said you would do the same thing to the poor in your own country - drive them out, get rid of them."

For once, Joe-Bob was speechless.

"We are getting off the track here," complained Dickie. "Joe-Bob, give us the American perspective on the war."

"Alright. I guess we thought it would be a piece of cake. President Jefferson himself said, 'it is a mere matter of marching'. Henry Clay of Kentucky, speaker of the House and leader of the American War Hawks, said 'the militia of Kentucky are alone competent to place Montreal and Upper Canada at your feet'."

"And so, being over-confident in typical American fashion, and still believing in citizen-soldiers, you sent old militia generals against us, relics of the Revolutionary War, one so grossly fat he scarcely could mount a horse."

"Jesus, God, Dickie, I hate it when you are so arrogantly right. The old generals were among those who counselled the next President, Jimmy Madison, to go to war. In January 1812, he authorized an increase in the regular army to 35,000 men; in the next few months, 10,000 militiamen were called up, and another 50,000 short-term volunteers were signed up. Finally, on June 18, he declared war on Great Britain."

"But there was general apathy about the war in your country, so that you had to offer a bonus in order to encourage your young men to sign up. And as Charlotte told us, New England did not support the war at all, even though some of its ships had been seized by the British. The Lieutenant Governor of Nova Scotia, Sir John Sherbrooke, was quick to recognize this, and he made a de-facto peace with the states concerned. Neither did those states seem to mind when Sherbrooke invaded Maine later in the war, and occupied much of it until peace was signed."

"My ancestor Judson in New Hampshire was disgusted with the attitude of New Englanders, and he ran off to join the New York militia."

"Yes, Joe-Bob. And now, we should move on to the conduct of the war. There were hardly more than 5,000 regular soldiers in the Canadas, some of whom were fencibles."

"Dickie, have pity!" Josée pleaded. "Fencible?"

"My dear Josée, a fencible was a soldier who volunteered to fight only in North America. A regiment of this type from Newfoundland was stationed in Lower Canada at that time. To go on, there was, in addition, the militia, but as we have discussed, they were underarmed, and in fact, most of them were not embodied."

"For God's sake, Dickie, I thought we had cured you of military detail," I objected. "Is this necessary to the story?"

The hurt look. "Well, I believe it is necessary, and so let me finish. Some militia were embodied, which meant they were in training; some were select-embodied, which meant they were actually in service, then there were the flank companies, invented by Isaac Brock. Oh, but we haven't even talked about him yet.

"Let me introduce to you Isaac Brock, popularly known as 'The Hero of Upper Canada'. He was a huge man for his times - over six feet tall - massive build - blue eyes - reddish-blond hair - born into a military family on the Island of Guernsey in 1769, the eighth of nine sons, not to mention his four sisters. He grew up to be a champion swimmer and boxer, and his other pursuits included sailing, fishing, hunting, and reading. He was fluent in French, having learned the language in Rotterdam during his years in school, and that would prove to be an asset for his service in the Canadas.

"At the age of 16, he became an Ensign in the 8th Regiment of Foot; in 1789, at age 21, he was a Captain in the 49th Regiment of Foot, and was sent to Barbados. There, he survived a duel, but not the fever, which was rampant in that part of the world, and he was sent back to England in 1793 to recuperate. By that time, England was at war with France, but Brock, because of his illness, could only look after the regimental depot. As was the custom of the day, he bought his major's commission in 1795, and when his regiment returned from Barbados in 1797, he was promoted to Lieutenant Colonel."

"Say, not bad for a soldier who hasn't fired a shot in anger yet. Or did he, in that duel?"

"No, not even in the duel. He made his challenger back down by insisting they fire pistols at each other over the width of a handkerchief."

"Over the width of a handkerchief? You mean, they would have been only a few inches apart?"

"That is correct. To carry on, it was in 1797 that Brock justified the faith his superiors had in him. First, he nipped a simmering mutiny in his regiment in the bud, and then he fought with distinction against the French at the battle of Egmont-op-Zee. For that, he was made the senior Lieutenant Colonel of the 49th. His next action was at Chagen, Denmark, in 1801, and while no land forces were involved, he found his model in the young naval officer, Horatio Nelson, who later would defeat the French at the pivotal battle of Trafalgar. Nelson pretended he didn't understand his superior's instructions to break off a furious naval engagement with the Danes, and he eventually bluffed the enemy into surrender.

"Like all keen officers of the day, Brock dreamed of battling Napoleon, but those hopes were dashed in 1802 when he was sent with his regiment to the Canadas. And there he was to remain, apart from a period of leave, until his death. Between 1802 and 1807, he alternated between Quebec City and the sparsely populated backwoods of Upper Canada, where his chief concern was keeping the members of his regiment from deserting to the United States."

"By this time," Josée interjected, "he was 38, and still no hint of romance?"

"My dear Josée, none, although the records suggest he was always welcome at social events in Quebec City."

"He must not have been normal."

"Be patient. With the retirement of Governor Haldimand, Brock found himself, a mere colonel by this time, in charge of the defences of all British North America, or, rather, the Canadas, Upper and Lower, and possibly New Brunswick, because the navy out of Halifax looked after the rest. One of the things he did during this period was to strengthen Quebec's defences, such as establishing the Royal Battery of 36 pound guns that could fire on Levis. Never again would an invading army be able to shell the city from there unchallenged, the way Wolfe did."

Josée resumed. "In 1807, the new Governor, Sir James Craig arrived, a complete contrast to the benevolent Haldimand. By his own admission, he tried to 'sink the French' by allowing English-speaking immigrants into the Eastern Townships, and he suppressed dissent ruthlessly."

"The Eastern Townships?" Joe-Bob queried.

"That part of Quebec, or Lower Canada as it was, that lies south of the St. Lawrence River. Dickie?"

"In his defence, Craig did not trust the Canadiens, or 'Habitants', as some of them called themselves, and was concerned that, should a French fleet come sailing up the St. Lawrence River, they would immediately rebel in support of Napoleon. By this time as well, war with the United States was looming. Craig kept Brock in Quebec City, knowing a good officer when he saw one, and was partly responsible for having him commissioned a brigadier in 1808.

With the deteriorating relations with the United States, Brock was sent back to Upper Canada in 1810 as Commander in Chief of the armed forces there. In June of 1811, he was promoted to Major General, and became the Acting President and Administrator of Upper Canada. The forces under his command at that time consisted of about 700 regulars, and a neglected militia with no weapons. Craig, like Haldimand before him, was afraid to arm the citizens, because so many were of American origin."

"It is my turn again," asserted Josée. "In 1811, to the relief of Canadiens, Craig became ill and returned to England, to be replaced by Lieutenant General Sir George Prevost, who soon corrected many of Craig's wrongs."

"Remember the name Prevost? Sir George, born in what would become the United States, and still with many friends there, was the son of Major General Augustus Prevost of Georgia infamy. Despite his years of satisfactory service in the West Indies, both as an officer and a governor, Sir George was a timid man, small in stature and mind. In relation to Brock, he played the same part as Gates did to Arnold: jealous of his subordinate's success, but quick to take credit for it. Prevost never was branded a traitor, but he showed a great reluctance to meet the Americans in battle."

"Say, let me tell you about the American commanders. Major General Henry Dearborn, the one who could hardly get on a horse, was in charge of the Northern Department. Under him were the militia officers Brigadier William Hull, Brigadier Stephen Van Rensselaer, and Brigadier Wade Hampton. Dearborn was eventually replaced by Major General James Wilkinson, a damn traitor, in league with the Spanish, and Hull was quickly replaced by Major General William Harrison, the Governor of New York."

"Thank you, Joe-Bob. We should now return to Brock and his difficulties. When war was declared, Prevost and others were convinced that Upper Canada would fall easy prey to the Americans, whose obvious strategy would be to take Montreal and Quebec. That, obviously, would cut off the lifeline from Great Britain to the Upper colony by way of the St. Lawrence River. For that reason, Brock was only given an additional 500 regulars and fencibles, bringing his strength up to about 1,200, while the remaining 4,000 battle-ready troops were held by Prevost.

"Now Brock, with his own flair and dash, and the example of Nelson in his mind, planned to keep the Americans off balance with a series of raids on key targets."

"You asked me to be patient," Josée reminded Dickie.

"Oh, yes, romance. From the time of his appointment as temporary President, etcetera, of Upper Canada, Brock often visited the home of Adjutant General Aeneas Shaw, and spent much time with Shaw's daughter, Susan, or Sophie, as some claim. It was rumoured they were to marry once the war was over."

"Normal, after all! But a tragedy is in the making."

"Yes, Josée. But Brock did not let love cloud his brain. He bought corn and flour in the United States to stock up the colony's larder, and the American farmers were only too glad to supply him in return for British gold! Joe-Bob? No reaction? As for the Upper Canada militia, on paper it was 11,000 strong, but Brock was convinced that no more than 4,000 would fight for Great Britain. In addition, the Assembly of Upper Canada, dominated by immigrants recently arrived from the United States, refused to give him permission to call up the citizen soldiers. In the circumstances, Brock could only, as he said, 'look big and talk in a loud voice'. After much wrangling, he devised an ingenious solution, convincing the assembly to allow him to train 2,000 militiamen, who would be formed into 'flank companies' to support the few regulars he had."

"Say, that obvious strategy you talked about earlier, Dickie, attacking Montreal and Quebec to cut off supplies to Upper Canada, was not obvious to the Americans. The Secretary of War, John Armstrong, bought Dearborn's four pronged plan, to invade Upper Canada at Detroit, Niagara, and Kingston, as well as Montreal in Lower Canada."

"Dear, oh dear. A four pronged plan."

"As a matter of fact, the whole idea of the war was taken too lightly. Just as an example, the Congress bought the over confident rhetoric of the war hawks, and slashed appropriations in half. Anyway, as part of Dearborn's plan, Brigadier William Hull was sent to Detroit with 2,000 men, and he crossed the St. Claire River into Upper Canada on July 12th, 1812."

"Big, red-faced Hull, who only learned of the war on July 2nd because his dispatches had been captured and sent to Brock. Imagine the humiliation, Joe-Bob! The US ship 'Cayahuga', carrying the dispatches and a military band, is intercepted by the 18 gun British sloop 'Queen Charlotte'. Our lads board, seize the dispatches, and force your band to play 'God Save the Queen'!

"Jesus, God, Dickie, there you go again!"

"Hull issued a typically bombastic American proclamation when he arrived in the Upper Canadian town of Sandwich, yet another Sandwich over here. Perhaps, Joe-Bob, you should read it out to us."

"I don't think it was bombastic. He thought the people, because so many had their origins in the United States, would join him. What he said was, 'Many of your fathers fought for the freedom and independence we now enjoy. Being children, therefore, of the same family with us, and heirs to the same heritage, the arrival of an army of friends must be hailed by you with a cordial welcome. You will be emancipated from tyranny and oppression, and restored to the dignified station of free men . . . I come prepared for every contingency, I have a force which will look down all opposition, and that force is but the vanguard of a much greater . . . The United States offer you peace, liberty and security . . . Your choice lies between these and war, slavery and destruction. Choose, then, but choose wisely.'"

"Bombastic or not? I rest my case. But to carry on. On July 27th, 1812, Brock dissolved the Upper Canada Assembly, declared martial law, and went to Fort George at the eastern end of Lake Ontario. Meanwhile, the Iroquois had declared neutrality, and the other Indian tribes were sitting on the fence, waiting to see which way the war might go - all, that is, except Tecumseh. He and his Shawnees were still smarting from the defeat the Americans gave them at Tippecanoe, and thirsting for revenge.

"Brock was sure he would need the Indians as allies, and he planned a pre-emptive strike, without the approval of Prevost, to secure their loyalty. He instructed Captain Charles Roberts at remote Fort St. Joseph, on the north shore of Lake Huron, to capture the American fort at Michilimackinac, on an island to the south."

Josée stopped typing. "Mishili-what?"

"M-i-c-h-i-l-i-m-a-c-k-i-n-a-c."

"Merci."

"Roberts took the fort on July 17th with only 46 regulars, aided by some 180 fur traders and Indians. This tiny victory had the effect Brock was looking for."

"I don't understand it. Lieutenant Porter Hank was in charge of Michilimackinac. He had 61 men and a good, stout fort, with cannon. He surrendered without firing a shot, and for that, he was to be court martialled. Anyway, Hull later wrote, 'As a result of Michilimackinac, almost every tribe and nation of Indians . . . excepting a part of the Miamies and Delawares . . . joined in open hostility, under the British standard, against the army I commanded, contrary to the most solemn assurances of a large portion of them to remain neutral . . . '"

"On the morning of August 6th, Tecumseh ambushed a mail escort from Detroit, and captured Hull's dispatches. The extraordinary thing about the engagement was that the Indians fired only 26 shots, but killed seven officers and ten men, and wounded 12 others. This show of marksmanship completely un-nerved Hull, and on August 8th, he withdrew to Fort Detroit."

"Hull was terrified of the Indians, and his men thought he was a coward."

"Brock arrived at Fort Malden at the head of Lake Erie on August 13th, after the usual arduous, week long journey from Fort George by boat, on foot, and on horseback. And that is where he met Tecumseh for the first time. He was much impressed, describing him in these terms: 'A more sagacious or more gallant warrior, does not, I believe, exist'. Tecumseh promised to obey the rules of war, and to keep his warriors from drink, and Brock welcomed him as an ally.

"Brock, with the example of Nelson in mind, and aware that Hull was terrified of the natives, particularly Tecumseh, next set about to bluff his opponent. On August 15th, he mounted an artillery barrage on Fort Detroit, then sent an escort under a flag of truce to demand its surrender. Hull refused. All that night, Tecumseh and his warriors danced to the beat of drums on Bois Blanc Island in the Detroit River, and the noise wafted across the waters to Hull in his fort. Early on the morning of August 16th, armed with a map drawn on birchbark by Tecumseh, with 3 six pounders and 3 three pounders, or grasshopper guns, and supported by the 18 gun sloop Queen Charlotte, and the 12 gun Brig General Hunter, Brock crossed the river with 300 regulars, including 250 men of the 41st regiment, and 50 from the Royal Newfoundland Fencibles."

"No, Dickie."

"I insist. He also had 400 militiamen who were disguised in old red army tunics to make the Americans think they were regulars, and he was supported by Tecumseh and his 500 or 600 warriors, depending on which account you read. On the assurance that he would be spared from the Indians, poor, frightened Hull gave up after only a two hour bombardment. The only good news, perhaps, was that Porter Hank, awaiting court martial for surrendering Michilimackinac, was killed by a direct hit on the guardhouse."

"What a spineless excuse for a soldier Hull was! Fort Detroit was one of the strongest frontier posts in America. It was over an acre in size with palisade, ramparts, bastions, glacis, and forty cannon, all surrounded by a deep, wide ditch."

Joe-Bob was beginning to sound like Dickie.

"He should have attacked Brock, rather than the other way around. His officers were beside themselves, but there was nothing they could do. Hull was later court martialled and sentenced to be shot, but he was let off because of his revolutionary war record. Dickie, I hate to hear what you're going to say next."

"The British took over 2,000 prisoners, 39 field pieces, not counting the cannon mounted on the walls of Fort Detroit, and enough muskets to arm the Upper Canada militia. More importantly, the victory at Detroit convinced many doubters that Upper Canada could be defended against the Americans. And as a postscript, Brock sent the captured regimental colours of the 4th U.S. Regiment, the one responsible for Tippecanoe, to Prevost, and gave his scarlet sash to Tecumseh. Let's call it a night, then."

Over drinks, we plotted up our next moves. "Joe-Bob," Dickie began, "we should at least fly over Michilimackinac, or Mackinac, as it is now known. At the same time, we can gain an appreciation of the Great Lakes and the country adjacent, essential to an understanding of the 1812 war. Can we do that tomorrow? Then we should go on to Windsor and Detroit."

"Jet's laid on. We'll check out in the morning, rent a car here, and park it at the airport while we're off on our flight." Joe-Bob was organized, no question.

A north wind was blowing when we took off, pushing the industrial smog back to where it came from, thus giving us a cool, brilliant day. I had never really thought much about the Great Lakes before - oh, I flew over them many times during my working years, but they were just part of the scenery. Now, from the windows of Joe-Bob's jet, I began to appreciate how huge they were. Along with the connecting rivers and the canals and locks of the St. Lawrence Seaway, they opened up the whole eastern half of the continent to commerce. Dickie brought into focus for us their importance in the war of 1812.

"Whoever controlled the Lakes had a huge tactical advantage in the movement of men and supplies. As the war developed, the United States gained undisputed control of Lake Erie, and that made the British position there untenable, as we shall see. Lake Huron remained a backwater of the war, but for what it was worth, the British maintained control of it. Lake Ontario was where the bulk of the action was, and a furious shipbuilding race there by both nations resulted in more or less of a stalemate. Ah! There is Mackinac Island off to the left."

We swung around over the island, a speck in the blue waters of Lake Huron, and headed south to the wedge of Ontario, or Upper Canada as it was, its point the southernmost part of Canada. Jacqui served lunch when we turned east to fly down the middle of Lake Erie, while Dickie pointed out a cluster of battle sites in the Detroit area, and others around Niagara Falls. On we flew over Lake Ontario, down the St. Lawrence River to the Quebec border and beyond, until there were no more battle sites on the ground below us. "And Fort York," Dickie concluded, "which is now Toronto. But we must keep everything in order, and Fort York comes later."

"How far did we fly altogether, Joe-Bob?" I asked, when we got back to Pearson International Airport.

"Pilot says about 3,000 miles."

We caught the 401 near the airport in our rented van, and joined the madhouse of transport trucks and passenger vehicles, all driven by maniacs darting from one lane to the other, with one foot on the accelerator and the other on the brake. Joe-Bob was impressed. "Say, this is just like the States. You've done a good job on this highway." That was a matter of opinion.

At London, we branched onto the 402, which took us to the petrochemical complex at Sarnia and the broad, flat St. Claire River, which forms part of the border between Canada and the United States. From 130 kilometres an hour, I slowed down to 40, and we meandered down the St. Claire Parkway, surely one of the prettiest drives in all of North America. Amongst stately broad -leaved trees on the Canadian side were large estates with houses to match built of brick, and Josée proclaimed she would be willing to live in any of them. Here and there were places where we could pull over and park, and we stopped several times to admire the river, and to watch the long, narrow tankers heading upstream for Lake Huron, or downstream for Lake Erie.

The St. Clair River; Lake St. Claire; the Detroit River; all the same water, draining out of Lakes Superior, Michigan and Huron, the road west that the voyageurs followed, and before them, the Courier-de-Bois, and before them, the Indians. From the windows of our hotel in Windsor, we could see the river and the city of Detroit on the other side, where Louis Bonin and his half-Bonney wife lived out part of their history.

"His work done here," Dickie told us over a late dinner, "Brock left Colonel, later Major General Henry Proctor in charge at Detroit, and returned to York. On the way, on the vessel Chippewa, Brock was heard to say by an officer of the York militia, 'If this war lasts, I am afraid I shall do some foolish thing, for I know myself there is no want of courage in my nature. I hope I shall not get into a scrape'. That quotation is at odds with others, such as that recorded by my ancestor, Major John Bonney, who served with Brock. In his diary, he quoted Brock as saying, 'If I fight and live to die an old man, no one will remark my passing; but if I die gloriously in battle, perhaps they will erect a splendid monument in my honour'. Which was the real Isaac Brock, do you think? We must take a position in the book, one way or the other. But enough of that for now.

"Curiously, Brock took Detroit while a cease-fire was in effect, as arranged on August 9th by the timid Prevost and the obese Dearborn. Brock had no way of knowing this, as news could only travel as fast as a ship could sail, or a man could ride. The cease-fire continued until early September when it was rejected by President Madison, but while it lasted, it forestalled Brock's plans to attack Sackets Harbour, the American Naval Headquarters on Lake Ontario, and Fort Niagara at the head of Lake Ontario, just across the Niagara River from the British Fort George. At the same time, it allowed Dearborn to reinforce his commanders in the field. Prevost even apologized to the Americans for the fact that Brock had pursued Hull into the United States, and ordered him to evacuate Michigan. Brock had the good sense to ignore the order."

"Why the cease-fire?" I asked.

"As I said earlier, the orders in council authorizing search and seizure of American vessels had been repealed, and Prevost thought that might be cause to end the war. That little weasel of a man! When news of the victory at Detroit reached London, Brock was knighted, and Prevost quickly took the credit!

"Tomorrow, we will visit Fort Malden and then go on to Queenston, where another pivotal battle in the war of 1812 was fought, and where Brock's fears and hopes were realized."

I had seen only one picture of Brock before, a profile of the head and upper body suggesting that he was massive, dark-haired, and stern, and had a protruding lower lip. That impression was dispelled the next morning when we visited Fort Malden. Military museums were becoming old hat to us by now - weapons, artifacts, uniforms, and paintings displayed in old forts, or in premises built for the purpose, as was the case here. It was the lone picture of Brock, facing ahead, that made this museum different, at least for me. As Dickie had suggested, he had reddish-blond hair, and the artist had captured a twinkle in his blue eyes, and an almost mischievous smile on his lips. I felt the same kind of fascination looking at this great soldier as I felt at Grand Pré when I stood before the statue of Evangeline, and I wondered if Brock had, as legend held, sacrificed himself at Queenston for the sake of a monument. He had already achieved high military rank, fame, and a knighthood. Susan Shaw was waiting for him. Why would he deliberately die?

Dickie looked over my shoulder. "Hardly a handsome dog, but an interesting face. His family meant a lot to him, you know. They had run into some financial trouble, and he saved them from ruin with his share of the spoils of Detroit. But you can't stand here all day, Fred. There are several other rooms to look at, and the cannon outside, the evidence of the old earthworks. Come along, or they'll give our rooms away at Niagara Falls."

From Fort Malden, we drove along the north shore of Lake Erie on Highway 3 passing prosperous looking farms, tidy small communities, and copses of trees, the remnants of the mighty mixed forests that covered the area before settlement. Here and there, we branched off on secondary roads so we could have a view of the water, such as at Point Pelee National Park. "The most southerly point in Canada," I was glad to contribute, "is Pelee Island, out there in the lake."

One of our detours took us from Simcoe to Port Dover, where Dickie said to us, "Remember the north shore of Lake Erie for future reference." After we rejoined the highway, we crossed the Grand River, "Where some of the Mohawks were resettled after the American Revolution," and farther on, we stopped to admire the canal at Welland which allows water traffic, by a series of locks, to rise over 300 feet from Lake Ontario to Lake Erie. At last, we came to Niagara Falls on the Canadian side, still crowded with tourists after the weekend.

It wasn't six o'clock yet, but they had already given our rooms away. Joe-Bob soon fixed that by creating a small scene, and threatening to make it a bigger one. "Who owns this hotel?" he demanded of the girl at the reception desk.

The girl didn't seem to understand she was in trouble. "I don't know," she replied, tossing her head.

Joe-Bob raised his voice. "Then, missy, where the hell is the manager? If he isn't here inside of 30 seconds, I'm going to buy this flea trap and sack you both!"

She looked at Joe-Bob's belligerent face, got the message, and dialled the manager, who soon appeared, looking annoyed. That only lasted two seconds. "Say, whatever your name is, some goose in your organization has given our rooms away. We want them back, now, and we're going to keep them till we're damn well ready to leave. You understand, or do I have to talk louder?"

I was embarrassed, but we got our rooms back.

Dickie allowed us the luxury of dinner in the dining room, which overlooked the falls, both the Horseshoe and the American. The first were so much more spectacular than the second that I'm sure every visitor from the United States wondered why they weren't theirs. But dinner was one thing, a night off another. Dickie marched us off to his suite the second the last drop of coffee was drunk, and before we were even seated, he began, "Prevost's cease-fire ended on September 14th, but nothing really happened for the rest of the month. Joe-Bob?"

"On October 8th, the Americans burned the British brig 'Detroit' off Fort Erie, and seized the 'Caledonia', an armed schooner."

"For that incident, Brock sacked the commander at Fort Erie, but his main concern was the activity on the American side of the Niagara River, opposite the village of Queenston. Clearly, something was afoot, and Brock reviewed his defences." Dickie sketched the scene for us. "Here, the village of Queenston. Across the swift-flowing Niagara River, 200 yards wide at this point, were the Americans. Here, the British battery of 24 pound guns at Vrooman's Point, and here, near Queenston Heights, on the Niagara escarpment, which at Niagara Falls is 326 feet above Lake Ontario, the redan with the 18 pounder."

"Oh, I wish this book was finished!" What, please, is a what-do-you-call-it redan?"

"A gun emplacement protected by low earthworks or a rock wall, my dear Josée. Guarding the redan was the light company of the 49th Regiment of Foot, the light company of a regiment consisting of, Josée, the most agile men. Farther down the escarpment was a company of the York Volunteers, militia, that is, and in Queenston, the Grenadier Company of the 49th - the tallest men in the regiment, you remember, Josée - as well as another company of militia, and a detachment of the 41st regiment, with two grasshopper guns, altogether about 300 men. In addition, American-born Major General Roger Sheaffe was in reserve at Fort George with 1,000 men. Joe-Bob?"

"The Americans had over 6,000 men, mostly New York militia under the command of now Major General Stephen Van Rensselaer. He had no experience in war, but he outranked the regular army Brigadier, Alexander Smyth. In fact, Lieutenant Colonel Solomon Van Rensselaer, Stephen's nephew, and Lieutenant Colonel Winfield Scott of the regular army were the real leaders.

"The American strategy was to establish a bridgehead on the Canadian side of the Niagara River by taking the village of Queenston. In the early morning darkness of October 13th, through the rain and mist of a fall storm, some 600 men, 300 militia and 300 regulars, crossed in bateaux - right, Dickie? - and landed upstream of their objective."

"Joe-Bob, you make it sound like a smooth operation. The crossing on October 13th was actually the second attempt. The first ended in comic failure when the boat with all the oars in it got loose, and drifted down the river. And on October 13th, three boats full of regulars, their oars sheared off by a militia boat, ended up far below the village. They were hardly to be a factor in the engagement."

"It doesn't say all that in my book!"

"It does in my notes. But to carry on. A sentry at Queenston spotted the invaders, and the word spread up and down the river. The Canadian militia began to fire sporadically, the 18 pounder at the redan opened up, hitting the lead boat, the 24 pounders at Vrooman's point joined in, and the detachment of the 41st, with their grasshopper guns, moved to intercept the enemy."

"The Americans scrambled ashore and took cover. The battery at Lewiston on the American side began to fire back when it was obvious surprise was lost."

"The Americans were trapped against the river bank, and began to take casualties. The militia below the redan moved down the hill to join in the battle, a serious tactical error."

"Solomon Van Rensselaer was wounded six times, and yielded command to Captain John Wool, a man the equal of Brock in size, and a natural soldier."

"Van Rensselaer was wounded only four or five times."

"Damn you Dickie, we should know how many times he was hit. Wool realized he had to put that gun at the redan out of action or the Americans were finished, so he took 150 men and started up the hill through the trees. Luck was with him. He found a path which allowed him to outflank the militia coming down the hill, and got above the redan."

"Meanwhile, at Fort George, Brock was awakened by the sound of gunfire, and set off within minutes for Queenston, leaving orders for Sheaffe to follow him. Brock first inspected the battle site, then, with a handful of men, rode up to the redan."

"He was met with a hail of American bullets! Wool was already in position!"

"Brock and his men, including the gun crew, retreated, but not before he had spiked the gun. At the bottom of the hill, he gathered another 100 or so men together, and led them back up the slope."

"Wool was ready for them. They were met with serious fire."

"But they kept coming, Brock in the lead, a huge man with the gold epaulets of rank on his red tunic, and that insane officer's hat on his head."

"And that's when my ancestor Judson stepped out from behind a tree, only 30 yards away, and shot him through the heart."

Dickie looked crestfallen. "What in God's name was a Major General doing leading a motley crew of militiamen up a hill into certain enemy fire? I'm sure only he knew the answer."

"The American position was precarious. Only 1,000 of them made it to the Canadian side. The rest, when they saw the grapeshot hitting the boats, the smoke from British fire on shore, the bloody wounded returning, lost their nerve, stood on their constitutional rights, and refused to fight outside their state. Both Solomon Van Rensselaer and John Wool were so badly wounded they had to be evacuated, and Winfield Scott was sent to replace them."

"After another unsuccessful attempt to retake the redan, the British regrouped at Queenston and waited for Sheaffe to get on the move. That wasn't until two in the afternoon. He advanced on Queenston, picked up the forces there, and marched up the escarpment without casualties. He then turned toward the river, driving 600 Americans before him. The other 400 were in Queenston, doing nothing."

"The bloody Mohawks were on the left flank, screaming and waving their tomahawks."

"It was the steady, disciplined fire of the British regulars, directed by my ancestor, Major John Bonney, that inflicted most of the casualties, and frightened many of your men into flinging themselves to certain death off the cliffs into the Niagara River."

"Scott rigged up a white flag and ran through the Mohawks to surrender."

"My notes say he was caught later hiding in Queenston."

"God damn you and your notes. The Americans suffered nearly 200 casualties."

"The British and Indians suffered only 14 casualties in capturing over 900 Americans. Thus ended the battle of Queenston Heights, the second threat to Upper Canada successfully defeated, and for all intents and purposes, that ended the campaigns for 1812."

"What about Dearborn's attempt on Montreal? That was on November 23rd."

"Attempt? Joe-Bob, I'm surprised you even mentioned it. Again, the New York militiamen invoked their constitutional rights, and refused to cross the border. Anyone for the bar?"

"What happened to poor Susan Shaw?" Josée asked.

"She lived to a ripe old age, but never married."

"I have a headache," Josée informed me when we got to our room. She looked pale, tired, and dispirited, and I could almost believe her, even if it was the first time she had ever used that excuse, or any excuse, for that matter. Since she recovered from her third menstrual period of our life together, hardly a day had passed without us making love, whether I was aroused by feelings of jealousy, or by a flash of thigh or breast when she readied herself for bed. There now seemed to be an urgency, a purpose to it all, not just sex for sex' sake, although, God knows, the sex was wonderful; and when we were finished, she always seemed satisfied, making me believe that, if nothing else, I was a good lover. She would hold me close to her for several minutes, with her eyes closed, and when she opened them, she would look at me in a way that I could not interpret. Once, I thought it was a look of love, and I told her I loved her, and she told me to shut up, and she punished me; but if it wasn't love, what was it? Faith, or hope, trust perhaps, but faith, hope or trust in what?

We were part tourists, part historians the next day. We had, of course, to visit the Horseshoe Falls, not the biggest in the world in terms of either height or water flow, but easily the most spectacular. We strolled with the crowds along the edge of the Niagara escarpment, through the mist and spray thrown up by the tumbling water, and looked across to the American Falls on the other side. Below us, three 'Maids of the Mist', the honeymoon boats, bobbed about in the current, and I suddenly wished we were aboard one of them, Josée and I, she with diamond and gold rings on the fourth finger of her left hand. I put my arm around her, and as if she read my thoughts, she said, "Shut up, Fred."

As for history, we drove down the Niagara Parkway to the flats of Queenston, still a village 18 decades after the battle when Brock was killed. From there, we could clearly see his monument on the heights, a great statue of the mysterious soldier himself on the top of it in heroic pose, complete with sword in hand, and it towered so into the sky that it must have been visible on the American side half-way to Plattsburgh, New York. Returning to the top of the escarpment and to the park where his memorial stood, we finally found a place to leave the van, and walked up to it. "It is 210 feet high," Dickie informed us, "with a museum and a staircase inside. Must climb to the top. You coming, Fred?" And we all went with him, even Joe-Bob with his limp, along with a busload of tourists.

"We must see where he was killed," Dickie said, as we descended to the ground. "The redan was just across the Parkway and down the hill a bit." It took no more than ten minutes to reach the spot, now marked by a plaque, a replica of the 18 pounder, and a low stone wall. What looked to be a grade school class was gathered around the gun, listening to their teacher explain its significance.

Quietly, so as not to disturb them, Dickie told us, "As we know, Brock and his men came up the slope from Queenston, he on horseback at first, but dismounted just before he was killed. As you can see, the area is heavily wooded as it was then, and we are within feet of the place where he fell. We should observe a moment of silence." Josée made the sign of the cross and we bowed our heads, raising them again when Dickie cleared his throat. "Just beyond the redan is the shear drop down to the Niagara River."

Joe-Bob walked over to the edge of the escarpment and peered downward. "Jesus, God, how did Johnny Wool get past here without the Brits seeing him?"

"A fine piece of soldiering, for certain. Poor fellow was shot through the buttocks, all the while. Just as a footnote, the Americans fired a salute from their guns at Fort Niagara the day of Brock's funeral at Fort George. His body was moved up to the heights in 1824, to the base of the original monument, but that was blown up by persons unknown in 1840, probably someone unable to accept that the Americans didn't win the war of 1812."

"But we did win the war! We've never lost a war in our history!"

"Where is the proof? What territories did you conquer?"

"Why, we occupied Upper Canada after we won the battle of Lundy's Lane."

"You think you won the battle of Lundy's Lane? We shall see about that. And do you think you won the war in Viet Nam? Ah! Silence! But back to Brock. His new monument was completed in 1845 and again, his remains were moved. At one of the last meetings of Queenston veterans, held here on the Heights, this resolution was passed: 'Resolved - that we recall to mind, with admiration and gratitude, the perilous times in which Sir Isaac Brock led the small regular force, the loyal and gallant militia, and the brave and faithful Indian warriors, to oppose the invader - when his fortitude inspired courage, and his sagacious policy gave confidence, in despite of a hostile force apparently overwhelming.'

"Now, because we will be talking about it quite a bit, we should visit Fort George, which is just a few minutes away."

"We'll have to be through with that by noon," Joe-Bob surprised us, "because Jacqui has made us a tee time at one of the best courses here."

So it was back down from the Heights on the Niagara Parkway, past the village of Queenston to the reconstructed Fort George, another National Historic Site, this one strategically located on the Niagara River. On the way to the massive timber gates, Dickie pointed out a wedge-shaped earthwork called a ravelin, which, he explained, was designed to split attacking forces into two, thus making them easier to deal with. Inside the gates was an enclosed area not near the size of Louisbourg but more than double that of Fort Beausejour, I estimated. For the next hour, we walked about the grounds and in and out of blockhouses, barracks, and bastions, not to mention the powder magazine and the artificers' building, the stronghold of such tradesmen as blacksmiths and carpenters.

Discipline was harsh in old Fort George, as it was universally in the armies of the times. Deserters were shot, and sinners were flogged in the 'punishment triangle' behind the guardhouse. Josée was especially fascinated by the married quarters, where the only privacy consisted of blankets thrown around the bunks. "Mon Dieu!" she said to me, suppressing a laugh. "Can you imagine making love behind that blanket while all around you, within a few feet, others are doing the same thing?"

"No, I can't imagine it, but if that's what we had for privacy, I guess we would do it."

The animator present explained to us that only a small percentage of enlisted men were allowed to bring their wives and families to the fort, something like six out of 100. And before a man could marry, he had to have two service stripes, each worth ten years of his life, so that if he enlisted at the age of 15, he would already be 35! His chances of bringing his wife to a place like Fort George were better if she had some training in the kitchen or in housekeeping, because she could then be employed in the officers mess, or as a maid in their quarters. As for the officers, they lacked few comforts on the frontier. Their mess table groaned with good food, and their liquor cabinet was stocked with the finest brands of the day, while the men subsisted on bully beef and biscuit, with a ration of spruce beer to prevent scurvy.

Joe-Bob shook his head. "Why would the enlisted men put up with that kind of discipline and these kinds of conditions?"

"The alternative was to starve to death on the streets of London, or rot in prison, or die destitute in a poor house," Dickie answered.

Across the river on the American side was Fort Niagara, the guns of Fort George designed to lob shells directly into it and vice-versa. It looked like a no-win situation to me. We strolled down to the riverbank where the Provincial Marine Base was located in 1812, and Dickie told us, "A volunteer service, the Provincial Marine. After the Americans gained control of Lake Ontario, the British sent out a naval officer to take charge, Commodore Sir James Yeo, along with 500 officers and ratings. From then on, the advantage on the lake shifted back and forth, depending on who had just finished building the biggest ship."

The golf game, with Josée thankfully on the winning side, used up the rest of the afternoon, and we spent the evening writing up the battle of Queenston Heights, and the ancestors' part in it. Just before nightcaps, Joe-Bob needled me. "Where were all the Bonneys from British North America while Judson was fighting for the United States?"

"All back in New Brunswick, where a truce was in effect with New England. But one of them got involved when the truce was broken."

"Oh that comes later," said Dickie. "Right now, I am developing a migraine trying to decide how not to get ahead of ourselves. With action taking place in 1813 all the way from Lake Huron in the far west to Lower Canada in the east, that is impossible, so we may as well finish off the far west first. We'll get a start on that tomorrow."

It was already August the 12th when we assembled in Dickie's room the next morning for a session on the book. Where had the summer gone? We'd covered thousands of miles and visited dozens of historic sites, but we were hardly half finished the book, going by Dickie's outline. As for the War of 1812, Joe-Bob began for a change.

"You remember that William Henry Harrison succeeded Hull out in the west. In January of 1813, he took an army of over 6,000 men to Detroit."

Dickie, looking miffed, continued. "You remember the Americans burned one ship, the brig 'Detroit', and captured another at Fort Erie. For all intents and purposes, even thought the 'Detroit' was salvaged, that gave the Americans control of Lake Erie, which meant that the British had to move supplies to the west end over almost impassable roads. That doomed the British forces and their Indian allies there now under Major General Henry Proctor, but he did not give up without a fight. As the American army approached, he crossed the Detroit River and killed, wounded or captured the entire advance guard of 900 at a place called Frenchtown."

"During the fighting, the Americans moved their wounded into the homes of the settlers, but when the survivors of the advance guard surrendered, the Indians went into the homes and murdered our helpless boys - carved out their livers and scalped them. That savagery provoked a violent reaction in the United States."

"Unlike Brock, Proctor was not able to control Tecumseh and his Indians. You remember our drive to Niagara Falls on Highway 3? That violent reaction Joe-Bob mentioned, was directed at the settlers along the north shore of Lake Erie, and it was led by a Canadian renegade of American ancestry named Joseph Willcocks. Homes were burned and civilians were murdered, and with little British military presence of any kind, there was no way to stop the atrocities. But back to Proctor. He would have been powerless without the Indians, and they needed him to supply them with food, but because of the American blockade on Lake Erie and the poor harvest in 1812, the situation gradually deteriorated, until all were facing the threat of starvation. In the circumstances, Proctor's first priority should have been to raid Harrison's supply depots, but instead, he frittered his strength away in a series of raids on less important objectives. As food supplies dwindled, he used his rank to persuade the poor, one-armed navy commander on Lake Erie, Lieutenant Robert Barclay, into attacking the American naval establishment at Put-in Bay. He had only one real ship, the 'Detroit', and four other makeshift craft."

"Commander Oliver Perry, the American commander at Put-in Bay, repelled the attack on September 10th, 1813, and captured all the British ships."

"Perry had bigger guns and the wind was in his favour, and poor Barclay lost his other arm in the engagement. Now, Proctor's situation was hopeless. He allowed the militia to go home to look after their families, abandoned Fort Detroit and Fort Malden, and fled eastward toward the town of London. With him were some 900 regulars of the 41st regiment, and Tecumseh's Indians."

"Harrison, with over 3,000 men, including a detachment of Kentucky cavalry, set off after them, and caught them on October 5th at Moraviantown. Where the hell is that on the map?"

"It doesn't exist any more. Nearest place is Thamesville. See there?"

"Alright. Anyway, the Kentucky cavalry came at the British out of the woods, and savaged them."

"Savaged them, and destroyed the town. Proctor lost more than 600 of his men, and with the remnants, made it to Burlington Heights, there, on Lake Ontario, after a journey that only desperate men could survive. Tecumseh was killed, and the surviving Indians scattered to the four winds."

"Say, Dickie, you have to admit this was a real American victory."

"I have to admit it was, but it was of no lasting value. Harrison withdrew back to the United States, his militia units disbanded, and he spent the rest of the war boasting about his one success."

"You just have to belittle it, don't you?"

"I think my judgement is fair. Now, we should go to Thamesville, or near there, where there is a monument to Tecumseh."

So back onto the freeways we went, first the Queen Elizabeth Way, then the 401 at Hamilton, with the same cast of maniacs in transport trucks and passenger vehicles, until we found the off-ramp to the sleepy little town of Thamesville. Just to the northeast were the remains of Moraviantown, so called at first because of the Christian Order that settled there, but more recently known as Fairfield. What was left of the village was now a National Historic Site, complete with a battle museum in a house built of rocks, and the staff inside were only too pleased to show us around. We got the impression they didn't get many visitors. Outside, about a block of the old main street had been gravelled, and along it were marked the locations of the houses that had been destroyed by the Americans. There was even a replica of one of the buildings, a tiny cabin built of logs, and a sign ironically proclaimed the street the 'Avenue of Peace'. At one end of it was a small, concrete block monument to the Moravian Mission, and nearby, two smaller memorials to Tecumseh. What a contrast to the gigantic monolith for Brock! Yet Tecumseh, the last hope for an Indian homeland in eastern North America, fought and died just as courageously.

"I suppose Judson was with Harrison, was he?" Dickie asked, when we got back to the hotel.

"Well, he was. He was a sergeant when he was captured at Queenston Heights. Got traded back for some Brit of the same rank, along with Winfield Scott and a bunch of others."

"Like all your family, he had a nose for action then."

"Say, Dickie, are you setting me up for another of your blind-side hits?"

"Not at all. Just making an observation. But the day is still young. We have time to finish 1813. Let's get rid of the minor engagements first. In February, the Glengarry Fencibles, a regiment formed of immigrant Scottish veterans based at Fort Wellington, there on the map, crossed the St. Lawrence River on the ice and attacked Ogdensburg, New York. History suggests it was all taken in good humour, because after they chased the American troops away, the normal river traffic and smuggling resumed. In April, the American Commander at Sackets Harbour, Commodore Isaac Chauncey, with temporary naval superiority, having bottled up the Provincial Marine navy in Kingston, escorted 1,700 men to Fort York hoping to capture a vessel under construction there. But our old friend Roger Sheaffe burned it."

"The Americans chased Sheaffe and his men out of the town, but the dastardly British, before they left, blew up a powder magazine and killed 100 Americans, including General Zeb Pike."

"Using this incident as an excuse, the Americans burned the Assembly Buildings and looted churches before they left."

"We haven't been to Fort York," I reminded Dickie.

"Right near the CN tower in Toronto. Next time we're there, we'll visit it, that is, the reconstructed version. In any case, Sheaffe was relieved of command as a result of this defeat and replaced by a succession of officers, the last and most important of them Lieutenant General Gordon Drummond. More of him later. Meanwhile, Governor Prevost and the new British Naval Commander, Sir James Yeo, attacked Sackets Harbour."

"And they were driven off by good old 'Smuggler' Brown, a brigadier in the New York militia. He was drafted into the regular army after that. Next thing that happened, the Americans landed near Fort George on May 25th, and took it, along with the village of Queenston."

"But they weren't clever enough to catch Brigadier John Vincent, who escaped the battle to regroup at Burlington Heights."

"Poor leadership, that's what. Colonel Winfield Scott, by now Chief of Staff to Dearborn, was in the lead group and wanted to chase Vincent, but he was over-ruled."

"The Americans eventually did follow Vincent, though."

"Yes. After a hard march, they camped at Stoney Creek, which is now a suburb of Hamilton, and the treacherous British attacked them in the middle of the night."

"We shall visit Stoney Creek on our way back to Toronto. Nice memorial there, I understand. During the engagement, the two American brigadiers were captured, one of them a fellow by the name of John Winder. Remember that name. The rest of the Americans retired in disorder to Fort George."

"How do you know it was disorderly?"

"More humiliations to come, my overbearing friend. On June 23rd, some loose-tongued American officers from Fort George were talking in a Queenston bar about a raid. A woman named Laura Secord overheard them, and, ostensibly driving her cow to pasture, went by a circuitous route to warn the British. The planned raid degenerated into disaster the next day when an American regiment ran into an ambush of Caughnawagas, Mohawks, and a single company of the 49th Regiment of Foot. This became known as the battle of Beaverdams. During a parlay, the British officer commanding, Lieutenant James Fitzgibbon, offered the Americans protection 'from the tomahawk and the scalping knife', and nearly 500 of them surrendered."

"You arrogant Brit! More treachery!"

"Laura Secord's family emigrated to Upper Canada from Massachusetts," I offered, "and she's had a chocolate company named after her. There's also a monument to her on Queenston Heights, remember?"

"Oh, Lord, yes, Fred."

"Jesus, God, from Massachusetts! How could she support the British?"

"Married to a member of the Upper Canada militia."

"Well, if that likeness of her on Queenston Heights was a true one, she was downright ugly."

"Time to visit her cottage, and that will wrap up hostilities on the Niagara Peninsula for 1813."

Back to Queenston we went to the mild tourist trap of Laura Secord's cottage, a private enterprise consisting of a reception centre and the home where Laura lived. We bought admission to a kind of play put on in the home by some young actors, who recreated the story of her journey to warn the British. Joe-Bob shook his head from time to time during the performance, still apparently unable to understand the foolishness of the Americans, or the lost loyalty of a woman born in the United States.

By now it was late afternoon, already a long day for us, with two excursions thrown in, but there was no use begging for mercy. Back at the hotel again, Dickie said, "Just two more engagements of note in 1813, the first in Lower Canada, the second in Upper. Joe-Bob?"

"Meanwhile, President Madison and War Secretary Armstrong gave up on Dearborn and replaced him with Wilkinson, sort of like jumping out of the frying pan into the fire. Wilkinson showed no inclination to press his advantage in manpower, and wasted the rest of the summer before reporting to Sackets Harbour. He was supposed to attack Kingston, but decided on his own to mount a two-pronged attack on Montreal, the other prong to come from Plattsburg, where Brigadier Wade Hampton had 4,000 men waiting. Even though Hampton hated Wilkinson's guts, he obeyed his orders, but to find feed for his horses, he had to change his line of advance into Lower Canada from the Richelieu to the Chateauguay River."

Josée perked up. "At last, the Canadiens have a chance to prove themselves! Waiting for Hampton, in well-entrenched positions near the town of Ormston, was Colonel Charles-Michel d'Imberry de Salaberry. A regular British officer, he was none the less a Canadien, born near Quebec City of a well-known family. He had convinced governor Prevost to let him recruit his own militia regiment, the Voltiguers, and at the battle of Chateauguay, they formed part of his force of some 2,000 men. My ancestor Lionel was one of the Voltiguers."

"Yes, Josée. Besides the Voltiguers, de Salaberry had two companies of select embodied militia, one of Chasseurs, or scouts, which included a few Indians, and some units of sedentary militia called up for the crisis. Only about 350 men manned the barricades he set up, which consisted of a lunette of logs and earth, and earthworks reinforced with abatis. The rest of his men, about 1,400 of them, were in reserve."

"Yes, Dickie."

"Say, let me tell you about the Americans. By this time, it was late October, and their period of enlistment was coming to an end. They were still in summer uniforms, their supply lines were stretched to the limit, and so when they ran into de Salaberry's defences on October 25th, they were not in good fighting shape. But Hampton's strategy was sound. When he learned that so few men manned the barricades, he sent a detachment under a Colonel Purdy to outflank them, and cut them off from their reserves. To do this, Purdy was supposed to make his way to a ford downstream, and cross when he heard the shooting from a frontal assault."

"But he never got to the ford. He became lost that night, and in the morning, found himself in front of de Salaberry's defences. When fire was exchanged, Hampton attacked, but was beaten off in the end by a stiff bayonet charge. The Americans then fled in panic, pursued by the Chasseurs and Indians, leaving behind most of their equipment."

"I sure do get tired of Americans fighting like a bunch of sissies. Wait till we get to Lundy's Lane."

"There are more American successes, but one of them was not Lundy's Lane."

"You'll have to prove that."

"I intend to. But one more battle in 1813. Remember Wilkinson?"

"How could I forget him? Here was the situation. Chauncey, never one to take a chance - say, that's almost funny - no chaunce from Chauncey, get it? Alright, alright. Not funny. Anyway, he succeeded in chasing Yeo and the British fleet into shelter at Burlington Bay by the fall of 1813, so the Americans had control of Lake Ontario. In October, Wilkinson put his army of 8,000 men on bateaux, and, by passing Kingston, which he was supposed to attack, he started down the St. Lawrence River to join Hampton. Imagine it! He had 14 regiments of infantry, two of cavalry, or dragoons, right, Dickie? - and three more of artillery! He should have been unstoppable!"

Dickie, looking as if he were trying to suppress a smile, continued. "But he was stopped. As he floated like an Egyptian Pharaoh down the river, he was dogged by 900 British regulars under the command of Colonel John Morrison, with Major John Bonney at his side. Like a gadfly, was Morrison, and he annoyed Wilkinson."

"Jesus, God, do I have to do this next part?" asked Joe-Bob, looking anguished. "Alright. Wilkinson sent 3,000 men to get rid of Morrison."

"They met at Crysler's Farm, near Morrisburg, on November 11th, 1813, where Morrison's 900 soundly defeated Wilkinson's 3,000, and the Americans withdrew to winter quarters with their tails between their legs."

"Wait till we get to Lundy's Lane!"

"Meanwhile, with each passing day, it became surer that Napoleon, after his disastrous march into Russia, was going to be defeated, and soon, the United States would face the wrath of the British army's veterans, released from years of combat on the European continent."

"And I have to do this, too. Even before their enlistments were ended, and before their replacements arrived, American militiamen were leaving their posts for home. The Americans had to abandon Fort George, and with it, their last toehold in the Canadas."

"Well done, well done, all of you. As a reward, let's have dinner in the dining room, and then we'll thrash through all the notes you've taken, Josée, this evening. We have a Bonin involved, and Major John Bonney. What about Judson Bonney?"

"After Moraviantown, Judson volunteered for Montreal. He was promoted to Lieutenant and was with Wilkinson. I hate to admit it, but he was one of the ones sent to stop Morrison."

"Good. Tomorrow, I think we should drive down to Montreal, visit the various battle sites we have talked about."

"How about letting us enjoy the country a little while we're at it?" I asked. "We should take a cruise through the Thousand Islands on the St. Lawrence, for example. That will bring to life the route first Amherst and then Wilkinson took to Montreal."

"Oh dear, a rebellion brewing. A good suggestion, the Thousand Islands, but later. We must keep our noses to the grindstone until we finish the War of 1812."

"Say, we could cover this end, take the jet from Toronto to Montreal, and work our way back. That would save some time."

"Capital idea, but we will have to backtrack from Morrisburg to Cornwall so as to avoid some later history. Can the jet pick us up there?"

"I'll get Jacqui on it."

Beaverdams, Stoney Creek, Fort York, Pearson Airport and the flight to Montreal, enough in a day for most people, but not Dickie. We were right up to date with our story by bedtime, but there was to be no sex that night in the same Montreal hotel we stayed at on our earlier visit, with Josée again seeming tired and unenthusiastic. The next morning, in yet another rented van, we did the National Historic Site at the Chateauguay battle site near Ormston, Quebec, where an earnest young man was concerned that his English wasn't good enough for us. He took us expertly if hesitantly through the battle with the help of a diorama, and we told him to stop worrying about his English.

Avoiding the traffic coming out of Montreal by sneaking across the bridges at Salaberry de Valleyfield, we continued on back roads along the St. Lawrence until we came to the Ontario Border. At that point, where Quebec Highway 20 turns into the dreaded 401, we were forced onto the freeway briefly, but left it at the first exit, and continued on Ontario Highway 2 to the Upper Canada Village near Morrisburg. Maintained by Ontario's St. Lawrence Park Commission, the village was designed to show what life was like at the time the Loyalists arrived, and it proved to be a lengthy diversion. Adjacent was the site of the Battle of Crysler's Farm, as represented by a visitor centre, a few old cannon, and some small monuments. In the visitor centre, we paid the modest fee and watched a 15 minute audio-visual presentation of the battle, then walked up the sandy riverbank to examined the monuments. "This is as close to the actual battle site as we can get," advised Dickie. "Crysler's Farm was flooded when the St. Lawrence Seaway was built."

Somehow, I was becoming averse to backtracking, as we now did to Cornwall. Surely, there was some better way to organize our travels, but then, nobody asked my opinion. Whatever, the jet had us back in Niagara Falls for a late dinner, and this time, when he heard we'd come back, the manager came to the desk to greet us with a broad smile.

Our night session brought us to the conclusion of the War of 1812. "You remember," Dickie began, "the Americans withdrew from the Niagara Peninsula at the end of 1813, but they commissioned that Canadian renegade, Joseph Willcocks, to burn the town of Newark, now known as Niagara on the Lake, after they left. You will also remember that the new Administrator and Commander of the armed forces in Upper Canada was Lieutenant General Gordon Drummond, who had something of Brock's style and dash, and the distinction of having been born in Quebec City. He immediately set out to revenge Newark, and in the dead of night, on December 19th, he attacked Fort Niagara."

"It was another damn treacherous attack. The British bayoneted our boys in their beds, then went on to burn the village of Lewiston."

"But Drummond wasn't finished yet. On December 29th, he burned Black Rock and Buffalo for good measure, and made this proclamation: 'There shall be prompt and signal vengeance for every fresh departure by the enemy, from that system of warfare which ought alone to subsist between enlightened and civilized nations.'"

"Now, if that isn't bombastic. But meanwhile, the Americans weren't finished either. Chauncey had control of Lake Ontario, and was building a new ship, the 'Superior', that would outgun anything ever built before."

"At Kingston, Yeo knew about it, and the only answer he had were the two much smaller frigates he was building. He advised Governor Prevost to do something about it, but that cautious man stayed safely at home in Quebec City. Yeo then found an ally in Drummond, and the two of them were authorized to attack Oswego, New York, which they did on May 6th 1814, hoping to intercept the guns for the 'Superior'."

"But all they got were some supplies. The guns had been loaded onto bateaux, and were being moved along the shore with a strong escort."

"Yeo, risking his fleet, sailed off to blockade Sackets Harbour, leaving Commander Stephen Popham behind to search for the guns."

"The bateaux carrying the guns took shelter at a place called Sandy Creek."

"American prisoners, Joe-Bob, told Popham where the bateaux were."

"And Dickie, your stupid Popham went after the guns, got caught in an ambush, and surrendered his whole outfit, ships and all."

"Yeo lifted his blockade of Sackets on June 6th and retired to Kingston to build an even bigger ship than the 'Superior', the 112 gun 'St. Lawrence'. By that time, the allies were in Paris, Napoleon had abdicated, 1,500 veteran British troops were on the way to North America, and Prevost had new orders from Lord Bathurst, the British Secretary for War and the Colonies. We will leave those orders for the moment."

"The Americans were not impressed. Led by good old General Smuggler Brown and Brigadier Winfield Scott, they came back to the Niagara Peninsula in the summer of 1814."

On July fifth, Major General Phineas Riall, based at Fort Erie, met Scott at a place called Chippewa, not far from Niagara Falls."

"And he got a nasty surprise. For months, Scott had been training his men until they were just as disciplined as the British, and he dealt Riall a sharp blow, gave him 500 casualties out of a total force of 2,000. Scott, with fewer men, lost less than 300."

"And now for the definitive battle of the war, fought on July 25th, 1814, on the Niagara Peninsula, at a place called Lundy's Lane."

"While Brigadier Winfield Scott was beating up on Phineas Riall at Chippewa, Smuggler Brown was advancing on Fort George and Fort Niagara, both now in British hands. Brown expected that cautious Chauncey to support him, but he never showed up, so he abandoned the idea."

"He was forced to give up the idea because Drummond showed up with fresh troops. Drummond and the remnants of Riall's men regrouped at Lundy's Lane, a low ridge just to the west of Niagara Falls."

"On July 25th, like you said, Dickie, as evening was coming on, the Americans, even though outnumbered, attacked, and the battle raged back and forth."

"The two forces were equal, both about 3,000 men. It was hand to hand, long into the night, with cannon firing at point-blank range."

"Brigade after brigade of Americans came at the British, and long about midnight, they drove them off the ridge. Like you said, Dickie, this was the defining point of the war, when our boys proved once and for all they were the equal of the redcoats."

"A nice fairy story indeed. True, the Americans almost prevailed, but at the last moment, the last British regiment in reserve, with Major John Bonney in the van, was thrown into the fight, and turned the tide. The Americans were forced to give ground, and if only Drummond's men had not been exhausted, they would have destroyed Brown and his regulars."

"You arrogant Brit! You are revising history!"

"Alright, you overbearing Yank. If you won, why did Brown withdraw to Fort Erie?"

"His supply lines were over-extended."

"Rubbish! Your timid Chauncey still controlled Lake Ontario, and it was Drummond who was over-extended. He had to be supplied over roads made almost impassable by heavy rains, and those rains continued until August 15th, when he attacked Fort Erie."

"And you can't deny that he failed, and don't deny either, because I know, that one of his regiments refused to fight, morale was so bad."

"Yes, it cannot be denied. The British suffered 500 casualties in the battle and withdrew to Chippewa, but you Americans were also demoralized, and you abandoned Fort Erie in late October. By that time, the British had taken back control of Lake Ontario with the completion of the mighty vessel, the 'St. Lawrence', but she only made one run before the end of the war, and that was to take supplies and men to Fort Niagara.

"Now, to finish up, we should record what was happening farther east. Prevost's new orders were to attack the American Naval Base at Plattsburgh, and you all remember Plattsburgh, on Lake Champlain. He set off from Montreal at the end of August with more than 10,000 men, most of them veterans of the Napoleonic Wars. He should have waited until a powerful new ship was completed - no, not the St. Lawrence, because it was impossible then for ships in Lake Ontario to sail down the river to Montreal - but for once, he was impatient, anxious no doubt to please Lord Bathurst. Any naval attempt on Plattsburgh without the new ship was a risky venture at best, but Prevost, like Proctor before him, used his rank to bully another naval officer, Captain George Downie, into giving it a try."

"Commodore Thomas McDonough was in charge at Plattsburgh, and when the British sailed into his bay, he was ready for them. By skilfully manoeuvring his ships, he disabled the four that the enemy had, and captured them."

"The British only had three ships. At any rate, poor Downie was killed in the engagement, and his ships did surrender. Meanwhile, Prevost lost his nerve and retreated, excusing himself with a torrent of rhetoric. That rhetoric did not save him from a court martial, but an untimely death did.

"To the Atlantic coast now, where the Americans were suffering a string of humiliations. No reaction, Joe-Bob? Governor Sir John Sherbrooke of Nova Scotia cancelled his truce with New England, invaded Maine on July 11th, and by war's end, occupied it as far south as the Penobscot River."

"And my ancestor, Abiel Bonney, was a captain in Sherbrooke's forces," I contributed.

"Thank you, Fred. A month later, a British Naval squadron escorted a 4,000-man army under Major General Robert Ross into Chesapeake Bay, brushing aside a feeble attempt to stop it. Ross landed on August 19th and advanced on Washington, soon to be confronted by our old friend, William Winder and 5,000 men. Alas, Joe-Bob, poor Winder was routed, leaving Ross to accomplish his mission, which was to burn and ransack Washington's public buildings, including the White House."

"The rest of the world was outraged by this uncivilized act, damn you, Dickie."

"Oh, but the British explained, it was in retaliation for the burning and looting of Fort York."

"Fort York! A wilderness outpost! What was that compared to our national capital?"

"Sow the wind and reap the whirlwind, as the saying goes."

"But that was the end of your successes. Ross tried to take Baltimore, and failed."

"Lost his life trying."

"And that gave Francis Scott Keys the inspiration for our national anthem - 'the rockets' red glare, the bombs bursting in air'."

"Meanwhile, peace negotiations had been going on at Ghent in the Netherlands since the summer. Both sides finally agreed that all captured territory should be returned, more to the benefit of the Americans, with much of Maine in British hands, and nothing of like value in American. Perhaps the most significant feature of the treaty was that the boundary between American and British interests beyond the Great Lakes was to be the 49th parallel of latitude all the way to the Rocky Mountains. In retrospect, it was an insane decision, a straight line through drainage after drainage, with no consideration of natural features. Lord! Look at the time! Now, even I have had enough. Let us retire to the bar."

"Just one more thing, Dickie." Joe-Bob looked like a bridge player about to ruff a trick with the ace of trumps. "Three weeks after the war ended, a British army of 8,000 landed near New Orleans, and old Hickory, Andrew Jackson, just beat their ass, gave them 25 per cent casualties."

"What you say is half true. This expeditionary force had no way of knowing that the war was over, and neither did the Americans, who were aided and abetted by a corps of French military engineers. It was the French who designed Jackson's defences, and taught him enough strategy to carry the day."

"Jesus, God, I never saw a man who refused to admit anything like you refuse to. Our story is it was the long frontier rifles we were using. We were picking your officers off at unheard of distances."

"I will admit that. And I will also admit that New Orleans probably convinced Great Britain that she should never again go to war with the United States. Now, tomorrow, we will visit Chippewa and Lundys Lane, finish the War of 1812, and get the chapter off to Basil."

We had our drinks and went to our rooms, and Josée was no friendlier than she had been the last few nights. "Before you ask me what is the matter, I cannot explain," she said, with an air of resignation.

"Nothing I did, or said?"

"No. Maybe if we weren't lost in the middle of the damn book, the damn book. It seems so hopeless."

Sunday, Sunday, Sunday again. Josée went off early to church, leaving the rest of us, as usual, to our own devices. Dickie phoned Roger and Joyce, and spoke to her for some minutes with a smile on his face. He next phoned Basil (who gave his love to Josée and his regards to me), assuring him that another chapter would be in the mail in the morning. Joe-Bob also spoke to Basil in that business-like manner of his, and seemed satisfied with the answers he got.

When Josée came back, we visited Chippewa, where the American and the Englishman agreed on what took place, but at Lundy's Lane, they agreed on very little, except that it was a shame there was no memorial. "The most important battle of the War of 1812, and nothing to mark it," deplored Dickie.

"I agree. The United States should do something about that."

"I don't think we would welcome a foreign power erecting a memorial to their armed forces on our soil," I suggested.

Dickie nodded. "Seems to me the Americans wanted to do that somewhere else in Canada - Louisbourg, I think it was, but they were rebuffed. Just not done, old chap."

"Well, I don't see why not."

By the end of the day, the War of 1812 was in an envelope ready for mailing, and we savoured our drinks in the bar with satisfaction. The next chapter would cover the period between the end of the war and the creation of the Dominion of Canada, and in the course of writing it, we would travel extensively not only in the east, but also to British Columbia, my home province. It would be good to see it again, that sea of mountains, the city-state of Vancouver with the wilderness at its back door, a chance to visit the girls and their families. I would introduce Josée to them, and I laughed inwardly at the reaction that would provoke.

Josée and I went to bed with a perfunctory kiss, and I fell into a deep sleep, and began to dream one of those wild, technicolour fantasies that began in Duxbury. This time, I was walking a high wire suspended from two towers, one on either side of the Niagara River, and below me was the redan where Brock was killed. Balancing myself easily with the help of a patio umbrella, I was utterly nonchalant about it all, I, Fred Bonney, who'd never spent a nonchalant moment in my whole life. Below me, I could plainly hear the sound of gunfire, and the New York Militiamen declaring their constitutional rights, and refusing to cross the river.

Suddenly, from up the slope, there appeared a celestial vehicle, rather like an overgrown bumper boat, with two huge American flags, one on each side, fluttering in the breeze. The vehicle stopped, and out of it stepped a tall, imposing man, be-medaled and dressed in 1812 officers' gray. He saluted in the casual American way, while an invisible brass band played '76 Trombones led the big parade', and he said, "I am Winfield Scott, the hero of Chipewa and Lundy's Lane." Another bumper boat appeared, this one coming up the slope and distinctly larger than the first, with two huge Union Jacks, one on each side, fluttering in the breeze, to the accompaniment of an invisible choir singing 'Rule, Britannia, Marmalade and Jam'. And out of it stepped a massive man dressed in the red serge of a British Brigadier General, with a hole in the tunic over the heart. "I am Sir Isaac Brock, the Hero of Upper Canada, and do excuse the uniform. My Major General's one was delayed in the mail. Winfield, old chap, I heard you saying that you were the hero of Lundy's Lane. Be honest. Admit it. Drummond gave you a drubbing, and shoved you off the ridge."

"I will admit no such thing."

"Oh very well. How do you like my monument?"

Scott looked up the slope at the towering monolith, and broke into tears. "It's the most beautiful fucking monument I ever saw in my life. Why didn't they give me one like that?" And with his body wracked with sobs, he climbed back into his vehicle, and disappeared up the slope.

Isaac Brock looked up at me. "By the Lord Harry, Fred Bonney, you've finally shown up. Come down here." And I floated to the ground under my umbrella as if I were a feather, and landed gently beside him. "Fred Bonney, you bear a striking resemblance to the man who shot me. He was a shirt-tail relative, was he?"

"Yes, Sir Isaac, his name was Judson Bonney. Tell me, Sir Isaac, did you deliberately expose yourself to death for that monument?"

"What do you think, Fred?" And he smiled an enigmatic smile. "But tell me, how many steps are there to the top of my monument?"

"I don't know. I didn't count them."

"Then you shall climb up and down them until you get the number right."

And I climbed up and down those stairs a dozen times, counting "one, two, three, four, five, six, seven and eight," until I was out of breath, but still, I always lost count.

"By the Lord Harry, I should have you flogged, Fred, for failing this test, but I will forego that. I need you for a most important mission. You know, I am sure, that I never married. Ah! Poor Susan, my darling! Withered on her maiden stock, pined for me until the day she died. It is my only regret that I did not take her for wife before the wretched war, and leave her, at least, with a child to fulfill her life. But there is no use crying over spilt cream. Did you know that I loved cream with a passion?"

"No, I didn't know that."

"But to your mission. Had I lived, I would have been much concerned about the future of British North America. American Imperialists will never cease to covet what has become Canada, and will take it by any means possible, be it armed force or economic power."

"What do you think can be done to stop them? They already control nearly half our commerce, and we are dependent on them for 80 per cent of our export trade."

"Remember the old expression? If you can't beat them, join them?"

"But I thought you wanted to keep us independent."

"I am suggesting the reverse, that they join you. You must think big, believe it is possible, as I believed my tiny army could hold off the Americans in 1812."

"You aren't serious? How can we make them join us?"

"Fred, the average person cares not a fig about loyalty or patriotism. They want freedom, yes, but besides that, they want a chance to succeed in life with the least amount of interference from government. Do you realize that millions upon millions of people in the republic to the south are descended from Canadians, both French and English? You must lure them back, by making this country more attractive as a place to live than the United States."

"You can't be serious! But if you are, how can we do that?"

"Don't forget about global warming and all the savage storms that beset the United States, which will make large parts of it dangerous to inhabit before long, nor the hatred against America that is fostered by terrorists. These factors will draw many Americans to this country. Then, you must have a leader who will captivate them, a leader with charisma, bilingual of course, of both English and French heritage, with a splash of native blood thrown in. Remember that without the Indians, we never would have won the war of 1812. He must be a strong leader, with an A-alpha personality, for the Americans like strength, and I would suggest that he should first of all be a champion athlete like I was."

"Not a woman?"

"Fred, Fred! Remember my times! Women were hardly considered persons."

"What else?"

"You must establish a climate in which government gets out of the lives of ordinary people as much as possible while still retaining your excellent social programs, you must make your tax rates competitive, and you must capitalize on your bilingualism. But enough of this. I have already chosen the parents of the leader who will meet my criteria, and who will do what must be done.

"As I look back through history, I am much impressed with your ancestor, Joel, for he was strong, just, and indefatigable, and looked a good deal like me. His genes run strongly in your blood, Fred. You shall be the father."

"You expect me to father your reincarnation?"

"Exactly. And the mother shall be, and I want you to know I have considered this carefully, the mother shall be Evangeline."

"But Evangeline doesn't exist! She is a figment of an American poet's imagination! Neither did she, figment or otherwise, have any native blood in her!"

"Ah, but she does exist, and she has a smidgen of Iroquois in her. You must go to her immediately, Fred, for she is in high oestrus, and ready to receive your sperm. Now, simply raise your bumbershoot."

"But my son! Your son! He won't have to die like you did, will he? He won't have to die?"

Suddenly, a great wind sprang up, and I was spiralled up into it under my patio umbrella, the while being suffused with an alien DNA, and all at once, I was in Grand Pré, standing before the statue of Evangeline. Her head was still turned as if to look over her shoulder, and she was as motionless and mute as the stone she was fashioned of. Bewildered, I looked about me, and discovered another statue in the distance, near to the church, where there had been none before. As I approached it, I could see that it appeared to be identical to the real one, yet somehow even more life-like. Suddenly, the figure on the pedestal spoke in a clear voice, "Fred Bonney, I am going to punish you for Le Grand Dérangement, for sending my people into exile."

"But I had nothing to do with it! I am not even British! I am Canadian! And my ancestor Lorenzo Dow let you escape!"

"You are as guilty as any, and handy. Take off your clothes, and lie down on your back."

In fear and trembling, I did as I was bid; and then, with her head still averted, she floated down from her pedestal, lifted her skirts, and straddled me. "But you are only a statue!" I objected.

"Do I feel like a statue?"

"No, you feel like flesh and blood. But Josée won't like me doing this for you."

"On the contrary, she will enjoy it as never before." And Evangeline turned her head, and looked at me with a lascivious smile. Josée! It was Josée!

I woke up in a hot sweat, shouting her name, and she shook me awake. "Fred, what is the matter?" And I took her in my arms, and we made the most marvellous love, until we were both exhausted, and even after that, she held me close for a long time, and then she looked at me with that look that I could not interpret. I had to ask. "Jos, what does that look mean?"

"Fred, cher Fred, I had hoped, I was hoping - but I guess - but I talk too much."

Chapter 9.

The Dominion of Canada

We all had a letdown after we finished the war of 1812, and Dickie declared a holiday. Joe-Bob said to him, "Say, come with me to Atlanta, and I'll show you a real war."

"The American Civil War? What a capital idea!" And off they flew in the jet to attend to 'business', and to tour the battle sites of the war between the States. Josée and I, meanwhile, took the rented van to Ottawa, and unloaded suitcases full of the clothes Dickie and Joe-Bob bought for her along the way. "Now there will be room for more," she said with satisfaction. As for her Impatiens, they were absolutely blooming in the summer heat, proof that Gino had been watering them faithfully. Because we had been away for weeks, however, the furniture was covered with dust and there were cobwebs in the corners of the ceiling, and by the time Josée dealt with them, the tantalizing mixture of smells - Impatiens, potting soil, polish and soap - filled the apartment.

We went to the local pub for supper, actually happy to eat hamburgers and chips again after all the fancy restaurant food, and we met Gino there with Raffelina, his pleasingly plump fiancée. We paid his bill as thanks for looking after the Impatiens, and I was glad to see, although he cast the odd pensive glance at Josée, that he seemed happy.

A low-pressure area sucked hot, humid air up from the gulf in the evening, the beginning of a mid-August heat wave, and we threw the clothes off our loveless bed during the night in an effort to keep cool. I spent the next morning catching up on bills and other business, which included dealing with a request from my renters to get out of their lease agreement the 1st of October. Joe-Bob would have been better at handling the situation, I guess. I just told them, alright. Josée in the meantime shopped and had her hair done, coming home a kind of brownette, a colour I didn't think suited her very well. In the afternoon, more as an excuse to get into the comfort of the air-conditioned van than anything else, I took her around to look at the house, and she was captivated with it, at least from the outside. "Not as grand as those places we saw on the St. Claire Parkway," she said, "but it looks like a home. You were happy there, Fred?"

"Yes, it was a happy time, raising the children."

Her expression changed from pleasure to dismay in an instant, and for the first time since we met, she as quickly looked her age. With obvious effort, she composed her features into a smile. "It would have been so nice to live there."

"We can move in the 1st of October, if you want. My renters are leaving."

"You don't mean it!"

"I do. You can have the apartment rent for clothes."

For no apparent reason, she burst into tears. I put my arm around her and patted her on the back until she got control of herself.

That evening, Josée again seemed disinterested in sex, as if that wonderful night in Niagara Falls were enough to last her indefinitely. We watched the late news, then a silly movie, and quietly went to bed. I was almost asleep when she asked, "What are we going to do for the next three days until Dickie and Joe-Bob come back? Sit and look at each other in this stinking hot apartment?"

"We could stay in bed and make love."

"Fred, be serious."

"We could go up to the cottage."

"You have a cottage? Why didn't you tell me before?"

"You never asked. Uncle Bill left it to me when he died, along with that trunk in the attic. He was a funny old duck - stepped on a land mine on the Normandy Beaches, never was able to have a family of his own - so he kind of adopted me."

"You mean he lost his balls?"

"Jos, you never cease to surprise me. Yes, he lost his balls. He was an archivist in the Parliament Buildings somewhere. I guess that's where he became interested in family history. Anyway, I should have sold the cottage, I guess, but I never got around to it. Always thought I would spend more time there, but with the kids grown up and gone, and Beth - well, there didn't seem to be much point."

"Where is it, the cottage?"

"Past North Bay, on a lake near Temagami."

"What's it like?"

"Old Bill built it by himself, except for the couple of weeks I helped him one summer. He encouraged us to use it while he was still alive, and we did, even after the kids lost interest. It's made of logs notched out and overlapped at the corners, and inside, there's just one room, about 20 feet by 24 feet, with a narrow staircase up to a sleeping loft. Because of the loft, the roof has a real steep pitch to it, and it overlaps the decks on each end. No power, just kerosene lamps, wood stove, no telephone either, just the way old Bill wanted it. Do you want to go up there?"

"I can't wait to get away from this heat!"

"O.K. In the morning then. We'll need to take casual clothes, bathing suits, and we can pick up what we need in the way of groceries in North Bay."

Old Bert at the lodge smiled when he saw me, and nearly swallowed his chew of snoose when he saw Josée. "Fred!" He recovered himself. "Long time no see! You want me to run you and the new missus over to the cottage, I guess."

Missus sounded good to me. "This a good time for you?"

"Good as any."

The cottage was on a little wooded island only a few hundred yards down the lake from the lodge, the only other improvements there a rickety old dock and a woodshed. Bert helped us unload, then roared off in his runabout, and I knew that everyone in Temagami country would hear by midnight that Fred Bonney had himself a fancy new woman. Josée seemed lost for words for a moment.

"Oh, I always wanted a cottage on a lake, some place to get away from the heat in the summer. But on an island, your own island, Fred!"

The door creaked on its hinges, and as it swung open, it revealed a disaster inside. The squirrels had got in and made nests all over the place, and the floor, the counters, even the beds upstairs were covered with dried mushrooms and cone scales. Josée took one look and a steely glint flashed from her eyes. "Fred! Where's the broom and the dustpan? And I'll need a mop, and some cloths, and that cleaner we bought in North Bay." And while the squirrels' mess came flying out the door, I got out the old wooden ladder and searched the outside of the cottage to see where the little devils had got in. There was a hole, alright, just under the eaves, and I covered it with a scrap of one by four.

Beth was a good housekeeper, but I knew the cabin had never been as clean as it was when Josée finished with it. As for the cooking, I dusted off the old barbecue and fired up some briquets, and about seven that evening, I lit the mosquito coils on the deck, and we sat down to salad and steaks and potatoes roasted in foil, and we washed it all down with a bottle of red wine. When we were finished, we stayed on the deck looking out over the lake at the sunset, and as the shadows lengthened into twilight, a pair of loons began calling to each other in the distance.

"Oh, Fred, how could you stay away from this place? It is so beautiful, so restful, so cool!"

"Not much fun by yourself. Not much fun, either, when the flies are bad. Sometimes the mosquitoes and the black flies drive you crazy, not to mention the horse flies. Anyway, tomorrow I'll clean out the rowboat, and we can try the fishing."

"There are fish in this lake? But you really should do some work on that dock."

"Fish first, dock afterwards. That's what cottages are all about, I used to tell myself, but the truth is, Beth and I did little else but work when we were here to keep the place up. It was the kids who got to play."

"Listen! What's that noise?"

"Coyotes yipping."

"Now there's a different noise! An owl?"

"That's a big owl. Used to scare the kids when they were little."

"Let's go for a swim. The water can't be that cold."

"It'll get your attention. Alright. Let's get our bathing suits on."

"Who will see us in this light? Let's just take off our clothes and go in."

"Alright. Off the dock? There's a ladder on the end."

"As long as I don't get what-do-you-call-it splinters."

"Slivers would be better."

We dived in and met each other under water, and wrapped our arms around each other as we bobbed to the surface, and I pressed myself against her wonderful, familiar body. She pushed me away with a laugh and swam off, churning the lake with powerful strokes, and try as I did, I knew I could never catch her. At last she had enough, and we crawled up the ladder onto the dock, and dried ourselves with big, fluffy towels, and when we got to the door of the cottage, I picked her up with inspired effort, and carried her over the threshold. The cottage and the lake did the trick, made her sexy again, but only for the first night we were there. The rest of the time she seemed preoccupied with her body, as if she were listening to it, waiting for some kind of message from it. It all mystified me, but I knew there was no use asking questions.

We caught a fish the next morning, or Josée did, with squeals of excitement, and we had it for lunch, and then she helped me replace some boards on the dock, and I cut down a couple of dead trees with my old swede saw, and bucked them into firewood. While I was doing that, she cut out some underbrush to improve the view, and when we got too hot, we jumped in the lake with our clothes on for an instant cool-off. By the time Friday afternoon rolled around, my little cottage looked as if someone loved it again, and I was reluctant to leave it. As for Josée, she cried when Bert came to take us away, as if she would never see the place again.

Three weeks of August were already behind us when we drove to Toronto that Saturday morning. Dickie and Joe-Bob were waiting for us in the hotel near the Skydome, and there were hugs and handshakes all around. Dickie frowned. "I know you are all anxious to finish the book. It has been a long session. Let's get at it right away. First, however, to finish up the war of 1812, what about Brock? Did he sacrifice himself deliberately at Queenston Heights?"

"Dickie," I replied emphatically, "he simply believed he was immortal and could not die. His ghost, restless because he left no issue behind him, still haunts the heights."

"Oh, come on, Fred!" objected Joe-Bob. "He may have believed he was immortal, but let's not get into ghosts."

"Alright," finalized Dickie. "He thought he was immortal and was wrong. Let's leave it at that."

In Dickie's day room, trying to concentrate and be constructive, we carried on through lunch and on into the afternoon. He flattered me by asking me to introduce the post 1812 period. "Because of the atrocities committed on the north shore of Lake Erie," I began, "immigrants from the United States were banned from British North America for a time after the War of 1812. Instead, settlers were recruited in the United Kingdom to counter the already strong American presence, especially in Upper Canada.

"In contrast to the situation in the United States, British North America was stagnant and in a state of depression, which fuelled resentment against the colonial governments. As I pointed out earlier, the British gave governors and their appointed councils access to their own funds, so they were largely able to govern without the consent of the elected assemblies, and that simply added to the resentment. Further, governors sent out from the old country generally went along with the policies in place when they arrived, rather than trying to actively govern on their own. With little interference from the executive level, councils and senior members of the civil staff in Upper Canada became inter-grown and arrogant, and were branded as 'Family Compacts' by the frustrated voters. In one case, a governor interfered in an election to keep a friendly crew of Tories around him. Josée?"

"The situation was particularly bad in Lower Canada, where Anglais dominated the council and Français the assembly. In 1822, there was a move to amalgamate the two Canadas, which, as you can imagine, met with fierce opposition from the French. In 1834, Louis Joseph Papineau, the leader of the Patriote Party, won a huge majority in the Lower Canada assembly, and pressed for republican-style reforms such as the election of militia officers. The governor continued to go along with the existing structure, however, and that brought open talk of rebellion. Dickie?"

"The governor was no fool. He knew that if he agreed to the election of officers, the militia would soon be controlled by the Patriotes. As for the military situation, Great Britain negotiated a naval agreement with the United States in 1817, the Bagot-Rush agreement, which limited warships on Lake Champlain and the Great Lakes to one or two, 1 gun gunboats."

"Jesus, God, one or two, 1 gun gunboats. You serious?"

"Made of wood, with sails. And since it was hardly needed any more, Britain closed the dockyard at Kingston.

"From 1812 onward, the threat of American invasion waxed and waned over a number of issues, Great Britain reacting to each crisis by sending over enough troops to match those in the United States regular army, then withdrawing them when the crisis was over. And always, there were the two problems of desertion, and the unpopular use of the military to support the civil authority. You see, in those times, two justices of the peace could call out the armed forces, whether to deal with a popular uprising, or a head-breaking confrontation between the Knights of Columbus and the Orange Lodge.

"Meanwhile, the defence of British North America was based on the building of numerous canals linking the rivers and lakes of Upper Canada, elaborate citadels at Halifax and Quebec City, and additional fortifications at such places as Kingston and on the Ile aux Noix, that is, Fort Lennox, which we have visited, as you will all remember. The cost was staggering: one fifteenth of the British budget each year, and the program had to be cut back. Fred?"

"Dickie, Colonel By built the Rideau Canal from Ottawa to Kingston, and his expenses were seven times those estimated. At Kingston, only one of six planned forts was built, and that was Fort Henry."

"Yes, Fred. We will visit Fort Henry in due course, but there was rebellion brewing in Upper Canada as well, was there not?"

"Yes. A bunch of disgruntled farmers led by William Lyon Mackenzie, a politician fed up with the abuses of the Family Compact, marched on the unguarded armoury at Fort York on December 7, 1837 with the intent of seizing weapons. The militia was called out by now Colonel James Fitzgibbon of Beaverdams fame, who routed the rebels. Two of the ringleaders later were hung, while several more were sent to the British penal colonies in Australia. Mackenzie himself fled to the United States, where he found support for his cause among young Americans, who were forming 'Hunters' Lodges', secret organizations dedicated to the ending of British rule in North America. Within days of Mackenzie's arrival, some of them occupied Navy Island above Niagara Falls. And I do like this story. Militia Colonel Allan Macnab called out a few men, routed the invaders, and sent their supply ship, the 'Caroline', careering over the falls."

"I don't understand it," said Joe-Bob, shaking his head. "That was an act of war. The 'Caroline' was an American ship, and we did nothing about it!"

"Oh, you overbearing Yank, you did nothing except look the other way when members of the Hunters' Lodges raided your armouries! But in Lower Canada, Josée?"

"The rebellion heated up in the fall of 1837 when some Patriotes occupied a seigneury on the Richelieu River near the village of St. Charles. It should not be assumed that all these rebels were French, for in fact, the military commander at St. Charles was an Anglais called Thomas Storrow Brown. Dickie?"

"Lieutenant General Sir John Colbourne, in charge of the defences of the Canadas, sent two columns against the rebels, the first under his Quarter Master General, Sir Charles Gore, who travelled by steamer from Montreal to Sorel. With him were flank companies of the 24th Regiment of Foot, a detachment of Royal Artillerymen with one 12 pound howitzer -"

"Dickie!"

"Perhaps 300 men, and the necessary two magistrates, with warrants for the arrest of the Patriote leaders. Josée?"

"Gore proceeded upstream to St Denis, where he was soundly defeated on November 23rd, 1837, and lost his howitzer to the Patriotes."

"The other column was under Lieutenant Colonel George Wetherall, with four companies of foot, three from the Royal Regiment, yes, yes, I know, and others, including a small detachment of Royal Montreal Cavalry, and some - oh, damn it, with two 6 pound field guns, altogether about 350 men, with the indispensable two magistrates. They crossed the river at Montreal, just as we have already done, and proceeded down the Richelieu. Colborne, meanwhile, ordered Wetherall to retire after Gore's defeat, but the message was intercepted by the Patriotes. Wetherall, with some minor reinforcements from Chambly, you all remember Chambly, which we could not find, carried on through the fall rain and the mud, and after a spirited engagement, carried the Patriote position at St. Charles. Josée?"

"At St. Charles, Wetherall had over 400 hundred men, the Patriotes only 250. But the defeat did not stop the unrest; it continued, and it was not extinguished even by a crushing defeat of the rebels at the battle of St. Eustache, a suburb of Montreal, on December 5th, 1837. Dickie?"

"Perhaps the unrest continued because the rebels, unlike the situation in Upper Canada, were treated leniently, Josée."

"Perhaps. In 1838, Papineau, now in exile in the United States, was deposed as Patriote leader, and replaced by more radical men like Robert Nelson, another Anglais. While his agents in Lower Canada formed a secret society of 'Chasseurs', to which disaffected young Canadiens flocked, Nelson plotted another uprising from the safety of the United States."

"Say, there you go again. Every time you Canadians wanted protection from your own government, you hid out in the United States."

"Meanwhile, Colbourne reacted to the threats of Hunters and Chasseurs by bringing in troops from New Brunswick, leaving that province vulnerable to expansionist Maine lumbermen. Great Britain sent reinforcements to the Canadas as well, the militia was called out to guard the borders, and the Indians volunteered in droves to help out.

"Meanwhile again, there were a number of incidents in Upper Canada. Early in 1838, the militia captured an American ship loaded with stolen weapons, and later, with the help of a few regulars, attacked rebel positions on Pelee Island, and you all remember Pelee Island. In late May, some Americans led by a Canadian renegade named Johnson seized the steamer 'Sir Robert Peel', robbed her passengers, and set her afire, shouting 'Remember the Caroline'! But the closest thing to an invasion was staged by members of the Hunters' Lodges, led by the vainglorious Charlatan, Nils Von Schoultz."

"Mon Dieu, mon Dieu, mon Dieu! A vainglorious charlatan?"

"Sorry, Josée. A boastful, vain, fake. Originally a Swede, he abandoned his family, enlisted as an officer in the Polish army, and then emigrated to the United States, where he became a bogus pharmacist, and committed bigamy. On November 12th, 1838, he and hundreds of fellow lodge members commandeered some ships and crossed the St. Lawrence River from Ogdensburg, New York, to the vicinity of Prescott in Upper Canada. Having been brainwashed into thinking the people would welcome them as liberators, Von Schoultz and his men were stunned when they were met with derision and armed resistance. Their escape route cut off by British ships, they were forced to take refuge in a stone windmill near Fort Wellington, and they surrendered after a shattering bombardment."

"Say, but not without giving the Brits some casualties."

"And suffering some of their own. Altogether, 160 were captured, including Von Schoultz, and they were imprisoned in Fort Henry at Kingston. Fred? You wanted to say something?"

"Just that at his trial, Von Schoultz was defended by John A. Macdonald, the drunken father of our country. Von Schoultz was found guilty and hanged."

Joe-Bob, looking amused, asked, "A bad lawyer was the drunken father of your country?"

"He might have been a good lawyer, but in any case, he was the father of our country."

"Yes, Fred. Now, Josée, finish up, will you?"

"The second rebellion in Lower Canada broke out on November 3rd, 1838, when Robert Nelson crossed the border south of Montreal with a small force. He was soon joined by over 3,000 Chasseurs including my ancestor Lucien, and they began to march north. Colbourne, through his network of bilingual spies, knew they were coming, and soon confronted them. I regret to admit that the Patriote leaders abandoned their men, who were left with no choice but to try to fight their way back to the United States. Colbourne caught them at a place called Odelltown on December 9th, and broke, once and for all, the Patriote movement."

"Yes, and there was to be no more leniency. Patriote prisoners were hauled by the wagon-load to Montreal and tried for treason, 12 were hanged, and 57 or 58, depending on which account you read, were sent to the dreaded penal colonies in Australia. Was your ancestor one of those, Josée?"

"No, he escaped back to the United States and stayed there until the amnesty of 1844, leaving his family to fend for themselves. It was either that or face the hangman's noose."

"Thank you. Now, that brings us to the end of the rebellion and insurrection period, though perhaps not to the sentiments it engendered. In fact, Josée, there was a lingering distrust and bitterness against the French, was there not?"

"Yes, Dickie. As a result, thousands of them left the country for the United States and elsewhere."

"Alright, then. This evening, Joe-Bob, can we fly again to Montreal? From there, we can hire a car and drive down the Richelieu River to the key sites of the Lower Canada rebellion."

"Why not fly to Quebec City?" suggested Josée. "From there, we could drive the south shore to Sorel and then up the Richelieu. I am sure I can find Fort Chambly driving up the river, and I could spend a night with my parents, go to early church with them, and see Yvan."

Not Yvan, still! My heart sank, while Dickie and Joe-Bob glared at Josée as if she were a traitor. "Say, we can do that," Joe-Bob said at length, "if that's what you want. It will give me a chance to touch base with Pierre."

With Dickie and Joe-Bob off looking for 'souvenirs' again, I spent another night alone in the Chateau Frontenac, wondering what Josée was doing, hoping she wasn't in bed with Yvan, but not at all sure that she wasn't. For all that, it was a pleasant night, and on a whim, I went for a walk on Dufferin Terrace. A big moon lit up the surroundings, turning the St. Lawrence into a broad ribbon of silver, and painting the Levis escarpment on the south shore with patches of ghostly light. I knew, in the back of my mind, that I was hoping to run into that girl with the come-hither smile again, although I didn't really know what I would do with her if I did. She didn't appear on the terrace, and after half an hour, I took the tram down to Rue Petite Champlain where I wandered about, looking in the shops and cafes. And suddenly, there she was, on Joe-Bob's arm, heading into a bar with hips swinging high, and laughter on her lips!

I had trouble looking Josée in the eye the next morning when we picked her up, which seemed to amuse her, and she laughed and joked with the others at my expense. I kept my mouth shut while I drove south-west to Drummondville, took the off-ramp to Sorel, and turned onto the 'Chemin des Patriotes', the main thoroughfare on the east bank of the Richelieu River. The waterway was busy with pleasure craft at the time, and of interest was the fact that the countryside adjacent to it still showed evidence of the old strip farms dating from the early days of New France. Throughout the area were stately homes on well-kept grounds, many of them with real estate signs on their lawns, and Joe-Bob noticed the bargain prices. "Say, Josée, why are all these places for sale?"

"Probably Anglais moving out of Quebec," she guessed.

Joe-Bob took his cell phone out of his briefcase and recalled a number. "Say, John, would you do something for me? I need a survey done in New England and New York State. I want to know what percentage of the population has roots in Canada, French from Quebec in particular, what kind of incomes they have, and whether any of them would like to buy property cheap back where they came from. Hey, extend that question to include people who would like to learn French, or live with French culture. Yes, along the Richelieu River, near Montreal. You never saw a prettier scene - on the canal system that will take you all the way to New York City - marinas - and you never saw nicer homes for the price. Would make great summer places. When can you get this done? In a week? Make it five days, and I won't argue about the bill. Be seeing you."

Joe-Bob ended the conversation and recalled another number. "Say Pierre, it's Joe Bob. Does your company charter allow you to deal in real estate? No? Look into buying one that can do that, then. And sometime soon, take a run up the Richelieu River. All kinds of places for sale cheap. Maybe we could buy and sell them for summer homes to ex-Quebeckers living in the United States. What? The province of Quebec has some control over immigration, and that might be a problem? Jesus, God! You Canadians are crazy. Anyway, check into that, and I'll call you again in a week or so."

At the village of St. Denis, where the Lower Canada rebels triumphed in 1837, we found a monument to them in a small tree-shaded park, on it the names of those who had died along with the epitaph, 'Honneur aux Patriotes'. An old woman shuffled into the park and looked at us vacantly, as if she didn't understand the significance of the place, or why we were there. Leaving her to eat her bag lunch, we drove up river to St. Charles sur Richelieu where the Patriotes were defeated, but there was no monument to mark the spot. Celebrate only your victories - a sensible philosophy.

True to her prediction, Josée found Fort Chambly from the downstream side without incident. "I knew you had to turn right just past that bridge," she said, looking self-satisfied. By chance, we arrived at the Fort, the National Historic Site on the banks of the Richelieu River, on August 22nd, the day the Feast of St Louis was being celebrated. Dozens of tents were set up on the grounds with costumed animators outside them stirring huge pots-full of food, while others were making such things as furniture and shoes with primitive tools. Still others in uniforms dating back to the first regular regiment in Canada, the Carignan-Salieres, drilled or strutted about, while bands of fifes and drums played intermittently. And a Mohawk warrior dressed in little more than a breech clout, his face painted and his muscles rippling, looked appropriately fierce. Inside the stone fort, we found a small courtyard surrounded by the usual barracks, officer's quarters, and rooms for artisans, now all converted into a museum. Through all this Josée moved gracefully, stopping here and there to chat, taste, and admire, bringing smiles to everyone, just like a politician.

It was well past noon by this time, and we bought a 17th century lunch from the concession, and sat down to eat it under the shade of the big trees beside the river. The Richelieu, now at its midsummer low, whispered by on its way to join the St. Lawrence, and I reflected on the wealth of history the eastern part of Canada had lived through. Josée, leaning against a tree for support, was in conversation with a group of children, and I wondered where our history together would lead. I shut my mind to the question. For now, I was experiencing the most wonderful period of my life.

Drums sounded, and a troupe of Mohawk dancers took to a stage. We watched them shuffle and pirouette for an hour or more, and listened to their strange chants, until Dickie dragged us away to our car.

The jet, this time, was waiting for us at Mirabel, the white elephant airport near Montreal built with taxpayers' money to buy Quebec votes. The flight to Brockville, Ontario, the closest point to our next revisits of history, was short, giving us a long evening to work, but we ran out of inspiration early, and repaired to the bar of our hotel. In fact, it seemed to me that we were all suffering from frayed tempers and fatigue, in spite of our recent holiday. An extra drink didn't help, either, and by the time we got to our room, I was feeling belligerent. "Well," I started in, "Did you go with Yvan last night?"

Josée threw her blouse on the bed. Not like her to do that. An opening gambit. "You want me to say yes or no?"

"I'm beginning to wonder if I care any more. But tell me the truth."

"No, I did not go with him."

I cared alright. "I saw that girl again last night," I said.

"Did you go with her?"

"No. She was with someone else."

"If you want to make love, I am tired, not in the mood, I have a headache, pick your excuse."

The heat wave continued the next day as we drove east along the St. Lawrence, through picturesque small towns with tree shaded streets and gracious old houses, the United States just the width of the river away. At length, we came to Fort Wellington, another in the vast network of National Historic Sites, and once the base of the Glengarry Fencibles, who attacked Ogdensburg, New York, in 1812. We paid the modest entrance fee, watched an historical documentary, and then toured the buildings and grounds. Dickie was beside himself, if I could judge his state of mind. "Oh, look at the horizontal fraising on the ramparts - and it has a caponnière!"

The 'Windmill', where Von Schoultz and his men were cornered after their attempt to invade Upper Canada, was less than a mile downstream from the Fort. Another National Historic Site, it was manned by an earnest young fellow who looked as if he were starved for company. We climbed the stairs and looked across the River at Ogdensburg where the invaders came from, and I wondered how they convinced themselves that they had any chance of success. Before we left, Joe-Bob made the earnest young fellow's day by buying two bags-full of gifts for his kids, including toy cannon and tee-shirts.

"Alright, Fred," said Dickie as we left the Windmill, "it's your turn. Where can we find a ship that will take us around the Thousand Islands?"

"At Gananoque, just a few miles up river. There's a nice inn there that I stayed at once, and it's handy to the docks." Such a nice little inn it was, and I hoped that it would infect Josée with a little enthusiasm, but, for yet another night, I was disappointed.

Our gleaming white ship, over 100 feet long with five decks, pulled away from its mooring at precisely nine o'clock the next morning, and headed out into the St. Lawrence River, more than three kilometres wide at Gananoque. From the bilingual commentary coming over the speakers, we learned that there were actually more than 1,000 islands along our route, from small rocks barely clearing the water to some many hundreds of acres in size. An island was defined, on the Canadian side, as anything over two acres with at least one tree growing on it, and it was not permitted to build on anything smaller. No such restrictions applied on the American side. After we crossed the international boundary, we saw buildings perched on rock ledges just large enough to accommodate them, and in some cases, only two or three feet above the water. The difference in the quality and value of the buildings was also obvious, or was it simply a reflection of attitudes? On the Canadian side, most of the cottages were small, snug and inviting, like a refuge from the cares of the world; on the American side, there were cottages, yes, but mansions, too, by the hundreds, with elaborate docks and boat sheds, and even a castle or two.

The four of us spent much of our time on deck in the brisk air, enjoying the breeze caused by the motion of the ship, the vivid blue colour of the water, and the endless variety of island architecture. Still, Josée seemed sad for some reason, and I asked what I could do to improve her outlook on life. "Buy you some new clothes?"

That brought a smile. "Clothes always cheer me up. You could try that."

Dickie overheard. "Of course. We'll find a shop in Kingston tomorrow. But to change the subject, when first Amherst and later Wilkinson came down this stretch of river, it was much more treacherous than it is today. There were rapids here and there which have been largely modified by the locks of the St. Lawrence Seaway."

Back on land again, we drove on to historic Kingston, once the outpost of New France called Fort Frontenac, where Lake Ontario empties into the St. Lawrence River. After a long evening of editing in our comfortable hotel, we retired to the bar, and as we were savouring our first drinks, I asked, "What's for tomorrow, Dickie?" It was my country, and I was still asking a Brit what we were going to do next.

"We'll be tourists, visit Fort Henry, Fort Frederick, and the Royal Canadian Military College at Kingston, then drive back to Toronto. Oh yes. And find some new clothes for Josée."

"While we are in Kingston, we should visit the house where Sir John A. Macdonald lived."

"Ahead of yourself again, Fred, but very well. We won't likely be back here again."

Fort Henry, on the other side of the Cataraqui River (where the Rideau Canal ends) from the main part of Kingston, was first built after the war of 1812, in case the Americans should attack again. Inside the stone battlements, our animator-guide took us through detention cells, officers' quarters, what could only be called the dormitory for the married men, and finally the schoolhouse. There, he explained that children were considered grown up and ready for the outside world by the time they were 14, so the boys enlisted as drummers or became apprentices in a nearby town, while the girls either married or went into domestic service. On the parade square, he told us that soldiers were paid a penny a day for their services, while it cost officers a princely sum in the early years of the 19th century to maintain their commissions. To come up with the amount of money necessary, most of them had to be subsidized by relatives or sponsors.

Although they had quarters in the fort, most officers lived in Kingston with their wives. If they committed some breach of discipline, they were merely confined to quarters, but the men, even for such minor crimes as being drunk and disorderly, were forced to carry cannon balls from one end of the parade square to the other and back again.

Before we left, we were treated to a gun salute, and we climbed to the top of the walls for a view of Lake Ontario, the St. Lawrence River, and Wolfe Island, named after the victor of Quebec.

With a snack in the soldiers' canteen to keep us going, we moved next door to the Royal Canadian Military College where our country's officers were trained, and Dickie ingratiated himself with the guard to the point that we were given a conducted tour. On the other side of the college was Fort Frederick, a round 'Martello' tower built about 1846 in response to another threat of war with the United States. Now converted to a museum, there were displays in it of weapons and uniforms, pictures of ships and officers involved in the War of 1812, and on the gun platform, three massive 32 pound guns on traversing mounts. After all our time together, Dickie finally explained what the pounds meant in relation to cannon. "Simply, a 32 pound gun fired balls that weighed 32 pounds."

In town again, we, or I should say Dickie and Joe-Bob, bought some new outfits and accessories for Josée, and we did take time to visit the house where Sir John A. Macdonald lived. Then it was on the road once more and back to

Toronto. We again avoided the freeway, following instead the 'Loyalist Parkway' to Trenton, a route that took us through rural, small town Ontario almost as it was when it was Upper Canada, and brash young Americans were joining Hunters' Lodges.

"We must carry on for a short time tonight," Dickie told us in our Toronto hotel. "It is necessary before we fly to British Columbia tomorrow. As I said earlier, the threat of war with the United States waxed and waned over several issues, after the rebellions and invasions of the late 1830's. There was the undeclared 'Aroostook War', in which Maine lumbermen tried to take over the interior of New Brunswick. No military action resulted, but the Americans did gain some territory in the Webster-Ashburton treaty of 1842. Meanwhile, navies were re-established on the Great Lakes, both nations agreeing that the earlier gunboat rules did not apply to iron ships."

"On the political front," Josée contributed, "Governor Lord Durham revived the idea of uniting Upper and Lower Canada, with the expectation that the French would be absorbed. Not a popular idea, as you can imagine, with the French."

"Yes, Josée. But Durham prevailed, and the Canadas were united into the single colony or province of Canada. But to get on with it, the most serious threat to peace came from beyond the Rocky Mountains, where both the United States and Great Britain were free to exploit the resources of that vast area, as provided by the Treaty of Ghent, which ended the War of 1812. To back up a bit, we already talked of the fur trade, and Mackenzie's explorations into the Arctic and to the Pacific Coast on behalf of the North West Company. Meanwhile, the Hudson's Bay Company was 'sleeping by its frozen sea', losing furs to the younger, more vigorous firm, and suffering losses to its territory as a result of the War of 1812."

"You talking about the Red River?" asked Joe-Bob.

"Yes. The Hudson Bay drainage includes the Red River, which flows into Manitoba from the Dakotas, and so that part below the 49th parallel obviously was removed from the Company's empire, and awarded to the United States. To partly compensate the Company, it was given rights to the unclaimed territory beyond the Rocky Mountains. To continue, in 1824, the two fur companies merged taking the name of the older, that is, the Hudson's Bay Company, which we shall henceforth refer to as 'the Bay'. By that time, it had trading posts throughout New Caledonia, the name used for the territory before it became British Columbia, and a headquarters at Fort Vancouver on the Columbia River in what is now Washington State. All the furs from the interior were brought to Fort Vancouver by the fur brigades, coming down the rivers by canoe and over the mountains by packhorse."

"Is this going to last much longer?" I asked, yawning.

"Fred, you lack stamina. We must understand what led to the treaty of Washington in 1846 before we quit. While the Bay was content to harvest furs beyond the mountains, and maintain a few hundred employees scattered over an immense area, American settlers by the thousands were heading for Oregon Territory, as they called it. In 1843, reading the writing on the wall, that is, realizing that Great Britain was not going to accept its advice to press for the logical boundary of the Columbia River, the Bay moved its headquarters to Victoria on the south end of Vancouver Island."

"Say, President Polk of the United States had a lot to do with that. He came up with the slogan, 'Fifty-Four-Forty-or-Fight', meaning go for all the country west of the mountains as far north as Russian Alaska."

"Yes, Joe-Bob, you overbearing Yanks made Great Britain compromise. By the Treaty of Washington in 1846, the 49th parallel of latitude was extended from the Rockies to the Pacific Coast, with a slight diversion to leave all of Vancouver Island in British hands."

"But that wasn't the end of it, either, was it?"

"Not quite, but we can leave the rest for our stay in British Columbia. What time do we leave in the morning, Joe-Bob?"

"The usual, nine o'clock. With the difference in time, that will get us into Vancouver early in the afternoon."

It was a good day for a flight across the country, with the sun behind us most of the way. Beyond the Great Lakes, the pilot assumed a course on the Canadian side of the international boundary, and the great expanse of the prairies passed beneath us, a mosaic of square and rectangular grain fields in various shades of gold and brown, soon to be ready for harvest. At one point, we could see Winnipeg in the distance and the big lakes beyond it: Winnipeg, Winnipegosis, and Manitoba. Joe-Bob craned his neck to take it all in, and whistled. "Jesus, God, some big piece of country. Any fish in those lakes?"

"All kinds," I answered. "Char up to 40 pounds and more, I've heard."

We droned on over Saskatchewan and Alberta until we could see the Rocky Mountains, the rugged peaks all pink in the still rising sun. Beyond them was British Columbia and more mountain ranges, the Purcells, the Selkirks, and the Monashees, separated one from the other by narrow valleys, their peaks rising from forest-clad flanks; and beyond them was the massive jumble of the Coast Range, 100 miles wide and more. As spectacular as the Rockies were in the morning sunlight, no less so was our first sight of the Pacific Ocean, the bluest blue, stretching out into infinity, all encrusted inshore with forested islands. We followed the mighty Fraser River as far as Abbotsford, then circled over the north-shore mountains, the granite knobs called the Lions not yet with their winter coats, and looked down on the city with the most beautiful setting in the world, according to the Chamber of Commerce: the Port of Vancouver.

"How big is this place?" asked Joe-Bob, craning his neck again to take in the scenery.

"Over a million people, if you throw in all the suburbs. Barely big enough to be major league."

We booked into a hotel downtown with a view of Burrard Inlet and the mountains, and after a hearty lunch, four hours late by Ontario time, we were herded into Dickie's suite for a history session. "We have already talked about the Treaty of Washington, which extended the 49th parallel of latitude from the Rockies to the Pacific Coast. Fred, as a native British Columbian, something of a rarity, I gather, tell us how Great Britain managed to hold on to this part of the country in the face of American imperialism."

"Say, now, that stings, calling us imperialists!"

"The shoe fits, you overbearing Yank. President Polk had hardly threatened Great Britain out of Oregon Territory, with only 8 American families in all of what is now the State of Washington, when he turned on hapless Mexico. By force of arms, he took from her much of Texas, all of New Mexico, Arizona, California, Nevada, and Utah, most of Colorado, and part of Wyoming."

"May I begin?" I asked. Silence. "We were able to hang on to this part of the country because of two remarkable men, the first being James Douglas, later Sir James. A man of uncertain origins, thought by some to have black blood in him, he came from Britain's Colonies in the Caribbean to work in the fur trade. He eventually rose to the rank of Chief Factor, that is, the top dog for the Western Compartment of the Bay, and he supervised the move of the Company's headquarters from Fort Vancouver to Victoria. In 1849, Vancouver Island was created a Crown Colony and the Bay was given the task of settling it, and when Douglas became Governor two years later, he resigned from the Company to devote all his energies to politics. Not all the colonists liked him, but whatever they thought of him, he was a big man with an immense physical presence, strong as a bull and absolutely fearless.

"In 1857, gold was discovered on the Fraser River, that is, on the mainland, and Americans by the thousands came to get their share. But they soon began hassling the local Indians, who appealed to Douglas for help. His response was to declare himself Governor of the mainland as well as the Island, to impose a fee of ten shillings a month on the miners, and to march up the Fraser with a small escort to settle the trouble. Somewhere near Yale, he ran into a large party of heavily armed Americans, who could easily have killed him and his escort had they chosen to. Instead, over-awed by the big man, they listened while he lectured them about their conduct, and told them he would see them escorted from British Territory if they caused any more trouble.

"In 1858, the mainland was created the colony of British Columbia, with Douglas officially appointed Governor. In this vast territory, Douglas needed someone to maintain law and order, and he found the man he needed in Mathew Bailey Begbie, a trained lawyer from England. A crack shot and almost a match for Douglas in size and strength, he was born for the frontier, and would have been a complete misfit in his native land. As the colony developed, mostly, in the early days, as a result of gold discoveries, Judge Begbie rode circuit from one tiny community to the other, presiding at trials without jury, and making the kinds of decisions that were the rule in those days. He became known as the 'Hanging Judge', and more than one attempt was made on his life by resentful Americans, but he was like a cat with nine lives, and always managed to escape.

In one incident, he was reported to have dumped a chamber pot from a balcony on his would-be murderer."

With Dickie's help, I completed a picture of the early history of British Columbia during the afternoon: the amalgamation of the Island and Mainland Colonies; the gold strikes; the building of the Cariboo Road through the Fraser Canyon; the naval establishment at Esquimalt; Douglas' proposal to buy Russian Alaska, rejected by the British Government; Douglas' recommendation that he retake Oregon Territory during the American Civil War, rejected by the British Government; the slow population growth and economic development of the region; the decision to retain most of the land base in public hands.

"Let me get this straight, Fred." Joe-Bob looked incredulous again. "You say that the province of British Columbia still owns 95 percent of the land base?"

"That's right, forests, mountains, the lot, except for five per cent. I know because my father was a Forest Ranger, worked for the government."

"Why, it's as if you were a communist country, as if you didn't trust the citizens to own land."

"And the environmentalists like it that way, because the government is easier to bully than thousands of landowners."

"Extraordinary indeed, Fred," Dickie agreed. "But I see it's five o'clock, and I know you want to visit with your daughters this evening."

"Say, Dickie, we have to be back by noon tomorrow because Jacqui's got a golf game lined up for us here in Vancouver, but why don't we fly down to Portland for the night, have a look at the Columbia River while we're at it. Need to get that local flavour."

"Capital idea."

We left the two of them in the lobby arguing about the ceding of Oregon Territory to the United States, and took a cab to my younger daughter's place. Josée was not too thrilled with the idea of visiting my children. "Do you really think you should introduce me to them?"

"Yes, I do. I want to show you off."

"But will they understand? Will they accept me?"

"Expect a mixed reaction. Grace will be warm and friendly. Louise may be horrified."

"Alright, but I am nervous."

"I love you."

"Shut up Fred, shut up."

Grace's husband, Bill, was a Vice President of a big forestry company, and they lived in the posh neighbourhood of West Vancouver known as the British Properties. When we got there, the grand children aged five and three, were still up, and for once, they were quiet and well-behaved. They were shy with me but soon were at ease with Josée, who seemed genuinely charmed with them. As predicted, Grace lived up to her name and embraced us both, while Bill winked at me when no one was looking, and clapped me on the back. Then Louise, looking cold and frosty, her husband Jack not looking as henpecked as I remembered, and their four year old daughter Jenny, looking spoiled and bored, arrived. After introductions, Louise all too obviously herded me out to the kitchen and hissed, "For God's sake, Dad, what are you doing with that French tart?"

Louise looked much like Beth, but she was much fiercer. Since her mother's death, she had appointed herself my custodian, but I had no intention of being brought up by my elder daughter. "She screws me and I love it."

"Dad! I've never heard you use language like that before."

"No more Mr. Nice Guy."

"What's come over you?"

"Middle-aged madness or male menopause. Lighten up, Louise. I've never been happier in my life."

"But what about your friends? And how could you do this to mom?"

"I don't have any friends. And your mother is dead. When she knew she was going to die, she told me to get married again."

"Oh, no! You haven't married her, have you?"

"Only because she won't say yes."

"She looks young enough to have children. You are taking precautions? What a disaster if she were to have a child!"

"Don't worry. She's impregnable. But why would it be a disaster if she had my child?"

"I don't believe what I'm hearing. Our inheritance - Grace and mine - and the grandchildren."

"Oh, come on. Josée and I have an agreement, but even if she weren't in the picture, you'd only get a few thousand each from me. Aren't Jack and Bill rich enough for you?"

Her manner changed suddenly, from the usual take-charge self-confidence to dejection. She sighed, "Oh, Dad, it isn't going well with Jack's business. He's invented this marvellous pump, but he can't get the financing to produce and market it. And - and, oh, Dad, I'm too hard on him, I know, but I can't seem to back off, our marriage is a mess, we don't sleep together any more, I wanted to try for a son, but I can't do it by myself. It's even worse than that. I think he's - I think he's screwing one of the girls at the office."

"Dad's solution. Let's go out there and claim those drinks Bill was mixing for us, and you get Jack to tell us all about that pump."

In the living room, Josée was singing 'Frere Jacques' with the kids, and Grace looked entranced. She took my arm and said, "She's utterly gorgeous, Dad. And what a lovely voice!"

"You don't mind all the makeup?"

"I don't know why she wears it, because she doesn't need it. You really care for her, don't you?"

"I love her, Grace."

At dinner, Louise tried to change her stripes. She reached across the table to pat Jack's hands, and told us, "Jack has invented this marvellous pump, and it's going to make us rich. Tell them about it, darling."

With an amazed look, Jack stuttered for a moment, then explained in halting words why the pump was such an innovation. "It uses 15 per cent less power, would save mid-sized communities with subdivisions up in the hills hundreds of thousands of dollars a year. Of course, it's one thing to invent a pump, it's another to produce and sell it. Our company can't do that with the resources we have, and so far, we haven't been able to convince the banks to help us."

Josée looked at me with a question in her eyes. I nodded, and said, "Maybe a friend of ours could help."

Louise pounced. "A friend of yours? You said you had no friends."

"Well, a kind of a friend. You see, as I've told you in my letters, Josée and I are writing a book with the help of a couple of shirt-tail relatives. It just so happens they are both millionaires."

"Dad! Quit the fiction! This is serious business!" Louise bristled.

Uncharacteristically, Jack cut her off. "Alright, Louise. Let's hear Fred out."

"One of them, the American, is investing in Canadian businesses. He's no fool, Jack, but if you've really got something, he'll recognize it and give you a hand."

"On what terms?" Jack again.

"His policy is to leave the existing management in place for a year. If by then the company is not making at least a ten per cent profit, he moves in and appoints his own people."

"Fair enough."

Louise looked frightened. "But Jack, you could lose the business!"

"I know you don't have any faith in me, but I think I can meet those terms."

There was an uneasy silence. I could see Louise wrestle with herself, come to a decision. She stood up, walked around the table and put hands on her husband's shoulders. "You're wrong, darling. I know you can meet those terms."

Jack looked amazed again. "Where is this mystery man with all the money, Fred?"

"In Oregon, but he should be back tomorrow. I'll get him to give you a call."

Josée was quiet and withdrawn on the way home, and I resigned myself to another night without love. Back in the hotel, we got ready for bed with a minimum of conversation and crawled in, each of us lying on our own side of the king-size bed, with our heads propped up on our arms. Sleep was about to come to me when she said, "Your grandchildren are so beautiful."

"Little monsters, really, especially Jenny. You simply charmed them."

She sighed, and sighed again, and then she turned to me, and came into my arms. "Fall is coming. Before we leave here, I'm going to con Dickie and Joe-Bob into buying me some new clothes. There is such a nice shop in the lobby."

As the balls fell, it was my turn to play with Josée again the next day, and we lost by a shot, and I wondered if I would be punished that night. Certainly, she was less than friendly by the time we finished.

We all had dinner with Jack and Louise that night, then toured Jack's plant. Joe-Bob was so impressed with the new pump that he wrote a cheque for a million dollars on the spot, cashable as soon as the necessary paper work was done.

Back at the hotel, our evening session brought us to the brink of Canadian Confederation and the event that sparked it, the American Civil War. "Yes, the American Civil War, fought between the North and the South between 1861 and 1865, led to the creation of Canada," Dickie affirmed.

"Say, now, that was a real war, wasn't it, Dickie? Like I told you when we were in New Brunswick, my great great granddaddy fought for the North, and became a carpet-bagger after it was over."

"Yes, Joe-Bob. An unscrupulous opportunist, I believe, is the definition of a carpet-bagger."

"That's what he was. He knew the timber business from New Hampshire, and he bought up thousands of acres of pinelands in Georgia dirt cheap. That was the start of the family fortune."

"As for the war, the British supported the South, the Confederacy, because of the high-handedness of the North, as represented by the Union Government. In April of 1861, for example, a Union warship stopped a British merchant vessel on the high seas, and removed two Confederate envoys on their way to London. For a time, it looked as if there would be war over the incident, but the Union Government backed down and released the captives, concerned perhaps about becoming sandwiched between two hostile forces, the one in British North America, the other in the south. Then there was the Alabama incident, the Alabama being an iron-clad Confederate warship built in England, which, the Union Government claimed, the British let escape instead of interning it. The fact that the Alabama was on the loose extending the war for three years, the Unionists later claimed, at a cost of four billion dollars, and British North America, they suggested, would be fair and just compensation. Influential northern newspapers, meanwhile, began to threaten revenge on British North America, once the south was disposed of. Finally, the Unionists at one stage invited the Russians to use bases in the United States so that they could attack British North America."

"Say, how about the St. Albans Affair? Confederate renegades in Canada raided St. Albans in Vermont in 1864. They weren't even given jail time, and they even were allowed to keep the money they stole."

"Meanwhile, Great Britain, barely extricated from the nightmare of the Crimean War, and facing the threat of hostilities with Prussia, was looking for ways to make her colonies in British North America less of a financial and military burden. Fred?"

"Britain encouraged the expansion of the militia, only to have the Assembly of the United Canadas refuse to pass the necessary money bill, with the excuse that the poor relations between Britain and the United States were not its fault."

"Thank you. Now, after reviewing the daunting task of defending the long boundary with the United States, the British decided to promote colonial confederation as a means out of their dilemma. Fred, again."

"But the push for union originated as much in Canada as Britain. George Brown, leader of the Protestant Reform Party and publisher of the newspaper the 'Toronto Globe', was inspired to suggest it by his new wife, so the story goes."

"Ah, a love story led to the creation of Canada! How, what-do-you-call-it?"

"Fitting, appropriate, my dear Josée. Go ahead, Fred."

"We do know that Brown wanted to split the Province of Canada into its two original parts so that the French and English could go their separate ways, and having split them, join them together again as equal partners in a federation. In any event, in the late summer of 1864, the Maritime colonies, that is, Prince Edward Island, New Brunswick, Nova Scotia and Newfoundland, at the prompting of Great Britain, arranged to meet in Charlottetown, the capital of Prince Edward Island, to discuss a federation. Politicians in the colony of Canada by that time had formed a coalition, and on hearing of the meeting, asked if they could attend. Led by Brown, John A. Macdonald and Etienne Cartier, they arrived with a boat-load of booze and a plan for the joining of all the colonies in British North America, including, eventually, Rupert's Land, that is, the lands of the Hudson's Bay Company, and the new colonies on the Pacific Coast. Brown said later that, as the Canadian party came ashore from their ship, he felt a little like Christopher Columbus."

"I suppose he might," mused Dickie. "A grand undertaking."

"Say, in 1864, the United States had a population of over 30 million people. How many in British North America?"

"Between three and four million," I answered, "and that ratio, ten Americans to one Canadian, has more or less persisted down to the present time."

"What ten Americans could accomplish, surely one true blue Loyalist, or one tough Canadien could also do."

"Now, don't you start needling me, Dickie."

"Who, me? Why Joe-Bob, the thought would never enter my head. Besides, as we shall see, Canadians will have need of you Americans."

"Let Fred go on," Josée chided. At least she was speaking of me, if not to me.

"Thanks, Jos. The Canadian idea of creating a nation from sea to sea, an empire to rival the United States, an economic entity that could borrow money and finance such desirable symbols of progress as railways, caught on with the Maritime Provinces. At a further meeting in Quebec City in October, where the Fathers of Confederation, as we call them, partied as hard as they worked, the idea was fleshed out into official proposals for union. These were taken to London in October of 1864, and almost immediately adopted by the British Government."

"Fred, I must interrupt you," apologized Dickie. "We must digress here to talk about the Fenians, those American-Irishmen who took it upon themselves to revenge their homeland by attacking British North America. Many of them were veterans of the Civil War, but most were more adept at talking a good fight in the bar than actually staging one. As proof of that, they started out five times to invade, but only once did they cross the border in enough force to cause alarm. That resulted in the engagement at Ridgeway, near Fort Erie in Ontario, during which Roger Patterson's great grandfather was killed.

"Between 800 and 1,000 Fenians, under a Lieutenant Colonel John O'Neill, crossed the Niagara River on June 1st, 1866, and took up a strategic position near Ridgeway. The next day, they were attacked by an undisciplined, inexperienced potpourri of militia units, including the 13th Infantry Battalion of Hamilton, the 19th of St. Catherines, the Caledonia Rifle Company –"

"Dickie!"

"Perhaps 1,000 men altogether, commanded by Lieutenant Colonel Alfred Booker. Things went well enough for the militiamen to begin with. They extended into line of battle, and were advancing steadily, until someone falsely reported that a detachment of Fenian cavalry was charging them. In the resulting confusion, the Fenians, who had no cavalry, chased the militia back to Ridgeway, and then retired to the vicinity of Fort Erie. There, they beat off an attack by the Welland Field Battery and the Dunville Naval Brigade, both units coming from aboard the steamer, the 'W.T. Robb'. Knowing that regular soldiers were coming from Toronto - including the 2nd Battalion, Queen's Own Rifles - alright, alright, I hear your grumbling - O'Neill and his Fenians retreated across the Niagara to New York State, where they were arrested by United States marshals.

"Now, we have a day in hand before we fly to Niagara Falls again, where we will meet Roger and Joyce, and accompany them to Ridgeway. Fred, we should take this opportunity to see a little more of British Columbia. Any suggestions?"

"Well, I'd like to visit Kamloops while we are out here, my home town. We could drive up the Fraser Canyon on our way, over the route of the original wagon road to the Cariboo gold fields."

"Agreed, then, and off to the bar."

And I did get punished that night, and then rewarded. Our relationship was back on track

Late summer in British Columbia: cool mornings; warm days; a hint of smoke in the air from uncontrolled forest fires; inadequate highways clogged with holiday traffic. As we droned eastward through the Fraser Valley, with the mountains on both sides of the river pinching in on us, Dickie asked me to describe my home province 'in a few words'.

"It is really two distinct geographical units: the coast on the mild, wet side of the Coast Mountains; the Interior with a more continental climate on the other side. Population about three million, over half in greater Vancouver and the Victoria capital region, the rest scattered in small towns along the main traffic corridors. Only five per cent of the land area is suitable for agriculture, and a big chunk of that is in this valley. The other 95 percent is mostly wilderness, half of it commercial forest, half not good for much besides downhill skiing. Our main industry is forestry, with tourism and high tech gaining, while mining and fishing are on the decline."

"No dog sleds, Fred? And what kind of trees?"

"No dog sleds, Joe-Bob. And the trees are mostly conifers like Douglas fir and Pine."

"And is it bigger than Texas?"

"Yes. Less than a quarter of the population, but almost one point four times as big. If it makes you feel better, Alaska is bigger than B.C."

"Alaska was my ace in the hole - bigger than any of the Canadian provinces except Quebec."

The Fraser Canyon, an awesome gorge carved out of the granite rock of the coast range, provided the easiest access between the coast and the interior in the early days. Two trans continental railways were blasted through it as well as the Trans Canada Highway, which perilously skirted the canyon walls for 60 miles when it was first built. Seven tunnels have since been bored through the most treacherous stretches to improve both alignment and safety, but it was still a tough stretch of road when we drove it, subject to rock slides in the spring and avalanches in winter.

We stopped at Hell's Gate, took the air tram the 500 vertical feet down to the river-level restaurant, and while the mighty Fraser surged by, had a lunch of poached Pacific salmon. "The fish ladders you see were installed after a massive slide narrowed the channel here in 1917," I explained.

Back on the highway again, the character of the country began to change radically, from heavy forest to scattered pine trees and grasslands. Beyond the small town of Lytton, we left the Fraser and continued up its major tributary, the Thompson, with its own style of canyon, until we reached the dry bench lands at Cache Creek, just a short hour away from Kamloops.

"Say, nice looking place, Fred," Joe-Bob commented as we rolled into my home -town. "I like the hills, the dry look of it. How big is it?"

"About 80,000."

"What do they do here? With all the grass, must be some ranching."

"Ranching, yes, but a minor part of the economy. Forestry is king like it is in a lot of B.C. towns, and the railways also provide a lot of employment."

"Any golf courses here? We've got time for a game before supper."

"Several of them. I'll call my old club, if you like, and see if we can get on."

"Oh, we really should do some editing," cautioned Dickie.

"Golf first, then editing, Dickie," Joe-Bob over-ruled. "Let's make it skins today."

With Josée back from early communion, we took off in the jet from the Kamloops airport the next morning, headed back to the coast, and took a swing around the south end of Vancouver Island so we could have a look at Victoria. "San Juan Island, the little one below us there, was the subject of the 'Pig

Wars',", Dickie told us, as we turned north again, "a bloodless standoff between Britain and the United States that lasted 13 years. The island was awarded to the United States in 1872 under arbitration by the German Kaiser. And that's it for British Columbia, where I am sure we could spend more time if we had it. Now back to Ontario and the Fenian raid on Ridgeway."

Roger and Joyce Patterson came from Buffalo to join us for dinner in our Niagara Falls hotel, he looking pale and drawn, she seeming happy and excited, with her cheeks flushed a becoming pink. In the evening, over drinks, we brought them up to date on the book, and Roger insisted on giving Dickie his great grandfather's papers, saying, "Nobody else in the family would be interested in them."

I drove everybody to Ridgeway the next morning, and there we found a monument marking the place where the Fenians met the Canadian militia in 1866. Roger walked slowly from one end of the little park to the other, communing, we supposed, with his ancestor, while the rest of us waited. After some minutes, he beckoned to me and said, "I suppose it was a crazy idea they had, expecting the people to support them, believing they could conquer British North America. You people are different, still have respect for appointed authorities, not nearly so irreverent as we are. Go your own way in peace."

The Pattersons invited us for dinner that night aboard the 'Lady Joyce', at dock on the Erie Canal in Buffalo, and Roger said to us as we were leaving, "This may be the last time we all get together. Just in case I'm not around much longer, good luck with the book." We protested, of course, but he really did not look at all well. "Keep in touch, won't you?" said Joyce, looking at Dickie with a tear in her eye.

"We certainly shall," he replied, and I don't think, at that moment, he realized that she was in love with him.

The jet that afternoon took us to Charlottetown on Prince Edward Island, the smallest province, so small in fact that Joe-Bob didn't even ask for a comparison with Texas. As we resumed our writing in the evening, I began, "On March 29th, 1867, the British North America Act created the self governing Dominion of Canada by joining Quebec and Ontario, the two parts of the old Province of Canada, with New Brunswick and Nova Scotia. Prince Edward Island joined in 1873 on condition that the Federal government assume its railway debt, but Newfoundland opted out, and didn't join until 1948. John A. Macdonald, soon to be Sir John, the leader of the Conservative or Tory party, was our first Prime Minister, and the capital was moved from Montreal to Ottawa. The government, though federal, was on the British parliamentary model, with a House of Commons and an all-powerful cabinet, or Privy Council, made up of the elected leaders of the governing party, while an appointed Senate took the place of the House of Lords."

"Thank you Fred for your brief and to the point summary. I should tell you also that, after studying the example of the rebellious American States, Edward Cardswell, the Colonial Secretary responsible for the British North America Act, included in it a 'Peace, Order and Good Government' clause, which gave Canada a strong central government. Further, foreign policy for the new Dominion was still under the control of Great Britain, and remained partly so until after the Second World War. Lastly, Canada committed itself to spend one million dollars a year on defence, in return for a guarantee of British help in the case of invasion from the United States, and agreed that the militia should be headed by a career British officer. Now, Fred, tell us about Rupert's Land, the empire of the Hudson's Bay Company."

"The Americans wanted to buy it for a reported 40 million dollars, but the British wouldn't allow the Company to sell to them. Instead, they accepted the Canadian offer of one and a half million, guaranteed the loan to buy it, and forced the Bay to accept it."

"You arrogant Brits! We bought Louisiana from Napoleon Bonaparte in 1803 - that's most of the whole Mississippi drainage - 800,000 square miles - for 15 million; we bought Alaska from the Russians in 1867 - that's another 615,000 square miles - for seven million; and you turned down 40 million for the million square miles in Rupert's Land?"

"Ah, yes, Louisiana. You remember that the French ceded it to the Spanish in the secret treaty of Fontainebleau, but they got it back, as planned. As for Rupert's Land, Joe-Bob, as you say over here, I believe, eat your heart out."

"As part of the agreement," I continued, "Canada had to give one twentieth of the most fertile lands back to the Bay. But there were soon problems. The Northwest Territories, as Rupert's Land became known, was already settled, not only by Indians but by Métis, the descendants of mixed marriages between French voyageurs and Indian women."

"Let me continue," Josée demanded. "The Métis, such a romantic people, Canadien in outlook and culture, even to the point of dividing the land along the rivers into narrow strips. Buffalo hunters and freighters for the Hudson's Bay Company, they depended on the rivers for fish and for transport, and it was the threat that government surveyors would force them off those rivers, or worse still, not recognize their rights to any land at all, that caused them to react. Their leader was Louis Riel, a mystic of sorts, who would later spend time in mental institutions in Quebec. He seized Upper Fort Garry, a Hudson's Bay post on the Red River north of Winnipeg, and held it until he forced the Canadian Government to agree to his terms."

"Now me, again," I said. "Some recent settlers from Ontario were accused by the Métis of trying to re-take the fort, whether or not that was true. One of them, an Orangeman named Thomas Scott, was shot for his part in the affair, which greatly upset the Protestants in Ontario, who put a price on Riel's head. Macdonald passed the Manitoba Act in 1870, creating what was at first a postage stamp of a province, and granted the Métis most of their demands, but he refused to give amnesty to Riel, which greatly upset the French in Quebec."

"Let me do this, Fred," smiled Dickie. "Macdonald sent a mixed contingent of militia and British regulars from the 60th Rifles, formerly the Royal Americans, to show the flag, under Lieutenant Colonel Garnet Wolseley. Travelling like the 'Courier de Bois' of old, it was a triumph that they even reached their destination."

"Now me," Josée broke in. "Riel fled to the United States, fearful that the soldiers, most of them from Protestant Ontario, would seize him. Later, in 1875, he was given amnesty by Governor General Dufferin, subject to five years' banishment from the county. Meanwhile, even though lands were reserved for them in Manitoba, the Métis were not happy with the steady - influx? - of Protestant settlers, and many drifted west to the Saskatchewan River country."

"And so ended the first trouble in the North West Territories."

"Thank you, Fred. Now, tell us about the entry of British Columbia into Confederation."

"To go back a bit, the colony of Vancouver Island was merged with British Columbia in 1866 under still-governor Sir James Douglas, Victoria winning out over New Westminster as the capital. In response to overtures from Canada, a delegation was sent to Ottawa in 1870, via San Francisco and American railroads, to discuss terms of union."

"Say, glad we were able to help out again. But you know, old Polk should have taken British Columbia when he had the chance. Damn shame you folks are still in the way between Washington State and Alaska."

"Yes, Joe-Bob. Macdonald was ill with gallstones, or a hangover, so the delegation met with Cartier, his deputy. When the British Columbians timidly asked for a wagon road to unite them with the rest of the country, Cartier laughed. 'A wagon road? Why not ask for a railway?' And so the wheels were set in motion for the construction of the Canadian Pacific. British Columbia joined Confederation in 1871 on the condition that the railway be completed within ten years, more or less."

Dickie grinned. "Joe-Bob, it will interest you to know that the driving force behind the construction of the Canadian Pacific was its American general manager, William Van Horne."

"I can understand that. We'd already built lots of railways."

"Later on, he became Sir William, and he remained in Canada for the rest of his life."

"I don't understand that."

"We're not going to go into the railway are we?" I protested. "Books have been written about it to end all books. All we need to say is that it was privately financed with loan guarantees by the government."

"But Fred!" Dickie objected. "The romance of it! Breaking through the granite of the Canadian Shield, forging at breakneck speed across the prairies, searching for passes through the sea of mountains in British Columbia – "

"That is sufficient," the rest of us agreed.

"Oh, very well. Now, there were more threats to Canadian sovereignty, Fred."

"Yes. American hunters at this time roamed freely through the Northwest Territories, buying hides from the Indians with rot-gut whiskey, or poisoning wolves so that their pelts would not be marked with bullet holes. In 1873, an altercation between the 'Wolfers' and some Indians broke out, and several Indians were killed in what became known as the Cypress Hills Massacre.

"This was a touchy situation. Macdonald knew that if he took action against the whisky traders with the army, it would likely bring the American cavalry over the border. Instead, he created the North West Mounted Police to establish a Canadian presence in the Territories. This force was unique in its conception in that it combined law enforcement, judicial and military functions. I'm happy to say that my great grandfather Thomas Bonney was one of the first 150 recruits, who followed the same path as Wolseley's men to Winnipeg, and spent the winter of 1873-74 training there."

"Fred," suggested Dickie, "for the sake of brevity, let us call this police force 'The Mounties'."

"Good idea. At the end of 1873, the Conservatives resigned over what was called the 'Pacific Scandal', in which they tried to buy votes with money given to them by the Canadian Pacific, and they were replaced by our other major party, the Liberals. The Ontario members of the party, including the Prime Minister, Alexander MacKenzie, were concerned that their province was footing the bill for all this nationhood, and sought ways and means to cut costs. MacKenzie thought that he could save money by asking the Americans to help bring law and order to the Territories, if you can imagine it. Fortunately, the Governor General talked him out of it."

"Say, how could the representative of the Royal family interfere like that?"

"He was a representative of the British Government, rather than the monarchy, with executive powers limited to signing laws passed by the Canadian Parliament, but early in our history, he could and did exert considerable influence, especially when it came to foreign policy. To go on, MacKenzie grudgingly sent another 150 recruits west in 1874, who had to travel part way on American railways, and all 300 members of the force embarked on the famous trek west to Fort McLeod and Fort Edmonton in what is now Alberta. Not much romance in that, Dickie - creaky Red River carts breaking down all over the place, hordes of prairie mosquitos, and bad water - but the presence of the Mounties alone was enough to bring law and order to the region. From the original posts, they spread out and established many more throughout the Territories, including Fort Walsh in the Cypress Hills. It was from there that they handled the delicate negotiations with the Americans when Sitting Bull and his Sioux Indians fled into Canada. That was after they massacred Custer and his army.

"By 1878, the Canadian electorate had enough of the Liberals, forgave Sir John A. for the Pacific Scandal, and voted him back into office. With this new mandate, he formulated what was called the 'National Policy', which consisted of a framework of tariffs to protect Canadian industry against American imports."

"Say, Fred, what about free trade?"

"Also called 'reciprocity'. Nova Scotia tried that successfully as a colony, but the Liberals lost the election of 1878 over it. You Americans established tariffs on our goods after the civil war, and you were 'Slaughter Selling' or dumping your excess goods into Canada."

"Alright, enough on our plate for tonight," Dickie yawned. "Tomorrow, we should head west."

"Say, we can't leave Prince Edward Island without a game of golf! Jacqui's got one laid on for us tomorrow, right near Charlottetown."

"And surely," I added, "we should stop in Ottawa on the way to see what the country's capital looks like."

"No, no," replied Dickie with finality. "That will be our last stop before we finish the book."

Chapter 10.

The Final Boundary

The last day of August: a new day, a new week, another adventure. After our morning golf game on Prince Edward Island, which ended in a tie, the jet took us westward over the Canadian Shield of northern Quebec, a desolate granite wasteland scoured by glaciers, dotted with thousands of ponds, and covered by scrubby forests. In the distance, we saw James Bay, and when the great Manitoba Lakes came into view, we turned south to Winnipeg, the city not quite big enough to be major league. "So Fred, what do they do in Manitoba for a living, and how big is it compared to Texas?" asked Joe-Bob, as we were landing at the airport.

"According to my automobile club book, Manitoba has one of the most diversified economies in Canada, based mostly on agriculture. It is almost the same size as Texas, but there are just over a million people."

In our downtown hotel, we assembled in Dickie's room for a writing session. He began, "Two more threats to sovereignty, Fred, and we are done. The first?" "Yes. The Saskatchewan Rebellion of 1885."

"Ah, yes, Saskatchewan, the heart of the prairie grasslands, traversed by the mighty branches of the river of the same name, which join together before flowing off to Hudson Bay. Note these places on the map which we will be talking about, some of which I've had to add because they weren't shown: Red Rock, Qu'Appelle, Regina, Fort Walsh, Fish Creek, Batoche, Saskatoon, Swift Current, Saskatchewan Landing, Battleford, Cut Knife Hill, Prince Albert, Frenchman's Butte, Steele's Narrows, Fort Carleton, Duck Lake, Frog Lake, Calgary, and Edmonton."

"Let me begin," Josée volunteered. "The Métis way of life was being threatened again. Surveyors insensitive to their preferences had caught up to them, the buffalo on which they depended for food and part of their income were disappearing, and the men who freighted on the rivers for a living, including my great grandfather Pierre, were being replaced by paddle-wheelers. Though not Métis himself, he was married to one, and threw his lot in with them. Fred?"

"Settlers from the east were also pouring into the Saskatchewan country, but they had their own problems with Ottawa, not the least the fact that they had no representatives in parliament. Their grievances, like those of the Métis, also fell on deaf ears, but the worst off were the Indians. With the buffalo all but hunted to extinction on the prairies, they were on the brink of starvation, and waiting for promised government aid that didn't come. Jos?"

"In 1884, the Métis brought Louis Riel from Montana, where he served his period of banishment as a school teacher, to help negotiate with Ottawa. He prepared a petition listing grievances and proposing remedies, but he also was ignored. Once again, he established a provisional government, this time at Batoche on the South Saskatchewan River, and recruited as allies some desperate

Indians nearby, two bands of Crees under the Chiefs Poundmaker and Big Bear. Even the white settlers supported him at first, but as soon as it was clear he was leading a rebellion, that support melted away.

"Riel's first act of war was to demand the surrender of the Mounties' detachment at Fort Carleton. They of course refused, but were forced to abandon the post on March 28th, 1885, after being ambushed near Duck Lake by Gabriel Dumont, the so-called Adjutant General of the Métis. Dumont was a skilled horseman and rifleman, and his men formed a very effective light cavalry. As for the Indians, Chief Poundmaker attacked Battleford on March 30th simply to find food for his people. And on April 2nd, some of Big Bear's tribe massacred nine whites at Frog Lake, including two Catholic missionaries, and took some prisoners. Fred?"

"Prime Minister Macdonald ordered the army to crush the rebellion. By this time, the Canadian Pacific Railway had been extended from Ontario across the Territories to Calgary, except for four gaps through the Canadian Shield on the north shore of Lake Superior. Dickie?"

"At the end of March, Major General Fred Middleton, the British appointed head of the Canadian militia, set off by rail from Toronto with the 'North West Field Force'. With him were 3,000 to 3,500 men, depending on which account you read, including the Queen's Own Rifles from Toronto, 'A' Battery of the Regiment of Canadian Artillery from Quebec – "

"No, Dickie!"

"The men had to leave the comfort of the railway cars at each of the four gaps in the line, almost 100 miles in total, and proceed by sleighs and on foot through the bitter remains of winter. Finally, at Red Rock, they were able to board the train for the last time, and travel all the way to Qu'Appelle in the Territories, arriving there on April 6th, 1885. In the west, another 4,000 men, in round numbers, had already been recruited, so that Middleton had over 7,000 at his disposal. He then set in motion a plan for a three-pronged attack. A column under Lieutenant Colonel William Otter continued on the railway to Swift Current, and marched north from there to the relief of Battleford. A second column under Major General Thomas B. Strange, dubbed 'The Alberta Field Force', proceeded north from Calgary to intercept Big Bear and his Crees. Middleton himself planned to take the rebel capital of Batoche."

"Say, another three-pronged attack. A popular choice. Who's next? Fred?"

"Several Mounties were seconded to the Alberta Field Force to act as scouts, and given military rank for the occasion. Major Samuel B. Steele, fresh off looking after security for the Canadian Pacific Railway, was in charge of this group, which included my great grandfather. Sam Steele was a native born Canadian, one of those big, just men like Brock and Douglas who stand out in the history of this country. We will hear more about him later in connection with the Klondike gold rush, and the settling of the border with Alaska."

"Yes, Fred." Dickie again. "Dare I say, without provoking a vociferous reaction, that all the columns had a few pieces of artillery? How about Gatling guns? Mounted infantry? I can see I'm pushing my luck. Very well. Let us dispatch first with Otter's column, nearly 600 officers and men. When he reached Battleford on April 24th, the townsfolk, who had taken refuge in the Mounties' stockade, demanded he attack Poundmaker and his Crees, which he did, against Middleton's orders. At the Battle of Cut Knife Hill on May 2nd, Otter's cannon collapsed on their rotten carriages, and Poundmaker drove him off in humiliation.

"As for the Alberta Field Force, Strange and his men reached Edmonton on May 2nd, and, after a frustrating chase, caught up with Big Bear at Frenchman's Butte. But the wily native escaped, and Strange chased him again, finally catching him at Steele's Narrows, where there was an inconclusive engagement.

"Finally, Middleton, with about 800 men, indicating he had many in reserve. Using the Hudson's Bay paddle wheeler the 'Northcote' to help move supplies down the South Saskatchewan River, he advanced cautiously toward Batoche, to the frustration of his men. On the way, he was ambushed by Dumont at Fish Creek, suffering 55 casualties, which made him even more cautious. Finally, on May 9th, he was in position at Batoche, and began his attack on the rebel stronghold. Well, hardly a stronghold. Dumont had perhaps 300 men, half of them Indians, and for protection, only hastily dug rifle pits. Let me draw the scene for you. Here, the South Saskatchewan River; the East Village of Batoche, on the east bank, obviously, where the fighting took place; the church here, where the Métis women sheltered, with the graveyard behind; the house of Letendre dit Batoche, where the Métis held their prisoners; the cable ferry, which used river current for power; and finally, the West Village.

"The battle plan called for the 'Northcote' to paddle down-river with part of 'C' Company from the infantry training school in Toronto – "

"Dickie!"

"Who would attack at nine in the morning, in concert with Middleton. But the river had other ideas, and pushed the little steamer to the target an hour early. The Métis lowered the ferry cable when she appeared, which sheared off her masts and wheelhouse as she drifted by, while the men aboard exchanged rifle fire with the rebels. They were soon out of range, however, as their vessel continued downstream, and she didn't stop until she got to Prince Albert, 100 miles away. There, the American captain resigned, saying that he wanted no part of any Canadian war.

"At precisely nine, Middleton's cannon began to fire from his position above the village, with little effect, and he was forced to take shelter behind his wagons by a fierce rebel charge. But numbers would tell the tale. Two days later, tired of inaction and the rebukes of their leader, militia commanders took matters into their own hands, poured down the hill, and overwhelmed the few defenders who were left. Josée?"

"Dumont, left to make his own decisions, would have carried on an effective guerrilla campaign, would never have allowed himself to be trapped at Batoche, perhaps would even have cut the railway line, thus slowing the approach of the troops. But he was constrained by the half mad Riel, who listened to the voices of spirits rather than to Dumont's good advice. In any event, Dumont escaped, and went on to fame as a member of Buffalo Bill's Wild West Show in the United States."

"Sheltered another one of your political refugees, did we?"

"Riel stayed to pray to his gods, was captured, and tried for treason in Regina, and for the murder of Thomas Scott in 1869. Found guilty on both counts, he was hung, and Catholic heretic though he was, he became a martyr to Quebec. As for Dumont, he was pardoned, and returned to Batoche many years later to die."

"What about your great grandfather, Jos?" I asked.

"He also escaped, and never returned to Batoche. The family story is that he said to himself, 'If you can't beat them, join them', and he became a scout for the Mounties."

"What about his Métis wife?"

"Who knows? She was not my great grandmother. He later married Josée Lévesque of Montreal, and I am named after her."

"My word!" Dickie smiled.

I carried on. "Meanwhile, both Poundmaker and Big Bear surrendered, and were to spend the next two years in jail, while those Indians who took part in the Frog Lake massacre were captured, tried and hung. I should say here that this campaign opened the eyes of eastern Canadians to the potential of the vast Northwest Territories, and the need to settle it to keep it from the Americans. And the Canadian Pacific Company, still scratching for money to complete its railway got lots of free advertising and testimonials of support from the men of the Northwest Field Force."

Dickie glanced at his watch. "Enough for now. We will edit tonight, and tomorrow, before we leave Winnipeg, we must visit Louis Riel House, the Hudson's Bay archives, and Lower Fort Garry, where that fellow Scott was murdered by Riel's men."

"Why the Hudson's Bay archives?" Joe-Bob wanted to know.

"Also known as the 'Here Before Christ Company', the Bay dominated the Northwest Territories and British Columbia until long after confederation, and its records constitute the best information available for both during that time period."

"Where are we going after that?" I asked.

"We are going to take the train from Winnipeg to Regina, as the Northwest Field Force did. Well, actually, they went only as far as Qu'Appelle."

"What about Fort Walsh?"

"Oh, heavens, we haven't time to go there. As I pointed out, it's off in a far corner of south-west Saskatchewan, and from Regina, we'd waste three days driving there and back. Can we fly over it in the jet, at least, Joe-Bob, on our way to Saskatoon? That would be tomorrow afternoon."

"I thought you might want to do something like that. It's available."

"Good. From Saskatoon, we will be off to visit Fort Carleton, Duck Lake, and Batoche."

With the help of the staff at the Hudson's Bay archives, we were able to find references to Josée's great grandfather, who was reported to be the best of the Company's freighters. Small thanks that brought him when the paddle wheelers took over. We also read some fascinating profiles of Company officers, young men trained in book-keeping in Scotland who came out to the wilds of Canada to seek their fortune. Many took native women in unblessed 'Fur-Trade' or 'Blanket' marriages, 'in the custom of the country', to keep their sanity during the long winters. The usual practice was to abandon these women at the end of a posting, or to sell them by what was sardonically called a 'dowry' to the succeeding officer. The ambition of nearly all was to retire to the old country after their tour of duty and marry. Some made provision in their wills for their natural children born in Canada, but most did not, while a small minority married the native women, and stayed here.

We found Louis Riel House on the east bank of the Red River, and for a donation, one of the staff, a good-looking young woman named Jocelyn, showed us through the two storey place. Originally built of logs and now covered with board siding, it had, like most homes of the period, a summer kitchen as well as a winter one. "This was the house of Louis Riel's mother, and he never actually lived here," Jocelyn told us. "But after his death, his body was brought here to lie in state for several days. It is the legend that the clock on the mantle stopped at the moment he died."

It became apparent from her off-hand comments that Jocelyn was an ardent feminist. After the tour, Joe-Bob asked her about herself, I thought fascinated with her figure. "I am of French descent, and I live in St. Boniface, the French area of Winnipeg," she told us. "We form a large part of the population of the city. Over the years, we have struggled to keep our identity, our separate schools, and I am happy to say we have managed to do this."

"Say, are you still in school yourself, little lady?"

"Yes, I am studying political science at university."

"You can't be financing that from what you make here as a guide."

"No, I am hard-pressed to find the tuition fees for the coming year."

"I'd like to help. How about I write you a cheque for, say, five thousand American?"

I thought Jocelyn recovered from her surprise very quickly. Through an icy smile, she asked, "And in return for that?"

"You interested in acting at all?"

"Why yes. I belong to an amateur theatre company."

"Then all you have to do is take a screen test. I'll take your name, address, and phone number, and some of my people will be in touch within the next few days."

Lower Fort Garry lies a few miles north of Winnipeg on the banks of the Red River, and the buildings at the National Historic Site there have been preserved or faithfully reconstructed. Stockaded and bastioned, but never involved in military action, it gave us a good picture of the way the Hudson's Bay Company operated during its tenure. Structures included a blacksmith shop, retail store, fur loft, sales shop, men's house, and several others, but the 'Big House' where the Governors of the Company lived was the main point of interest. In its day, it was staffed with all manner of servants, from cooks to chamber maids, and it was a fit residence for the most powerful man in the Northwest. Each of its many rooms had its own fireplace, and we were told by our guides that fifty cords of wood were burned each winter to keep it warm. We ended our tour by examining the remains of one of the Company's big freight boats, used on lakes and the more navigable rivers in place of canoes.

The Via Rail train travelling from Winnipeg to Regina was hardly an extravagant experience, but one, Dickie told us, that was essential to appreciate the events of the late 1800's. We were fortunate enough to find seats in the crowded dome car, and while we sipped our drinks, we listened to some impromptu music provided by a couple of Albertans. 'When it's Roundup Time in Sunny Old Alberta', 'The Good Times are all gone, and It's Time for Moving on', and Gordon Lightfoot's 'The Railway Trilogy' were among our favourites. The musicians just happened to have some tapes for sale, and naturally, we bought one, or Joe-Bob did, with two American twenties. And afterwards, Josée and I had a nice night in our compartment.

Regina, once known as 'Pile of Bones' to the Cree Indians, sits in the middle of nowhere on the dusty Saskatchewan prairie. At the time of our visit, it had a population of less than 200,000, but it was the largest city and the capital of the province. The Royal Canadian Mounted Police Training Centre was there, with a museum adjacent featuring stories and pictures on murals of the force's accomplishments, along with displays of old weapons and uniforms. We spent most of the morning in the museum, and stayed on to watch the Sargent Major's parade in the early afternoon, where the cadets were put through their paces.

Later, in the jet, we flew to the Cypress Hills on the Alberta-Saskatchewan border, the highest point in Canada between Labrador and the Rockies, and over Fort Walsh, one of the earliest Northwest Mounted Police Stations in the west. Below us was the short grass prairie of southern Saskatchewan, almost treeless and broken up with coulees, those abrupt little draws and canyons where deer and antelope can hide by the thousands, and where cattle seek shelter from the incessant winds.

On course to Saskatoon, we passed over historic Saskatchewan Landing, where Colonel Otter and his men crossed the south branch of the river, bound for Battleford. As we continued north, the country changed subtly, becoming flatter, with more tree cover between the cultivated fields, and while towns were small, few, and far between, each had a grain elevator or two, standing out on the skyline like Brock's Monument on Queenston Heights. The farm buildings almost universally were protected by shelter-belts of planted trees, isolating them in a way from the vastness of the prairie, and I began to sense the loneliness of this land. Joe-Bob, I thought, began to sense it too. "Why, there's no one out here where there's room for millions, Fred. Why is that?"

"Hardly a million people live here, actually, in a province almost as big as Texas. It's the winters, I suppose. They are cold, and with nothing to stop the wind, they get some awesome blizzards. Then, too, it's almost all dry land farming out here, and they need big acreages, I mean sections of land, to hedge against crop failures."

"What else do they do out here besides farm?"

"Mine potash, and they have some oil and natural gas. In the north, in the Canadian Shield beyond the prairie, they have forests that support some industry."

The air was fresh, clear and a little on the cool side when we left Saskatoon for Batoche the next morning. The landscape of grain crops was broken here and there by windbreaks and the occasional pond, and it seemed that no matter how small the pond might be, there was a family of ducks in it. Our first stop was Fort Carleton on the North Saskatchewan River, a former Hudson's Bay post named, we presumed, after the infamous governor, and now maintained as an historic site by the provincial government. Occupied by the Mounties at the time of the Métis uprisings in 1885, it consisted of a stockade enclosing an acre or so, with bastions on each corner, and some reconstructed buildings. While Joe-Bob grumbled about the latest hatch of black flies, the rest of us listened attentively to the native girl who acted as our guide.

Some 20 miles to the east, we came to Duck Lake, and an interpretive centre dedicated to the battle, which took place nearby. By the time we left there for Batoche, it was raining, and the dirt road to the tiny community of St. Laurent on the South Saskatchewan River was muddy and slippery. The ferry that crossed the River there was a simple contraption, little more than a scow held to its course by overhead cables, and it pulled itself back and forth on the cables by means of a small engine. It was operated by a tall, dark, young man with a moustache, who greeted us in English in an accent that sounded French-Canadian.

"Comment ca va?" asked Josée.

The ferryman's face lit up with a broad smile. "Bien, eh bien! Etes vous de Quebec?"

"Oui. Etes vous Métis?"

"Oui. Je m'appelle Denis Dumont. Et vous?"

"Josée Tremblay." Switching to English, she asked, "You are a descendant of Gabriel?"

"Yes."

They carried on a spirited conversation during the short crossing, while the rest of us looked at the river, about 200 yards wide at that point, I guessed. "So important, these rivers, the North and the South Saskatchewan, to the early exploration and commerce of the Territory," Dickie commented.

"Yes," I said, "but what a boon the advent of roads must have been! Today, we can drive from Fort Carleton to here, a distance of about 25 miles, in half an hour. To do the same thing by river, we would first have to go 100 miles downstream on the North branch to the junction, then upstream on the South branch another 100 miles, at an average speed of maybe five miles an hour."

"Say, then it would take 40 hours to get here, or most of two days."

By the time the ferry nosed into the dirt landing on the other side, the rain was coming down hard, turning the country roads into a greasy challenge, and I was thankful it was only a few miles to blacktop and Batoche. At the National Historic Site there, we found an elaborate interpretive centre complete with restaurant and bilingual staff, while close by was a replica of the church that served the community at the time of the Northwest rebellion. We browsed through the centre and had a snack, hoping for the rain to stop, but it didn't, so Dickie dragged me out onto the former battlefield, marked now with signs explaining the action, while Josée and Joe-Bob visited the church. I tried to concentrate on what Dickie was saying, but somehow, I couldn't shake the uneasiness I felt about the other two being alone together. "You see, Fred, the militiamen up here were exposed on the skyline, thus making them easy targets for the Métis sharpshooters below, but they, the Métis, were running out of ammunition, and some were forced as the end neared to use rocks for bullets. Now, over there was Jolie Prairie, where Middleton took his cannon – "

Our editing session was over, our itinerary was set for the next few days - Battleford, Edmonton, the Territories - the drinks had been drunk, and Josée and I were alone in our hotel room in Saskatoon. "No hanky-panky in the church today?" I had to ask.

"Other people were there. How could we?"

"You would have if they weren't there?"

"Who knows?"

"Are you trying to make me jealous again?"

"Of course."

"What do you really think of Joe-Bob and Dickie?"

"I know they want me."

"Why don't you tell them they can't have you?"

"I like to have men wanting me."

"Alright, you've succeeded. I'm madly jealous."

"That makes you a better lover, n'est ce pas?"

"Let me prove it to you."

Battleford was 100 or so miles away, and we were there the next day by the time the old fort, built on similar lines to many we had already visited, was open for business. On a gray, windy afternoon, we drove from there the 40 miles through the Saskatchewan countryside to the Chief Poundmaker Historical Centre and Teepee Village, near the town of Cut Knife Hill. A descendant of the Cree warriors who humiliated Colonel Otter showed us around the elevated, gently-rolling battle site, marked here and there with plaques and monuments, and gave us the Indian view of history. He pointed out a buffalo jump, a ridge over which, in the days before the advent of firearms, the Indians use to stampede the animals to their death. With the buffalo gone, he said, his people were reduced to wards of the state. Returning to the Interpretive Centre, we admired the outstanding displays of native arts and crafts, and Joe-Bob bought a small fortune's worth for his children.

As planned, we drove on to Edmonton, arriving there early in the evening. As we sped over the flatness of the prairie, we sang along with the tape we'd bought from the Alberta group on the train, and I told the rest what I knew about the province from my automobile club guide. "Almost as big as Texas, but with only about one sixth the population - less than three million. Almost half of them live in the two principal cities, Edmonton, the capital, and Calgary, neither of them really big enough to be major league, although they both have teams in the National Hockey League and the Canadian Football League. It's Canada's 'have everything' province - oil, gas, good agricultural land, forests, the Rocky Mountains, and lots of red-necks."

"But less than three million people?" asked Joe-Bob.

"Yes, but it's one of the fastest growing provinces, with many corporate headquarters moving out to Calgary from the east."

"Fred, tell us about the settlement of the prairies, in general," said Dickie.

"After the North West Rebellion, the Federal Government started promoting immigration from central Europe as well as Great Britain. Thousands of Germans came, and they now are the third largest ethnic group in Canada. Many Ukrainians came as well, and they are another major ethnic group, proud to be Canadians, but still maintaining their culture. If you haven't seen a Ukrainian dance group in action, you've missed a treat."

"Where can we see such a group?" asked Josée.

"Edmonton would be a likely place."

"But you were talking about the settlement of the prairies, Fred," Dickie reminded me.

"Thousands of Americans came, too, Joe-Bob."

"Say, it's a wonder all these American immigrants haven't taken over your country, and presented it to us on a platter."

"It's my experience, Joe-Bob, that the descendants of American immigrants are the most rabidly anti-American citizens in Canada."

"Why, now, I find that impossible to believe."

"Lots of people have both American and Canadian citizenship. What do you think of that?"

"Dual citizenship? How can the government of the United States allow that? Say, when I go home next, I'm going to look into that. But what did you do with the Indians out here?"

"Made treaties with them, moved them onto reserves. Put their children into residential schools run by the churches, where they were physically and sexually abused, and forced to speak English, all in an attempt to assimilate them. It didn't work."

"Say, you've mentioned several ethnic groups that came to the prairies, but what about all those orientals, East Indians, and who knows who else walking around in Toronto?"

"Well, we have a pretty generous immigration policy."

"And you're making the same mistake we made, allowing anybody into the country."

While we were registering in our hotel in downtown Edmonton, Josée asked if there was a Ukrainian dance group performing in town. She was locked into her one-track mind. As it so happened, there was: the show would be starting in a few minutes at a nearby theatre, and Joe-Bob got us tickets. And what energetic entertainment it was, with the men flying through the air, and the women whirling about the stage, so pretty in their traditional costumes and red slippers.

Late though it was when we got back to the hotel, it was not late enough to deter Dickie. He insisted on finishing up the story of the last boundary, the one between Alaska and British Columbia, and allowed me to introduce the subject.

"There were two versions of the boundary, American and Canadian, and I would stress Canadian. As Dickie has made it clear, the British decided after the battle of New Orleans that they should not go to war again with the United States, and they weren't about to change that policy over a fog shrouded part of the north-west coast. As for the boundary, Canada believed that the Lynn Canal area was part of British Columbia, based on negotiations between the Russians and the Hudson's Bay Company. Joe-Bob?"

"And the United States knew it was part of Alaska, because they, like the Russians before them, occupied it in terms of the communities at Skagway and Dyea."

"Because you were there didn't mean it was yours. But it was the discovery of gold in the Yukon that forced Canada to seek a settlement, for fear the Americans were just going to walk in and take over the whole of the territory."

"And we would have, too, if it hadn't been for the Mounties."

"To go back to the beginning. The Canadian Government approached Washington in 1892, and an agreement was reached for a joint survey of the Alaska boundary, with a report to be made in 1895. Mounties represented Canada on the survey, and maybe that is where Americans first learned to respect them."

"My great grandfather Pierre was on the survey crew," Josée threw in.

"And so was my great grandfather! They must have known each other, then! But where was I? To settle the jurisdiction of Lynn Canal, a tribunal was struck with representatives of Great Britain, the United States and Canada. Meanwhile, President Teddy Roosevelt talked quietly and carried a big stick, convincing the British that he was willing to go to war over the issue, so the British sided with the Americans, and we lost Lynn Canal. But the United States did not get the Yukon, which was carved out of the Northwest Territory in 1898. At the beginning of the great gold rush, the Mounties posted men at the top of the mountain passes that the miners were coming in on, imposed conditions of entry, and collected duties. And my great grandfather Thomas was one of the Mounties serving at the top of the Chilkoot Pass. Sam Steele arrived to take charge of the territory while this was going on, and based in Dawson City, he maintained law and order with an iron though just hand."

"That wraps it up, then," Dickie said, with a surprising air of relief. "Canada, the rump of British North America, is now complete. All we have to do is finish the last chapter. I believe a celebration is in order."

"Not quite complete," I corrected. "Alberta and Saskatchewan were carved out of the Northwest Territories in 1905, and made into provinces."

"But how are we going to end the book?" asked Josée. "The settling of the last boundary leaves us nowhere."

"As usual, we were going to leave that to you, Josée," said Dickie, with a trusting look.

"Let me try. My grandfather Jean is made restless by the stories his father tells him, and travels to the west, to Saskatchewan. He visits Batoche, and discovers his half brothers and sisters. He homesteads in the area and tries to farm, but encounters prejudice against the French wherever he goes. He therefore returns to Quebec and becomes a separatist. That is the way it was."

"And if Quebec separates," I said, "that leaves the rest of us to be gobbled up by the Americans. Jos, I don't agree with you. Surely, there has to be a reason why this country should survive, after the heroism of Wolfe and Brock, de Salaberry, and Sam Steele. You know I have been dead set against fiction from the beginning, but now is the time for fiction. This book is not a simple military history, you've made it into a romantic, generational novel, so it should end romantically. Besides that, we have identified that the single biggest problem Canada faces is the French-English one, and we should provide some closure for that. End by having Jean fall in love with an Anglais, a Bonney of course, and becoming a strong advocate of a bilingual country. Have him encourage Quebeckers to inherit the whole of Canada, and his wife to convince the rest of us to learn French, for that is what really separates us from the United States."

"Say, I like the idea of taking over Canada, except for Quebec. And we'd get Quebec, too, after awhile, because she would be all alone. Then all those people there would have to learn and speak English."

Josée glared at him. "Jamais!"

"Jesus, God, what does that mean?"

"Never!"

"Joe-Bob, be content with dominating us economically," I advised. "We are different, besides the fact that we are one quarter French. Even Roger Patterson recognized that. You know, when I was young and foolish, I toured Europe with a friend, and wherever we went, we could sit down with people from Britain and other Commonwealth countries like Australia and New Zealand, and we could drink with them and get along famously. When it came to Americans, we couldn't get along with them at all. They just didn't fit in, somehow, I think because they were boastful, pushy, too individualistic, too demanding, even downright rude. They were quick to complain about the service they were getting, even if it was good, for example. The Revolution made you different, I guess. Anyway, you don't belong in the Commonwealth Club any more."

"Bravo, Fred!" Dickie applauded, while Joe-Bob shook his head.

"I will sleep on it, and decide tomorrow how to end," Josée said with finality.

"Say, how about one last grand tour of the country before we break up, Dickie?"

"Capital idea, Joe-Bob. Fly over the Alaska boundary, for example?"

"How about the Yukon, and what's left of the Northwest Territories?" I offered. "But we'll have to get some warmer clothes, because winter in coming on up there."

"New clothes?" Josée perked up.

"Then on to Winnipeg, and drive back to Ottawa from there, so we can see on the ground how the country changes from west to east," I added.

"Just so long as we get home before curling season," Josée said firmly.

Anticipating Joe-Bob's question, I explained, "Curling is a game played on ice with granite rocks. The Scots invented it, like they did golf."

"Say, we haven't played golf in Alberta, Saskatchewan, or Manitoba yet."

"Nor the Territories," I pointed out, "but we might still be able to play the course at Yellowknife."

Dickie stood up with a look of anticipation. "Let's retire to the bar and discuss this!"

It was Sunday again, and as usual, we were waiting for Josée to come back from church. What was unusual was the article in the paper that had Joe-Bob fuming. "I just don't believe what I'm reading. This rancher near Edmonton has been put in jail for defending his property. Four young no-goods crashed through his gate with a four-by-four in the middle of the night, and started turning doughnuts in his yard. He woke up, came out, and ordered them off his place, but they just laughed at him, and made a run at him with their vehicle. He's got his gun with him, so he takes a shot at them as they are coming on, and they take off. The next day, they file a complaint with the police, and he is charged with careless use of a firearm, and attempted murder! Worse yet, he's convicted! You Canadians are crazy! Jesus, God! Every man has a right to protect himself and his property!"

"There's a big debate in Canada over tightening up the gun laws. Most people are in favour," I told him.

"Well, I can tell you, nobody's going to take my gun away from me."

"You carry a gun, Joe-Bob?"

"Believe it. Remember that night in Albany, when we almost got mugged? I had it in my hand."

To pass the time, as we usually did while waiting for Josée on Sundays, Dickie and Joe-Bob made phone calls, and I wrote to the girls. Then the three of us went for a walk, and the nip in the clear morning air brought a sense of anxiety to me, as if I were a squirrel and had yet to lay in enough nuts for winter. Maybe it was the kid who walked by toting an enormous bagful of hockey equipment that made me realize fall was upon us.

When Josée reappeared, we went from store to store looking for warm clothing. The rest of us found what we wanted without much fuss, but she took her time, trying on outfit after outfit until she was satisfied: dark blue wool slacks and vest, matching wool lined jacket with hood, two long sleeved blouses, and a pair of lightweight winter boots.

Our route that afternoon took us over the glory of the Rockies at Jasper and the forests of central British Columbia to the small town of Smithers, where we topped up the fuel tanks. From there, we followed the Skeena River through the granite peaks of the Coast Mountains to the port of Prince Rupert, then swung out over the Pacific for a look at the Queen Charlotte Islands, the misty home of the Haida, perhaps Canada's second most famous Indian tribe. We landed at Masset, and took time to admire some of their artwork: inscrutable cedar totem poles; small replicas in argillite stone; bracelets of silver inlaid with abalone shell. Joe-Bob, of course, bought a small fortune's worth of trinkets for his kids. Returning to the mainland, we flew north along the Alaska panhandle until we could look down on towering Mount Logan, the highest point in Canada, "Say, but not as high as Mount McKinley in Alaska." By the time we landed at Whitehorse, the capital of the Yukon Territory, it was dusk, and the temperature was well below freezing.

In our hotel room that evening, we finished the book, with Josée adamant that her grandfather Jean be as he was, a separatist. My grandfather, by the same token, became what he was, a red-necked British Columbian, who thought the French should learn to speak English. "So," I said sadly, "We end up admitting that the country doesn't work, because we can't solve the language and culture problem." Still, I was vaguely unsatisfied. "Should we really end it there, back in the early years of the century, or bring it up to the present? Canada is vastly different today than it was then. Then, we were still British, ready to go to war in aid of the mother country at the drop of a hat."

"That is not true!" Josée objected vehemently. "Except to defend ourselves, as we did in the war of 1812, the French in Canada were never ready to go to war for Great Britain!"

"Except for a few gallant men in units like the Vingt Deuxième, the Royal 22nd Regiment." Dickie looked heroic as he breathed the words.

"Say, if you're not British any more, what are you?" Joe-Bob wanted to know. "We've been travelling around this country now for weeks, and I still don't know what Canada is all about."

His question annoyed me, but it was a good one, and I took some time to come up with an answer. "I have to go back to the Second World War and its aftermath. Before the Americans were involved in the war, they were sending supplies to Britain through Canada under the Lend Lease Agreement. That moved us closer to the Americans and away from the British. After the war, the process accelerated until, I guess, if you want to be extreme about it, we have become little more than a vassal of the States now, with 80 per cent of our exports going there. On the other hand, we have done some pretty big things on our own, like fighting two world wars with valour, and coming up with the funding for the St. Lawrence Seaway, even if the Americans did become involved later. And we have some status in the world as a nation willing to help preserve peace. I guess you could say that the average English-Canadian's outlook on life is as if he had an English mother and an American father."

"Never forget the French fact in Canada," Josée reminded us. "After France abandoned us, we became as we are, a people who have a unique language and culture in North America."

"Fred, never forget either," Dickie reminded me, "that until only a few years ago, there was an obscure colonel in the bowels of defence headquarters in Ottawa drafting plans to repel attacks from the United States. But perhaps we should hold off sending Basil the last chapter until we make up our minds about the ending."

The day dawned cautiously and late on this Labour Day Monday, the sun already well on its way south to the Tropic of Cancer, soon to leave the north in the gloom of winter. We flew east until we picked up the MacKenzie River. "The third largest in the world, Joe-Bob, and the Mississippi is not the first or second." Using it as a guide, we winged north over stunted, cold-tortured forests to the Government Centre at Inuvik, and over the vast MacKenzie delta to the Beaufort Sea, until we landed amidst the 'Pingos' and the Arctic tundra at Tuktoyaktuk. Once an important link in the radar network protecting North America, this western Eskimo community of less than 1,000 now relied on trapping and welfare for its continued existence.

There was already snow on the ground, and the indoor swimming pool had been closed since the middle of August to prevent it freezing up. People were bustling about, getting their trapping gear ready for the coming season, and the house yards were thronged with friendly, half-grown husky pups, soon to be initiated into the sledding trade. We walked from the airport to the beach, and with screams and shouts, dipped our bare toes into the Arctic Ocean in the style of tourists, and it was there that I remembered the last threat to our sovereignty. "In 1969, the United States sent the ice-breaking oil tanker, the 'Manhattan', through the Northwest Passage in a kind of show of force, telling us, in effect, that we were too puny a nation to assert our jurisdiction over it and the Arctic Islands. But once the decision was made to build the Alaska pipeline from Prudhoe Bay to Valdes, we heard nothing more about it."

We were airborne again at two o'clock in the afternoon with a sense of relief at being able to flee the onset of winter. Following a south eastward course over the pink granite of the Canadian Shield, we passed near Great Bear Lake, larger than Erie or Ontario, and landed in the gathering darkness at Yellowknife, the mining centre on the north shore of Great Slave Lake, also larger than Erie or Ontario. In Yellowknife, the capital of the Northwest Territories, we attended a concert that evening given by a promising young Inuit singer and songwriter, and when Joe-Bob was finally convinced that she really was what we used to call an Eskimo, he negotiated an agreement with her manager to produce a tape. Later, over nightcaps, we continued our discussions, trying to define Canada, but we were no closer to an answer by the time we went to bed.

In the half-light of the Arctic morning, we checked out of our hotel, took our belongings back to the jet by taxi, and set off on a walking tour of Yellowknife. With a population of 18,000, it had most of the amenities of a much larger city, including a new 'Tim Horton's', and I observed that Canada could be defined in part as the country with the most doughnut shops per capita in the world. Further, many Canadians were hockey fanatics, while many more loved the outdoors and outdoor activities like canoeing and skiing, easily accessible almost everywhere in the country. But Canada was, in the last analysis, a debate between French and English, between Separatists and Federalists.

At the suggestion of the staff at the visitor centre, we toured the Legislative Building, a round structure intended to evoke the image of an igloo. Inside were displayed exquisite Inuit or Eskimo carvings, wall hangings, and paintings that further distinguished the place from any other seat of government in the world. The assembly chamber itself was not divided into two sides in the traditional manner, but arranged in the round to promote consensus rather than confrontation. Behind the speaker's chair was a wall of zinc, the principal metal mined in the territory, and a polar bear rug graced the floor.

The last stop of our tour was the Prince of Wales Northern Heritage Centre, a museum of northern cultures, natural history and resources. Of particular interest were the many paintings and sketches of A.Y. Jackson, a member of Canada's famous Group of Seven, who travelled extensively through the territory before the middle of the century. "Say, this is some hell of a country up here," Joe-Bob observed, as he examined one of the paintings. "Like Alaska, in a way, but wilder and more natural. But say, Jacqui's got us a tee time at the golf course here. They got a tournament on, so all she could get us was nine holes. Time to go."

The nine-hole Yellowknife golf course, in a setting of scrubby Jack Pine trees, was like no other we had ever seen. We had to play shots from the dirt fairways on a piece of indoor-outdoor carpet rented from the pro shop, because the only grass on the layout was a narrow collar around the greens. The greens themselves were made of artificial turf, so to prevent approach shots from going into orbit, the correct strategy was to sneak up on them by bouncing shots off the grass collars. Other hazards included a flock of croaking ravens, who seemed to delight in making off with our golf balls, and we had a hilarious time that afternoon trying to outwit the birds and shoot a decent number, failing on both counts. The good news was that Josée was on the winning side.

At three in the afternoon, we lifted off in the jet and flew south again over the flatness of Alberta, with the foothills of the Rockies visible to the west, arriving in the booming city of Calgary for dinner. On the way, Jacqui made reservations for us at a hotel near the airport, and a tee time for the next day at the resort community of Kananaskis, some 100 kilometres away. From there, we would go on to Banff for the night, the jewel of the Canadian Rockies, where we would stay at the prestigious Banff Springs Hotel. Over drinks that evening, we planned the rest of our trip: return to Calgary from Banff by car, fly to Regina in Saskatchewan for a game of golf; fly from Regina to Winnipeg in Manitoba for another game of golf; drive from Winnipeg to Thunder Bay, and then along the north shore of Lake Superior to Sault St. Marie; fly from Sault St. Marie to Ottawa, where we would tour the Parliament Buildings, the National War Museum, and the National Gallery. And that would be it. We would break up, and go our separate ways.

The next few days disappeared in a blur of golf (but curiously, no punishment, even when Josée lost), travel, and soul-searching about the ending of the book. Canada, we determined, was not a homogeneous mosaic, but rather, except in Quebec, a sea of English with French enclaves, like St. Boniface in Winnipeg. Otherwise, Canadians' outlook on the world was dominated by relations with the United States. We were full of admiration for Americans, but fearful of them at the same time, especially when some loose cannon vying for political office began to threaten us. Where Americans applauded economic success, we were jealous of it, suspicious that it could not have been gained honestly; yet the true mark of achievement for a Canadian seemed to be to 'graduate' to the wider opportunities in the United States. "What you have up here," Joe-Bob summed up, "is too much government. Government is involved in too many things that the private sector or individuals could do better, and that's why your taxes are so high. You can't expect to compete with the United States, to be equal partners in this free trade, unless you play by the same rules. You know what this country needs? More billionaires who can make things happen in a cost-effective way, instead of all this inefficient government enterprise."

Still, we kept returning to the biggest problem Canada had to face, the bilingual one, the one that threatened to split the country.

On our way east from Winnipeg, Joe-Bob complained about the quality of the seemingly endless, winding, two lane roads through the Canadian Shield in western Ontario, so he was more than glad to pause for one more National Historic Site, old Fort William in Thunder Bay. "After the war of 1812, when the 49th parallel of latitude was extended as the international boundary from the Great Lakes to the Rockies, we lost Grand Cache to the Americans. Fort William then became the rendezvous point for the fur brigades," I explained to him.

Beyond Thunder Bay, we drove hour after hour on more winding, two lane roads through the Canadian Shield on the north shore of Lake Superior, the while continuing our discussions, our attempts to define my country. Was there another Canada, a place where Francophones and Anglophones lived together in peace and harmony - indeed, where they spoke both languages? New Brunswick, where many Acadians spoke English, might qualify. I suggested we might find another such place in northern Ontario, where many people from Quebec had come in search of work in the mines and the forest industry, and we decided to go there. "Jesus, God, but not by road!" Joe-Bob exclaimed. He summoned the jet when we got to 'The Sault', and we flew north from there on the morning of September 13th to Kapuskasing, an industrial town of about 10,000. The population there, we were told, was 80 per cent of French origin, but almost 100 percent bilingual, and everywhere we went, we heard both languages, the people switching from one to the other as Josée and I unconsciously did. But it was the French who were adapting more than the English. Would English-speaking Canadians, where they were in a majority, ever be willing to learn French in the same way?

In Joe-Bob's jet, for the last time together, we flew from Kapuskasing down the broad valley of the Ottawa River to our capital city, arriving there at last light. From the airport, the limousine delivered us to our last hotel, the Chateau Laurier, not so magical as the Chateau Frontenac, but built in the same mould. Over dinner and on into our nightcaps, we argued and postulated about the book's ending, without convincing Josée to make any changes.

The Gothic grandeur of the Parliament Buildings, perched on a knoll overlooking the Ottawa River, impressed both Joe-Bob and Dickie the next day. "Designed, naturally, by an English architect," Dickie boasted. The House of Commons was in session, and with the help of a friend, I got us passes to the visitors' gallery. From our vantage point, I explained the proceedings to Joe-Bob: Government members on one side, opposition on the other; the role of the speaker; how business was conducted. He shook his head. "How can those politicians get anywhere when some of them are talking one language and some the other?"

"The ones that speak only one language can get a translation over an earphone if they want it," I explained. "Sometimes, they don't want to understand what the opposition is saying."

"And this Bloc Quebecois party you talked about. They openly want to split the country? Why, they should be tried for treason instead of being allowed into the national parliament!"

The War Museum was within walking distance, so we hoofed it over there, and browsed through the three floors cramped with exhibits. Isaac Brock's red serge tunic was on display, and I stared for a long time at the hole in it - from its location, I had to believe the musket ball must have blown his heart apart and killed him instantly. Of interest to Joe-Bob was the First World War battle of Vimy Ridge during which Canadian troops, where the British and French had failed, succeeded in driving the Germans off a strategic point of high ground in the spring of 1917. "Cost us over 10,000 casualties, but it was the turning point of the war, and a defining moment of Canadian nationhood," I said.

"But the Americans won the war."

"By the time the Americans arrived on the scene, the storm was over, you overbearing Yank," Dickie needled. "You hardly suffered more casualties altogether than the Canadians did in that one battle."

"Dickie, you arrogant Brit, I don't care what you say. We did win the Second World War for you."

"Credit where credit is due, but you did need some help from the rest of us."

The steel and glass edifice known as the National Gallery of Canada stuck out like a sore thumb in the midst of Ottawa's more traditional architecture, but it housed fine exhibits of both aboriginal and European-Canadian art, from Inuit carvings to modern contemporary paintings. We spent the rest of the afternoon there, enjoying in particular the Group of Seven's interpretations on canvas of the Canadian countryside. It was then that Joe-Bob and Josée seemed to distance themselves from Dickie and I, and to talk in tones so low that I could not hear what they were saying. My heart sank. They were setting the stage, making plans for a relationship. After some time, they rejoined us, and Josée said with a smile, "I have to make some little changes to the book. See you at supper."

It was our last night together. Tomorrow, we would drive Dickie to the airport, and he would fly home to England with the last chapter. Joe-Bob would fly home to the States in his jet, and I was convinced that Josée was going to go with him. She was the last to arrive at the dinner table, and I had to look at her twice to recognize her. Her hair was brunette again, she wasn't wearing any makeup, and there was an aura about her, a kind of serenity that was at odds with her nature, as if she had just been to church. We started off with a fine meal at the Chateau Laurier with cocktails before, wine with, and liqueurs after, except that Josée refused anything alcoholic. Long before our normal bedtime, she excused herself, saying she still had some work to do on the book, and I was left with Dickie and Joe-Bob, who were Colonel and Major again, and deep into the Rusty Nails. "Here, Fred," said Joe-Bob, "try one of these," and he pushed his fresh glass over to me. I had to admit it tasted good, so I soon had another, and before long, I wasn't feeling a lot of pain.

"Say, Dickie and Fred, come on up to my room. I've got something that will interest you. Waiter, bring a pitcher of these rusty nails up to 802." And Joe-Bob threw a half-dozen twenties on the table.

"What have you got hidden up there?" asked Dickie, with a cackle. "Oops, we can't have Fred tempted to be unfaithful to Josée, now, can we?"

"No, not women, Dickie, not real women anyway. I've got the screen tests for Nancy Garcia, Jocelyn Martin, and Amee O'Brien. You remember them? Nancy was at Job Burnham's Pub in Machias, Jocelyn was at Louis Riel House, and Amee was at Castle Hill on Newfoundland. Come on."

We followed him into the elevator and to his room, where he took three cassettes from his briefcase. "Now, all the girls go through the same series of skits, from comedy to drama to skin. Let's start with Nancy," and he plugged the first cassette into the VCR. "Hey! Here come the Rusty Nails."

"Gentlemen," Dickie slurred, "Charge your glasses before the cimena begins." Nancy came across as amateurish but engaging, and when, as the script called for, she readied herself for bed, she removed her clothes shyly, revealing a pretty pair of breasts. As for Jocelyn, she seemed overly aggressive, and when it came time to take it all off, she balked. 'That's as far as I'm going to go!' she said to the camera belligerently, when she got down to her brassiere. We were left to imagine the delights that lay beneath. Then came Amee, who waltzed through the cycle of skits with sharp wit, style, and class. At the end, she disrobed gracefully, as if she were in private, and not even Josée had such a perfect body.

Joe-Bob chuckled, then laughed. "That Amee O'Brien! Never saw the beat of that little lady, so pretty, so full of sauce, asking me if I wanted her to be my mistress! Some have it, and some don't. Amee's got it. She's got star written all over her, and that's just what we're going to make her into."

I stumbled off to my room long after midnight, hoping Josée was already asleep and wouldn't get on my case about being drunk, or complain about the gas attack I was having. She was breathing easily, and I slipped as quietly as I could under the covers. Almost immediately, I fell into a fitful doze and started to dream a series of nightmares related to the book. When I woke in the morning, she wasn't there, oh my God she wasn't there! I screamed out, "Josée! Jos! I'm sorry I got drunk! I'm sorry for the gas! I'm sorry! Don't leave me! Don't leave me!"

I dressed as quickly as I could and rushed down to breakfast, hoping against hope that she had simply got up early. Only Dickie was waiting for me, with the last chapter of the book in his hand. "Seen Josée or Joe-Bob this morning?" I asked nervously.

Dickie looked surprised. "No, I haven't. Josée not with you? She left the last chapter for me at the desk." He chuckled. "I read the last few pages, and she accepted your advice. Her grandfather marries a Bonney!"

"Maybe she went to church - but it's not Sunday," I remembered. We ate in relative silence, and I wondered if Dickie also suspected that the other two had run off together. I waited in the lobby for him while he collected his bags and checked out, and drove him to the airport for his nine o'clock flight. I could have left him there on his own, I guess, but maybe he was the only friend I had left in the world, so I waited. He seemed nervous, and finally broke the silence.

"Fred, I have a confession to make. One night in Boston, when Joe-Bob was off on business, you got drunk, and I did something I am very ashamed of. I tried to take Josée from you. I just couldn't help myself. She is the most fascinating woman I ever met. She let me down so gently, with such sensitivity and class, that I am doubly ashamed. Will you ever forgive me?"

I went through a gamut of emotions from rage to pity to emptiness. "Sure, why not. It doesn't matter any more."

"Oh, but it does. I know you are afraid she has gone off with Joe-Bob, but I am sure she hasn't. She had an agreement with you, she said, that she could not break."

A ray of hope. It flickered and died as they called his flight. We stood up, and uncharacteristically, he embraced me. My last friend, even if he tried to take Josée from me. I hugged him back.

I walked with him to the security gate, and he talked urgently on the way. "Now listen to me, even if I have betrayed your trust. You have a wonderful thing going for you here in Canada - a beautiful country, two principal cultures that have managed to get along for over 200 years, and many more ethnic groups that enrich your diversity. Don't give it up. Don't let Quebec separate, because then you will be swallowed up by those bloody Americans, who are all descended from deserters from the British Army, thieves, and religious fanatics. Encourage your young women to have children. Bring in more immigrants. Especially, encourage those who have gone to the States to come back. Increase your population by 20 million, and you will be self sufficient enough to tell the Americans to mind their own business."

"That's what Isaac Brock told me."

"What?"

"Have a good flight back to Britain."

"Britain? Oh, not till day after tomorrow. Joe-Bob got me an invitation to West Point, and I'm also going to New York to see Roger and Joyce, the Pattersons. He's very low, not expected to live more than a few days."

"You know that Roger has picked you for his successor? Joyce is in love with you."

Dickie looked stunned. "In love with me? That charming woman, that wonderful Baltimore accent? Oh, you must be joking!"

"You're the only one who doesn't know. Just ask Roger when you see him."

I didn't want to go back to the hotel. By now, Josée would be packing up if she were in our room, but I couldn't believe she was there. I thought of driving to my old house in the suburbs - the people who were renting it would be moving out at the end of the month - and what would I do with the damn place now? And what would I do with myself? "You can always start talking to yourself again, Fred Bonney."

I could go to the apartment, but there were too many wonderful memories there - that haunting scent of Impatiens, potting soil, soap and furniture polish; Josée in bed; Josée in the shower; Josée cleaning house. Funny, that last one was the best memory of all. I knew that if I went near the place, I would break down and cry. I drove slowly back to the hotel and turned the car in.

It was eleven in the morning when I got there, and with mixed feelings, I saw Joe-Bob come out of the elevator. Josée wasn't with him. "Well, if it isn't 15-handicap Fred." He looked at me steadily for a moment. "Come have a cup of coffee with me."

For two cups, he threw a twenty on the table. After a couple of sips, he gave me another long look, until I couldn't stand the suspense. "Seen Jos this morning?"

"No, I haven't."

He took another sip, then another long look at me. "Fred, I don't know whether you're hung like a horse or what, but you sure got something going for you. I have to tell you I tried to take Josée away from you the night you and

Dickie got drunk in Albany. She listened to my sweet-talking for quite a while, till I said, 'And of course, you can't speak that French in the States'. Then she started in on me, talking French a mile a minute, till I asked, 'Jesus, God, Josée, what did you say?' And she said, 'Joe-Bob, I called you a son of bitch, and a lot worse.' Well, now, I'm not used to women saying no to me, and I couldn't believe I couldn't have her, so I tried again yesterday in the art gallery. Like the first time, she listened to me for quite a while, then she said, 'Joe-Bob, would you be faithful to me?' And I said, 'Why, Josée, I would try to be faithful.' And she said, 'and you would fail, you would be just like that scum Paul, who said he loved me but needed other women. Joe-Bob, I won't go with you.' Hey, Fred, where are you going?"

She wasn't in our room. I went back down to the lobby and the doorman got me a cab. When the driver let me off at the apartment, I could hardly get my key in the door, my hand was shaking so badly. She was there, unpacking, and my heart nearly burst with relief. She had set aside all the clothes we bought for her on our trip, by the look of it, and I recognized the suit she'd changed into as the one she wore when we started west. "What's with the clothes?" I asked.

"The Sally Ann thrift shop is going to pick them up."

She walked over to the window and stood looking out on the street. I followed her, and put my arms around her from behind. "Josée, Jos, I love you."

"Fred, for the last time, shut up."

"No, I won't shut up. I've finally managed to put things together. Remember when I first moved in with you, and you said you often wondered what it would be like with me?"

"Yes, I did say that."

"I remind you of your father, don't I?"

"Yes, you do look a little like him."

"And you could never please him, but I am a pushover. You please me just by breathing."

"When I was young, he made me practise until I cried, and then he would make me practise some more. You are so easy to please - except when I make mistakes reading a map."

"And you didn't tell me about Pierre because you were afraid I would be frightened away. You care for me, don't you?"

"It is hard to be intimate without caring - a little." She turned from the window, and she looked positively radiant. "You sexy Bonney men, fathering children into your fifties and sixties. It wasn't me, it was that scum Paul all the time. And now he's sued for divorce. I went to confession this morning, and the priest said I should marry you when I am free, if you agree the child will be raised Catholic."

I was aghast. "What are you telling me? That you're pregnant, and you don't know which one of us did it?"

She looked at me with a Mona Lisa smile. "Oh, I know which one. It is like in hockey. The other two just get an assist for making you so jealous you wanted to make love all the time. And then there was Yvan, who gets an assist too. I said goodbye to him after we went to the cottage. You see, the doctor told me the only way I could get pregnant was to make love every day. And if it's a boy, we will have to name him after my brother, and after Isaac Brock, because I was dreaming of him when it happened that night in Niagara Falls."

"Josée!" She's impregnable. She can't be pregnant. But she is. My God, I'm going to be a father again. My kids' inheritance. My Puritan ancestors will turn in their graves when they realize a child of mind is being raised a papist. Josée! She might die trying to have this baby at her age. I couldn't stand it if she died.

I sank down on the couch in a state of shock, and recoiled from something sharp. It was the corner of a hardcover cookbook.

POSTSCRIPT

I sat down in my favourite chair, in my old house in suburban Ottawa, and sighed. Except for that telephone call, this January 20th in the year 2001 had been a good day. E-mail from both the girls. Louise had long since forgiven me, and was busy raising the twin boys she and Jack had after they sorted out their marital problems. More e-mail from our co-authors. Dickie and Joyce wanted us to come over for the launching of his new book, 'The Military History of British North America', based on the notes and sketches he'd made while we were writing the novel. Joe-Bob finally made his billion with the help of the novel, and the movie he made of it starring Amee O'Brien. And the tabloids were speculating that she was indeed his mistress. But I was disappointed in the movie in one aspect - it stopped after the glorious American victory at Lundy's Lane, with Judson Bonney carrying Amee, his French-Canadian love (a descendent of Ephraim Bonney, of course) back across the border. Very important to Joe-Bob, too, I could tell, was that his eldest son, the starting quarterback for his college team, had got in touch with him. They were coming to Canada in the spring on a fishing trip, and they would spend part of that time at our cottage. As for Pierre, Josée's brother, now based in Montreal, his association with Joe-Bob had made him wealthy, but his dreams of fathering ten good separatists had been shattered. After having a boy and a girl, Geneviève told him that was enough, and that if he wished to have more, he should have married a sow. Worse, she had become a Federalist, and campaigned against the referendum in which the Quebec Government narrowly failed to win approval for separation. And a bit of irony. The Americans had repatriated Laura Secord by buying the chocolate company named after her.

I heard the back door slam, and barely had time to stand up before my son charged and knocked me back into my seat. I laughed and gave him a bear hug. "Playing Uncle Pierre again, are you, Pete?"

"When I grow up, I want to be just like him! I want to be the Canadien's enforcer!" He smiled contemptuously, struck a pose, and fought the air into submission.

I laughed. He just might make it, and more than just as an enforcer. Old John Hughes, our next-door neighbour and the coach of Pete's Atom League hockey team, watched Wayne Gretzky grow up, and insisted that Pete had all his moves, and was bigger and sturdier as well. "More like Mario Lemieu, Fred. I tell you, he's the best I've ever seen at his age." As for me, I just couldn't get over the energy of this boy. I made a rink for him in the back yard on which he skated by the hour, and if it snowed, he cleared it by himself, and then skated for hours more. Then there was golf. During the previous summer, we took him to visit his Bonin grandparents, and he got his hands on a club for the first time. After that, it was impossible to stop him hitting balls, whether on the practice range or around the greens, and tears came to his grandfather's eyes. "If Josée had practised like that, she would be in the LPGA hall of fame."

Still, I sometimes wondered about the boy. Was he really my son, or could he, by some strange, occult twist, be Isaac Brock's? I looked at him sideways while he put on his house slippers. Reddish-blond curls, blue, blue eyes, his usual expression one of determination, like Brock's portrait in the National War Museum. It didn't matter, really. I couldn't love him any more than I did, no matter whose son he was.

Pete looked serious. "Dad, Stevie called me a half-breed and a mongrel today, because I'm half French and half English. I told him to take it back, and he wouldn't, so I hit him."

"I know. His mother just phoned, and she's quite upset. He's got a black eye."

"Dad, is it true? Am I a half-breed and a mongrel?"

"No, you are a complete Canadian. You've even got a smidgen of Iroquois in you. You should be proud of that."

That seemed to satisfy him, and his thoughts turned to his stomach. "What's for supper, Dad? I'm starving."

"We're having baked potatoes, roast beef and Yorkshire Pudding. It won't be ready till six. How about a couple of cookies and a glass of milk to keep you going?"

"Cool."

I got him two of my mega-sized chocolate chip specials and poured his milk. With his mouth full, he asked, "Dad, how come you do the cooking and Mom curls and plays golf? Stevie's mom does all the cooking at his place, and she says that's normal."

"Well, let's just say I'm better at cooking, and your mom is better at curling and golf. She phoned a while ago to tell me she'd won her game. And we're going with her to a bonspiel in Montreal week after next."

"Cool! Can we stay with Uncle Pierre and go to a Canadien's game?"

"It's all laid on, sport."

"Really cool!"

"Now, Stevie is still your best friend, isn't he?"

"Well, yeah. He's lots of fun to play with. Except today."

"Alright, we better phone his mom, and the two of you can apologize to each other. And don't go asking if you can go out to play tonight. The Canadiens are on the TV."

"Cool!"

I phoned Stevie's mom, and soon the boys had apologized to each other, and were giggling over some private joke.

The phone was hardly back on the hook when the garage door opener started whining. "Ah! Votre mère est chez nous." Josée swept in, looking gorgeous in her slack suit, even with no makeup on, and that touch of gray in her hair made her look the part of a distinguished novelist. Our book, or her book, really, had been translated into ten different languages, and had made us more than comfortably well off. She gave me a quick kiss and hugged our son - Pierre Isaac Brock Bonney - Pierre to her, Pete to me.

"Fred," she said, "you've got to do something about that shutter in the attic. It's rattling again."

"Oh, that's just Uncle Bill's ghost trying to get my attention. I wonder what he wants this time?"

"What nonsense are you talking? Tomorrow, I want it fixed! Maintenant, nous parlons Francais seulement ce soir, n'est ce pas?"

"Oui, mama, we speak French only in the evenings so I will know both languages and be Prime Minister some day, and I will stop Quebec from separating, and I will save us all from the Americans."

Printed in the United States
72564LV00001B/11-38

9 780755 202386